Forge of Stones

by Vasileios Kalampakas

March 18, 2011

Published by Βασίλειος Καλαμπάκας, Vasileios Kalampakas
Copyright © 2011 Βασίλειος Καλαμπάκας, Vasileios Kalampakas
ISBN : 978-960-93-2923-1

Printed on demand through createspace.com

Available in print by Amazon Inc. and other retailers
Available in e-book form from *http://www.stoneforger.com*
and the Amazon Kindle store.
You can reach the author at this e-mail address:
kalampakas@stoneforger.com

Written and typeset with the L_YX document processor
from *http://www.lyx.org*

Cover made with the aid of the GNU Image Manipulation program
from *http://www.gimp.org*
The painting on the cover is "Clytie", from Lord Frederick Leighton.
Written under extreme pressure and varying temperatures.

with special thanks to my editor

who should have acted more like the City of Pyr

Αφιερωμένο στη μητέρα μου. Μπορεί να αδυνατεί να διαβάσει το βιβλίο, αλλά άς διαβάσει τουλάχιστον την αφιέρωση.

Θαρσεῖν χρή, φίλε Βάττε· τάχ᾽ αὔριον ἔσσετ᾽ ἄμεινον ἐλπίδες ἐν ζωοῖσιν, ἀνέλπιστοι δὲ θανόντες᾽

- Θεοκρίτου Ειδύλλια, Νομείς

Contents

Part I

Ex Principia

Prologue

"It is by fortune alone that man maintains his bountiful existence, unhindered by the forces beyond his grasp, unaware of what lies beyond. Once that veil is lifted, who can foretell the future?"

-Hilderich D'Augnacy, *Visions of The Aftermath*

The dancer

SHE reveled in the darkly lit chambers, her form so very much like that of a swirling dervish. The locks of her hair mirrored the precious little light with a warm sheen of honey and brown. An ethereal smell of roses and lavender poured out of her skin, intoxicating the senses. She moved as if the ground was a mere illusion to be disregarded with her arms faintly bent upwards in prayer, a caress for the lithe forms of young gods. Her face had the impression of unborn awe, mesmerizing to see,

3

inviolate to the touch.

She danced to the sounds of incessantly beating drums, in patterns and rhythms deep and rumbling that seemed to echo from the walls of her very soul. They seemed to follow behind a melody of strings as clear as an erupting mountain spring. Like a fresh dew that engulfed the chamber a band of flutes called out to unseen spirits, as if a ritual of old was being performed for her pleasure alone.

The music reached a crescendo, a ground-shaking climax. She became frenzied with passion, exhuming a mystical air of love, a beacon of a haven for all the ones who were unloved. An unseen pact with a muse beckoned behind each tempting gesture.

Her faint gossamer dress swirled, failing to contain her ethereal form in such a breathtaking way, that even the flames of the brazers around the chamber flickered in tune with her dancing form to cast shadows that seemed to have a life of their own.

The crowd around her was silent and still, wearing almost identical masks of brass, the few flames that illuminated the chamber adorning them with golden hues of honey and the distinctive glimmer of sunlight upon metal.

A single man stood at the edge of the dancing stage. He was robed in heavy linen, his face unmasked for everyone to see. Tears were running down his cheeks, welling under his chin in an unwavering steady flow. His face was a painful mix of sorrow and awe, his eyelids closed shut in a vein attempt to contain his tears.

At the climax of her dance, she laid her body down on the stone floor, and planted her feet and hands on the stage with her back forming an arc. She start to convulse in a familiar but never spoken way, the way of ecstasy. Her pelvis moved to the rhythm of the drums, faster and faster, as if an invisible lover was holding her aloft, their bodies mingling with lust.

The music came abruptly to a stop and utter silence filled the chamber. She springed herself on her knees, her hair concealing her face completely. The silence was almost deafening. Her ragged, fast breath was the only sound that could be heard. Then, the unmasked man spoke while bowing solemnly:

"Celia, I lack the words. The Chorus weeps in adoration. Let everyone be witness to this moment: Celia danced the Edichoros, and

4

the Gods were pleased. So says the Chorus."

In a transient moment of still time, the crowd of masks said in one voice:

"Aye."

As soon as the word was spoken, the masked men dispersed as if answering to a silent summons and melted into the shadows, as if they were never really there, as if they had been a mirage, a background for this dance alone. The dancer and the unmasked man still remained.

He extended his arms, palms facing upwards, a gesture to the dancer or mayhap the Gods themselves. She stood up on her bare feet slowly, her hands touching her thighs over her gossamer dress, strands of her hair upon her bare shoulders. He spoke softly now, as if not to be overheard, even though there was not a living soul around in earshot.

"Celia, my love. Come."

At his words, she touched his palms and drew closer to him. She looked upon his face, wet with tears and lit by flickering flames, her hazel eyes still glittering with ecstasy, alight with enthusiasm and yet forming a wizened look that belied her years.

"Amonas."

She uttered his name with a feeling of relief.

"It is done. You need not worry anymore. Men and Gods alike will remember this night for all time," Amonas said sweetly while gently caressing her head.

"And you, will you cherish those tears?"

A faint smile formed on her mouth, a playful expression shone on her face and her eyes darted around his face with glee.

"Need you ask?"

His eyes ran all over her features, to her smooth hair, her sculpted nose, the lobes of her ears, her slender neck, her measured lips and back to her stare.

"I am only a woman, Amonas. I have to."

She craned her neck to meet his lips, tall as he was.

"I'm not worthy of such a gift."

Amonas told her as he stood still with black eyes peering at her closed eyelids.

"Speak no more."

Celia said and hushed him by touching his lips with hers. She then embraced his neck with both hands, softly but steadfastly guiding him towards her. Afterwards, they made love on that very stage. The silence of the chamber was only broken by the sound of sputtering candles and flaming braziers.

The Curator

A man dressed in dark crimson robes and a sky blue sash made haste up the curatorium's long winding staircase. Perspiration covered his craggy old leathery face and his gray bearded chin was still awash with the wine he had spilled only moments earlier.

"Damn the fools, damn them!"

He kept repeating these words to the deaf, heavy-set stone walls, with almost every breath. The flickering flame of the torch he held cast shadows of his form over the stones of the stair's steps and the dank walls. It resembled the form of a stumbling, muttering old fool. Even the shadows seemed to mock him, crouching even lower than him as the staircase finally unwound onto the roof of the curatorium.

"So, it has finally come to this," said the old man as he caught his breath, and started off to find what it was he had come looking for. His mind was not as sharp as when he was young, and he was caught unprepared. He fumbled around the roof while the lukewarm dusk gave way to the chilling, gloomy cloudy night.

He kept straightening his beard with one hand, keeping his eyes closed. His other hand was raised, waving a pondering finger in a hazy, uncertain rhythm. It looked as if it was trying to catch up with a silent tune only he could hear. Suddenly, he opened his eyes and set off with his head intently searching the floor.

The air smelled of liquorice and the burned wheat stalks of nearby farmsteads. It was the planting season. He looked annoyed, trying to pick up what seemed to be a loose cobblestone from the roof. It

6

seemed to give no purchase and try as he might, he could not remove it.

Standing upright, he folded his arms and breathed deeply, his elbows sagging slightly, his chin almost touching his chest. He sighed, and then abruptly erupted with a flurry of curses, kicks, punches and stomps. Quite an unseemly attitude for a person of his stature.

A Curator. By mutual assent among his peers, not a very prestigious one, but nonetheless, a Curator. The men had chased him up the stairs with profound alacrity and ruthlessness. Their drawn swords looked dull in the little light that was left, but the white of their teeth seemed to shine uncannily behind their wide grins. Forcing himself to calm down, he drew a few deep breaths before standing over one ledge from the roof and shouting, almost in a screech:

"Hilderich!!Hilderich!"

An answering shout came from somewhere below: "Over here master Olom, over here!" The curator leaned over the ledge, searching for a face to direct his ire at to no avail. He shouted once more, throwing his fists wildly into the air. The men drew ever closer slowly but surely, an air of supreme confidence about them. They had cornered him and there seemed to be no escape. The chase would be over now.

"Hilderich, you mongrel! Get the keystone and run! Run like there's no tomorrow!", said the curator and Hilderich complied smartly to the best of his ability. The Curator felt a strange rush of stinging air, turned about slowly, and had time enough to yell one last time at his pupil:

"Run now! Find the one I dared not!"

As Hilderich ran outside the curatorium, his gaze locked with the despairing eyes of his master, whose last look implored him silently to live. One of the men lunged forward with his blade set to pierce the old Curator. The wizened form of master Olom for a moment seemed to sidestep the blow nimbly, but that was not so. The blade had struck true, and the old man fell on his back without grace. As the second man raised his blade for the final blow, they were both grinning, their faces showing their relish, their enjoyment. This was what they lived for, the rush of murder and the smell of blood. They went about it in revered silence, cherishing every moment.

Hilderich simply stood there for a moment, transfixed, overtaken by the speed and incredulity of what was taking place. Fear had crept up in him, and had saved his life. And it was fear now as well, that urged him to heed his master's order. In the next moment, Hilderich was running with eyes wide from horror, his hands gripping the green, flashy keystone with white knuckles.

"Had to make sure first," said the curator through the agonizing pain of the blade's blow while clutching his pendant. As the blade of one of his assailants came rushing down to meet his sternum, he was smiling with a glaze in his eyes, as if lost in a loving vision of the past. When he blinked next, himself, the curatorium, and the two assasins became a thing of the past. Bright white light suddenly filled the dusky plains accompanied by an eerie, unnerving silence.

Hilderich only felt a haze of feat and a tingling at the back of his head. He dared not stop or look back, he simply ran. And he prayed.

The jester

HE grand audience hall was fabulously lit through grandiose arched windows on either side. Sunlight glistened off the brass and gold etchings everywhere around the hall, from chandeliers to decorative ornaments, invariably marked with the livery of the Castigator. Crests and banners engraved with family mottoes finely crafted from materials of the highest quality, hung in carefully positioned places around the hall. They denoted the respective family's status, lineage, and deeds.

Sweet aromas of burnt incense, cinnamon and musk permeated the air. Bouquets of freshly picked flowers with the colors of the rainbow were abundantly strewn around in neat vases and edifices all around the thick marble pillars that supported the magnificently painted dome, depicting wondrous scenes from the history, mythology, and tradition of the Outer Territories.

A ruckus of tingling bells and a flurry of strung chords echoed in the vastness of the audience hall, a single tinny voice singing along:

> Five pieces of gold that shone, and the sight of her alone
> Another man atop his throne, how will he ever atone
> Bloody hands reach for the tome, will he ever dare to come home?
> This ballad may remind you of lore, I might even sound a bore
> The heart of it still remains, all will always be the same
> As long as clouds grace the sky, as long as He will never die

The jester played out the last part of the tune, merrily dancing around the main hall, a wide smile was carved on his painted, multicolored face. As he hit the last of the chords, he ended his performance with a wide curved bow towards the man who sat in the center of the audience throne, his sole spectator, and waited there, until he heard a morose voice:

"I tire of you too easily these days, Perconal. You used to be more, ah.. Fun", said the voice that belonged to the Castigator of the Outer Territories.

"I could do the leap-frog again, sire," the jester countered with a hopeful proposition.

"That only seemed funny when you leap-frogged onto the Patriarch and the Procrastinator Militant. Never saw a Procrastinator Militant fumble for his sword like that before," the Castigator responded absent-mindedly, his head resting on his left hand, a goblet of wine on the other.

"No crowd today, sire. Who could I leap-frog onto then?", the jester insisted while fumbling with his crown of bells, his smile turning into an ever more persistent grin.

"No crowd indeed. I believe I tire of crowds as well lately."

"Perhaps .. an orgy?", proffered the jester, shamelessly making a rude pelvic thrust in the air, his hands mockingly grasping an imaginary waist.

The Castigator seemed to offer a little time to the idea, but a disapproving nod of his head made the jester suddenly wear the face of a crying, hurt man, his shoulders slumped, hands knead together, as if pleading.

"No, Perconal. I'm not in the mood."

"Then games sire! Games are always fun! And a challenge! Or are you perhaps.. Afraid?Surely not!", the jester said in a booming voice, and then exploded into a series of mock athletic gestures, like running, jumping and javelin throwing, flexing pitifully thin muscles, kneeling and offering an invisible crown to the Castigator, looking as solemn and expressionless as a grave.

"Games, you say?", the Castigator seemed briefly intrigued, and now rested his head on both hands, his voice slightly muffled.

While he seemed to ponder the idea, the jester scurried soundlessly near the table where the goblet of wine lay, and with a wide grin forming on his shallow face once again, he mischievously reached for it. The Castigator took notice, but said nothing. Eyes darting to and fro, the jester sipped some wine off the goblet, his painted lips smearing its bronze, delicately decorated surface, with white powder, red and violet paint. As the jester closed his eyes and savored the exquisite vintage, he felt steel like ice hard against his throat.

"Feuillout usually leaves too dry an aftertaste, don't you think?", the Castigator said to the jester in all seriousness, the knife in his hand set against the jester's throat, its edge flashing bright from the sunlight.

"Sire. I transgressed", replied the jester with any hint of grin or smile cast out instantly from his fear-stricken face.

"You did, Perconal. I hate it when you do that. I thought more highly of you. I believed you to be above such things," said the Castigator in an emphatically disappointed tone of voice.

"I was tempted sire. I haven't tasted wine, any wine that is, since.. I really can't remember. Truth be told sire, I can't."

The jester almost cried out the last few words, his head bowing in submission, his hands fumbling with his chordus, careful not to touch any strings lest he sound a note.

"Well, no matter. Tomorrow you will be castigated, forty lashes should be enough. People have been hanged for less. Water is so scarce, yet you would risk your life to indulge in wine tasting, no less. I think I'm growing a soft spot for you, Perconal."

"Thank you sire, Gods bless you and your divine rule. Can I at least have another sip, sire? It is so sweet," said the jester with a half-formed smile and the hint of a gesture towards the goblet.

"Another sip? Ha! There you go Perconal, you actually made me laugh. Ha ha!", a hearty laugh creased the Castigator's usually bored, flat face and shook his chest and head, before throwing the goblet on a nearby column, wine spilling all over the shiny, green-veined, black granite floor.

"There you go! Lap it up, you fool! Leave none for the maidens!" shouted the Castigator, a furious laughter welling up, unable to contain it. And Perconal the Jester helplessly ran about the marble floor, trying to sip as much of the spilled wine as he could, his bells and jingles ringing and echoing in the empty hall.

The boatman

ONE of my business, young sir, but given the chance and all since I don't get many passengers through here this ferry, being so far away from the Basilica Road and all, might I ask where do you come from? Beg your pardon, too,"the boatman ventured in a fast talkative manner, affording his passenger a casual gaze, beating the boat's rows in and out of the water with a calm, slow rhythm.

"Nicodemea. Far to the west, if you haven't heard of it. Is this safe? The fog, I mean."

The young passenger answered in an absent-minded fashion, his question trailing off with a hint of worry and nervousness, his eyes averted from the surrounding fog and water, focused instead on the boat itself as if an invisible wall had made such an effort vain.

"Why shouldn't it be? The water's dead still and there be no rocks on the other side, just green grass, young sir. You carry nothing more than your person, so missing the platform shouldn't be a bother. A simple matter, sir. We'll be there before you know it too. Looking for a mule or a horse, by any chance? You seem to have a long way to go ahead of you, ain't I right?"

"But the fog. Isn't it.."

The young man hesitated to add his thought fully, and a sour expression appeared on his face.

"Thick? Damn thick fog this time of the year, lifts at around noon, sets in before dusk. Pretty normal, sir. Come to think about it, I didn't catch your name. Care to share it in a friendly discussion? Reilo's mine," the ferry man interjected with a smile part glossy silver, part cavernous lack of teeth.

"Ahem, I'm Molo. Thessurdijan Molo," the young man said after a small pause and some fidgeting about with his cloak and belt before he revealed a gloved hand, proffering it to the boat handler.

"Can't right now lad, kinda caught up in rowing, remember? But very much obliged to meet you nevertheless, young sir. I'm Reilo, Reilo the boatman. Don't get many nice people like you around here. 'Specially not from the western parts," the ferry man nodded in acknowledgement, underlining the fact he was rowing by enthusiastically flapping the rows ineffectually above the water's surface, before adding with a note of apprehension:

"Not to sound too promiscuous sir, but what's a nice gent like you doing crossing these no-good-parts for?"

"Well you are quite talkative a fellow aren't you, Reilo? I'm a curator, on an errand, that's all," the young man rearranged his cloak, and peered past the boat man, through the fog, without success of glimpsing anything else than a gray oozing atmosphere and a thin shiny sliver of murky water.

"Must be quite an errand to travel that far, eh?"

"That, it is indeed," said the young man sounding suddenly grave. The fog started to lift about then and a light breeze rushed around them, the feeling of chilled clean air a welcome change on their cheeks.

"There you are sir Molo, fog's lifting. Clockwork, eh?", the gaping mouth of the man lending little of the associated perfection to the word.

"If you say so, Reilo."

"And once you're on the other side, how 'bout resting your aching feet for a while, eh? I got a cousin, fine lad. He's got comfy beds, real straw and all. Sensible prices too, mind you," the boat man tried press on his advantage while rowing the last few yards towards the shore.

"I'm looking to keep on moving, thank you," Molo answered politely.

"Then a horse might come in handy? Got a nephew, has a couple o' fine workhorses he could sell you cheap if I put a word too. It'd almost be a steal."

Reilo blinked one eye in a way that could have offered an onlooker too many wrong connotations.

"I won't be needing any of that, thank you Reilo," said Molo, stressing his expressed gratitude as well as his gentle patience by accenting his thanks.

"Alright sir, hope there are no regrets later on," said the boatman, somewhat disappointed his far too obvious sales pitch didn't hit off as he had hoped.

"Believe me, no regrets," answered Molo, and stepped off the boat and onto the river's shore, one hand on his knapsack, a walking rod in the other one. Soon, he picked up a brisk pace and after a few dozen feet met the road going east. He checked his few belongings one last time as a late afterthought and he set off once again.

The Pilgrim

HIS feet were sore. Cold air rushed to meet his face, the flimsy cloak he wore offering a little less than adequate protection. Tall grass grew on either side of the rocky path through the hills. The cries of a crow accompanied the howling gusts of the wind and the sky was painted a bleak gray, just like it had invariably been for the last few days. He looked around, searching for some kind of shelter at least until the wind decided to die down. He knew he had to rest soon, his body ached and his legs felt like they were cast in stone.

He spotted the large bark of a tree. It looked like a large hollowed out oak, grizzly and old. He made a dash of strained effort to reach it quickly as it lay further up the hill. A little more pain and then he could sit for a change, he thought. Perhaps even sleep, cold wind or not.

The oak was a perfect fit, large enough to lay down with only a small opening that even a lean man had to go through sideways. He was lean. As well as hungry, cold, tired and groggy. He put down his knapsack and grimaced from the pain of stiff, overworked muscles. He lay down on the ground, and felt like all his cares and troubles in the world had been suddenly lifted. He felt light as a feather and a sweet numbness encircled his senses.

He stretched his feet and looked upwards, through a small crack on the bark that let the view of the sky seep in. His sight wandered to the clouds passing overhead, gray tinted whisps of smoke on a sea of blue and black, reminding him of forlorn shapes running through a twisting, foaming river.

He closed his eyes and muttered a prayer, thanking his God for the timely shelter. He felt as if he was being looked after and cared for. To him, it was as if his pilgrimage was an extraordinary thing, a matter of unusually grave importance. He felt the mission he had to carry out was a mission worthy of every help and mercy. All he had to do was have faith, and he would persevere. His God would keep a watchful eye, and provide.

Soon he fell asleep, laying there looking as dead as the wood around him. He dreamt, but he would remember nothing when he would wake up. His chest rose and fell with a slow, deliberate rhythm. All around the oak, the thin grass bend where the wind blew. The crows had stopped their crying and some of them were perched on the very same oak.

A few drops of rain started to fall, and pretty soon the drops turned into a drizzle, thin and almost refreshing, a shower of a gift that the earth accepted eagerly. He was dry, and he was warm. He thought to himself, 'God always provides' and fell into a dreamless sleep.

The City of Pyr

"It is the will of the Gods for man to live as such, to be
humbled by his misgivings and sins, to be laid low. For if
it was man's destiny to live free as he desired, he would
sooner rather than later turn upon his own, his desires becoming a fatal trap, a wretched condition any man worth
living strives to keep in check daily, with prayer and the
Law as his guide. For without the Law, what is man but
a cunning animal?"

- Arch-minister Feinglot XXIV, *Porfyria Voluntas, Vol.
II*

Dangers of the trade

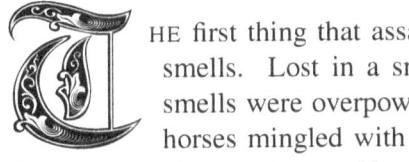HE first thing that assaulted Hilderich's senses were the
smells. Lost in a smelting crowd of city people, the
smells were overpowering: the acrid sweat of unkempt
horses mingled with rosewood and cinder scraps from
the carpenters' workshops. Heavy spices like cinnamon and uwe
flared his nostrils while an essence of oils and meats wandered

through the air. The smell of filthy beggars waxing and waning around every corner, its temporary absence filled in with incense from close by temples and intoxicating perfumes from passing, illustrious carriages.

The mix of sounds though felt familiar. It reminded him of bees buzzing through the meadows back home, whole swarms feeding on the nectar of roleva flowers over a golden carpet swaying gently under the evening gale. Now and then some voices stood taller than the rest, hints of tradesmen selling their wares and the ever present and watchful Ministers announcing laws, edicts, verdicts, punishments, and religious texts, all for the ears and minds of the good people of Pyr. The cacophony was further accented by the clacking sounds of hooves, the cries of pigs and the pleas of beggars.

Tall arches overhead cast angled shadows everywhere, the walls of the buildings like sheer cliffs towering over the palpitating mass of people and animals. Blue-gray rock and lime mortar dominated the market's landscape, the wear-torn cobblestones of the streets a hazy washed white wherever the grit and the mass of people allowed a small glimpse. Street after street, wall after wall, bronze engraved plaques embellished with holy texts and iconography hung on arches, balconies and posts, in favor of the Gods, in memory and glory of the Castigator and the Pantheon.

If the market was the heart of the city as its inhabitants claimed, then the popular piece of wisdom Hilderich had heard about Pyr being a heartless bitch seemed at once both right and wrong. Every single cast, class and type of man was to be found here: they were buying, selling, begging, stealing, killing, blackmailing and dying, all in one place. He had also heard there were parts of the market where the suns had never shown upon them since the city was built. There were dark corners where those who entered usually did not reappear, and when they did, blood that was not their own had soiled them. From what he was seeing before his eyes, no story could do the place justice. Everything could happen in the market of Pyr, that much he could imagine.

The beggars had become part of the landscape: blinds, invalids, all sorts of castaways and society's detritus were tugging away at embroidered hems, pleading with sore voices and grotesque faces. Those of them who bothered the wrong people time and again were soon beaten or stabbed to death by lackeys and guardsmen, left for dead on the same spot. As if that was not enough, they also seemed to attract the ire of the some merchants and artisans for not having the decency to crawl away from near their workshops and stalls and die someplace else where they would not put off potential customers.

But this was at the same time the place where everything of import came to be; this was where produce from the surrounding fields and indeed neighboring territories was gathered and sold to those who could afford it. This was where artisans created common everyday wares, materials and tools as well as delicate, commissioned works of art. This was the place were deals and partnerships were entered and broken, contracts signed and carried out. This was the place where everyone, whether a layman or a noble, had some kind of business.

This was the place were the Ministers' chants were heard every day, preaching, teaching, and enforcing the religion that is Law. The market in that sense, was a living representation, a miniature of where and how the people of Pyr lived their lives, and even how some of them lost them.

Hilderich was drifting along the current of people flowing incessantly through the market, occasionally bumping onto variably indifferent or protesting men, trying to take caution of the treads of carts, running heralds and practicing pickpockets. He could hear the Minister from the next street calling out a long list of names, while his eye caught two men in an unlit alley cracking another man's skull, their shadowy outline briskly contrasted with the lit background of the large street that ran behind the small alley. It seemed dishearteningly clear that this was business as usual in the market, that some code of practice had been followed and the formalities obeyed, killing a faceless man hidden away from the light of the suns.

His almost random course took him closer to the Minister's spot, an elaborate fountain made of granite, engraved with scenes of an historic battle from the Heathen times he could remember learning about as a child but could not immediately recognize. The Minister held a distaff on one hand, heavy-looking and oblique, and was still reading names off a long unwinding scroll fitted in some kind of extensible hook on the distaff that seemed purposefully designed. He wore a long robe made of violet velvet with a gold embroidered hem and a silver-lined crest of the Outer Territories woven on his chest. On his head lay a small black cap with a single emerald denoting his office, and both of the robe's arms were filled with holy texts written in Lingua Helica, the Territories' formal language, stitched in purple silk.

The ministers Hilderich had known made offerings to the Gods, upheld the Law and taught it to the people that looked to them for guidance in their daily lives. These holy men seemed somewhat distasteful, one might even call them pompous. He wondered what Master Olom's remark would have been and he was reminded of the duty he had yet to fulfill. He ignored the small mass of people gathered around the Minister as well as the rest of the still unfolding list of names, and lost himself once more in the throng of people. His senses had become acutely attuned by now, searching for a sign that would bring him a step closer to finding the one man he was searching for ever since that fateful night.

He conjured in his mind a brief glimpse of that night, an almost morbid recollection of what had happened. He had barely had time to stop and ponder the minutiae, while trying to get to Pyr as fast as possible, the place where he had to start his quite possibly fruitless search. The more he thought about what had exactly happened, the more he failed to grasp how everything had come crashing down like an avalanche: the perfect stillness in his life had been washed away by sheer and utter terror, an unavoidable terrible fate. Such was the end of Master Olom.

Even though he would not admit to it, he felt he somehow cheated death on that night, that it should have been him rather than his Master or at least he should have had the same luck, at least as a matter of principle. Thankfully wise master Olom, he thought, had believed otherwise and bought him time enought to live and make the most of his life. He would complete his master's lifetime work. He would not be doing it for his master's sake alone. If Olom had been right.. Hilderich could not imagine the consequences that that would imply.

Never pausing in his stride, Hilderich closed his eyes and clutched the keystone his master had entrusted him with ever so tightly. He had taken extra precautions ever since he had to carry the strange artifact with him. He always kept it on his person, and had fashioned a small metal holder with a small but sturdy chain fastened to his thick leather belt. The holder resembled the small cage of a sparrow. It was made of thin sheets of metal he had scrounged off the stables of an inn, the second day since he ran away from that explosion.

He remembered that vividly. An inexplicable explosion of light and heat, the sound of hundreds of steam engines going off at the same time. It must have been something ancient, there was no other logical explanation. But his knowledge of the Old People and their ways and artifacts was little compared to his master's and as far as he knew, no such examples were in master Olom's care. Hilderich had never seen or heard any hint of such awesomely destructive or powerful items since his apprenticeship began. Hilderich was starting to warm to the idea that it had perhaps been the Gods themselves that were responsible after all.

He let out a sigh without noticing. He looked crestfallen, his expression sour like unripe neranges. He had been so deeply engrossed in thought, that when he ventured a look around him he saw he was utterly lost, without a sense of direction in a part of the market conspicuously calm, lacking the overwhelming mass of people that at least offered him a false sense of safety that was nevertheless more welcome than none at all.

The far away din of the market proper could still be heard, but he had walked quite a distance and the crowd of people looked a little more than a milling sea of garments and bustling feet. With the corner of his eye he glimpsed a pair of shady figures that seemed to be stalking him, probably had been for a while, and from their earliest motions felt they were just about to gang up on him.

Hilderich was not a stoutly built fellow, and did not consider himself a man of action or someone capable of putting up a serious fight. But he had faith in his master's work, and his quest had to take precedence over everything else. He had to preserve his life in order to preserve the keystone, so he chose the most viable and logical course of action under the circumstances: he ran like hell.

He suddenly darted off towards the direction of what seemed to be a large bell tower, and ventured a slight look over his left shoulder to get the bearings of the figures behind him. They were just beyond hand's reach when he started running, his heavy cloak waving wildly, feet scurrying on the cobbled street.

One of them cursed profoundly and the other one shouted at him to stop, then both of them went on a chase after him. Hilderich went right and left crossing through alleys and larger streets, sometimes under the cover of shadow and others under the sunlight, trying to keep the tower that somehow seemed a public, safe place in sight, as well as give his pursuers the slip. He thought that surely, they wouldn't dare have a go at him in a public place in daylight. At least, that was what he was counting on. They seemed to prefer shadowy, lonely spots. He reminded himself to avoid the shadows.

The sound of boots on stone was still unmistakably behind him. Sweat had started to pour out of his body. He went past small houses, inns, and squares, while fleeing for what would certainly be his life. Curiously enough his mind registered that not a housewife or elder man ventured more than an indifferent look at the chase taking place in front of their eyes. Only the children paused in their play to look startled and amazed, point and giggle excitedly.

His feet started to ache and his breathing became short, almost painful. Fire welled up in his lungs and then he knew he could not keep this up for long. The tower he had set out to reach did not seem much closer than earlier. He ventured a slight look over his right shoulder, and couldn't see either of the figures chasing him. He listened intently for a few moments and could not make out the distinct noise of chasing boots, only rather his own two feet galloping achingly. He allowed himself a drop in pace and eased his breathing. He came to a slow stop near a shadowy wall, and bent over resting his hands on his knees. He threw scared looks around him, hoping that the chase had been over, that his assailants had somehow given up.

"Don't ever run off like that again."

The man's gruff voice seemed to come through the wall of stone, but he was only hiding deeper into the shadow of an adjoining alley. Hilderich instinctively turned around and saw a flash of light hinting at an unsheathed knife or sword, its wholeness under the cover of dark.

Hilderich drew enough of a breath to dart off again in another random direction, slipping away at the last minute like before, but then he noticed the other man: a red-haired bearded brute, pieces of armor showing underneath his shabby clothes with a jagged knife in hand. The big man stood a few paces to his right, steadfastly covering the only way out of his predicament.

With no real options left, Hilderich suddenly leaped on the man that had appeared from within the shadows, blade or no blade, in what could only really be a selfless last act of defiance. His mind flashed with the thought that he was soon about to die and fail his master for the last time. While he leaped he gathered his fist aiming for the man's head, trying to deliver as much pain as possible. His punch never connected.

The man still standing inside the shadows, expertly and calmly took a step back bending his back slightly, Hilderich's wild effort going awry. He hit nothing but air, lost his balance and made a counter-step trying to compensate. Just as he could feel his face freeze in astonishment, he brought his other hand backwards in order to try and have another go at punching his assailant. He did not manage that in any event though, because he winced and doubled-up at the paralyzing pain from the knee that had firmly and powerfully connected with his belly. He felt his stomach empty itself of its contents and his sight go blurry. A hint of red clogged his sight and his feet went limp and heavy, his breathing shallow. The last thing he saw before he passed out, was a grinning mouth and the icy clear flash of a steel blade.

She woke up with cold sweat on her forehead. Her temples damp, a few locks of hair glued against her face. She drew the bedsheets against her body, and curled up onto the empty side of her bed. She felt the unborn child inside her stir uncomfortably, as if awoken with terror by the same dream as her. She laid her hands on her belly and gently caressed it, feeling the child inside calm down and freely flow in a warm inner sea of love and protection.

The unborn child fell silent, its tiny heart barely stating it was alive and well inside its mother's womb. The mother, on the other hand, was still visibly shaken from her vision. She had seen rivers of blood engulfing her and her child, and fires bright as the suns all around her. She saw Amonas' head on a pike along with hundreds of other men's heads, hellishly put on display in a gory show. In front of them seething masses of animals, rather than men, were cheering with voices that echoed like broken glass brushing up against uncut stone.

The hair on her back was raised and she felt as helpless as a hawing flake of snow, unable to comfort herself and lay back to sleep. The shocking images in her nightmare had burned through her waking heart and mind. She stood up with some effort and with a slow attentive pace, went to the balcony. The night was invitingly chilly, offering a crystal clear sky. The few clouds overhead were like thin gossamer webs the Gods might have woven to catch a falling star.

She peered out over the never-sleeping city, its market always alight with torches and large common pyres. Strange shadows flickered on walls, while fleetingly illuminated faces with blank expressions as if in a haze of ecstasy whirled in the rhythmic dance of the city like strands of cloth spun in the air.

The Ministry Tower and the Disciplinarium were lit as bright as day, their proud banners flung high and wide. A procession of ministers was underway, and another festivity in the Disciplinarium's garden that sported tricks of fire and light was taking place, washing the rest of the city with golden red hues and splashes of green and blue light as if there was not a care in the whole world.

The rugged brown stonework of the balcony felt rough under her smooth touch. She moved her hand unconsciously across the stone while gazing at the city, vainly searching for her loved one among the sands of men. Her hand seemed to dance, ebbing and flowing to a melody even she herself couldn't hear, like conducting an invisible chorus of spirits of old that seemed to inhabit this very stone.

She closed her eyes momentarily and the image of Amonas' head haunted her, blood still pouring hot out of him. She held her breath and moved her lips in a silent prayer, wishing her dream was nothing more than simple fear and worry of whatever lay ahead. She thought to herself that her faith should not waver, that she must be strong enough for Amonas' sake and above all for sake of their unborn child. She wished for the good winds of fortune to carry them forward and hoped that all would be as it should be.

Her child stirred once more, soothing her soul and bringing a faint smile to her face. She went back inside and laid herself on her bed, her hands resting on the still empty side. Sleep overtook her in peace, her face a statue of serenity. She saw no more dreams or nightmares on that night.

Inescapable Reality

ILDERICH knew he was still alive since the men's voices echoed faintly inside his throbbing head. Pain was stabbing him in the back of his neck and his muscles were stiff from a prolonged unconsciousness. He opened his eyes and blinked furiously, his eyesight adjusting to a brightly lit chamber with sunlight pouring from tall arched glass windows and a radiant glass dome above.

A small table occupied the middle of the room and a flimsy looking cupboard adorned the opposite wall. The two men that had attacked him were looking at him with what looked like cautious curiosity and apprehension. The bearded brute was standing up with his hands in his pockets and the man with the gruff voice was sitting down at the table. A beam of light partly obscured his face, while dust motes whirled silently in the air.

Hilderich lay in a small stone cot carved into a recess of a far wall. The cot felt uncomfortable and his body protested slightly to his efforts at moving. He flexed his arms and legs momentarily, and realized he was not bound or restrained in any way. Puzzlement showed on his face, and then the man who had bested him in the alleyway addressed him:

"You were out for almost a day. I am sorry we had to take somewhat extreme measures, but we had to make sure you disappeared properly. Giving us the run did not help, so we had to make it look like you were being mugged. Hence the terrible headache you must be having. I apologize for being rather rough," the man's voice gruff but genuinely polite, almost friendly. His words were followed by a faint smile and what seemed like a condescending nod.

"Dunno if that put any sense innim though," the bearded man grumbled under his breath audibly enough, regarding Hilderich with a look akin to contempt.

"Philo.. Please," said the man in the friendly voice who appeared to be the better of the brutish red-haired man, someone in authority of some sort.

Hilderich noted the brute's name was Philo and watched him for moment, as he made a snorting sound and then crossed his hands across his chest. He then leaned against a wall and quieted down, as the other man had requested. The polite man with the coarse voice continued:

"My friend here thinks you are somewhat dim and unforgivably naive for a place like Pyr. That remains to be seen. I think you will prove to be very useful indeed, no matter what the initial appearances suggest," said the man, eyes level with Hilderich's who was now sitting upright on the small cot.

"Who are you people? I thought you wanted to kill me, and be done for. You said you wanted it make it look like I was mugged? Why would you want to make me disappear? Why am I here?", the look on Hilderich's face was contorted with eyebrows that almost touched each other. His puzzlement was now even more evident than before.

"Again, I apologize. My name is Amonas and this, as you must know already, is Philo. Let's leave it at that for now. There are things I can and things I cannot explain to you, at least for the time being. You had to disappear because you were at risk of being found by people with an agenda quite different than ours, one that you'd certainly have found to be at least disagreeable. Once I make myself clear you will understand our course of action was necessary for more significant reasons, as well as for your protection. Soon enough, you will need to reach a decision."

"What kind of decision? Am I being threatened? You did not bind my hands. Am I a being held as a prisoner? What exactly do you want with me?"

"You are in no way a prisoner. We just needed to talk to you in safety. Please, hear what I have to say first before you jump to any wrong conclusions and make up your mind in haste. It is a matter of grave importance, and it involves the keystone in your possession."

Amonas' tone carried a hint of pleading and urgency, his words almost becoming jarred against each other. At the mention of the keystone, Hilderich was left wide-eyed.

"Aye, we knew," Philo added, casting a severe look upon Hilderich.

They knew? Since when? The thoughts kept rushing through his mind. What should he ask and what he might reveal that he should not troubled him. Was there indeed real danger here? Were they telling him the truth? Was he being safeguarded? He instinctively reached for the chain on his belt but it was not there. They had taken it. They had taken the keystone. Had he failed already? Was there a point to all this? His face took on an expression of silent horror, mouth frantically opening and closing without a sound coming out, like a fish out of the water, the spasms of death upon it.

Hilderich shouted in a trembling voice that could have been mistaken for a shriek:

"Give it back! Thieves! You are nothing but common th eves!"

He was standing upright now, his head frantically turning from Amonas to Philo and back, casting looks of urgent accusation, wide-eyed and tense. He regained a measure of self-control, and clasped his hands together as if pleading for mercy. He closed his eyes and said in a clear, level voice:

"Please. Give it back. It is not of any significant worth as a gem. I can pay you in good time, I can make arrangements. But please, give me back the stone."

Hilderich had lied flat out to them for being able to arrange some sort of payment. Everything he owned he carried on his person and that much was the extend of his fortune. He hoped his bluff might work.

Amonas and Philo were exchanging dumbstruck locks with Hilderich's outburst having caught them by complete surprise. When they both seemed to be trying to answer, all they could do was break into a hearty fit of laughter. Philo while still laughing, managed to speak:

"Thieves! And the.. 'Please'? Listen to how that sounds, lad."

Amonas cut in with a motion of his hand and took a beleaguered Hilderich by the arm. A calming, reassuring voice issued from his mouth:

"Fear not. We mean you no harm. We consider you a friend, and if you'd choose so, a brother as well. The keystone is safely with me, I have it on my person. Here," and Amonas unclasped his cloak to reveal the keystone and chain safely tucked away in a pocket on his leather bodice, the chain firmly attached to a ringed metal bel .

The sight of the keystone calmed Hilderich somewhat, but he still seemed uneasy, willing to protest. His eyes darted around, a look of hurt feelings and pride in his eyes:

"What kind of friend hunts you down, knocks you out, and then robs you of your most valuable possessions?"

"Your new ones do, at least the first time around. Please, listen to me Hilderich. We know about what happened to your master. It pains me as well, I knew Olom personally."

Amonas let that sink in a bit, recalling a few memories of his own, and then carried on:

"There is trouble brewing ahead in the Outer Territories. What happened that night at your curatorium was neither singular nor a chance event. The keystones from curatoriums around the Territories are being stolen, and sometimes curators try to put up a fight. In some cases, like yours and your master's, there are deaths involved. The timing is too perfect to be a mere coincidence. We cannot yet ascertain exactly who is orchestrating this, but we have a pretty good idea."

Amonas glanced sideways at Philo, who nodded knowingly.

"You knew my master? Do you have any proof of that? Who is 'we'? Are you some sort of group? An organization? A cult? What is the Curatoria doing about this? I wouldn't like to attract your ire, but I can't exactly think a man who kidnaps people to 'have a talk' as trustworthy."

Hilderich showed his distrust even by the creases in his forehead. The people in front of him indeed seemed to him to make little sense and what he had heard so far felt very thin indeed.

"I knew him and loved him dearly. I'll show you proof if that's what will gain us your trust, soon enough. We are not a cult, Hilderich. We might be many things, but a cult we're not. You could call us a group, perhaps. We call ourselves Kin. Or Brotherhood of Old. Or Old-folk. We come by many names. Some help us stay hidden, some help us raise support. Your support, for instance."

Hilderich's face looked incredulous at best, right on the edge of laughing in disbelief:

"You want my support? And this is how you go about asking people for you support? Ganging up on them in the middle of the street? Support for what? Clubbing more people in the head?!", Hilderich's tone emphasised how incredulous this all seemed to him. Philo seemed especially displeased with his tone and remarks, while Amonas stayed calm and resolute, determined to make his point.

"We want your support in order to claim back our lands, overthrow the tyranny of the Castigator and expose the hateful lie that is Pantheon."

Amonas words came out like the rush of an unstoppable river, ready to wash away everything that might dare to stand in its path. He sounded earthly solid and unyielding, utterly determined and deadly serious. Hilderich was too impressed to actually register what the man had just said.

"Well, that is.. Did you just.. But, that's heresy! And high treason!"

Hilderich almost stammered the words aloud, unable to contain his shock, while Amonas replied in kind:

"Heresy is nothing but the leash that binds our blind brethren. Treason is the act of paying tribute to false gods, letting our Kin of Old fade like ghosts with nothing left for them to haunt.."

Amonas was in an instant transformed in Hilderich's eyes. What seemed like a calm, reasonable person, yet mysterious, shady and quite incredulous, had given its place to a fiery zealot of some sorely misguided cult of heretics. Hot embers seemed to have replaced instead his eyes, burning with the mindless passion of a fanatic with an untenable goal.

Hilderich wasn't sure of what to say to such a man, but he settled for what felt like the truth of things:

"You must be out of your mind then. Deranged. Or just very misguided. But no.. You would have to be crazy for all that to run through your head without it bursting at the seams."

Amonas was grinning with a faint smile now:

"Am I Hilderich? Or is it you that has been played like a fool? Like I had been before I saw the truth, and felt the righteousness of our cause? Like Philo was when he was still a killer for hire? It is shocking, I admit it. But by the end of the day, I promise you you'll see the truth of things as well. If you place any value in it, you will be given sight and hearing anew, and you'll be ready to decide for yourself. We can become brothers, or remain simply friends on separate paths."

"You seem too confident in what you say, and maybe you are a special breed of crazy. But I cannot even begin to imagine how you can prove that these aren't the rumblings of a madman, that Gods forbid, our religion is a lie. I must confess, I find some of the Castigator's and the ministers decisions and punishments harsh and unfitting, but I dare not judge their wisdom, or the Law as we have been taught it. It is one thing to doubt the people that uphold the Law, and quite another to judge what is Holy Law, inviolate and heaven-sent."

Hilderich was now exuding an air of authenticity and oratory skill, dressed with a rarely exhibited confidence, expressing an almost staunch belief. He looked like he knew he was right, and Amonas wrong.

Amonas grin would not go away when he nodded to Hilderich with a motion of his head and then looked up to meet a well-nigh defiant gaze. He told him in his hoarse, steady voice:

"The seed of doubt is already sown in your soul, Hilderich. Tonight it shall spring to bear fruit at last. It is a good sign, for I believed you would be too unwilling to see the truth, but this may yet prove not to be the case."

"I still think you are madmen. Suppose it is true, that the Law and the Gods are a lie? What then? If everything we've ever believed in is a lie, what will the people do? Where will they turn to? If you, for the case of argument, succeed in your purpose, with what will you replace everything that gives sense and purpose to our lives every day? Do you plan to overthrow the Castigator, and the army and all the nobles who will stand against you by mere force of conviction? Or perhaps you cherish a fantasy where all but a few will join your cause, and no blood will be spilled in the inescapable day of triumph?"

"You are more of a thinker than I had believed, Hilderich. Above all, you seem a man of logic. Your questions will be answered in due time. A bit of patience will go a long way. And in any case, we can't allow you to leave just yet, not before you witness what will invariably change your opinion, for better or for worse. You will come around to see that we are not crazy, and that we know that chaos and mayhem will erupt once we decide the time has come to act. I have no fantasies and will bear no misgivings: blood will be spilled inevitably, but not in vain. These are not the endeavors of bloodthirsty warmongers or power-hungry dissidents, Hilderich. We are hope incarnate, nothing more and nothing less."

"Hope incarnate? Doesn't that sound a bit presumptious? You certainly seem to lack modesty as well as sanity."

Hilderich's mocking tone was destined for an insult. His remark made Philo move and fidget with suppressed anger, shooting pleading looks at Amonas, clearly intent at putting the audacious little man in his place through the use of some non-crippling violence. Amonas would have none of that though and dismissed Philo's silent protests with an outstretched hand, replying in a serious and honest tone of voice to Hilderich:

"I can only force you to remain until my promise to you is kept, until I make you see. I need your help Hilderich, I need to know things that have been kept in the dark for too long. Olom was getting close, too close perhaps. I need you to make sense of what I cannot, Hilderich. If what I show you does not seem worthy of your time, then you can freely go your own way if you like. But the keystone has to remain with us."

"So this is not so much of an offer, as it is a blackmail. I can go, but the keystone stays with you? And you ask me to trust in you under these conditions? Tell me in earnest, would you think any differently if you were in my spot?"

"I have been in a similar spot like you and no, I did not think differently. That is why I believe you'll be our brother by the first light of dawn tomorrow."

Amonas smiled heartily for Hilderich to see, but the young curator's expression remained distant and withdrawn.

"You place too much on mere belief and court with arrogance, Amonas. I don't like all of this one bit. But it seems that I am at your mercy, for better of worse. Would you have me trying to wrestle my freedom and the keystone out of your hands? Whatever I may think of you, I'm no fighter and you seem to know that as well. I have no real choice in the matter, do I?"

"You will prove more valuable and insightful than I had imagined, Hilderich. It is exactly that false belief and that vaunted arrogance that we seek to expose, and since you place no value in those, I consider you a brother already, a man free of those poisons."

"We shall see, but don't bet on it."

Hilderich sat down on the cot once again, hands on his knees, seemingly resigned to his fate. He had tried to make a stand, send out a message that he would not succumb to such underhanded tactics. If not in essence, at least as a matter of principle.

"I am not a gambling man Hilderich, you need not worry. There is still some time ahead of us. You must be famished. Would you like to have something to eat? I know we have been less than welcoming so far, but the circumstances got the better of us. Please, indulge us."

Hilderich pondered this for a while and in his mind dismissed the idea that the food might be poisoned. If they had wanted him dead, they wouldn't have bothered with all these theatrics. It seemed somewhat of a concession to the man effectively holding him captive, but the inescapable reality of not having eaten for more than a whole day struck home in the end. He nodded in acknowledgement and then added verbally:

"That would be sort of nice."

Amonas smiled politely and told Philo to get some food and water for the three of them. Promptly the brutishly large man vanished behind a rather small wooden door, his steps faintly audible as he climbed down a wooden staircase.

"I'm told our most hospitable friends here have prepared a delicacy today: lamb stew with uwe and knop leaves. Should be rather tasty."

"I still think you are crazy, Amonas. Just a very strange and mysterious kind of crazy person, apparently with a culinary taste to match."

"Hilderich, I confess, I have a soft spot for uwe. It's an acquired taste, I know."

Hilderich just shook his head in disbelief, a small sigh escaping his lips. Amonas smiled ever more broadly at that particular reaction, and pretty soon the strong smell of boiled uwe wafted through, hinting at Philo's return. Amonas seemed rather expectant, and could not help asking Hilderich:

"If you don't like uwe I believe a different arrangement can be made. Perhaps some ham or bread-pie."

"Uwe lamb stew will be fine. I can manage."

Hilderich caught himself being actually irritated at Amonas' inexplicable insistence on food, which he found rather childish, further enhancing his opinion that the man was indeed deranged, if not outright mad.

"Oh well, I had to try and steal that extra serving."

Philo returned and entered through the door with some difficulty due to the fact he was trying to balance two plates of stew on his left hand and arm and a large bowl held with his right hand. He precariously managed to reach the safety of a nearby table putting the bowl down first, and then unloading the plate off his left arm. Seeing that no one cared to assist him he threw around a few looks of mixed hurt and mild anger, before pulling a chair and sitting at the table and then proclaiming:

"If you gonna join the table be quick about it."

Amonas sat excitedly in front of the bowl of stew, and Hilderich guessed the other plate was laid out for him and sat accordingly, but couldn't help noticing and asking:

"Shouldn't there be another plate for Amonas?"

Amonas had already dug in with a spoon, and seemed quite indifferent at anything else that went on around him and rather focused at enjoying his substantially rich meal.

"No point in using a plate if he's gonna eat a whole bowl. So I brought the bowl. Now, eat.", Philo said with a hint of retired disapproval.

Hilderich nodded slowly, shrugged and dug in like the others. He took a careful taste, and then started munching and gulping down large chunks of stew eagerly. It tasted delicious indeed.

Darkly lit night

HE Disciplinarium's large audience hall was exquisitely decorated with fine tapestries, hung from the columns and walls with golden ropes and aggrandized with silk laces, freshly picked fragrant flowers and all manners of decorations that go hand in hand with highly luxurious pomp and ceremony.

Though night had already fallen, giant ornate silver and brass chandeliers hung from the high ceilings illuminating the grand hall with the light of thousands candles. Their beams of light were enhanced and mirrored by all the brass, gold and silver decorations strewn around almost every object in the hall, making them glitter and shine, magnifying their splendor tenfold.

Delicately detailed lifelike oil paintings adorned each wall: previous Castigators and Arch-ministers, Procrastinator Militants and Patriarchs, noble supporter families of the Castigator. Every important person that was notably recorded in the zealously well-maintained history books was to be found here in the form of awe inspiring portraits, paintings and sculptures from the most talented artists of each generation from around the lands.

The mass of people was still flowing slowly but steadily into the hall, and for a time it would seem like the small swarm of men was going to swell to inelegant numbers. But the Castigator's people in charge of the eventful night, had meticulously planned who was to be given the praise of summons. They also decided on the time of each person's appearance as well as whether or not he should be given the privilege of being able to dine at the same table as the Castigator. Albeit always at an innocuous distance a table seating on the Castigator's table implied an immense increase of status and almost unrivaled political power.

As the time for the opening ceremonies for the grand festive night grew closer, all the needed preparations were being doubly checked and the gathering of guests efficiently monitored. Everything seemed to be in place, refreshments and drinks served in silver plated cups; sweetmeats, fruit, and fine pastries circulating among the crowd in golden platters by busy servants dressed in fine cloth wearing the green livery of the Castigator's office: a white eagle bearing a book and a key, a snake held in its beak.

People were chatting in low voices, politely exchanging greetings and news of the lands, though some of the more brazen guests that either lacked the knowledge of etiquette or were in a position to ignore it as a whole or in part, were already laughing heartily at jokes or anecdotes between friends and close acquaintances.

Everyone attending had been careful to dress as stylishly as possible, and according to wealth and status there were examples of extravagant overdressing, with some people closely resembling moving heaps of gold and silver, like treasure-laden mules.

Others preferred to overstate their presence with exotic cloths and tailorings, usually uncommon and outlandish, suggesting time and money had been spent just for this one occasion. Indeed everyone was wearing the best and brightest they could afford, and maybe some had even took on a loan to have something special tailor-made in order to try and stand out in the crowd, in a certainly desperate bid to improve their fame and fortune.

The atmosphere in the hall was generally convivial though mildly restrained because of the premises and significance of the night. The festivities were taking place in order to commemorate the Castigator's 25th Term in Office, which coincided with the anninversary of the Pacification of Zaelin, the last of the Territories to be enlightened and brought under the Law of the Pantheon.

Rumors circulated among the nobles' elite as well as people in the army and the Ministry that the Castigator would be announcing a decision of major importance that would stir up the relatively still and quiet recent affairs of the Territories, perhaps ushering a new era of glory to the Gods, and perhaps for the people as well.

In any case it promised to be an eventful night, with dancing troupes of wondrous abilities, unsurpassed technique and airy grace performing for its duration. Bards of worldly renown and enchanting voices had prepared to sing the Mythos in praise of the Castigator and the Pantheon, a telling re-enactment of the Pacification of Zaelin and the striking down of the last Heathen; Parnoth Larthiel, the Last Ignorant.

The re-enactment would also offer a kind of prize to one of the guests who would be lucky enough for his name to be drawn amongst hundreds: he would have the chance to play as the Castigator in the final duel with Parnoth, the unclaimed role filled in by a lawbreaker due for execution. The honored guest in killing the lawbreaker-Parnoth would be spilling heretic blood in the service of the Ministry, the Castigator and the Law. It was quite possibly the highest service to the Pantheon possible, save sacrificing one's self while enforcing or upholding the Law.

A huge oblong platinum chime resounded by the stroke of an ornamental ram swung by two Protectors, the Castigator's personally hand-picked guard, and judging by their imposing physical builds apparently chosen chiefly for their brawn. The sound of the chime drowned out the chatter of the milling guests; it reverberated with a majestic effect in the audience hall, and signaled the official commencement of the festivities. Acoustics was one of many things not left to chance when the grandiose chamber was built in the time of the Founding.

The crowd of guests went by in silence, ushered inside by dutiful servants and thick-set expressionless Protectors gathered on two opposing sides of the hall, leaving a wide stretch of room where the Castigator was meant to walk through when he would be announced. Indeed, the voice of the Chief Functionary boomed like a cannon in the night:

"All kneel or be chastised for now enters this hall his Holy Piousness, Olorius Menamon the IV th, Deliverer of Aconia, Pacifier of Zaelin, Proxy of the Gods, Procurer of the One True Law, and Castigator of the Outer Territories. Kneel or be chastised!"

The last words uttered with the gravity of a holy commandment, the obvious threat to be carried out with ruthless deliberation if the need ever arose.

At once and in concert, the whole of the crowd including the servants, Protectors, Ministers, as well as the whole of the Disciplinarium's staff, any and all figures of authority, military or religious including the Chief Functionary, knelt on both legs and bowed their heads deeply and solemnly, as if in wholehearted prayer.

The workings of some kind of a large mechanism probably involving gears and other mechanical contraptions rang through the audience hall. The massive copper tinted Gates of Leor opened slowly but steadily, revealing the radiant form of the Castigator breathtakingly dressed in the formal robes of his Office: a deep crimson color dyed in the blood of heathens and heretics, solid golden runes written in Helica Preatoria adorning the hem. The first two pages of the Book of Law covered its surface in so fine a silk thread that its weavers were known to have gone blind in the effort.

Above his robes the Castigator wore an immaculate platinum breastplate, without carvings, etchings or any other decoration whatsoever. On one side hung Urtis, the Mace of Judgment, the Castigator's long ago chosen tool of enlightenment and battle, that was said to have cracked as many heretic skulls as there are stones in the walls of the Disciplinarium. Indeed, some claim the very same skulls have been used in building the latest parts of the majestic building as a morbid reminder that All is Law.

The Castigator strode with a steady pace down the central lane where a raised block of marble floor had appeared in concert with the opening of the Gates. The only sound in the grand chamber was the sound of the Castigator's boots: a simple, utilitarian set of metal plated boots a soldier would wear, finely polished but otherwise quite common. When he reached the dais on which the Seat of Office stood, he surveyed the crowd momentarily, sat down and clapped his bare hands once.

"Stand and confess!", the Chief Functionary bellowed sharply, and the crowd complied smartly and fervently:

"All is Law!"

The Castigator echoed back the mantra in solemn ritual, his voice carrying unusual depth and mesmerizing melody for a single man, however powerful and unique he may be.

Those that saw the Castigator and had not been granted such an honor before in their lives, were immediately left awestruck. Some of them even broke down weeping, pious fervor instantly occupying their hearts and minds. Those that had been blessed so before, did not immediately stand but rather silently prayed with tears welling in their eyes, before being able to stand again erect. The people that kept closer to the Castigator, his immediate entourage, the Ruling Council, and his guards intoned the holy mantra reverently and resumed their places and functions.

The Castigator then addressed the crowd which stood there reverently, their excitement and waiting evident in their glittering eyes and tense faces:

"I shall call you my children, for I am like a father unto you. I guide you, protect you, offer you learning and sustenance, like a father does for his child. I ask you: Does not the Ministry keep a daily watch for the heretic, the heathen, the lawbreaker? Does it not preach the Law every day, for the continued enlightenment of all? The Army, does it not safeguard our lands, from enemies from within and from without? The Procrastinators, do they not wisely guide your every day lives, always watching over you lest you stray into a horrible path with no redemption in sight? I ask you again, am I not like a father unto you all?"

The Castigator's voice turned from a sweet melody into a harsh pragmatist's staccato tone, then back in a wavering, almost pleading tone, evoking sympathy and familiarity. The Chief Functionary struck down his distaff on the granite floor once, and spoke aloud while nodding surreptitiously, his bearded chin almost touching his chest: "Aye!"

The crowd followed in check, the audience hall reverberating from the loud voices of what now seemed to be almost a thousand people.

"This then I tell you as a father: For the betterment of us all, for the glory of the Pantheon, in two weeks time, the Holy and Righteous Armies of the Outer Territories shall march into the Widelands to bring it enlightenment, cleanse the land, and finally make the Land of the Gods whole, as is their mandate."

His voice rang true and clear around the chamber. His message rang inviolate and final, a decision that was to be carried out, not thought upon or discussed but a matter of fact that he had set in motion with but a few of his words.

Most of the Ministers, Generals and other officials of the Disciplinarium were apparently surprised, though they instantly recovered a measure of composure and if one had not been eying them constantly, they would have looked easily unperturbed by the announcement and its implications.

The Procrastinator Militant in his exquisite armor and fine silk sash was at a loss for words, and opened his mouth wide-eyed as if in protestation, but his disciplined service and training kicked in and he barely managed to save himself from embarrassment by nodding in the last minute and simply saying "His Piousness has spoken".

The other members of the Ruling Council, the Arch-minister, the Patriarch, and the Noble Representative had their gaze locked on the Procrastinator Militant, as if waiting for a sidestep or a slip that would bring him crashing down in a most shameful and undignified way, an affront to the significance of the night.

The Noble Representative, dressed in a simple green robe of the practical sort, his chest adorned with the signet brooch of House Remis suppressed a grin at the nearly unforgivable blunder that would have definitely incurred a public lashing and a year's donation to the Ministry, let alone probably kill the Procrastinator Militart's career on the spot.

"I have indeed! Now feast, enjoy and praise the Gods!", the Castigator raised his arms in jubilation and smiled broadly, the atmosphere in the hall warming up in the blink of an eye. People started to shuffle around seeking food, drink, or whoever they had been talking with before the Castigator entered the hall. The announcement of setting out to pacify the last wild region, the Widelands, was definitely going to spur debate however hushed it might be.

Lord Umsepyre Remis, the Noble Representative, was seated in the council in order to speak on behalf of the noble families of the Outer Territories. His was a purely consultative role, expressing current views among the noble houses, informing the Ruling Council of the ebbs and flows of power, wealth, and status, as well as the reactions and thoughts of the nobles on affairs of state, religion and Law.

Even though he had no voting rights in the Council, his input was often quite impossible to receive otherwise and any network of informers too crude in comparison. The Castigator seemed to consider him a quite valuable asset, judging by the special dispensations recently appointed to House Remis. Likewise, Umsepyre Remis was the insightful eye and ear of the Noble houses concerning the inner workings of the Ministry and the Castigator, and solid knowledge of what went on in the Disciplinarium sometimes could buy things money could not.

His was a unique position where he could not be accounted for practically anything since he was not part of the decision making process, but was amply able to exchange information and insight as he saw fit, to better suit the continued survival of his House.

He smiled brightly at the still uneasy Procrastinator Militant, and made a gesture to straighten his shoulder-high long black hair, in an almost overly bland demonstration of cool confidence.

The music that would accompany the dancing acts had started with a brass fanfare which soon settled in a soft string melody, oddly accented in parts by flutes and bass drums. The dancers performed practiced choreographed scenes from the Mythos, reliving the handing down of the Law from the Gods to men.

The Patriarch noted the interest on Lord Remis face who was more than visibly enchanted by the dancers' performance, while the Procrastinator Militant had hurriedly called for his chief aide more so in order to look busy and industrious, rather than because actual operational planning could happen at such a time and place. The Archminister was indeed busy on the other hand, a trio of scribes jotting down notes and letters to be sent immediately in order to notify key personnel of the imminent rush of preparations that needed to start as soon as possible.

"Lord Remis. A patron of the Arts should be more circumspect in his admirations, don't you think? Some may misinterpret your artistic admiration for mere lust. And lust is a sin, Umsepyre."

The Patriarch's tone was precipitously balanced between the whimsical and playful, and the vehemently dangerous and cunningly suggestive, his mouth and face a rigid, expressionless mask. The man was an almost complete mystery to Remis; he had to confess to himself that the Patriarch's remarks and suggestions always left an aftertaste of sourness.

Remis was not decisively put off and managed to respond appropriately, though the effect on the Patriarch seemed to be minimal at best:

"The day we look upon the Mythos with lust, Your Reverence, is the day all sin will be revealed."

"Ah, quoting Law back to me. I see. Am I making you uncomfortable, Noble Representative? Is there a reason about it that you would care to share?"

The Patriarch was now smiling genially with a nearly fatherly candor, eyes darting around Lord Remis face with a seemingly genuine worry apparent on the craggy old man's face.

"No, not uncomfortable Patriarch. I would say, curious," said Remis without looking directly at the Patriarch.

"Curious? Of the coming, final campaign?", the Patriarch ventured, raising his eyebrows and hinting he knew better than that.

"No. Of you, Your Reverence. You are always shall I dare say, fleeting."

Ursempyre turned and looked the Patriarch directly in the eyes, seeing cold pinpricks of blue that reminded him of icy death and men disappearing in a deep watery grave.

"Oh well then. I would dearly hate to spoil your idea of me," the Patriarch answered, his head and gaze locked in place in front of him and walked into the crowd, his figure soon blending in until the point it disappeared.

Remis was bereft of any other thought, trying to ponder what really went on in that man's head when the Castigator's voice reawakened him back into his immediate surroundings:

"Ah, my dear Ursempyre. Is the Patriarch causing you trouble?"

The Castigator touched one of Remis' shoulders, a rare gesture of unmatched camaraderie. Such an act could only mean he was indeed the Castigator's favorite for ascension. Ursempyre turned and bowed slightly, careful with the words he chose as well as his body language:

"Trouble is what a drunkard might cause, or a hapless wife. The Patriarch feels like a man who causes death, Your Holiness. He always seems to be, so detached."

"Ah, the toils of the Church. Holy Communion with the Gods can be too much sometimes. However gifted and trained a man might be. You say he reeks of death? I say if the Gods will it, I shall follow wherever I must. Won't you, Remis?"

The Castigator's look had been transfixed on him, awaiting a sure and clear answer that would dispell all doubt. Ursempyre indulged him accordingly:

"All is Law, Lord. Unto death and beyond. For the glory of the

Pantheon."

Remis recited the last phrase of the Oaths and crossed his hands over his chest, further reaffirming his loyalties.

"You are a good man Ursempyre. Now, drink! It is a night of feasting, and joyous celebration. Won't you join me?"

The Castigator's eyes suddenly turned ablaze with wrath and fury, menace hidden under his voice. Ursempyre was taken aback taking care not to show it, and simply bowed and said:

"Of course, Your Piousness."

The Castigator broke into laughter as if having heard a joke no one else could, and started the rounds of the audience hall, like a perfectly good host.

Ursempyre followed close behind, not so happy of his singular position as he would have normally been. He took a silver cup filled with mead and drank it in one go. There was a long night ahead of him.

The marble road

I T was hunting time for the owls, the wild dogs and the wengals. He sat down on the cold, humid grass with his legs crossed and a walking stick on his left shoulder. He rummaged through his ever lightening knapsack for something to eat. With little fuss, he managed to come up with a meager meal: worrain berries and a piece of goat's cheese, still fresh and spongy. He tried to feed as much on the land as possible, keeping most of his food supplies for the difficult part of his journey, the Widelands themselves.

The people in the village he went through last were the usual sort in these parts: animal herders mostly, and a few wheat farmers. Simple people that prayed solemnly to the Gods every day, wishing not for riches and power, lands and wives or other things that spelled vanity beyond their grasp. They wished that their child be spared of illness and harm, their herds be still whole come morning, the snow be light, and the rain plenty before harvest.

That was the sort of fools they were. He could feel sympathy like a man with sight feels for a man in the dark who has never seen golden fields in springtime and the piercing deep blue eyes of a young maiden, but nothing more. Even blind men wish for light to shine yet before their lives are ended. These folk just tread on, and never give things a second thought. He wouldn't spare them more than a passing thought.

His road was about to take him through the Widelands, an unforgiving place. Few had made the passing, and even fewer were left sane and unscathed in body, soul and mind once they did. There were stories and legends about the Widelands that were passed down from generation to generation, in many places and in many folk.

Most of them, he had determined, were the superstitious tales of simpletons and madmen: mere fantasies for common people to spent the grinding, toiling days, thankful for their safe, ordinary, almost pitiful lives. Some were invariably twisted second and third-hand tales of those who ventured somewhat into the accursed place and came back, surely not wholesome in spirit ever since.

Fact and fiction were interwoven tightly in such accounts but some probable, shared truths could be distilled from the broth of rumblings, mutterings, and assorted hearsay that permeated the inns and taverns all across the Territories. There were even a few written accounts by people who seemed to have genuinely made the journey and lived to tell the tale, becoming rich and famous in the process. Most of them seemed to be very talented liars and writers, the distinction between their works of little significance.

Only the Tale of Umberth could be counted as less than nefarious, since he set out with a hundred-score of men, of whom barely three survived: Umberth, his esquire Esphalon and a woman, then only a child, who Umberth claimed was found wandering alone, mute and dark-skinned, almost pitch-like in color.

Umberth had spent the rest of his days and sizable fortune trying to organize further trips into the Widelands. He made a few unsuccessful efforts to present the girl as living proof of his sayings of underground cities, height-defying towers and huge arching constructs, but the girl could not even speak her name. Her skin color was a singular phenomenon that more often than not provoked the wrath of the Ministers and the aversion of the crowds, speaking of heresy against the Gods and the bastard offspring of heathens and beasts of old that the earth unveiled from time to time to test the faithful and attract the blasphemer.

Not long after the Ministry had declared her as well as Umberth heretics, a relentless manhunt together with the watchful, ever pious and dutiful believers of the Pantheon bore fruit and Umberth and the girl were beheaded and their bodies burned to ashes in Pyr, in the winter of the third pacificum, 153rd annum, 51 days before the Solstice.

Esphalon, his esquire, had been sentenced to silence unto death and exiled never to utter a word in his life again, his tongue cut out. He had then wandered the northern lands, surviving on little more than worms and lichen, possibly wishing death for himself. It was while wandering the far north that he resolved to built a boat to travel to the End of the Ocean, and find the death he believed would free him of his troubled life.

Strangely enough, he insists in his work that he did build the boat, only to founder upon a land he had never heard of before, seemingly at first devoid of life. In those lands though he purportedly came upon a small tribe of nomads, wild men that knew not how to herd sheep and work with metal or clay, armed with wooden spears and no knowledge of fire.

From what Esphalon later wrote down and described, where he was trapped and caught like animal prey probably destined for a savage death, be it a sacrifice or plain and simple cannibalism, the savages noticed while they searched his clothing a small hand-sized plaque of metal with no discerning characteristics other than a circular notch in its center, a memento from the Widelands. When they noticed that, Esphalon was greeted among them as an equal, a member of the tribe that was lost and suddenly found.

He soon realized the importance of that plaque, and was further mystified. The savages used it to produce light and heat by placing an ordinary stone, even a lowly pebble, inside the notch. Pebbles and stones were the most widely used since they could be found in abundance in the northern rocky steppes were these people seemed to roam unhindered and unchecked. Sometimes they used animal bones or pieces of wood, mostly whatever was handy at the time.

Invariably, the said item slowly seemed to shrink and then vanish into thin air in a matter of moments, and then pleasant sunlight and radiant heat would emanate from the plaque for hours to come.

All this and much more was written in Esphalon's memoirs, a compilation of the things he saw and experienced in the wild lands coupled with what little time he spent with the savages. The plaque remained with the savage men who would not part with it in any way. Esphalon made a new boat and managed to reach an isolated fishing harbor facing the Pangalor Sea, half-dead from starvation and exhaustion, losing a leg and three fingers from frostbite in the process.

It was there where he wrote the Pangalor Scrolls, the single half-consistent work that contains enough about the Widelands to make it the single most useful resource in an attempt to cross it, and perhaps uncover more about this mysterious land, as well as surviving long enough for others to know as well.

His reverie was broken by the cries of a nighthawk swooping in to catch his prey, somewhere out in the star-lit fields of short grass and poppies swinging gently in the night breeze. He marveled at the arrogant precision and expert flying of the nighthawk which made no effort to catch his prey unguarded, but instead seemed to announce indifferently it was about to kill and then feast on a rather helpless and doomed animal.

He smiled thinly and then got up on his feet fastening his knapsack on his back. He picked up his walking stick and set off down the marble road. He looked overhead and saw the nighthawk soaring triumphantly with a small snake writhing in its death throes, captured in the hawk's beak. The nighthawk cried into the night once more and then disappeared over the distance, its faint silhouette mingled with the starry blue and black sky.

Under a livid sky

HEN they had eaten and after Amonas conferred with Philo, the burly man said he would be back soon. Hilderich had relaxed somewhat, but he could not for the life of him fathom the two men. It might be just as well, he thought. He wanted to believe that when he had seen whatever it was they wanted to show him, perhaps they would stick true to their word and release him, let go of him and consider him a friend. The chances though, were slim.

He wasn't sure exactly how a person who planned heretical plots to overthrow rulers of divine authority could afford to just tell people and then let them go and trust their good souls to tell not. He had a nagging feeling it involved some kind of pain and extortion, or simpler techniques involving knives or falling down.

It just struck Hilderich as odd. He felt he could trust this man, but his mind reeled at the prospect. I must be going slightly mad, he thought to himself. He was starting to think of ways he could snatch the keystone and make a run for it, but the more he thought about it the more stupid he felt. They had already outran and outsmarted him once. Certainly he was no match for either one of them in single, even unarmed combat. He now belatedly wished he had taken some time to practice his body rather than spent most of the time knee-deep in curatoria.

He decided his best chances lay in playing along, seeing what it was that they promised would change his mind and heart forever.

The faint dusk had just given way to a pure, clean night. As he lay there in his cot, he noticed Amonas had lit a large candle and was reading what seemed to be letters. He noticed the man had been rather drawn into his reading material and decided against indiscretion on his part. Amonas through the corner of his eye though was aware of Hilderich's mild scrutiny and without lifting his head from his reading, he said to him in an inviting, conversational tone:

"From my wife. She's carrying our child."

"I didn't mean to intrude, I just noticed you were very much occupied," said Hilderich almost apologetically.

"Still thinking of how and when to escape Hilderich? You are more lively than you already know, friend. There will be no need."

Amonas looked at him levelly, his gruff voice adding an air of authenticity Hilderich hadn't noticed so far. There was an unknown likeable quality to the man. Hilderich thought that perhaps he was being afflicted with a disease of the mind, something in the food.

But he felt alright otherwise, he did not believe he was poisoned or otherwise tampered with. He just could not believe he was somehow starting to like a person who was either mentally deranged or emphatically dangerous, a man who confessed to heresy nonetheless!

Hilderich's thoughts were interrupted by Philo who entered the small room wearing a hood on his head. He nodded to Amonas, who in turn said to Hilderich:

"Come. You shall see for yourself soon."

Hilderich stood up and Amonas offered him a hooded cloak, somewhat finer and more elegant than most. As soon as he wore it, Amonas was instructing Philo to lead them on and out into the city. Amonas would be trailing, and Hilderich would be in the middle, evidently a small precaution on their part should he feel a sudden urge to run like hell.

Philo lead them through somewhat shady alleys, light from far away lamps barely reaching them. They angled left and right, as if trying to evade unseen stalkers. Hilderich thought that perhaps they had caught whiff of someone he couldn't. He would not be able to see or smell anyone until it was too late in any case. So he trudged along. His knowledge of the city streets was perfunctory at best, but even he could discern that they were walking towards the Disciplinarium's hill. Even from a distance the sounds of music and festivities could be heard, and a light show of fireworks seemed to be underway as well.

Hilderich mused in spite himself:

"Are we invited then?"

Amonas smiled wryly and urged him forward with a gentle nudge, while Philo turned his head around and stabbed Hilderich with his eyes. His attempt at humor had gone unanswered.

The more they approached the Disciplinarium, the more careful they were in their approach, triple checking alleyways, hunching over shadows, their feet as light as cat-feet, not a sound other than shallow breathing. Hilderich was trying his best to follow the two men who seemed at ease with such practices. If he indeed attracted unwanted notice and they were caught, there was nothing to support he was an unwanting accomplice to their endeavor. Even if he could, he wasn't sure that would make much of a difference.

When they reached the base of the Disciplinarium's Hill, Philo signaled them to stop dead in their shoes. He let a guard patrol vanish behind the curve of the hill's base before urging them to rush for a certain part of the slope, where the shadow of the aqueduct overhead should conceal them.

They did so with a dancer's grace and reached the grassy part of the slope Philo had indicated. He took out a small knife from his belt, and Hilderich watched in still surprise as he dug out a small piece of tuft. A metal dial was to be found underneath, which then Amonas proceeded to twist left and right accordingly to some whim or unknown sequence.

Without making a single sound a small tubular opening appeared above the dial, large enough for a man to fit inside, but only in a prone position. It led into a shiny metal pipe or tube of some sort with a downward inclination whose other end was obscured in darkness. Judging from the light stream of air wafting through, it was a long pipe indeed.

Philo nodded to Amonas and said:

"I'll go on ahead."

Amonas patted him on his left shoulder and grinned:

"Are you sure you'll fit?"

Philo was already sliding inside the mysterious and intriguing metalwork, and muttered in a low voice what must have been a friendly obscenity. Amonas then ushered Hilderich inside, imparting a word of advice:

"Keep your arms glued on your body. Count to thirty and then take a deep breath and hold it. You're not afraid of water are you?", Amonas' low gruff voice barely revealing a hint of worry.

"Water? Why count to thirty? Do you mean fast or slow?"

"Go on then!"

Amonas had to shove Hilderich inside, whose protests became dangerously loud:

"You really plan to kill me!"

Hilderich's terror was evident in the shrill quality of his voice. It had all happened too quickly to try and hold back, so when Amonas pushed him down the tubing he tried to follow his advice: he held his arms stiff to his body and started counting to thirty.

The tubing angled downwards pretty soon and Hilderich felt he was riding a children's slide, with the slight difference that the end of the slide was nowhere in sight, and mad, possibly delusional, quite certainly heretic thugs, were shoving you down into one.

Hilderich heard a splash echo dimly in the metal tubing, and was suddenly reminded of Amonas instruction. He wasn't sure if he had counted past thirty or not, but his terror and anxiety mixed with his confounded thoughts was a recipe against keeping calm and cool-headed. He filled his lungs with air as long as he had time anyway, and just when he started to think he had grievously mistimed his breath, he splashed into water.

The feeling was one of quiet shock: the cold water encircled his whole body, seeping through his clothes. It assaulted his ears and nostrils, as it tried to enter his body without warning. His eyes had closed instinctively but then he opened them slowly, searching for the surface. His hands wobbled uncertainly, before a small primal fear of running out of air urged him to swim upwards, towards what seemed to be a faint source of light.

Within moments his head was clear of the water. He exhaled momentarily, then breathed in gasps until he could return to breathing normally once more. An outstretched hand seemed to be offering to help him out of the water. As soon as he realized it belonged to Philo he heard another splash of water roughly behind him, and turned his head to look even as Philo pulled him to somewhat dry land.

It was Amonas who as if he were intimately accustomed to the area needed no help and within seconds was among them, tiny rivulets of water still running down his leather vest, thick drops of water falling from his forehead.

"Let us move. Hilderich, I would beg your silence. We are relatively safe as long as we are silent," Amonas said in hushed tones while holding Hilderich by the arm in a friendly gesture.

"As if I've been screaming my lungs out. I'll keep my mouth shut.

Are we near whatever place you think will change my mind? Are we below the Disciplinarium, by any chance?", said Hilderich while vainly trying to squeeze off some of the water in his clothes Amonas responded promptly:

"We are. But we still have some way to go. Come now, you will dry yourself later."

They had fallen inside a natural cistern in a small rocky cave. Strangely enough, light seemed to seep through some cracks in the walls. With a closer inspection, Hilderich saw the cracks were more akin to lichen, faintly wet to the touch but rough like rocky sand. A sort of crystal formation seemed to lie underneath such spots. Philo nudged him onward, cutting his examination of the peculiarity short. It reminded him of some lesser kind of curatoria that his master was not particularly interested in, and thus were only lightly studied.

But the light they gave off was indeed enough, even though only barely, to walk the gently curving twists and turns of what seemed to be an extensive network of caves, an almost ant-like structure deep underneath the Disciplinarium's hill.

He noticed the steady, purposeful stride of Amonas before him and the dim blue and violet light that imparted a grim hue on everything around, including themselves. A feeling of eerie wariness started to seep in Hilderich. After some time had passed, he tapped Amonas shoulder, who paused in his gait to turn and look directly at Hilderich, a look of expectancy on his face but not a sound coming out of his lips. Hilderich asked in a low voice:

"Are we lost?"

Amonas did not answer but rather resumed his walk, taking them through caverns small and large through a path that could not be retraced unless one had a detailed map. The further down they went, the warmer it felt and soon walking in the caves felt like a warm summer night. Hilderich had by now lost track of their approximate depth, direction, or distance of travel.

Perhaps they were not lost but he essentially was and thought he would be unable to find the way back on his own if the opportunity ever presented itself. On a second reflection though, Hilderich thought it would be of little importance, since the tube was meant to go down and not up. Just as he let out a sigh of hopelessness, he could discern light pouring out from the next corner and feel their slight descend leveling out. By now his clothes felt almost dry with only a slight feeling of dampness remaining in his feet and arms. If anything at all, it was an improvement in the state of his affairs.

The light grew more intense, clear like sunlight. Hilderich knew it was impossible to find sunlight so deep under the earth, especially at night. They were only a few paces away from a corner in their path that shone with light. Amonas threw up one arm with his palm open, indicating a halt, and Hilderich followed Philo's example and stopped. Amonas leaned over the corner, and peered carefully for almost a minute. Hilderich assumed he was making sure it was safe for them to enter, though he doubted there was the possibility of a real threat against them in such a system of caves.

Amonas nodded to indicate that everything seemed as it should be, and walked out into the light pouring from around the corner. He blinked, his eyes flinching as they adjusted to the brightness and then gestured with his hand to Hilderich before he said:

"Come. We are here."

Hilderich stepped forward as well, the bright light forcing him to instinctively cover his eyes with his right arm, its small shadow the only shelter against such sudden illumination. A fragrant waft of air rushed around them, and as Philo joined them as well all three of them were slowly walking towards the light. As Hilderich's eyes finally adjusted to the light, he could see the rocky cave all around them give way to a smooth white surface that at first glance seemed much like porcelain.

These strange walls seemed to extrude themselves from the strata of the cave rocks, as if totally alien and utterly old in origin. Then Hilderich's eyes wandered a bit more, his gaze resting on the center of a huge chamber apparently made from the same ivory white material. The chamber was cylindrical in shape. From top to bottom stood a wide pillar which incredulously seemed to be made of pure light, a sight that defied Hilderich's sense of sight and filled him with astonishment.

"What is this place?", Hilderich asked Amonas awestruck, his gaze still locked on the pillar of light.

"This is the first pillar of truth, Hilderich," Amonas said while edging closer to the pillar. Hilderich stood a couple of steps behind him with his face brightly illuminated, but his eyes unflinching. Philo stood at the rocky entrance to the chamber, with his back indifferently turned to the wondrous sight in front of their eyes.

"The truth? What is this, Amonas? Is it Ancient?"

Hilderich's tone had a far-away quality, as if he was mesmerized, his mind off to some deep trench of thought.

"It is, my friend. A working piece of technology of the ancients, buried deep under the Disciplinarium. What does that tell you, friend?"

Amonas was looking intently at Hilderich's calm and entranced face, his every word glistening with expectation.

"Only what it should. This must be preserved. Documented. Studied. A Curatorium has to be built around it, scholars from around the lands should visit and-"

Amonas grabbed Hilderich violently from both arms demanding his total attention, his voice free of constraints:

"Studies! Scholars! Can't you really see what this means? Think of your Mythos! Think of your precious vaunted Law!"

Hilderich was visibly shaken as if coming around from a waking dream, eyes rolling around trying to come to grips with his surroundings and the man with the gruff voice in front of him was shouting at him, as if he was ready to snap him in two if he said the wrong thing.

He asked him to think of the Mythos, and the Law. The Law was the established religious canon that had replaced traditional secular law hundreds of years earlier. The Mythos was the recorded history of the Gods handing down the Law unto the forsaken race of man, to save it from destruction and withering, to help men reach their Gods at the Time of Conjugation.

The Law instructs man that those the people knew as Ancients were the manifestation of evil. That any tool or work of art or science whose workings cannot be seen with the naked eye or touched by naked hand are containers of evil. That there is only this land, and none other. That the lights in the sky were put there by the Gods, to make nights more bearable. That death is irrevocable and permanent and those who do not uphold the Law, will be shunt forever, their souls kept away from the Gods.

That any man, woman or child upholding belief in the Ancients or their works is a heretic, a vessel of corruption. That the Ministers, uphold and teach the Law to the people. That the people in turn, devote themselves and their lives to obey the Law. That the Patriarch declares additional Law as he sees fit, and he alone chooses his successor. That a Castigator rules above all: a man of wisdom and strength to lead the people, protect them; enlighten the heathens, punish the lawbreakers and the heretics, and offer praise and glory to the Gods.

That is what the Mythos and the Law say. Hilderich, though he did not consider himself the religious type, had always been careful not to attract the ire of the Ministers. He had memorized the Mythos and the Law as part of his training and education, as is the case with most who are fortunate enough to be allowed to read and write. He was fortunate enough to become apprentice to a Curator, a guild of men with a special dispensation to hold and maintain approved artifacts from times past. Some of those artifacts are of nefarious origins, and strict indices of what is stored where are kept.

Only ministers and certain officials of the Disciplinarium or the Army and then again only after special permission is granted for expressed purposes, can be allowed to even view a Curatorium from the inside. To think that now, he was looking at what seemed to be a working example of heretical technology was breathtaking. What troubled him was that he actually marvelled at it.

"They know about this? The people in the Disciplinarium know?", Hilderich asked feebly.

"Of course they know Hilderich! They have always known! Do you think this is the only place they have access to with an artifact of such origin? I'm sure there are many other places like this one."

"But, what does it do? And what proof do you have they know about things such as these? Much less use one?", Hilderich was being argumentative but slightly unsure of his words, his voice wavering as if he shaking from cold.

"Always the hard way, eh Hilderich?", said Amonas and shook his head in silent disappointment, nodding to Philo who winked back an acknowledgement.

Hilderich was considering the magnificent simplicity and awesome sight of the pillar of light in front of him. It was a bright pillar of sunlight not as blinding as the suns though, with a hazy rainbow of all colors on its edges, and a pulsating haze of tiny pin pricks rushing through some sort of invisible shell. He was interrupted somewhat violently by Amonas who neatly but decisively pushed him towards the pillar of light.

"What are you doing? Is this safe? Wait!", Hilderich seemed to protest in principle only, his mouth voicing concern but his feet offering little resistance.

"Don't really know, it's only my second time through one."

At that answer Hilderich's face took on an expression of exacerbated disbelief but only for a moment, because an instant later both his and Amonas' figures were vanishingly thin and elongated ghostly forms. In the next instant, all that was left of them was a smooth scent of uwe stew.

Philo turned and looked at the pillar of light, gave a derisive rough kind of snort, and continued his vigilant watch, unperturbed.

The first thing that Hilderich felt was a sinking sensation like the inevitable pull and grasp of a whirlpool, the dreaded voids of the sea that claim ships and men alike. Then he saw an explosion of light, swirling walls of light running up to meet him face on. Nothingness ensued for what must have been less than a heartbeat.

Then light filled his senses totally, even his smell. He could have sworn he could smell the light. Then his eyes seemd to adjust to the radiant sea of white enfolding him, and he could make out the outline of his hands. Then he heard a gravelly voice with serious undertones: Amonas' voice.

"Take a step forward Hilderich. Don't be afraid now."

He did and was left standing there. His eyes insisted that he was outside, on what seemed like a clear summer sky. How he could have in an instant walked past an underground cave as well as the grasp of night, he was unable to answer, not without gibberish coming out of his mouth. After a few more moments had passed, while playing back what had just happened, Hilderich was finally able to ask:

"Where are we?"

Amonas grinned as he was pointing at the single pale blue sun in the sky, and simply said:

"I'd love to find out."

Fulcrum

"A man with no purpose in life is like a river without a sea to lose itself in. Such is the meaning of purpose, hard and defining: to lose oneself completely in its threads. Immerse one's essence in a journey with no visible end in the distance. Anything less is bound to bring about ennui, the crushing realization of our discrete physical form and its inadequacies. Anything less than steering oneself through life like the only real obstacle is death itself, leads to early death of the mind and the soul. I ask you, would you live life or stand by idly waiting for death? I choose to vanquish death altogether."

-Thessurdijad Molo, *Life Unleashed*

A long and winding path

 HE mountain grew ever more unkind. Its many bare faces looked down upon a lonely figure, slowly but surely making its way through the rocks, gravel, low grass and loose dirt. His hood was down, revealing a stern but

humble face. Care lines dotted his forehead, and one could easily spot he was not a man prone to laughing easily. His face was adorned by a beard grown out of necessity, not choice, and his thin long hair was unkempt; a few wild strands jutted in strange directions.

The wind and the rain were thankfully absent on this day, awarding him the leisure of trudging along the mountainous path with only his sore feet and stiff legs to distract him from his effort. Indeed, he paused once again to rest for a moment and let his blood flow freely in his legs and feet; take a moment to pray to God for his good fortunes.

He sat down on the naked rock, his buttocks well used to such discomforts. He touched his forehead with one had and brought out a small piece of knotted string with the other. His lips then moved in a silent orison, asking for more of the same good fortune and perhaps a bush or nut-bearing tree from which to gather some much needed food.

He had not seen or heard signs of goats or other mountain-dwelling animals for days now. There was still some grass on these slopes, so it stood to reason there might be herds or families of animals feeding. Perhaps there were richer plains and slopes far below or plateaus with good grass his path had not taken him through.

Maybe it was pure chance that he had not seen a living soul, neither a bird or lizard and certainly not a goat. Maybe it was God's doing, testing him for purity of heart and strength of purpose to steel him further in order to come through the always perilous journey of Pilgrimage.

He was living on certain kinds of insects that were still to be found if someone knew how and where to look, and a few roots he had been able to identify as edible. The further deep inside the mountain range he trod, the stranger and more different the life he met became. At first the trees started to become bulky, water rich, taller and greener than the ones at the feet of the mountain. Then he noticed the animals: they were more stout and fatter; their meat sweet and richer in flavor, its color a vivid red. It was unlike the dark, stringy meat of the animals he was used to.

He decided in his mind that it was a sign: With his every step closer to God's Lands, the land was graced by his favor. The animals became fat and felt no hunger, the trees and plants grew tall and proud, the birds soared high and their voices were sweet as honeydew running down a child's mouth. It was His work all that was abundant, and all that was good.

This part of the mountains seemed to have fallen from His grace though, whether as another trial or for reasons only He could entertain. No matter; since his wisdom permeates the earth and the sky, the Pilgrim felt he could only accept and never wonder. That way lay madness, and a hard fall from grace into bottomless pits of despair and unworthiness.

He felt he was attuned, his soul resonating with the earth below his feet, the sky above and the stone all around him. He reached into his small sack and with little effort produced a small circular pendant, a thin slice of white marble or porcelain cast around a black mat surface, smooth and cold to the touch.

He held it firmly with both hands for a while looking intently at its black surface. A thin sliver of green started to pulsate on the black surface. A green line started to form in one edge of the small black circlet to end on another, forming a straight path. It was like the invisible brush of a painter kept stroking the same line, always in the same straight direction.

He looked at the thin, green line of light and then looked at the faint mountain path that made a zig-zag through the ever rockier slopes. His path was true, that much he knew. His pointing stone had not failed him before and neither would it fail him now, not on his Pilgrimage; not while his faith was strong and his prayer warm of heart and soul. That he knew, and little else would come to matter.

He took a moment to gaze at the lands resting below him. The great northern plains could be seen far away, a faint gray haze slightly discernible under a thin sheet of fog. And then rolling hills of auburn slowly lifting off the ground as if the very hand of God had touched and pinched the lands, his hand print faintly echoed in the timid, graceful slopes.

Between the foot of the mountains and the hills lay a deep gorge with a wild river running through it, twisting and turning as far as the eye could see further to the east. Its flow came from somewhere deep inside the mountains, further to the east, from places where the ice moves as if alive and the suns always hide behind the clouds. Places where neither man nor beast can endure for long without the mercies of God.

A sensation of wonder filled him for the works of God were magnificent to behold, and his Pilgrimage a unique journey of faith, beauty, wonder and duty. The honor he was blessed with was indeed so great he could have never thought it possible, much less aspire to be given it. Nonetheless, he was on a Pilgrimage to the Land of God. He was the Pilgrim, the one honored to pay homage to the Land of God and the resting place of their forefathers.

To him lay the duty of bringing back a Holy Forge, to pluck one out of the very famed Garden of Wonders! His eyes were suddenly lit at the very thought, even as his body still dully ached from the many hardships his peregrination had knowingly brought upon him and would bring him still. But he ignored all that which occluded his mind and he imagined himself, standing amidst the Garden of Wonders and quenching his thirst from the Unending Spring.

It would all be more than worthy of the pain, the cold and the rain. Just to lay his eyes on the Holy Gates, he would willingly give his life. But he could not and would not, until his Pilgrimage is complete, and his people have their Holy Forge anew. Oh, the joyous wonders he was yet to behold, not just the earth and the rivers and the mountains all wrought in unquestioned wisdom, but the craft of God Himself right in front of his eyes, at the touch of his hand from silver, and stone. From sand that never crumbles or faints, and never shall.

The Pilgrim's senses brought him back to the cold, harsh reality. He still had some good light left and he should not waste it. His journey was still many days and nights away from an end. Tarrying here in the middle of the mountains, daydreaming like a young selfish brat was not at all what any man would expect of him, the one so honored. His shoulders suddenly felt a bit heavier with so much resting on them: the future of his people, the life of the land, the children yet unborn.

A gust of the mountains' cold and wholesome air seemed to have infected him with renewed vigor. Within seconds he was already steadily climbing up the steep winding path that would take him between the two dominant mountain peaks, and afterwards probably on a shallow descend to the Land of God.

Those who had gone before him had followed the same path, and had passed on word of their travel and their journey. What mountains and ridges to pass, which rivers and springs to drink from, what strange growths and roots to eat, where to feel safe and sleep unhindered, as well as where to keep one eye open and your knife in hand.

He thought to himself then: 'But God provides, and always will. As long as we have faith, as long as we live our lives like we were meant to, taught to from father to child, as long as we go on the Pilgrimage when time and God mandate.'

Such thoughts occupied his head as he toiled onwards, even though under his thick pelted boots his calloused feet could feel every last jut of rock and bit of gravel. This was him now, this described him wholly. He was the Pilgrim, meant to walk the earth until he reached the Holy Place. Whether or not he would go back to his people and his previous life, that meant nothing. When he performed the Rites, the Holy Forge would be with his people. And then he could walk back, and live the rest of his days having witnessed the glory of God. He could then teach those that would come after him and if it fate would have it so, help the next Pilgrim prepare for his own difficult journey.

'Perhaps,' he thought to himself, 'I am getting too far ahead in my thinking. My journey is still far from over, and yet here I am: my feet dead as wood, my legs heavy like rock, once again on the climb. All I've loved and known left behind perhaps forever, and I am letting myself be fooled by visions of a future yet to unravel, with me at its center.'

Selfishness. Ego. A sign of malignancy, a precursor to evil thoughts and desires, accursed manifestations of Them. He prayed then to God, to watch over his people and lend him strength and clarity of mind and purpose. To think such thoughts was almost irredeemable. God was already pointing to the true path, when everything so far had proceeded along according to his divine plan, when the auguries had said it was a good time for a Pilgrimage. That he was a good man, that he would be a true Pilgrim, one that God would accept.

He felt he had to cleanse himself with birch and water, pay obeisance to his God with an offer of personal sacrifice. But he was already on his Pilgrimage, what could he do now that would not interfere with his holy purpose? He had no inkling yet, but he felt blood rushing through his veins, feeling guilty and shameful, almost soiled.

He pushed harder, the slope turning into an almost sheer wall of rock. The small, narrow path had degenerated into a granite crevice with pockmarks and surfaces of chipped rock that one had to climb using his hands as well as his feet.

In his mind it mattered little, because he felt like he would grow wings if he had to, if somehow the earth was without warning removed from his feet. He felt like he would grow gills and scales, and swim the oceans of the world if the skies suddenly opened and poured all the water of the world and the earth was covered in it. He felt that nothing, save God himself, could stop him now.

He steadily put one hand after the next, hoisting his lithe and supple careworn body slowly but surely, every step of the way a small death for Them. A death to their venomous influence that seeps into the hearts and minds of the weak-minded and the unfaithful, that spreads over the people of the earth like a rotting disease.

Perspiration glistened on his forehead and the small of his back was damp as well. Every muscle and joint burned from the effort and protested at his every leap and move. But he kept going, his mind focused; his soul was shielded and armed like a searing force of pure light stabbing through a heart of darkness, a pestilence of lies, deceit and wrong-doing.

He was fighting Them even as he climbed, even as he sweat and toiled. His whole Pilgrimage was a Holy War he now knew, and this very climb a fight, a battle. Like the War between God and Them, at a time before man. The same war; a million fights and a million more until God prevails, until the faithful have had their share of blood and toil. Until then he would climb for his people, His Faithful. Until then he would endure the forces arrayed against him, be they nature, men, or Them, in one disguise or many.

He would endure and he would prevail. Not to become a revered one among his folk, not to serve some delusional idea of a grandiose self in a small world and an even smaller land, among its few people. It was true; their numbers were dwindling and their women bore less children as time went by. Their lives were becoming shorter. The Pilgrimage was their hope of survival, he knew. He would endure the hardships of his path and the machinations of the enemies of God, for the good of his people and the will of his God.

He reached out with one hand blindly, his face wearing an expression of determination. It was a resolute, stout mask under which nerves flickered furiously with jabbing explosions of pain and anguish.

He tried to find a handhold in the rocks, a fissure, a jutting piece of granite or lime, but all he could grasp was the thin, cold rush of air. He made a leap and his face was caught in the stream of air: his hood fluttered wildly about his neck, sweaty locks of hair caressing his face. He had reached the neck between the two peaks, and he could now see a wide stretch of plain-like ground extending before him. There lay before him grim patches of grass, rocks and dusty gravel for days worth of travel.

He could feel the touch of God as he took the final step onto the plateau. He felt his soul drifting away by a divine wind, his aching body forgetful of its pains and trappings. He felt light as a feather, in body and soul. He remembered then the words of his Guide, his people's master of lore and faith, their holy man:

"Once you step onto the wide, gray mesa, a gust of wind will greet you and lift your soul. It will be God whispering in your ear; it will be a sign from God that your path is true."

Indeed then his path was true, the first of many perils he had just left behind. He let out a laugh in spite of him, a laugh he would soon look down upon with contempt as it bordered blasphemy. But it was a laugh that welled from the soul, a liberating act; a cry of thanks to his God and his protector, his ever watchful Father. He started walking with a steady, slow pace once more. What little light of day remained guiding him to a cluster of rocks where he might find shelter for the coming night. Once he lay down, he would pray to God and offer him his gratitude for saving him from disgrace and keeping him on the true path.

And then he would sleep like he hadn't slept in days, and dream of goat's cheese, berries, honey and mead.

Celia woke up as the beam of sunlight characteristically bounced off the gleaming, copper-skinned Ministry tower as was usually the case. Her long golden brown hair tangled as it was from last night's fretful sleep, resembled a flaming bush when the copper-tinted light cast off the ministry's tower shone upon her. Her visage was one of a fiery, avenging god-maiden of fury and destruction, an avalanche of wrath rushing down upon the wrongdoers and evil-makers that dared incur her retribution.

But that was only a fleeting impression, for when she touched her belly and felt her unborn child still soundly and safely asleep, her smile was like heavenly orchards that grew and bore ripe honey-sweet fruit in the blink of an eye. It was as if all the goodness in creation had come together in a still moment of time; a mother's smile, a power beyond reckoning and imagination, all that in the creases of a beautiful face and two comely lips. She who had seemed as a terrible force had been wondrously transfigured into a mother bathed in sunlight, radiating warmth and love; all hints of terrible awe a mere phantom now in the eye of the beholder.

After a few moments of silent contemplation as if communicating with the fetus growing inside her, she spent some moments of simple indulgence in smelling the morning fragrances and hearing the first sounds of day. Celia then threw her sheets away playfully and got out of bed to follow her usual routine: she took her morning bath and then offered her own prayer to her own Gods, thanking them for sending a man like Amonas to her, for the conception of their child. She also prayed for her husband's safe return and her child's first cry into this world.

She was then startlingly taken by the fragrant smell that had gently occupied her senses ever since she opened her eyes. She felt almost strange for not immediately taking notice of such a beautiful scent. With a familiar way she tried to trace the source of the strong, tasteful smell that seemed to seep through the walls and pour from balconies and windows. She peered over her stone balcony and saw that more and more people were starting to wade through the streets, the day ticking on in its usual rhythm.

She then spent her morning as was her usual routine nowdays: brooming and cleaning the house as much as her straining back allowed. Most of her time though she spent knitting clothes for her unborn child: winter clothes and baby gowns, blankets as well as a lenarion for Amonas. But her mind ever so often wandered to him, and when he would come knocking at their door again. She put her mind at ease knowing he had Philo with him, whatever they were doing.

Time flew by like birds in the spring. When she had felt tired once more, evening had beckoned. She was surprised that she hadn't felt any hunger, but her appetite was strange for a pregnant woman, she had known. Sometimes she could not stop eating whatever came to hand, and other times hours went by without a single bite of food. She decided to bring firewood from their small cellar and paused for a while before starting a fire anew for the day's meal. She mused about making some stew or perhaps a broth of beans and greens.

She stood with a few small pieces of firewood cupped into her arms, when the thought flashed in her head with a jolt: she was out of uwe, again! She left the tiny logs aside on the small kitchen table and went upstairs to fetch her small purse.

She then made sure she hadn't actually started off an untended fire and drew her broadly-hemmed cloak around her darting off towards the market.

The city crowd on the streets was shifting towards its nocturnal aspect, the people that rarely venture outside if the suns still abound and rarely crawl back to their domiciles before dawn is about to break. The Watchday would be over as soon as the suns set and the Merrynight would hold until tomorrow. Loud song and cheers, sounds of merrymaking and laughter could be heard at least once in every street that she passed on her way to Ves, a farmer that was her distant kin, a cousin in fact, and did not try to fool her like most others in the market did.

She wasn't sure if she would make it in time for at that hour Ves as well as almost everyone else with farms or animals to tend, had to leave for his farmstead to eat and rest. In the morning he would be getting up in the middle of the night to water whichever plants were in need, and then he would harvest those ready for the market. Then he would load up his cart and off he would be to the market once more to make some coin for his wife and children, so they'd not have to beg like some people who were cast adrift in the unfathomable torrents of fortune.

She could see those people: disheveled beings, sometimes indistinguishable from animals. Some of them brought a sore tear to her eyes. A few she helped as she could, a loaf of bread or her daily bottle of milk she would share. Sometimes she would leave a plate of food for those that drifted throughout the city and did not just await their end at some dark corner of the market.

As she turned the last corner before she reached Ves' usual stand, she could see she was too late: Ves as well as everyone else in the same spot had left for the night, leftover fruit and vegetable stalks amassing on the cobbled streets and a sour acrid odor wafting all around her. If nothing else at all, she had indeed taken a walk though at an inappropriate hour, and she should be getting home before long.

As she turned around to start walking back towards her house, she froze where she lay when a mailed hand seemed to stretch a shadowy crevice, some chasm in a wall she hadn't noticed in her dimly lit surroundings: it was a surreptitious figure that seemed well-disposed towards her, or else she would be already lying in a pool of her own blood for what little coin she carried in her tiny purse. She shuddered at the thought that worse things than an untimely death could have happened to her that she dared not imagine while carrying her child still in her womb. The figure spoke to her in a curt, hushed voice:

"Lady Celia, be still and fear not. I am Kin, and I bear news for you: Philo has been, but your husband is nowhere to be found."

Her voice quavered in shock and vibrated with disbelief:

"And Amonas?What of him?Is he dead?"

It was a well-practiced phrase in her head, her moment of fear was embodied in her low voice. She barely avoided a stutter and her lips trembled while her eyes narrowed down to small ovals. What little blue was left in them was exposed to the light of the lamps, flashing with terror. Her hands had instinctively gone to her belly hugging it closer than ever, as if she feared the child would be needlessly drawn away from her, a life unborn for a life taken.

"Hush milady, we know not. But no body to be found, or a trace of cloth, we can be sure. Have hope, Lady Celia. And let not a soul know of this."

The man left a hint of consolation in his voice but none of that would be enough for Celia now.

He was gone as silently and instantly as he had appeared through the unseen folds of the night, a messenger in the dark leaving grim and hollow thoughts in his wake.

She ran back to the house with tears running down her pale cheeks. Blood had left her face, and coldness crept in like endless tides of water running under a door. The laughing crowds that seemed to have taken over every street became a noise of sorrow in her mind and a weeping feeling choked her heart. She ran up to their bedroom feeling the child within stir uneasily, as if it knew something was amiss.

She lay down on their bed and put on her wedding gossamer tirval. She wept until she could weep no more, until her tears dried and her numb mind sent her into a merciful, dreamless sleep.

Of the Sun and Moon

E will get back."

"Well that's what you keep saying. Is it that difficult to accept the fact that we are now, thanks to
your efforts, terminally lost?"

Hilderich was picking ineffectually at the withering bark of a large
oak-like tree. The tree was slowly turning into ash, returning into the
dirt one very small piece at a time. Hilderich was quite fascinated by
what he was seeing all around him and that was probably why he had
not broken down in hysterical cries since their mishap.

Which was also why he could blame Amonas for their predicament in a steady, calm, and somewhat detached distant tone of voice.
Half his mind was infuriated close to bursting, because Amonas
seemed to have had inadvertently stranded them *somewhere.* The
other half of his mind was trying to make connections between the
flora and fauna of the place they had found themselves in, and the
various curatoria he believed he could remember having some kind of
relation in part or in whole.

Indirectly this was Hilderich's way of coping with the problem in
hand, partly to offset his mind and unburden it from the stress and the
anxiety as well as what he had learned to consider generally counter-
productive emotions.

On top of that he was actually trying to help in his own lateral
way by trying to identify anything he might be able to. His efforts
were based on the various curatoria he had studied or seen in his unfortunately short and, recent events not withstanding, uneventful apprenticeship. It seemed that apart from superficial resemblances and
some generic common traits, he had arrived at no particularly useful
conclusion. 'For the time being,' he reminded himself silently and
thoughtfully.

Amonas was sitting at a partly exposed root of a gigantic tree he
had trouble accepting that was real even though he had been sitting
right there on the same spot for the better part of an hour in silent
and thoughtful perplexity. Hilderich had spared little of the last hour
trying to talk to Amonas, or simply take notice of the man's face. If he

had, it would have been enough for even the most socially inept, slow-witted and sentimentally detached human to understand that Amonas was deeply troubled. In fact he looked morose, and it was not without good cause.

Insects abounded in this humid environment, the likes of which he had not known existed, not even in the southernmost bogs and marshes. Sweat poured from their bodies incessantly, making their every movement a sticky, messy business. It was the heat that really got to them. The heat of the desert combined with the the moisture of a lake or river. It was as if steam rose from the earth in a constant, endless motion.

They had seen no river whatsoever from the top of the hill where they had emerged, and had come upon no body of water in their blind search so far. The humidity and heat of the place was overwhelming though; Amonas had expressed the sound opinion that they should devote most of their time and effort into simply staying alive for the time being. He had objectified that into finding a source of clean, fresh water, preferably before nightfall. Water was not the only thing that occupied his mind though.

It buzzed incessantly with the same recurring thought; that all this was indeed his fault, and Hilderich had been right to accuse him. His initial purpose when pushing Hilderich into that infernal pillar of light, a machinery truly made in its makers image, was to force him to see the truth. It had not gone as planned.

The first time he himself had stepped through that beacon of light, he vividly remembered how he had been instantly transferred into a huge, deep cavern with walls of solid metal jutting out of the bedrock. He had wandered through a meandering labyrinth of large metal pipes, interconnections and all manners of weird machinery and constructs the likes of which he could not believe were made by mere men. They had to be the work of beings akin to Gods or their dutiful servants. The scenery around him was indeed as if it had been wrought out of the Mythos itself.

He had seen words in Helican Pretoria he had not seen before dangling in the air around him as if they had been stamped with a thick ink of light on a giant spider's gossamer web. He had seen visions of gruesome death, savagery and bloody toil, endlessly replayed as if it all was a theatrical stage, and he was the sole viewer. He had seen the likes of the Patriarch and the Castigator conspiring against the people, orchestrating deaths and mass executions as if people's lives were mere numbers on charts, maps and reports. And he had seen him vanish and reappear, wielding strange instruments of unknown origin that would have been deemed utterly blasphemous. Instead, he had wielded them like tools intimately known and regularly used. Apart from dangerous and cunning wolves he know saw the extended of their lies and deceit.

He had seen many things he could not fathom and explain. He had needed Hilderich to do that for him. Uncover some idea of the workings behind all that, perhaps use something against the Patriarch and the Castigator. He had seen so much more he needed to forget as well but could not, in fact dared not forget, lest the hatred for their jailers and captors, those madmen, would diminish ever so imperceptibly. He found out he lacked the words to describe the sickening mob of rulers who moved freely about like a sickle does unto stalks of wheat.

No such euphemism like dictator or killer would really suffice to describe them completely. He felt like he would have to leave that to someone else, since in the end he might not be able to slit their throats in person as he would have liked.

Without knowing he seemed to have been gripping his knife from its blade so intensely that he had cut himself: a small rivulet of blood and sweat ran down his wrist, droplets of rosy red falling down onto the constantly wet ground. Ever thirsty and never quenched, be it blood, water or both, these new lands seemed to feed on a man's desperation and sweat. His focus returned to the immediate reality around them and felt the sagging weight of the situation.

He had to have faith in himself, he knew. He was a man of action and he had already decided to forfeit his life if it came to that. Others were capable of carrying out the same mission as he was supposed to. If he could not do so in the end, he only felt it was wrong for Celia and their unborn child. What would happen to them, if he were to perish?

She was strong of mind and will, that much he knew and was one of the many reasons he loved her so. But he could not so easily cast her adrift without a second thought; she had suffered such impropriety in her life already. He wouldn't be a man if he did not take her and their child into account. What misguided sense of duty could overcome his true purpose? A world and a future free of slaves in body and mind. No, he would not die in this place, he set his mind against that. He had a mission to do and a family to return to. He decided that all his thoughts from now on would form around these two things, and he'd cast each shadow of a doubt like a drunkard from a barracks.

He looked up to the alien looking sky, so familiar but so different at the same time. He could remember his days of ignorance and blissful youth riding in the countryside, galloping fast and hard as if the world's end was rushing right behind him. The sky had a strange quality: a light blur or a haze of wonder. It looked as if it was merely a ceiling he could reach up and touch as long as he wished it hard enough.

He would keep his promises and find his way back, to make things right. He would free his fellow men. He would live his life anew, reborn, fresh and innocent as his firstborn would be.

He thought then that he had tarried on the matter for too long. It was time to act: they would secure any means of survival in this strange land and acclimatise themselves quickly. No one could know how long their journey back would take. They were completely lost, but he knew that nothing important ever happened on its own. They would have to have faith in themselves and their purpose, and anything would be possible.

Amonas thought to himself that it was Hilderich's purpose as well. He knew though that Hilderich could not have grasped the extend of the lies, deceit, and exploitation. His instincts and experience told him that he should be able to put Hilderich to some good use as well; the man who was a little older than a mere boy seemed to have some good qualities: he was smart and perceptive, suspicious but not predisposed, simple but not simple-minded. Amonas believed that Hilderich would do fine, that they would be fine.

There were some issues that defied explanations though and would probably be denied of one for a long time.

The suns seemed wrong, for starters, and that certainly said a lot about the grievousness of their situation. They appeared brighter than usual and smaller, the hue of its light a pale blue, as if a sickness had befallen it. That was what had caught their eye in the sky. But then there were the towers, or spirals, he wasn't sure how to describe them from all that distance. They seemed to be tall towers with double spires that seemed to form a roughly crescent shape, their base lost behind the thick foliage of the ever-present trees.

There seemed to be dozens of these huge constructs in regular intervals, as if an architect blessed with godly sight had deemed to place them all over the landscape which in itself was another peculiarity: as far as the eye could see the horizon was covered in shades of greenery, spotted in parts by yellow and red patches. It was as if there was nothing else to be found in these lands other than this hot and humid garden and its strange awe-inspiring structures. They sort of reminded him of giant bullhorns, if he had to describe them more plainly.

He had thought about broaching all these matters to Hilderich, but he decided against that for now. The detailed intricacies of their whereabouts, their actual location, the climate and topography of the region were merely academic issues if they could not provide them with a small shred of actual information that would lead them to somehow going back to Pyr, or any other recognizable place for that matter.

He was still absorbed in thought, his eyes piercing the tall canopy of thick foliage. The huge volume of the surrounding trees stood like rocky pillars between the sky and the ground. He was marvelling at their size when Hilderich literally slapped him back into the real world and felt his wet and sticky palm, his left cheek flushed red from the hit:

"Are you listening? Are you here? Gods help me, he was insane to begin with now he is catatonic! Amonas!"

Hilderich was shouting now, still thinking Amonas was daydreaming or far worse, had finally lost his fragile mind. As he swung his hand back once more to deliver another slap, Amonas turned his head ever so lightly and looked him straight in the eye and simply said:

"Don't do that, please. No need. I must thank you, actually. I was thinking. I was, overly engrossed in thought I must admit. Were you calling out to me for long?"

Hilderich was genuinely surprised at such an ambivalent behavior. Had Amonas been catatonic he would never have responded and then he would have been left alone. With his survival skills and his latest round of luck, Hilderich was certain that he would have perished in this steamy cauldron. If Amonas was indeed mad, he would have probably gone berserk and snapped his neck like a twig in the best case scenario. It seemed now that he was neither. He had been simply, as strange as it seemed to Hilderich at the time, hard at thought.

He sat down in front of Amonas on the leaf strewn ground which was wet and muddy. A continuous hint of rotting vegetation waxed and waned in the faint wisps of air, a fitting reminder of what happens to idle life. Hilderich cleared his throat and while looking at the ground, was toying around with a small branch, shooting idle looks at the ground before his feet. He asked with some reluctance:

"Amonas. This is real, right? This is not a trick, not some very elaborate way of forcing me to join whatever it is you mean to in the first place? Is it?"

Amonas bit his lip and outstretched his hands, an ornate ring of silver and copper catching the eyes of Hilderich for the first time. He seemed to draw some breath, and then paused briefly as if he intended to say otherwise before nodding in acceptance and telling Hilderich:

"It's real Hilderich. That is what has dragged me down in thought. I am sorry Hilderich, my intentions were quite different, and certainly did not involve both of us getting utterly lost, especially at such a moment in time. I know I have failed you so far Hilderich, so I will promise you nothing. I can only offer you my help in order to find a way home. We need to work on this together, whatever you might think of me so far. It was my fault, but I cannot undo it alone."

A bitter smile formed on his lips, and his head turned to look once more at the thick foliage, hoping to catch a glimpse of the strangely immaculate, perfectly cloudless sky.

When Amonas looked down again, he noticed Hilderich had fallen on his back giggling almost maniacally with his knees bent haplessly in a comical angle and his arms folded across his chest, clapping his hands vibrantly. Amonas face frowned quizzically. Hilderich's bizarre reaction to his statement had left him unable to understand or much less respond at all.

"*You*? You're offering to help *me*?"

Hilderich sat upright with his legs sprawled in a seemingly uncomfortable position, his hand pointing at his own face in sheer disbelief and his voice a falsetto. Suddenly his visage turned harsh and unforgiving, out of place with his normal self and then he raised an accusing finger at Amonas. He told him in a calm and studied manner, as if lecturing a lesser man of poor intelligence:

"Not to insinuate that you have done a very poor job so far, but please, indulge me. How can *you*.. Help *me*.. find a way home? Are you perhaps a magician like the ones that abound in the tales told to children? I think not, dear friend. If you were, then you would be in possession of a ridiculously cone-shaped hat. You would be talking gibberish even in your sleep, and you'd be constantly searching for your frog pills or something equally inane.

Another possible way in which you might be of help would be that you are in fact, a fallen angel of the Gods, who has yet to use his superlative powers in our favor because he is as ever trying to teach me a lesson in humility and religious awe, lest my soul is eternally condemned in the Catharterion, Damnation, the Twelve Wheels of Fire and so on. You seem to be missing the complimentary wings, shield, divine aura, and angelic face so I would say no, you can't help me like that.

I briefly considered that you might actually own this particular piece of land and are indeed *dying* to offload it to a dimwitted fool like myself who might mistake the extreme humidity, unbearable heat and overflowing vegetation for marshlands suitable for raising cotton, or something equally senile and outright dumb. Without trying to hurt your feelings or impede your vested interests in a manner most ungracious, I regret to inform you that I find your selling points lacking and will not be following up on your offer.

Now, unless I am mistaken in all of the above, and unless you are in possession of some pillar of light that does the opposite of what brought us here, I dare say we are properly doomed and good as dead and finished. Other more vulgar expressions pertaining to our present unfortunate situation come to mind, but I will not bring myself down to such inestimable depths of bad taste and linguistic ineptitude to use them like a debased wretch of lesser stature.

I will now formally and being in a state my predilections: one, that I wish to hang myself at the nearest opportune moment in order to escape further unneeded physical torment under these circumstances, and two, that I wish for my remains to be burned, as is customary under Law, even though I fail to see what a fat lot of good that would do."

All that Amonas could do, was blink wide-eyed at a loss for words. Hilderich was resting his hands on his knees cross-legged on the wet ground with an air of finality around him, as if he was a holy avatar that had just announced the end of the world.

Amonas shattered the uneasy silence with a question that was uttered in seemingly complete fascination. A glazed look of mock awe covered Amonas face and his gruff voice added tremendously to the intended comical effect:

"Are you sure you weren't studying to become a Minister?"

With that having being uttered they both broke down in hearty laughter, the strain of their situation and the accumulated fatigue almost vanishing as if washed clear away with one simple joke. An invigorating smile graced Hilderich's mouth before he answered in kind:

"Actually I had been thinking about it, but though I can handle the dramatics, I am not too keen on handing people over to the procrastinators for spilling oil or eating sugar on a Watchday."

Amonas thought there was a lot about Hilderich to muse over when time and circumstance would allow it, but there were other more pressing matters to attend to first.

"Hilderich, I'm sure we'll have quite some time to exchange tales and ideas. But we have to attend to our survival first. We will need fresh, drinking water. Something solid to eat, surely. Something that will not easily spoil in this heat and moisture. But our priorty should be water. At the rate we sweat, we will surely suffer the most without it. And too soon for comfort, I would wager. And another thing I only now noticed. There's something peculiar about the shadows in this place."

Hilderich nodded, and then looked carefully around them at the barks of trees and small rocks and hanging green overgrowths. He looked at what one would call a glen if it weren't for the awfully wrong conditions and the green overarching roof made from ostensibly ancient tree branches. The canopy was a mosaic of green and brown hues, the greenish light of the sun adding an emerald glare to the columns of light that shot underneath where Hilderich could see the shadows standing still.

Indeed he noticed that the shadows had moved little or not at all since earlier. He couldn't be sure, but he knew it was at least strange and probably another indication that they were very, very, far away from home. He pointed at a broken log with his right hand, a tall outstretched branch casting its shadow on a peculiar half-gray, half-bleached stone.

"What time of day would you say it is, Amonas?", asked Hilderich while still pointing his hand in that particular direction.

After little deliberation Amonas answered casually:

"I would say about noon. But I could be mistaken. A few hours ago, before we reached this place, night was well under way. And then when we came here, it had seemed to me like a bright summer day. My body and mind long for rest, my sense of time must be in disarray. But if I woke up right this instant, I would've thought I overslept into noon."

"That shadow was there when we went down from that hill and sat here first. I remember because I imagined pouncing your head on that rock," Hilderich added nonchalantly.

Amonas face wrinkled with wariness, but he did not press the issue. Instead, he nodded in silent agreement and then said with a careful choice of words as if musing on the matter:

"Then.. If shadows stand still.. Does time as well? Is this a limbo of sorts? A jail.. for our souls? If we return, will it be as if no time has passed?"

Amonas seemed troubled by these thoughts. Hilderich on the other hand had no qualms in throwing Amonas interpretation of facts out the window:

"That's nonsense! Even ministers would find that assumption idiotic! At best! Master Olom would have you scrubbing the horses for a week for even pondering such a connection! I do mean, scrubbing! Flayed brush and murky water for a week! Grooming a horse is no occupation for an aspiring Curator, mind you! And especially the horses' parts where.."

Amonas had the decency to interlope and cut Hilderich in midsentence, offering his timely excuse:

"I trust you will be more forgiving than dear Olom was and should the opportunity arise, I will be more than happy to be accordingly reproached for making such extravagant extrapolations. So, what do you make of it?"

Amonas' voice was finely and expertly tuned to defuse Hilderich's probable ranting and almost concede in a sincere fashion that he was out of his depth in this matter and it would be wiser to let someone who knows better find out what is going on. Hilderich took the bait, hook and sinker willingly:

"The shadows during the day are cast because of the suns' light. So, when the suns move across the sky, so do the shadows follow in hand and move accordingly. Would the suns stay still, so would the shadows. It is not entirely without logic to postulate that since we have witnessed only one sun, this is perhaps the reason for its inability to move, and hence the standing shadows and the continuous light. There it is, a much more simple explanation which as my late master would have said, is usually the right one. The sharper, the better."

"Like a razor then? Might you have called such a rule of thumb Olom's razor?", Amonas grinned to show he remembered the old man fondly as well, a shared memory they had yet to explore.

"You could call it that, I guess. It might prove to apply in more subjects of interest. It could be a general rule."

"I hope it does. To me, simplicity is a virtue."

Hilderich nodded in agreement:

"Indeed."

"Now we know it will be noon for an inordinate amount of time, is it not wise to assume that nightfall is nowhere near?"

That had not immediately dawned on Hilderich, and the revelation left him looking worried and puzzled, more so because he had not followed the train of thought completely. He ventured a guess for an answer:

"If that comes to be, then the heat will not dissipate and this will go on until we are able to return. A half-light, half-shadow under this monstrous canopy, sweat and grimy mass of rotting leaves stuck on our bodies. Or then again we might never leave this place. The prospect of spending days or weeks in such conditions, whether or not we will be able to go back, makes me want to once more consider adopting an inherently expeditious approach to going through life."

Hilderich was seemingly more humorous than before his words clearly not to be taken for granted, but Amonas had to admit to the fact that this strange sun and taxing climate would make their efforts even more strained and difficult that he had calculated. And still he feared, they had no solid idea of how to get back home. Survival would have to take precedence. That meant finding water, not sooner or later, but immediately. They had spoken enough of the matter.

"Come, we will find water.", Amonas said decisively and picked up his pace towards a seemingly random direction.

"Under different circumstances that would have involved my absence, I would have been impressed by your optimism, but I do have to point out that water is abundantly present, the problem being that it seems to lie thick in the air and the abundant plants. How do you plan to go about doing that, pray tell?"

Hilderich was already on his feet, following Amonas from close behind, careful with his steps, avoiding what seemed the most grisly pathways and wet spots that held soft matter of dubious origins underneath.

"We'll start searching where the plants look thicker, greener and more lively. There should be some source of running water, at least underground, like the places were we would look to dig a well back home. I guess that we can also use some of the fattier green trunks if we find some. We'll take it slowly, the more we exert ourselves, the worse it will be in the end if lady Luck keeps running out on us," Amonas said while plowing on ahead working his knife in one hand, hacking away any lush growths that proved to be obstacles in his path.

"I'm not very excited at what you are suggesting, but I cannot think of anything better right now, so I'll just trudge along," Hilderich admitted with a small hint of grudge in his tone, and an almost imperceptibly condescending sort of nod.

A few hours later, Amonas had ground their way through an ever thickening vegetation. He was now stripped naked to the waist, the heat and humidity insufferable to bear with his leather vest and chain mail underneath. Hilderich wondered at how the man had suffered to carry all that weight at all, never mind wearing all that in such conditions. It was a curiosity that he had only chosen to take off most of it only after they had been walking for the better part of an hour.

It seemed to Hilderich as if the man had grown literally attached to his set of armor, or that its prolonged use had left indelible stains on his body. None of those reasons it seemed, could withstand even light scrutiny. Amonas had answered when quesitoned that he had simply not taken them off because he hadn't felt inclined to. Hilderich thought that spoke volumes for the man's tolerance threshold, and what he was capable of going through if pressed hard enough. Hilderich knew he had no desire to learn of Amonas' limits though. He believed this whole experience would be if nothing else, sufficiently educational and vividly remembered if they did make it back.

Amonas seemed to be indefatigable. He had trod on through thickset lush overgrowths, greens and all sorts of wild vegetation using his indispensable knife and had neither complained for the steaming heat nor for the breath-clogging moisture. Hilderich had refrained from asking questions about the reasoning behind their apparently random course through this probably impossible to map land, which lacked easily identifiable characteristics to use as points of reference.

Except those towers that looked like bullhorns, or 'giant forks' as Hilderich had described them. Naming was of little importance and would probably do them little justice as well. Such majestic structures in the middle of this chaotic spread of plants was indeed a humbling sight. They were roughly headed towards the general direction of one of those structures. Structures that mere men could not have possibly wrought.

Hilderich's concentration was broken by Amonas triumphant voice, a hundred or so feet ahead of him, but still clearly heard over the distance:

"Water, Hilderich! I told you we will find water! Come! It might not be cold, but it's clear enough to drink! Come!"

Hilderich felt Amonas was not unreasonably excited about his finding, but he could not readily share the joy. His legs though he did not complain about it felt heavy and pained him, while his feet were a soggy, uncomfortably wet affair. His light boots had let all the moisture inside and their path had guided him through many mud-soaked footings. He could feel his skin was not up to the task and looked miserable to the bone.

Still, finding water was the first good thing that had happened ever since that fine uwe stew. To Hilderich the previous day seemed now like another age altogether. He managed a defiant smile which he hoped Amonas would not take too seriously, and carried himself to the small trickling water source where Amonas was washing his face:

"Finally then. My mouth feels like a Ministry's rug, like everyone's trod on it!", Hilderich said jokingly and cupped his hands under the small trickle of water running down through an old tree's bark. It looked almost as if someone had fashioned it specifically for that purpose. Their luck hadn't run dry just yet, it would seem.

After they managed to wash away some of the sweat and grit and more importantly quench their thirst and fill their belly with more water than it could handle, Amonas took Hilderich by the arm and suggested to him that they should try and make some sort of camp there, near the water. The rain would be coming he said even with the clear sky above, since there can be no water with no rain.

Amonas insisted they would have to keep dry, since that was how many folk in the sea died. He explained that their bodies were usually found almost dried out, nothing but dessicated husks. From what he knew, it was because water was attracted to water and the water in the body, the blood, the piss, the spit, was drawn away to the sea. The rich got richer even in nature, perhaps even in this weird land as well.

In any case, he had convinced Hilderich that it was wiser to stay dry, and it would indeed be a welcome change in any case. They would have to build a fire to do that and with all that humidity everywhere he could not for the life of him figure out how. They had found water though, so Amonas was optimistic that they would find a way to build a fire as well. Hilderich thought to himself that he found Amonas to be very convincing and reassured himself before feeling unmistakably hungry, his stomach sounding like a cauldron on fire with nothing inside the broth but bubbling water.

"We need to eat too," Hilderich admitted frankly to Amonas who nodded knowingly.

"I haven't seen a breathing thing yet, only biting insects and that's no good if they drink your blood. Trying to get back at them won't work either. No river or stream to try and find fish so far. We'll have to rely on you then, Hilderich. Try and find some kind of root, stem or plant in general you think might be safe to eat. I don't mean taste good, mind you. Just something that won't kill us by eating it, not right off anyway. I know I can leave you to it while I gather what wood and fiber I can manage to start working on that small tent of ours. Have faith in yourself Hilderich, we'll manage somehow," said Amonas in his usually gruff voice with a friendly tone prone to suggestion. It was the voice of a leader Hilderich realized, a man who seemed fit enough for the task at hand: keeping them alive.

Hilderich nodded and accepted the task, though as in most cases without knowing if he was really up to it. He turned though once before starting to rummage through the thickset leaves and lush bushes all around, and asked Amonas:

"I noticed we were roughly headed towards the structures we saw from that hill. Do you have something in mind about those?"

"You noticed, eh? I thought you would. I don't have something particular in mind, no. Just somekind of a feeling, an urge if you like. To be honest, what more is there to look for around here? If there's some kind of a device similar to the one that brought us here, we're better off looking at one of those things before scouring the whole damned land hoping to blindly stumble upon one."

Hilderich shrugged and nodded in agreement:

"That's true."

Amonas went about making his make-shift tent and Hilderich disappeared from sight trying to find something edible. Within less than half an hour Amonas had laid down a few logs, most of them half rotten and half dead but good enough for the job in hand. He had stacked them so as to make a simple crude roof of sorts and then covered the simple skeleton with freshly snapped branches and twigs. In the end, he overlaid huge thick leaves from the innumerable plants available all around them.

He hoped these would suffice and once he had massed enough pieces of wet yet not soggy wood, he piled it down neatly to form a fire stack, wishing his flint and stone would be enough to get the fire going. He called out to Hilderich to check if he had found anything at all. While he received no reply for a few moments, the moment he started to feel worried about his whereabouts Hilderich popped out of a cluster of bushes with what seemed to be an armful of large, thick mushrooms.

"There's more! Fantastic really! Of all places, renia mushrooms of this size, right here on this godforsaken place! My grandfather would have had a fit!"

Hilderich was shouting enthusiastically when he walked over the stacked wood, looking for a good place to leave his priceless armful of mushrooms. Displeased with the available options he decided to just stand there, a load of mushrooms twice the size of his fists carried on his arms.

Amonas smiled, greatly pleased and mildly surprised both for their luck as well as for the gleam in Hilderich's eyes. It was a genuine expression of happiness however transient and irrelevant it would prove to be in the long run, it was good for morale; Hilderich's and his as well.

"Put those down and help me get the fire going," Amonas nodded over the stacked wood.

"Oh, no. I've never started a fire in the woods before. I'd be useless. Always used a bottle of- Oh, you might be inadvertently correct in your proposal. I'm telling you though, you will be eating the ones that touch this sorry excuse for a ground."

Hilderich indeed lowered his body almost in a squatting position to put down the load of mushrooms as intact as possible. They formed a somewhat neat pile that did not immediately crumble when he let go of his arms. He then searched through the numerous pockets in his vest and procured a small metal flask which he in turn proffered to Amonas with a radiant, beaming smile.

"Gin. Fine grain, citrus taste. A distill of mine. I tend to drink a bit from time to time. Well, frankly, more likely when master Olom would be away on important business. But I insist, it really is my produce. He never touched the stuff," Hilderich's voice playfully mischievous.

"Well, you certainly have more about you than meets the eye Hilderich D'Augnacy."

Amonas grinned while taking the small flask and dabbing with it some more or less dry cloth from his own garments, then placing it where the fire should be lit.

"Which reminds me Amonas, you seem to know my name though

you haven't yet very well met me. You told me only just yesterday that Amonas was the name I needed to know, and the rest would be revealed to me in due time. I believe that time is long due, wouldn't you say?"

"You are right, friend. I do owe you that and some more still."

Amonas was busy with his knife and a nicely shaped and sized stone that seemed to spark properly. Thankfully, he always carried with him some flint and stone. With a couple of more efforts on his behalf, sparks flew into the gin-soaked piece of cloth and the fire leaped out as if beckoned by a spirit of old, rushing and blazing lively as it should.

"Amonas Ptolemy, a friend to those that wish it and an enemy to many, a husband to one."

Hilderich could sense the sorrowful note in his voice, his wife understandably a defining part of him, part of who he felt he was.

"I'm sure she'll be quite happy to greet you on our return, will she not?"

Hilderich's tried to say that with an uplifting, playful tone. A smile formed on his face even as he put a nice whole piece of mushroom through a stick getting ready to roast it over the growing fire.

"I am sure she will, just not as sure that she will be as happy as I will," Amonas answered in kind. He too, was skewering a mushroom head cut in slices with his knife through a stick with a size handy for roasting.

"Well I'm quite happy around these lovelies here," said Hilderich amusingly, gesturing at the small pile of mushrooms with the hint of an innuendo that would have made master Olom instantly bash his head with whatever he would have held in his hand at the time.

They ate until they were full and their sense of taste and smell satisfied beyond mere hunger. The fire was burning well now and they had hung their clothes overhead using a well balanced piece of wood and some of the hanging green ropes of vegetation. The clothes had seemed to dry adequately.

Hilderich had laid down on top of his cloak with feet outstretched, letting them dry out close to the warmth of the fire. Amonas had lit a pipe with what he thought passed for uwe around the place and puffed away leisurely, lost in thought. He had offered some to Hilderich who politely refused, choosing instead to down a few sips of his own distill of gin. As if it had been bothering him for days on end, Amonas turned and asked Hilderich:

"Don't you feel like sleeping now? You must be exhausted from all this. I was a soldier once, I've known similar hardship. But you, you should have been half-way home in a dream by now."

"I know what you mean. I feel like a press was weighing me down and now that I ate and laid myself to rest, it has been lifted. I should have fallen soundly asleep, as you say."

"What's keeping you then, Hilderich?"

"Nightfall. There's no bloody nightfall for me to sleep."

Machina Segnis

HE suns seemed to have risen earlier on that particular day or at least the Castigator's people definitely had. At every level of office and hierarchy, the living mechanisms of the Ministry, the Army and the Procrastinators were of a singular mind and purpose: The Castigator had announced that in two weeks time the wrathful military might of the Outer Territories would be ready to march for war, the likes of which had not happened in the past 25 years.

In every single office and chamber of the various organizations of people and ruling institutions, the situation was almost the same even if one cared to take into account the multitude of minor variations in disciplinary strictness, interpersonal roles and affiliations, as well as structural differences and the specific nomenclature of each branch of service.

Lesser officials busied themselves with arranging communiques, writing down orders and manifests and then calling for couriers or perhaps taking it upon themselves to forward the appropriate documents and even matériel to their intended recipients. It would be anathema to any one in that overwhelmingly complex machine of sorts to should singularly fail especially in simple orders.

If anything were to happen to this whole enterprise, this majestic war footing, this Holy Campaign that had been blessed by the Gods and commanded by the Castigator himself, it would not be because a lowly clerk or young lieutenant forgot to sent out some matériel requisition form or a call-to-arms teller. Indeed, if such a Campaign were to fail because of a human error in such a catastrophic way before it even began to put itself into motion, it would not be because of the lowly gears in the machine that worked above and beyond their human capacities.

Diligence was considered a virtuous characteristic and most Law-abiding parents tried to hammer that into their children if they had to, so as to become people worthy of upholding the Law whenever they could, whatever their place in society might be. Those that the Gods seemed to favor most were selected to enter public service as

Ministers, Procrastinators, or Army officers, according to how well they performed at the Agogeia.

Select officials from these three embodiments of rule and order taught at the Agogeia, schools for those that could afford to become something useful in their lives. After the basics, such as obedience to Law, reciting scripture and fairly simple counting and sword-fighting skills, the best of each class of children were selected for progression: that was done according to the inclination, receptiveness, and skill they showed at the various tests and games carried out to separate those who were capable of serving the people and the Gods and those who simply could not.

Some of those who were better skilled in memory, oration, the use of language and emotion, and showed a certain ability to swaying the hearts and minds of their fellow students, were further trained to become Ministers. They were inundated into the teachings and trappings of the Law and were tought how to best interpret Law according to need. They learned the intricacies of teaching, enlightening, and chastising the layman. They were most importantly shown how to impress and guide hundreds, if not thousands of people as the Law, the Ministry, and the Ruling Council dictated.

They were responsible for the enlightenment of the people, teaching them Law and helping them avoid the temptations that would lead to blasphemy, heresy, eternal damnation, and a most probably gruesome, demeaning execution that would serve as a reminder and a lesson that All is Law and no one and nothing is above it. The Ministers also tended to the daily running of the Territories as administrative officials, collecting offerings and making amendments to the lesser decrees of the Law to better handle the multitude of people and the realities the land of the living required, with its needs of economy, trade, and resources.

The spending of coin for public works would be decided and then dispersed accordingly to those noble houses that could field enough manpower to make things happen. Things like roads, bridges, canals, buildings, walls, mills and workshops and every other piece of structure that would make the Territories grow and prosper, for the glory of the Pantheon. One day, one of their number would be chosen from the Castigator with the blessings of the Patriarch to be the next Arch-minister, the one blessed to be the voice and heart of the Ministry.

Those of the Agogeia students who were energetic, athletic students, and showed exceptional stamina and strength; those who exemplified martial prowess both with blade and bare hands, those who were blessed with possessing a sharp and decisive mind, those having proven their faith to be unfailing with a stone-hard dedication to the Pantheon, those were in the end chosen as fit for service in the Army.

Rigorous training in all the known aspects of warfare was their sole occupation unto death. Whether or not they would be called upon to act, to kill or be killed in service to the Gods, they would train with sword and spear, shield and horse until the ailings of old age would force them to continue serving by training others of their kind. In matters such as the planning and design of warfare where a mind should be much more fit than the body, their experience and long years of service were unmatched, and those traits they used when passing the torch to the ones that would succeed them.

Their training began with single combat techniques utilising many different weapons, under different situations and varying levels of duress. Then they progressed into infantry squad tactics in the open field against other types of units like cavalry, or steamers and artillery. And then they would rotate into the rest of the units in order for their training to be complete and be able to use everything from bare hands to a complex steamer machine. Such a practice also made them knowledgeable in the weakness and strength of each type of unit, making them able to select the best course of action and the kind of men, machines and animals it would require to be successful.

These were the core lessons they were taught: strength in knowledge, success in adaptability, glory in death. As they progressed through the standings of the Army always according to their merit and degree of success in their duties, they always kept in mind their faithful devotion. Through their accrued experience they learned more about handling men, matériel, and equipment; they became excellent organizers, designers and planners with tens of thousands of men in their mind as one day they might be called upon to lead the whole Army as Generals, in the name of the Pantheon first, and the Castigator second.

Those that did not excel in anything but showed average skill at wielding a sword and could learn enough of the Law as it was needed orally, those did not learn to read and write like the Minister's did, nor did they train any further in order to excel into combat. These children were strictly chosen for their ability to follow the letter of the Law blindly and unerringly, to keep a watchful eye for signs of heresy and insubordination as well as any element that was an affront the Pantheon and the Law, or anything that might defy the Law or its upholders in spirit or in letter.

These were the ever watchful eyes of the Castigator, the arm that made the Law reach into every heart, body, and mind: the Procrastinators. Their training was simple, crude, and effective. It hammered into them the utmost loyalty to the Law, and tought them how to use people in order to learn all that was needed: the rumors, the happenings, the weddings and deaths, births and oath-takings.

Everything that went on not just in Pyr, but everywhere in the Territories, they made it their job to know. If the need arose they disciplined and re-enlightened. At times they would bring to the Ministers those they deemed suspicious or knew to be genuinely guilty of sin. Then they would enforce the Law and the divine will of the Ministry with unflinching loyalty, following the credo that All is Law. If they performed their tasks impeccably, surely they would have a chance at being given the honor of becoming Procrastinator Militant: part of the Ruling Council, the left hand of the Castigator himself.

All that was a structure that had been handed down from the Gods themselves. That meant that its purpose and form were Holy, and any talk of reform, change, or deviation from the established norm was treated at best as blasphemy but usually it was deemed heretical, and was treated accordingly by public torture and death.

None were exempt from such punishment, especially the men in the Ruling Council who were meant to be the paragon of Law itself for all the people to see. Such a hideous concept was not unknown, that a man in the Ruling Council would denounce the Gods by committing or speaking heresy: it had happened long ago, in a past almost rightly forgotten and excised from the Annals of the Territories. Its memory still lingered though in the people's minds as Shan's Betrayal, a myth to frighten the children into obeying, a fable to instruct and put the fear of the Gods into the soul of men, but indeed part of a history long forcefullty cast into oblivion.

Shan had been a General of the Army at a time when the Territories had not grown past the lands around Pyr. When the Ruling Council decided it was time to enlighten the nearby shores of Urfall, Shan was reluctant at first. The story says he was publicly chastised, with a hundred lashes to his back; the chastisement had brought him to the brink of death.

Because he was deemed an exceptional strategist and a peerless tactician, he was once more asked to lead the armies that would enlighten Urfall, instead of being stripped of office and rank and live on the streets as a beggar. He had been given the opportunity to redeem himself in the eyes of the Pantheon, the people, and the Castigator. He acceded and the armies marched off, gleaming in their metal armor, the blessings of the Castigator sung over the Southern Gates of Pyr. Within a few weeks Shan's armies seemed to have been lost, and no message of the war had reached Pyr; not a single messengers sent from Pyr ever returned.

One day, Shan appeared over the hills encircling Pyr, and had with him not only the armies he had marched off with weeks before, but horses as well, and men, catapults and hellish contraptions that spurted fire and death. He had spread his heresy to the armies like the mythic whores of old spread disease; like a cancer that spreads from the roots of a tree to its leaves and brings about its death. And he had the Urfalli with him, their machines working in ways unfathomable, the heinous products of heretical pacts with the forces of evil.

He reached the Gates of Pyr and demanded the surrender first and foremost of the Ruling Council. The man also had the ineffable audacity to accuse the Council of lies and crimes to the people, twisting the word of the Law and spewing forth horrific untruths. It was an attempt to poison the minds of every man, woman, and child in the city as well, promising that none of those who surrendered willingly would be hurt in any way, and that a fair trial would be arranged for all.

Except for the Council, who would be executed after their supposed lies had been exposed and their non-existent crimes against men proven unquestionably. Such heretic lies had never been uttered before and never would be again, their venomous treachery so base that the Castigator himself is said to have cried in desperation, for he had never thought a dearly loved brother like Shan could fall from grace like a star falls from the night sky.

The city was utterly defenseless save but a few procrastinators and old army tutors. The rest of its defenders were lowly farmers, herders, artisans and traders that had not yielded shield, spear or sword for once in their lives. The armies of Shan had cast away all form of decency or honor and had turned into a rabble of heretics. They had begun to scour the lands pillaging, raping, and burning, before they dug their teeth in what they thought would be the grand feast of Pyr itself.

But they never managed to sink their putrid claws into the immaculate flesh of the City of Pyr for it was protected by the Gods, as are all their faithful and humble servants. For when the time was nigh and all seemed lost, the Castigator Hanul Ofodor the 1st, retired from the halls of the Disciplinarium and went deep into the Sacred Vaults, where he and the Patriarch offered their blood to commune with the Gods and ask for deliverance in that time of need.

For a day and a night, while the heretic hordes of Shan looted and pillaged the lands, while the outer walls of Pyr were about to fall, an angel sent from the Gods appeared in their image, and cast brilliant rays of cleansing light annihilating the armies of Shan who had no other recourse but to flee like the vermin they were. None escaped the angel's wrath, who spread the cleansing fire to every last part of Shan's army.

When the Day of Redemption had passed, the City of Urfall and its majestic harbor and proud workshops were all extinguished in a ball of light so pure in its wrath that those who saw it with bare eyes went blind, and would forever be praised for the rest of their lives as Martyrs of the Wrath of the Gods, spreading the tale of Shan and what they had seen to everywhere they went. And such was the way the story was told from one generation to the next, as a reminder of the fallibility of even the most righteous and pious of men. The official Annals never admitted or recorded it, since Shan's betrayal should never have happened in the eyes of the Gods; and so it seemed as it never really had.

Such was the tale of Shan Lagus, the Betrayer; proscribed from history, but alive in the memory of Law-fearing people. People like the Arch-minister La Vasse, a wide, big-boned man, dressed in an opulent surplice with holy texts in High Helican weaved around its sleeves and a Seal of Office hanging round his neck in a pendant made of platinum and emeralds, fittingly pure and clean to represent the qualities an Arch-minister should possess.

He was presently sitting at the Strategium Proper in the company of the General of the Army and the Procrastinator Militant. His embarrassing near-blunder at last night's festivities at the announcement of the Last Holy Campaign as it was officially now named, had not gone unnoticed: it had become the subject of sarcastic comments and irony even at the lower echelons of the Ministry and the Army, but had only naturally been ignored by the Procrastinators in whole.

The General of the Army had not been present at the event due to having received news of the Castigator's decision from beforehand: he had indeed spent the night hard at work putting his most trusted and capable people together, rousing them up from their sleep in order to lay down the priorities of planning and start orchestrating the massive preparations involved in such an endeavor as a Holy Campaign.

He had of course learned of the Procrastinator Militant's blunder and even though second hand accounts rarely manage to do justice, he had exchanged knowing looks and smiles with the Arch-minister that had gone largely unnoticed by the Procrastinator Militant; a somewhat alarming fact if one would care to extrapolate the level of the Procastinators' vigilance from the qualities apparent in its most senior member.

The three of them had been there from before dawn, the Arch-minister and the Procrastinator Militant arriving together even though they had rode in separate coaches, having left from the Disciplinarium once proper etiquette was adhered to and the reenactment of the Pacification of Zaelin thoroughly completed, with all the bloodletting and the prayer that ensued.

They were now sipping fresh hot uwe tea comfortably seated at the General's planning chamber, all sorts of charts and maps laid out over a grand table. Heaps reports and still unsigned orders were amassed upon the General's desk which was a utilitarian piece of furniture like most around the chamber, sturdy and well-made but otherwise unadorned and plain.

The Arch-minister was seated in the only luxurious chair available: plush velvet adorned its back and the sitting surface. Elegantly inlaid pieces of ivory, black granite and tether-wood intertwined in flowing designs on the stylish armrests. The Procrastinator Militant sat at a simple stool which was much more accommodating for a soldier in search of a few moments of peace for resting his legs, rather than a man of such office as a Procrastinator Militant.

The General had briefly apologized to the Procrastinator Militant for lack of a better seating apparatus, and had at length explained that any and all equipment deemed to be of an extraneous nature was being dismantled to be put into other uses with the preparations for the campaign demanding every last bit of reusable material. That even included finely crafted chairs made from young sycamore wood and inlaid with ivory, granite, and tether-wood, not unlike the last one available for seating persons of importance, of which the Arch-minister seemed to be putting to such good use.

Not that he implied at any point, the General had continued, that the Procrastinator Militant was not a person of incalculable importance but alas, the Arch-minister had seniority according to the Law of Founding. It was Law that essentially demanded the Arch-minister to be seated in the proper way, while he would have to make do with what little was available at such a time of need.

At that, the Procrastinator Militant withdrew from any thought or intention of protesting, and simply accepted the proffered stool graciously. By looking at the Arch-minister, if one didn't know better he might have misinterpreted his slight grin as an indication of silent enjoyment of the unfortunate predestinations of the Procrastinator on his behalf. Such a man though was beyond base thoughts of that sort; he was certainly merely grinning at the studious labor going on around the Strategium Proper, indirectly praising the high spirits of everyone involved and personally congratulating the General of the Army for kicking off the preparations in a way that only expected of him:

"Well done, Tyrpledge. I see that you are already thinking of using all the available material. Even using the ivory and granite in such a fine chair. Hard to find materials, are they not?", the Arch-minister inquired with his nose delicately poised over his cup of uwe, letting the aromas seep in of their own volition. The General replied in earnest:

"I am more than honored, indeed I feel blessed, to hear such praise from your Excellency. Yes, they are most valuable, as well as the tether-wood and the sycamore. From what I know of the artisan's techniques, the ivory is used in delicate steamer parts without which the damnable things would blow up before going on for ten feet. The sycamore and tether-wood are used in the construction of the siege engines, and the granite is turned into pellets for the steamers' sling-shots."

The hint of a smile formed on the General's face and his eyes darted back and forth between Gomermont, the Procrastinator Militant, and La Vasse, to whom he added as an afterthought:

"Is the uwe to your liking? I can always call up the cook to present himself and receive proper chastisement if he has failed you. He was specifically instructed on the required quality of the uwe and your precise likings. It would be an affront to the Council if he could not serve uwe of the proper quality."

"There will be no need, General. Please, call me La Vasse. We rarely meet on official business as it is, with you spending most of the time on exercises away from Pyr and me always busy at the Ministry and the Disciplinarium. I believe that in such an important time, we should dispense with the tiring mannerisms of protocol and etiquette and get on with the business in hand to better serve the Law and the glory of the Pantheon, naturally."

The Arch-minister's tone was polite, level, and straightforward. He seemed to regard the General as his peer, which was strictly speaking, not so.

Tyrpledge was visibly as well as pleasantly surprised; his look widened and his face brightened up a tone. Gomermont seemed to fidget uncomfortably at his stool, unable to arrange his body in a manner both sufficiently comfortable and befitting of a Procrastinator Militant.

La Vasse and Tyrpledge largely ignored Gomermont's discomfort and Tyrpledge replied in kind to the Arch-minister:

"I am more than grateful for that dispensation then, La Vasse. It does help a great deal when going to war to not have to devote precious time on finding the right chair, serving the proper tea and using the protocol-bound appellations of rank and office all the time," the General said while easing up on his chair, his body assuming a more relaxed position.

"Oh, make no mistake Tyrpledge; my rank, office, and related trappings of my status as Arch-minister still hold and I expect you to diligently administer the proper respect. At least in public when we are not planning together, exchanging information and agreeing to our next best course of action. Be reminded of course, that the Castigator is always briefed on our meetings and though we have been given executive control of the Holy Campaign, whatever course of action we decide on has to be ratified by His Piousness. In grave matters of battle that is, since currently I have been empowered with freedom to act as the Castigator's proxy in these preliminary stages of the preparation."

La Vasse's voice had assumed a harsher tone, the weight in his voice and words punctuating his heightened status of authority. His strict but fair tone was indicative of his intentions: He would be reasonably cooperative and would dispense of the pleasantries and honors where applicable, but that would not bring Tyrpledge up to the same level as him, the proxy of the Castigator.

He also seemed to limit this dispensation to Tyrpledge alone since Gomermont, apart from being a relatively useless dolt which was widely regarded as the most common type of Procrastinator, his office also was not immediately pertinent to the Campaign; he and his men would remain in the cities and townships, ever watchful for signs of insurrection and heresy when the Castigator and the complete armed might of the Territories would be in the Widelands.

Tyrpledge was simply a soldier, a sword to be wielded like a tool, bending to the master's will. He had never had any misconceptions of his status, and the Arch-minister's words didn't carry a different message: he would still be following orders diligently and respectfully, he just didn't have to stand at attention the whole time.

Once La Vasse's words settled in, Tyrpledge said in a simple, straightforward manner and a genuine voice of calm acceptance:

"I understand perfectly, Arch-minister."

Gomermont was standing up having given up on the stool and he was languidly peering over the milling mass of soldiers, artisans, and laborers outside at the huge staging fields. He was sipping on a freshly poured cup of uwe. He asked no one in particular, in a rather rude manner without turning to face either one of the men he was supposed to be working closely with:

"These are the Army's infamous steamers then? They do seem clumsy and unwieldy. They lack that polish I thought the Army insists on fervently. How do you fit the horses inside that? How do they breathe, is it through those pipes? I'm quite curious."

General Tyrpledge rolled his eyes in an almost shocking expression of unadulterated lack of esteem. The Arch-minister was smiling, sipping almost indifferently at his uwe when the General sighed and replied in as much seriousness as he could muster:

"They are called steamers because they use steam, which is very hot water. They do not use horses. They are not polished because if they were, they would give away their position hours away before reaching their intended targets, giving away the position of our forces. The pipes are part of the system of steam-works."

Gomermont was as adamant as he was ignorant:

"Ah, I see. Still, clumsy pieces of machine. I'll never understand why you insist on using them."

"I can accept that in good grace, Procrastinator Militant," said Tyrpledge and left the dead-end exchange of words at that. Tyrpledge resumed his thoughts even as Gomermont took in more of the vast area where work intermingled with a large camping area. At an opportune time, the General asked the Arch-minister:

"La Vasse, I need to know. You are closest to the Castigator. You are his proxy, as well as probably the only reliable person I can talk with meaningfully. The Widelands are wild lands, there are no people living there. No sane people that I know of, at least. No cities, no towns to speak of; nothing to capture and maintain. With no population to enlighten, no known forces arrayed against us, what objectives should I designate? What provisions will I require? What manner of equipment should I gather, what should the disposition of our forces be? How will our forces move? What, exactly, will we be going up against, Arch-minister?"

Tyrpledge's tone showed his anxiety. Some of the words burst forth rapidly behind the others. He was not scared, La Vasse could see that. He simply needed a target to focus on. He was a soldier after all.

"I am much at a loss as you are, General. I have had little foreword of the Castigator's decision, and though privy to most of his thoughts and discussions, I have to say that the Patriarch is better informed than I am. All I can tell you is that you should commit the totality of our armies, for a reconnaissance in force."

Tyrpledge frowned in disbelief before asking to make sure, the surprise in his voice more than evident:

"The totality of our forces? In two weeks?"

"I have not been known to impart His Piousness's words imperfectly. The sum of our armies Tyrpledge, in two weeks time."

"But.. There is no precedent of such a mobilization.. The artisans and laborers at my disposal cannot cope with such a workload even if I drive them to death thrice over! It is not a matter of ability, it is simply a matter of-"

The general's protests were politely interrupted by the Archminister waving a dismissive hand and saying as he reached for another cup of uwe:

"The Army has been granted special dispensation to use any and all capable men and resources that can be found across the lands, for the period of time up to and including the Holy Campaign with the blessings of the Ministry and the cooperation of the Procrastinators."

Tyrpledge was stunned in silence and was instantly awed at the power put forth by the Castigator, effectively forcing every able bodied man to serve as labor and offer his belongings for the express purposes of this Last Holy Campaign. Truly momentous times they were living in, he thought. Then he started mentally calculating the manpower he would need to use to have everything ready in time, when the Arch-minister commented on his tea:

"Fine uwe, Tyrpledge. You have a fine cook. If the rest of the army proves as capable and as willing, the Pantheon will smile upon us."

The Procrastinator Militant spoke then suddenly out of turn, sounding morose:

"I prefer keplis to uwe, really. It upsets my stomach."

The longest errand

HE previous night's walk had exhausted him. He had laid down to sleep right after dawn with sore feet. His legs were leaden with the weight of all the distance traveled so far. It was indeed a long journey from the western lands, from Nicodemea south through the great farmlands of Rubnis. Then he had crossed the great river Shielwa onto the rough country of Ilonas, the shepherd country. It was a land filled with animals, hill and rock where few hardy men lived.

This was where the marble road leading into the Widelands begun. This was where his quest had taken him so far. For weeks he had been on the road, suffering fools too gladly sometimes, subjecting his body into a trial of strength of will and body. He had been traveling on foot almost half-way through the lands. Indeed, it was a feat in itself. But that was merely the means to far greater a prize, the complete knowledge of which still eluded him despite all the years of studies and inquiries, both his and his master's.

The marble road started off as a narrow, thin road, small edges of pure white marble-like material delineating its boundaries. It was not really made from marble, for if it was it would have been stained, shattered and chipped away bit by bit long ago. It had defied though the machinations of man and had stood throughout time as immaculate as it must have been once first laid out.

It was a sleek, shiny white-gray road that felt cold to the touch but also fine and delicate, like glass-work. There it was: unbreakable, unyielding, unscathed by time, man, and nature. A foreign body so exquisitely crafted that it was indeed unique. No artisans of any time and no empire that ever rose and fell ever managed to construct such a piece of perfection, truly as some ancient poet had once said, "for the Gods to walk upon the lands".

It was, and had always been, part of the lands but alien to them as well. The people had always known of the marble road, just as they knew of the trees, the mountains and the rivers, the forests and the glens, the fields and the wheat, the goat and the cow, and the suns and the clouds. But these things were of nature, and the marble road clearly was not; for nature abhors uniqueness. Animals come in pairs, rivers abound, and so do trees. But there is only one marble road. A perfect thing; a leftover from the time Gods had walked among men. Or even so, before men alltogether.

What reason was there behind it? Why does it lead into the Widelands? What is it made of? Who build it? With what tools? They was the proper word because this must surely have been the work of thousands. No single man could have ever hoped to accomplish such a work in his lifetime. Perhaps most rightly so, the road was the work of the Gods. To try and unravel their reasoning and purpose could only lead to madness brought forth from vain, fruitless searches of the lowly human mind.

Molo decided to leave these thoughts that had been troubling him aside; thoughts which beget questions begging for answers that could not be found. At least not before he ventured into the Widelands proper, until he could find what Umberth described as the Necropolis where inestimable knowledge was waiting to be uncovered to the world. Knowledge of a time unknown before man had ever walked the lands, the Time of the Gods.

It was already a fascinating sensation walking upon the very same road that even the Gods might have walked upon once. What other man, apart from him and Umberth had dared walk the marble road unto its terribly unknown end? What other man had lived long enough to tell the tale, only to be hunted down as a heretic, a blasphemer? Would his own end be as tragic and miserable?

He grinned wickedly at these thoughts for they were immediately followed by the echo of his resolutions: He wouldn't perish neither in the Widelands. Nor would he be torn by the hands of a fanatical mob or made to disappear by the ever watchful Procrastinators. He would not succumb to any torture the Ministers might put him through, for when all his trials and tribulations had come to pass, he would be a simple man no more. He would not be hunted down or exiled; he would become a feared and terrible man.

When all the power and majesty and magnificence of the Gods was unveiled and made manifest through him, he would be transformed into a being of awe and power that the lands had not witnessed since the beginning of time. He would become a living deity, an avatar of the Gods to be loved, cherished, and worshiped as a God among men should.

He knew the truth of it, he could feel it in his heart and bones, see it in his twisting dreams. Dreams of cleansing light and fire, himself a creature of wrath and glory with terrible power at his hands and unimaginable purpose in his mind. The purpose of the Gods, their divine plan unfolding through him alone, their chosen instrument of will. He would not fail them, for his lust of the promised power burned deep withing, deeper than the need to breathe indeed.

He had to find the Necropolis first though and that task seemed ever so slightly more difficult with each passing day. Last night he had found the marble road and had eagerly walked under the stars for a long stretch of time without giving pause. He had seen the trees give way to bush, the grass wither, and the sounds of animals grow weaker, fainter, and fewer still. He knew he was entering the Wide-lands proper, the signs visible around him. It had been the same with Umberth, according to the tale that had been recorded so many years ago.

He laid down to sleep near the marble road under the skinny old withered bark of a tree, a small cluster of rocks sheltering him from the howling winds. He laid his cloak under his head like a pillow, and drew his blanket high enough to cover his face from the rising suns. He slept lightly, with a smile on his face like a happy, carefree child.

When he woke up in the afternoon, the suns were still high. He got up and stood gazing towards the far end of the road. The marble road that he would follow for as long as it proved wise to him. Though nothing about his journey had ever seemed wise. He had even been called a madman by his master, when he had told him he would follow Umberth's steps.

What of it, if he was indeed a madman? What of it indeed? Mad-men answer to no one, only to the Gods. And so would he answer if he was called for. The Land of the Gods beckoned. They tested his mettle. Only someone mad enough to challenge such authority can truly knock on the Gates of the Necropolis. He was all alone out here, in the Widelands.

He would play. He would play with the rules of Their choosing. He would find the Necropolis, at any cost. Wherver these people who had been worshipped as gods had been finally laid to rest, he would find them. Once he had set out, he knew he would be attempting a feat that no one had succeeded at before. And even if he did, as Umberth might have had, nothing was certain of the power therein and how it would finally become his own.

His thoughts wandered to a passage from Umberth's tale:

"Only a few nights after we had definitely passed into the Widelands, we lost track of the road. We decided to camp quite a distance away from it, towards what had seemed to be a natural spring in a rock formation. After we had laid to rest, in the morning we had lost sight of the marble road. We were doubly misled, since the spring had dried out and there was no water to speak of as well. The maps had failed us early on. Terlet went mad and master Umberth ordered me to put him out of his misery. Nubir and Vamden probably got lost trying to find the road, or simply decided to run back to civilized country before we went deeper into the Widelands. In any case, we never saw or heard of them again."

This place was unforgiving. The road was like a lifeline, his only hope of making sense of direction in such a place. He would keep on it for as far as it took him, and try to make sense of the other signs in Umberth's tale to find his way. He would not become lost like him.

The exact location of the Necropolis was a mystery to him, but he knew that it lay further deep into the Widelands; into its Dunes, the desert proper. He hoped the road would eventually take him there. He was worried that food and water would become even more scarce in the endless sands.

He still had a ready supply of honey-laden bars of nuts and sesame; it was a confection most appropriate for traveling long distances; generally invigorating when consuming one's energy. His water sack was still full from yesterday, but he knew now he had to ration his water perhaps allowing himself no more than two mouthfuls a day.

The more that the Widelands turned into a desert, the more imperative it became for him to conserve his water. That is why he had chosen to travel at night: because it was cooler and the walk not as demanding, especially concerning water.

He believed it would be possible to find sources of water as he went along, at least until he reached the Dunes. He doubted any water could be found in that place at all, for days on end. And that was where he would either perish or triumph. Deep in the desert dunes of the Widelands, searching for the Necropolis.

As was his preferred way, he waited for dusk to come and the suns to disappear from the sky before he would start walking again. He picked up his knapsack and his walking stick and started off once more, feeling he had won a small battle. Renewed vigor and determination coursed through him, each one of his steps brimming with confidence. He felt like he needed no road to find his path and he could carve himself a path worthy of his own legendary tale, forever sung in the eons to come.

The stars were shining bright soon, and he felt the future could only hold a taste of that glimmer. Somewhere up there, in the firmament of the stars, there shone a star for him alone.

Part II

Per Ardua

Wishes of the Unholy

"A soldier can serve the Gods, the Council, and the people in one of two important ways: that is, he can either be dead or alive, but he will still serve. A soldier might choose either but one of the two has proved extremely popular, and for good reason. As a soldier myself with as much experience as any can hope to amass over the years, I can only share with you a rough guideline on how to live long enough to write your own manual: Avoid the meaningless battles, and especially politics."

-General Ret. Normo Mimmot, *Didagmata*

Circumstance and happenstance

 E hasn't spoken a word, your Reverence. He could be a mute for all we know," the man with the bloodied iron scraper said to the Inquisitor. Bits of raw flesh were still hanging off the tool of torture, the man shackled to the wall limp, probably passed out.

The Patriarch stood still, his attention drawn to a few pieces of clothing and some belongings that were gathered on a shabby old table with jutting splinters and worn-away cuts all over its rough surface. He picked at some of the clothing with the edge of his patriarchal Rod, the sigils and High Helican scripts etched on its golden knob top barely visible in the dim torchlight of the torture chamber.

He sniffed the air around the ragged, bloodied clothing, and a grimace of distaste and scorn appeared on his otherwise solidly expressionless face. Some said he sometimes looked as if he was wearing a mask, rather than a real human face. And then there were the tales of him sitting idly in the dark without ever sleeping, or that he never asked for food or drink to be served. Fewer still feared he might not be a man. It was indeed wondrous what the human mind could attribute to persons of unimaginable power. The rumours made the Patriarch laugh sometimes.

None were brave or stupid enough though to point out such troubled thoughts in the presence of his Holiness. Others were too eager to circulate such rumors as well as the names of those who commented on such impertinent views of the Holy Avatar, the Patriarch.

All these kinds of curious, imaginative and disrespectful people who could not impose self-discipline and mind their own business ended up in deep rivers, forever reaching for breath. Others met a similar fate in shallow graves, their bones exposed for wild dogs to chew on. Some simply vanished with neither body nor bone left behind, not even as a gruesome reminder.

The Patriarch smiled at the thought of people being capable of voicing such audacity and felt almost impressed. Naturally, such phenomena had subsided considerably after it became a well-known fact that people with much to talk about can be heard the most. There was a popular saying that applied well to that fact: 'When people talk, the Patriarch listens'. Still from time to time people tend to forget what has come to pass before their time, but they are on occasion grimly reminded not to speak of the Holy Avatar in anything less than reverent hymns to his Holiness, divine origin, and purpose.

The Chief Inquisitor stood in reverent attention a few steps next to the Patriarch with his head bowed and his gaze averted from the Holy Avatar's face. It was a sign of reverent servitude and deference, which was in fact nothing less than proper adherence to protocol. Before speaking, the Inquisitor cleared his throat and licked his lips momentarily, his forehead glistening slightly with perspiration. He stood in a bowed position with hands knitted together, hidden inside the sleeves of his surplice. With a deep voice full of worshipful tones, he simply said:

"Your Holiness."

The Patriarch was still examining the small pile of clothes; the contents of a leather pouch and a small sack that were found on the man shackled against the wall, seemed to attract his attention. His visage showed a man detached from his surroundings, seemingly deeply engrossed in a detailed cataloging of what the prisoner was carrying on his person. It was as if he was searching for something his servants and people might have missed, something important that he had to make certain of himself alone.

There followed a brief period of silence with only the sputtering flames of the torches and the hollow sound of drops of water on damp stones accentuating it. A faint echo filled the otherwise almost empty chamber.

The Patriarch then spoke, addressing the Inquisitor without turning his head or gaze with his examination of the prisoner's belongings uninterrupted and now seemingly even more thorough:

"Hmm? Speak your mind Inquisitor."

The Patriarch's voice was commanding but calm, quite unassuming.

The Inquisitor then bowed deeper before speaking. There was stiffness in his voice, the words coming out of him as if with pained difficulty:

"The prisoner, your Holiness.. He has not given up any information yet, sir. The procrastinators found him where you indicated he would be, but there was no sign of his accomplices, your Reverence. His name is Philo Dutur. These are his belongings you are examining sir, in case you didn't know."

The Patriarch cast a gaze of subdued anger at the Inquisitor, his otherwise serene face the cause of a disturbing, fearful sensation. The effect was rather unsettling and the Inquisitor bowed deeper still as a physical reaction to the Patriarch's menacing look. It was evident he felt real fear afflicting him to the bone.

The Patriarch took notice of the Inquisitor's fear and felt pleased. Fear was a most useful tool he liked to regularly employ. He paused his examination of the items on the table, and turned to face the Inquisitor offering him his complete focus and attention:

"You should be careful not to recite the obvious, Chief Inquisitor. One might have mistaken you for a blabbering fool of little use beyond shoveling dung in the heat-pipes. Or even for someone committing blasphemy in taking me for a fool. That would be most unpleasant. I would have to choose a new Chief Inquisitor and the technicalities of such an affair, though I sometimes I must admit find somewhat pleasant, tend to bore me. Not to mention there are ongoing issues that demand my attention and there's little precious time. So please Chief Inquisitor, spare me the mundane and tell me something I can make use of."

The Patriarch seemed calm and restrained but his last phrase was uttered with such venom and malice that his uncannily melodic voice suddenly took on a sickeningly sweet quality. It felt like his last few words dripped of thick, clotted blood.

The Chief Inquisitor who in his long years of service had witnessed and performed countless acts of relentless and inhuman torture, was apparently terrified at the prospect of incurring the Patriarch's wrath. He physically recoiled and took a step back before kneeling to the wet, hard stone floor, pleading in all fours:

"I beg your forgiveness most revered and wise of All, the Holy Avatar of the Gods. I have nothing more of interest to offer you, your Holiness. I spoke out of nervousness and feel ashamed for my failure. I have faith, you know it in your heart to be true. Shall I ever once again even imply blasphemy or sin strike me down with all your might, but not because of a slip of the tongue, merciful Luminous One."

The Patriarch could see the man was visibly trembling. He was just another weak minded fool. He would have to dispensed of sooner rather than later, but not immediately. Other matters would have to take precedence. These were the traitors, more aptly sinners, that liked tp pronounce themselves as rebels. The Kinsfolk, he believed they called themselves now. Delusional fanatics, sprouts of a seed long thought extinct, dire remnants of a long lost cause.

He should have personally eradicated the lot of them, a long time before they developed the propensity to spread their mewling half-truths and insidious propaganda. Their riotous myths were always the preferred fodder of the easily deceived masses. He knew, he used such tactics himself.

He had knowledge of certain noble Houses to be either sympathetic or actively participating in the heresy. Remis would have to be made acquiescent in this matter, compliant and pliable as the Patriarch believed he was. If needed though, he would be forcefully removed.

He thought that he should have known better, he should have seen it would come to this before long. But there were niceties to be observed, rules to be followed before they were bent and finally broken. 'There were always the rules,' the Patriarch thought with a hint of exasperation in his brow.

His hands were finally, figuratively speaking of course, loose. He would break down their spine, their will, and their determination. He had the means to accomplish that and with some careful steps it would all seem so natural, so typical of all failed revolutions; blood-soaked affairs of chasing wild dreams that turn into ashes when the night is through.

His part would be small as always; the stage would be filled with other characters, some willing and some not very so. But he would conduct the opening and closing lines of the chorus, and they would all dance to his tune. It would be a performance truly fit for Gods, if only for a limited audience. Nevertheless he felt he would genuinely enjoy crushing the fools utterly; they would offer a fitting diversion indeed.

He had been absorbed in these thoughts for a rather discomforting period of time, the Inquisitor hanging by his ever word and even their absence. None dared break the forced uneasy silence and his apparently thoughtful concentration. The prisoner stirred, awaking from a merciful sleep.

His moans drew the flogger's attention who immediately reached for a barbed whip from a motley of tools and instruments, some evidently specific in their use and other much more common items put to such a use with surprising ingenuity.

As he distanced himself back from the wall to have more room to lash out to the chained man, a shout from across the chamber halted him with his whip barely halting in mid-air:

"Stay your hand!", the Patriarch's voice boomed deafeningly, matching and perhaps surpassing the authority he was imparted with however impossible that would sound. The torture chamber reverberated with his voice for mere moments, the flames of the torches quivering in response as if the air had been momentarily sucked out of the room.

The flogger set down his instrument of torture and bowed reverently as fast as it would seem prudent, and then stepped completely away from the chained form of Philo, standing still and averting his gaze from the direction of the Patriarch.

The Inquisitor managed a slightly expectant look towards the Patriarch, awaiting for the casual flick of the Rod that would sentence him to excruciating torture at the hands of the Patriarch himself, who had far more delicate and much more painfully agonizing unseen methods of torment at his disposal.

No such move was ever made. The Patriarch instead motioned with his left hand, the one unadorned, his Mourning hand, for the Inquisitor to rise, before he added:

"You are a pathetic fool, Inquisitor. Stop groveling, it sickens me. I never suffer fools gladly, but by necessity I shall. Serve your purpose and you might be able to redeem yourself and avoid my personal chamber of torture. You might even be able to save your insignificant little life you seem to value so much. I might feel less inclined to throw you to the boars, if you actually provide me with some names."

The Inquisitor was a middle aged man, lean and of austere face. Normally he would have looked menacing and unyielding to a common townsfolk in his elegant robes embroidered with his sigils of office and rank; he would have looked like someone important and powerful, someone to be feared and respected.

He now seemed instead a hollow, reduced man: his surplice spoiled and mudded, his face contorted from the imagined agony in the hands of the Patriarch. His feet were barely able to support his weight and slight tremors coursed through his body. He simply managed to croak:

"As is your bidding, your Holiness. But we need more time with the prisoner. He has proved, quite resilient."

The Patriarch was studying the prisoner intently with a deeply frowned face, as if trying to uncover everything he needed to know merely by watching him hard enough. His right hand, the one adorned with the Holy Diadems, was scratching his chin in a rather detached and insouciant way, in stark contrast to his earlier searing demeanor. He addressed the Inquisitor without turning around or barely moving his head, his voice carrying hints of aggravation:

"What you need Inquisitor, are lessons in silence. You would have killed him without getting a word out of him. I will break him myself. Your crude methods can only serve as instruments of death, nothing more. Vacate the chamber now, the both of you."

The Patriarch's voice carried a finality that could not be challenged. The flogger did not even bother picking up his tools, bowing once more hastily but affording time enough for what would seem to be proper reverence and then quickly heading towards the badly lit staircase that led to the upper levels of the tunnels.

The Inquisitor had no intention of uttering a single sentence that could very well be his last and with a series of deep bows and small steps made his way to the staircase as well, being very cautious not to turn his back to the Patriarch at any one point. The moment he reached the base of the stairs as ready as he was to turn and hurriedly run them up, the Patriarch raised his left hand and with his gaze still fixed on Philo, he asked the Inquisitor:

"The men you sent after the sinners deep into the tunnels, did you take care of them as instructed to?", his tone sharp like clear ice.

The Inquisitor stood at the base of the stairs with one foot already on the steps. He bowed low and replied in a somewhat controlled voice, rather than in the earlier whimpering tone:

"They were blinded with hot iron, their tongues were cut out, their arms were chopped off and their teeth smashed to the last. As you commanded me, your Holiness."

"I see. There are tasks even the likes of you can accomplish then. Let it be known that these men were chastised for witnessing one of the Holy Grounds with tunclean eyes and touched its walls with bare filthy hands, disturbing it with their impure voices. Parade them through the City tomorrow. Let the people see what happens to sinners and blasphemers."

The Inquisitor answered meekly after a small pause:

"Thy will be done, your Holiness."

"Of course it will be done. I will tolerate no interruptions Inquisitor, not even from the Castigator himself. If he threatens you with death, remember that I will be less merciful."

The Patriarch's last words struck true. The Inquisitor managed to simply nod and rushed up the stairs as if swaths of fire were behind him. A dull metal thud echoed, the large door to the chamber closing right behind the Inquisitor. The Patriarch then walked closer to Philo who was still alive and currently awake, unable though as he lay with his face towards the wall to look at his captor. A grin that threatened to tear the Patriarch's face apart suddenly appeared on his face revealing his immaculate pearly white teeth for no one to see.

"Alone, at last. Philo, was it then?"

His next steps took him closer to Philo, the Patriarch's boots barely making an audible impression on the stone floor. He noticed the pool of clotted blood lying under Philo, his back a horrible mess of deep gouges and bloody wounds.

Rivulets of blood stained his whole body, from his shoulders down to his legs. His feet were bare and bruised livid underneath, the skin so deeply stained crimson that it was almost impossible to know whether there was any of it left. Philo's thickset body had lost its healthy color a pallid skin implied he was less than feeble.

Philo did not answer verbally, neither did he nod. He simply spat vehemently and a thick mix of blood and saliva landed on a pool of his own blood, the little splash audible enough to register as an action of defiance or even possibly indifference.

"These amateurs who worked on you were thorough enough, I'll give them that. But amateurs still. Bleeding a man to death can only achieve in killing someone. Not in confessing his sins. Will you do that, Philo? Will you confess?"

The Patriarch had leaned closer to Philo and was standing on his right side, looking at him with bright enthusiasm; a yearning expectancy loitering timidly in his voice. The Patriarch wished dearly for an easy answer, a "yes" that would make things smooth and civil. He wanted to see a recognition of being outplayed, an acceptance of defeat, the knowledge of pointlessness proven in Philo's resignation from the fight before it could even really begin. There was such joy to be had in the feeling of superiority, that the Patriarch almost trembled with anticipation.

But he also knew Philo would not choose the easy way out. He was too proud, too ignorant and too stupid to do so. He was unable to spare himself from the immeasurable heights of pain he would fail to endure, the unbearable humiliation; he would suffer the final destruction of his mind, body, and soul.

He must have thought himself already a martyr for his cause, a proud shining beacon against the darkness. Someone for the others to follow as an example; a stoic fighter, a proud man that could not be brought low.

How embarrassingly naive, the Patriarch thought to himself. He decided that he would leave Philo's tongue and throat intact for as long as possible. Their own screams always became insufferable to them. Philo would be driven mad by the time he was through with him. A mad, witless fool. Not a martyr, but a wretched sack of flesh. An utter nothing. He would obliterate him completely, in the most literal sense. Philo Dutur would be in all manners erased, as he had never even existed, or indeed been born.

Ah, the small mercies, the little joys of his life and work. That was what kept him interested, what made him tick. In the end it would all have been worth it, just for these bright moments of uninhibited truth and voracious feelings.

When the cries blanketed all the senses, all thoughts and feelings. When the reality of pain promoted a higher sense of self; when those who had received his attention were indeed enlightened, their forms pure and bright right before they ended, like the last light of dying suns.

It was, the Patriarch thought, an art form. He wished he could make Philo understand before he began, but that would be an exercise in futility. Words would not affect him; Philo's ears and mind had been closed shut to him, that much was certain. It was of little conse-quence, because soon he would become so much more receptive, like a child only now beginning to learn. Philo Dutur would learn so much about him in so little time.

The Patriarch was filled with a fleeting sensation of jealousy: he told himself in his mind how blessed indeed these people were, to be stripped down to their essential self. How unique to be able to see clearly for just once; to understand what everything meant, the truth of life bared naked before their crying souls.

He almost wished he could experience that first hand, but he had the knowledge ingrained in him. The pain and sensation were not worth as much as the revelation ever did. He felt almost violated; robbed of his right to discover, experience, and learn anew.

It was as if he was a mere tool, that should never amount to much. A useful but otherwise uninteresting tool. These people here, he considered so much more intriguing, entertaining; pure mysteries definitely worth uncovering.

An inner rage that had been left neglected for too long flared up again. He could use that rage; he would use it to make Philo really *believe*. Not just acquiesce, give up his friends, his family and all that he loved and held dear. He would make him a true believer, a man happy to die in servitude at long last. The Patriarch told him then, with a laugh and a grin:

"I'll make you believe, Philo. I'll save your soul. You'll see. Faith, Philo. Faith can work miracles."

Philo concentrated what little strength remained in him and smirked derisively before adding in a low but steady, unwavering voice:

"I spit on your faith. I will die a free man. You can cage me no more."

And to accentuate his point, Philo did spit once more; reddish saliva came out of his mouth with broken teeth and the wounds inside it still open, bleeding freely.

The Patriarch replied in a candid way, as if exchanging opinions with a peer:

"Oh you misunderstand, dear Philo. I was talking about faith in one's self. And I do have faith in myself, Philo. Here, I'll show you."

That having being said, the Patriarch reached for Philo's chains; a mere touch of his hand unlocked the first one and Philo's body swayed immediately to his other chained side. It was all very sudden and Philo barely had time to put his feet down to be able to stand instead of slumping on the stone floor.

When the Patriarch unchained his remaining hand, Philo tried to act as fast as possible. His right side, he believed, was nearer to the Patriarch; he mustered all the strength that he could and focused it on his elbow, suddenly jutting it towards the Patriarch's groin.

As he did that, he was already clenching his left fist, trying to gather some momentum by twisting his torso and perhaps landing a good punch on the Patriarch's face. He knew that this was probably his last and only opportunity, so he thought he'd make it count and go for the kill as well, his mind focused on reaching the motley arsenal of torturing tools available.

His elbow did not connect with the Patriarch's groin. Instead, he felt a rush of air as if a void was suddenly created where the Patriarch had been standing. As his torso swooped around in its instinctive movement, his feet swiveled to accommodate the sudden move and his left fist came rushing down only to meet thin air. His body was awkwardly positioned now and precariously balanced, openly inviting hits of retribution.

The Patriarch was not where he should have been and was instead at Philo's left side now; it was as if he had instantly sidestepped him with inhuman speed, impossible reflexes, and divine foresight. As Philo turned his bruised head around to see, he had one eye completely hidden behind swollen tissue. His other eye was damaged and bled almost beyond recognition, but still it seemed to function. Evidently surprised and dumbstruck, he managed to ask the Patriarch:

"No one can move that quick."

The Patriarch let out an almost hysterical laughter, his shoulders bobbing freely up and down in an unseemly lack of decorum. He then added, still snickering intermittently:

"And yet, I did! A wonder made manifest! Praised be the Gods!"

And yet another smirk before he stretched out his right hand, his adorned hand, the Hand of Tribulation, to grasp Philo from his forehead.

Philo went limp almost instantly, his big bulk sagging down onto the floor; his legs were sprawled awkwardly and his arms simply rested against his body, barely touching the bloodied floor.

His face, or what was still left of it, tried to take on an expression of pain; he flinched and his visage contorted violently. Suddenly his face slackened and his mouth opened up to reveal his broken teeth and the numerous open sores and wounds. He started to mewl incoherently, blood and saliva dribbling down his chin; he tried to voice incomprehensible words sputtered in blood.

The Patriarch smiled. His face lit up at the sight of the broken Philo and he seemed pleased that his work was beginning to take form now. He asked Philo in a sweet, inviting voice:

"Who else was with you in those caves Philo? Was it someone I know? Who were your friends, Philo?"

Philo seemed to twist his body a little as if trying to escape an invisible grasp, and his head shook with involuntary tremors. The Patriarch tightened his hold on him, and his voice became a venomous hiss:

"Who was it? I'll pry it anyway from your dying mind you wretched fool, so tell me of your own volition! Unburden your soul! Who was it?"

Philo let out a deep moan and his eyes tried to let tears flow, even though it was nearly impossible. His eyes were practically swollen shut and the tears welled up constantly, making what little vision he had left, a complete blur. His groaning became deeper, and his body started to shake involuntary; he could feel the spasms of death approaching, washing over him.

The Patriarch screamed in hellish fury and the air around them cracking audibly. Small arcs of fierce blue lightning flickered between the Patriarch's ringed fingers:

"Who was it? Who entered the caves with you?"

Philo's skull was throbbing and enormous veins jutted from his head which seemed ready to burst apart, his scalp beginning to turn red hot. His throat managed to let out a few audible words while his head was still grasped tightly, forming an odd angle with the rest of his body as if it was about to snap:

"Amonas.. Ptolemy.. Hilderich.. the curator boy.. Please.. End it.."

The Patriarch grinned appreciatively, and then almost immediately his face wore an expression of mild disappointment. Resentment accentuated his poisonous words:

"This Hilderich fellow, a Curator's apprentice? How quaint! A schoolboy and a romantic!"

He let go of Philo who instantly regained some sort of composure, however drained he was of his vitality close to the point of death: his heart was barely beating and his every breath had become copious and painful. His voice now little more than a whisper, Philo said amidst weeps and moans of pain:

"End it.. Kill me.. You have your names now.."

To which the Patriarch replied with a brilliant smile adorning his face:

"But Philo.. I knew their names all along.. I just wanted to hear them from you.. Can you feel it? The stain of treason? It will go away before the end. Have faith, Philo. You know I do."

The Patriarch grasped Philo's head once more. The screams filled the chamber, echoing around its damp stone walls.

The guards above the torture chamber were used to the cries of the sinners. But not to whatever it was that they were hearing now. They became uneasy. Before long, one of them vomited.

When the other guards came to relieve them, the screams and voices could still be heard. And that went on, and on, all through the night.

When the Patriarch emerged from the door of the torture chamber, the guards posted there were almost ashen in color but still managed to stand to attention briskly enough. The Patriarch said to the first one he laid his eyes on:

"You. Send for Ursempyre Remis to my personal chambers. And you, clear up what is left down there."

Both saluted and bowed deeply before silently rushing to perform their assigned duties. The Patriarch walked down the long corridor that would bring him to the staircase leading to his chambers. He felt stiff from the effort, but satisfied.

He smiled to himself, before musing aloud:

"Oh, Philo. What a charming little soul you once had."

By the horns of the bull

ILDERICH had finally slept, his protestations about the lack of a night sky were silently put aside when his fatigue took over and the anxiety and nervousness subsided after their thirst had been quenched; when the warm, tasty meal of mushrooms sat comfortably in their bellies.

He was snoring heavily and though it would have normally been less than a pleasant sound, under the circumstances it was mildly comforting. It let Amonas know that not everything was amiss, that some things were still normal albeit frustrating and hard to deal with.

Such a thing was the sound of Hilderich's snore. Amonas tried to picture a future lady D'Augnacy going to sleep next to the somewhat handsome young man, but failed to end his train of thought in anything other than a grin or a hearty laughter.

He nodded to himself thinking it was a good thing that Hilderich had slept after all that had befallen him; he definitely needed to sleep more than he did so himself. Not that he didn't wish for sleep to come and bless him with a few precious hours of oblivion and rest, but he could cope while Hilderich could not.

He had a nagging feeling, he knew; rest would not come even in his sleep. Nightmares would haunt him as long as he was away from Celia, as long as he couldn't know what fortune held in stock for her should he fail to return. He had to entertain the idea that he could be stranded in this lush version of hell with Hilderich as his sole companion for the rest of their lives. The thought alone was unbearable. It wasn't because of Hilderich, the man kept interesting company; living without Celia though would be impossible for him. He'd rather take his own life than be forced to live with memories of her alone, each waking moment.

Amonas was sitting cross-legged without the cover of the small makeshift shelter he had fashioned; most of it was taken over by the sprawled figure of Hilderich who seemed to be thankfully quite at ease sleeping on the almost bare ground, with nothing but his already muddied and stained cloak as a mattress.

On the other hand, he could not let himself surrender to sleep. It was not the lack of night or the invariably harsh conditions of continuous lighting, unbearable heat, and sticky moisture that prevented him from having some kind of much needed rest.

It was, as was the case most of the time, his mind that could not be appeased, that could not be turned off as it should. The immediate necessities had taken their toll of thoughts already. The water, which he still didn't know whether or not was indeed drinkable; the food he hoped would not prove much of a problem now that they knew there was at least something edible to be found.

But it was not just the simple minded anxiety of surviving: it was this strange new environment, totally unlike anything he had experienced before. Certainly nothing he had ever known to exist, not even on the most faraway of lands.

The suns were wrong as well. He was beginning to accept the possibility they might not even be on their own world. The thought had unconsciously been formed before, when they had first seen that clear, harsh sky. Now though, it took form and voice; he could hear the thought ringing loudly in his head. 'This might be another world'.

The ultimate truth was revealed in form and substance all over him. And he had no one to share it with but Hilderich, who might even hold it such a fact as suspicious but implausible at best Another world with no animals to speak of and no people, however queer or similar, friendly or hostile they might have been.

He suddenly felt terribly alone; the thought of them being the sole two individuals on this other world was weighing him down grinding him to the damp, muddy ground. Just the two of them wandering like castaways on a strange and mysterious island where no ship would ever sail to. An uncharted land with its existence always hidden away, never to be revealed; a future that would see their bones bleached and turned into lime for the wild growths to set their roots in.

His gaze turned to the tiny flickers of the fire; a few coals were still red hot and thin lines of smoke rose from the perpetually wet wood. He focused on the fire, marveling at its simple avarice. It consumed the wood steadily and unperturbed, without a care for the world at large. It was a force of nature, a universal truth: eating away as much as it can and then perishing of its own accord, accepting its nevitable fate to end.

How he longed for such simplicity in his own life. Away from this world, as well as the world he had known as home. Away from the Castigator's tyranny and its false Gods. Away from poverty, the coming war and the misery that would ensue no matter who the victor was. How much he had wanted to get away from all that with Celia by his side. Had she been with him here, he could have let the world burn for all he cared. Just like fire, burning through wood.

He smirked despite himself, thinking he was letting himself down somehow. Perhaps he had been too morose in his thoughts; their plight so far had sunk his feelings even more than he had realized. Such a mood would do him no good, that he knew. No matter whether any of these thoughts hold any truth, in the end they would do him no real good.

He knew that thinking too much and acting too little had somehow brought everything to this point. A rule of tyranny, based on lies and deceit. People dying everyday of famine, people rotting away in eternally dark dungeons for stealing a loaf of bread, having children without the blessed permission of the Ministry.

He shook his head. Permission was needed to create life. As if any God would need to hinder the inevitable, unimpeachable, unstoppable force of life that permeated everything, from the worms in the ground to the stars themselves.

It was indeed a sad moment when a star fell; he remembered having heard though that another one was born at the same time. He had no way of knowing that for sure though; who could count the innumerable stars or the grains of sand in a beach? But he knew it in his heart to be true.

Life just keeps happening. Whether anyone permits it or not, it doesn't seem to care; it blindly goes on whatever the cost. Even in this place. They might have encountered no animals so far, but the vegetation was astounding. Lush, vivid green, everywhere the eye could see. If it wasn't so damn hot and humid he could have felt like living here for ever. Him, Celia, and their children. The many more to come after his firstborn.

Would he ever live to see all that come true?

He sighed. He knew that thinking in such an almost saturnine way did not suit him. He stood up and decided to clear his mind, flush it clean of any thought. Any kind of action would do his spirits good. Since he couldn't rest or sleep, a mild activity that would not drain him of much energy would be a welcome change in pace.

He would go for a walk, in a way to explore their immediate surroundings. Perhaps, he thought, he could even scout ahead their path to the bull-horned structure, that huge fork that had seemed so impeccably dominating even from afar.

Hilderich stirred in his sleep mumbling something inaudible; he licked his lips and smiled lightly. 'He must be dreaming,' Amonas thought.

The fact that Hilderich could sleep as if nothing of import had transpired over the past few days brought a smile of hope to Amonas' lips. Perhaps not everyone looked on things so dourly, and had good reason not to. So did he, he thought to himself, bringing an image of lovely Celia to his mind.

Lovely Celia; her hair touching her slender body with grace enough to make any man weep from the joyful sight and instantly adore her beyond reason. Her face would have had a sweet and mellow taste if his eyes could swallow her whole, and forever feel her smile. Celia beloved, and to the death his mate and pair. His firstborn's mother to be, his miraculous haven where every storm subsided, where all the seas came to rest and all the rivers ran home.

She was not far from giving birth to their child and though they had known bloody times of fire, steel and death were drawing close, he at least had the surety of her touch and her smile to count on to meet life or death by.

Now he was denied of her touch, the smell of her breath, the feeling of her body clasped against his own. He could not look upon her gaze locked with his own and see the oceans of time passing by in mere moments. Damn them! For that hurt alone, he would make them pay. Whoever was indeed behind all the lies and curtains of deceit. Behind the Castigator. He could feel there must be something to the Gods. Every lie, he had observed, has been sown from some sort truth.

As he walked about the place, he noticed more and more beauty; life was celebrating in this otherwise simmering cauldron of green. Small colorful flowers with overgrown petals and fat, juicy stems.

Lithe trees that could be easily bent without being broken, and thick overgrown plants that dared climb the huge trees hugging them, curled around them like charmed snakes.

It was indeed a place teeming with life. It remained a mystery to Amonas why they had come across no animals at all and barely enough insects to simply make their unwanted stay even more miserable. He mused for a while at the strange color of the suns, and decided he could not come up with anything resembling an explanation other than this was another world to their own indeed wholly alien and undecipherable, at least with the knowledge at hand.

Perhaps they could learn more of it before they returned, but that would be something more relevant to Hilderich's domain and not his own. He was more interested in solving problems, not analyzing them thoroughly and documenting them for posterity and further study.

He thought with a smile that it would be a strange day indeed when he would be able to sit in a chair and tell his grandchildren stories of the other world. Or maybe even worlds. If there are indeed more than one, why should there only be two?

The walk had made him thirsty and he felt like maybe it was time for him to return; with his mind put a little bit at ease perhaps he would try and get some restful sleep. Even though he was used to hardship, he did not think sleep was not essential and he knew no one could go more than a day or so without even a few minutes of sleep.

He had also climbed up an inviting tree in an effort to see over the canopy if at all possible and get their bearings, so they could start off in the right direction for the nearest bull-horn. Getting the direction wrong while already being lost would be a blow to their morale, let alone a waste of precious time and meager resources.

His thoughts suddenly ran back to his brothers in arms: back in their own world, the Kinsfolk were about to strike for the first and hopefully the last time. Years of planning had led to this culminating point, and an untold number of his brethren had lost their lives in the effort of keeping it a secret alone.

He knew they were being followed, he knew they were being watched. But he also knew they were waiting for the right time to act and catch them all in one fell blow, root them out forever, crush them utterly and dispense with the notion of a rebellion for untold generations to come.

He had to be there when the time came, that much was at the least expected of him. And he'd rather die trying rather than abandon and shame his blood and soul brothers, or face the wrathful scorn of Celia; no, that alone, he could never suffer.

A weak but warm smile crept on his face as he imagined such a scene, Celia engulfed in all-fiery wrath, her gaze searing, boring through him as if he were made of powdery snow. He laughed despite himself, loving memories of her rushing through him like a stream of water on parched land.

As he approached their tiny camp he could hear Hilderich screaming his name over the top of his lungs, sounding terrified at the thought that he had gone and left him there to die all alone, the final twist of an incongruously ill fate. He answered back, his strong gruff voice undimmed by the blanket of vegetation all around them:

"Coming, Hilderich! I just went for a walk!"

Without yet being able to actually see him, Amonas heard Hilderich cry out in a near falsetto:

"Damn you I thought you'd left me here to rot!"

A few more steps brought Amonas nearer to their camp where he could see Hilderich quite evidently disheveled, his thin blond hair in wild disarray from the sleep and the humid hell they had to endure, his clothing almost unrecognizable by now, a uniformly gray and brown mud covering most of it. Amonas waved a dismissing hand from afar, laughed heartily and replied playfully:

"I'd never leave you behind to rot, Hilderich. Simmer a little perhaps, but never rot!"

His good humor went largely unnoticed by Hilderich, whose spirits where in sharp contrast. He looked genuinely hurt, glum and uninspired, giving Amonas a picture of how he must've looked a couple of hours before. The thought sobered his mood, and thought he had better make Hilderich bounce back from what must have been a seriously rude awakening.

Hilderich was keeping silent, casting a look of rightful accusation at Amonas, who thought it to be a little childish and perhaps somewhat unbecoming of a man. But their situation was indeed unique and perhaps he had been asking too much of the man already. He cast those blemished thoughts aside and instead spoke from the heart, seeking to calm Hilderich and soothe his fear:

"I am sorry I left you alone, but I could not sleep. I went for a walk, but I was close by. I heard you when you called, didn't I? I could not have been very far. You were as safe as I could vouch for in such a place. So please, accept my apologies and think no more of it. It only helps to aggravate you, and lower your spirits. Here, have some of this."

Amonas reached into his small sack and brought out a small roundish object covered in what seemed to be something like hair, thin strands of wood or brown parched grass. He used his knife to chop off a small slice from its top, then offered it to Hilderich.

Hilderich made a gesture to take the proffered little ball of what could have been fruit. It looked to be white on the inside, but he shook his head and gave it back to Amonas with a hesitant look on his face and a quavering quality in his voice:

"You try it first."

Amonas' pride was stung: Hilderich seemed to imply that he might be trying to poison him. He was about to go off on a rant unfitting his character, about how misguided and foolish a person must be to still be unable to trust him after what had befallen them, but wisely decided against that. After his initial surprise and shock lifted from his expression, he took the strange cross between a hairy nut and a fruit in his hands and drank a good mouthful.

After he had quite thoroughly sloshed it around his mouth in an evident display of the juice's potable quality, he swallowed and offered it back to Hilderich who accepted it even though with some reluctance. He sniffed the watery liquid inside the strange fruit and kept his eyes on Amonas, who tried to appease his fears:

"It's sweet and refreshing. Almost better than water. Drink up, you'll like it."

Amonas was motioning with his head for Hilderich to drink, urging him to just have a taste, while Hilderich slowly brought the fruit to his lips, constantly eying Amonas warily.

After a brief pause and a small period of uncertainty Hilderich finally took a small sip, swallowed, and then surprising even himself in the process proceeded to empty the small ball of a fruit of its watery content.

Amonas grinned in a relaxed manner as he laid down to the ground to enjoy at least a few minutes of sleep. After closing his eyes and covering his face with one arm, he said to Hilderich:

"I wouldn't kill you with fruit Hilderich. There were ample opportunities with better tools. We need to trust each other to make it back, that much I can assure you."

"Oh, I know about your assurances so far. I can see them all around, sure as hell."

Hilderich's tone was rather that of a grudging complaint rather than a gross accusation. 'He might be right', Amonas thought, 'but now was not the time to settle such a score'. He hoped that they would make it back, become friends, and Hilderich would forgive him for the misfortunes brought upon him. But until then, Amonas' patience would be tried and tested at almost every chance. He replied in kind, eyes still covered by his arm:

"Opportunities may arise once more, don't make me want to take advantage of them."

Hilderich opened his mouth wide in what seemed a mock expression of shock before he composed himself once more, straightening up and saying in what seemed to be his formal tone:

"I'll restrain from further commenting on the problematic issue and instead focus on more worthwhile endeavors, such as getting back."

Amonas smiled even as he said in a genuinely friendly tone:

"That's more befitting a Curator now, isn't it?Let me catch some sleep, and then we will be off to those bullhorns."

The thought had occurred in Hilderich's mind but he had not given it much time. With the death of his master and half-way in his apprenticeship, he was now considered officially, though without seat, a Curator, with all the rights and responsibilities his office carried. It was certainly not an apt time but he felt somewhat proud, and suddenly all too grown up and a bit older than he thought possible. Amonas added as an afterthought:

"Don't fret over it. You can do whatever you like for a while, as long as you don't get lost. Study the trees or the insects, do something a Curator would do."

Hilderich nodded silently and appreciatively before heading off to a nearby log of wood half of it rotting away, creeping with maggots and worms, what he had been taught was the basis of a healthy and fertile ground.

Time passed quickly for Hilderich who uncovered all sorts of different layers of decaying wood, taking good notice of its grain and the various kinds of insects that used it as housing, food, or what seemed to be a combination of the two, eating tunnels through it on which then they laid what looked like to be their eggs.

It was fascinating he thought, to witness a whole civilization of insects in its various stages and levels unfolding in front of you in a simple piece of wood right in front of your eyes, at the tip of your very hands. How tempting it felt to push the eggs around and see how the insects would react, or douse them with water and see whether they'd drown. But he was taught that nature knew best, and men could only learn from it, not change it. At least not for the better. So he decided to let the insects be.

When he did so and paused his study of the insect-ridden log he noticed Amonas had quietly awoken, seemingly quite refreshed and energized. He asked him if he had slept well, to which Amonas answered laconically after briefly thinking about it: "Good enough."

Amonas then made some broth of what he had found to be an adequate substitute for uwe, and sipped appreciatively. Like before, he offered some to Hilderich who again politely refused, but did not resort to his small flask of gin. He wisely assumed that they would need more of it to light up a fire, and more than just once. So he kept Amonas some quiet company, until they would move on again.

Once they did so, Amonas led the way once more with quite deliberation, carefully choosing his path as if he could smell their destination however far it might be.

To Hilderich, it was unfathomable how any man could navigate practically blind, without a map or a solid point of reference, simply using his hunch and a general feeling of direction. Both seemed to be easily fooled in a chaotic mass of vegetation such as the one they were entangled in currently.

When Amonas felt Hilderich needed time to rest he paused, and made sure Hilderich was ready to move on before they set off again.

Hilderich felt quietly thankful of that small mercy and made every effort to proceed in a timely manner, never dallying for too long. Until they had walked for the better part of what would amount to a day in this accursed place, or until they had reached the bull-horned building he would try his best.

The heat was as always unbearable and the moisture nearly debilitating, but they trudged along hoping to strike lucky soon. If nothing else, Hilderich hoped they would soon rest for what should have been night time. Lost in thought and numbed by fatigue, Hilderich bumped unwillingly onto Amonas who seemed to have suddenly stopped. Hilderich apologized curtly and asked:

"Pardon me for running onto you like you were invisible, but why have we stopped? Are we here yet? I can't see anything like a wall or stones or something resembling a construction. So does that mean we can rest now?"

Hilderich's voice had an unmistakably pleading quality and though it would be indeed great if they had reached their intended destination, it would be nothing short of bliss if they could stop and sleep for now. Amonas knew what Hilderich was thinking from the look on his face and the expectancy in his voice, and replied curiously enough with a question:

"Did you notice something about this place?"

Hilderich was still catching his breath when he said to Amonas in a knowing manner, somewhat alienated from the strange question:

"It's too hot and too wet for comfort, what else is there to notice? That it's too green?"

"See here, I like some healthy irony from time to time but right now it's not what you should be doing. You should be feeling, with all your senses alight. What do you feel, Hilderich?"

Hilderich was about to make some comment in the same vein as the previous one, complaining about sore feet and an empty stomach, not to mention a dried out mouth.

But once Hilderich paused for little more than a moment, he felt it. A light breeze, chilly to the touch, a swift rush of air like a cloud from the heavens.

"The air is chilly. And everything's not as moist. It's like.. It's more like back home.."

Hilderich was genuinely surprised, and looked fittingly puzzled. As he tried to make some sense of it, Amonas added:

"Well it's not chilly. It's not that hot, cool would be a better choice of words. And the light is less intense, it's almost like an overcast sky. Like a shadow is hanging over our heads. We're in its shadow, Hilderich. The shadow of the bullhorns."

Hilderich was enjoying the cool breeze when he pleaded once more:

"Would it be then advisable to get some more sleep now?"

Amonas laughed out heartily at that display of good-humored single-mindedness, and feeling his spirits lifted laid down and started singing a tune his grandfather used to sing when they were fishing together, on a boat by the river.

Hilderich was complaining that his stomach felt empty, and that they had not secured a source of fresh water. He could also hear some grumblings noises about him doing all the really necessary stuff, and that Curators should be treated respectfully rather than being ignored profoundly. He stated then that he would nevertheless procure some sort of food since he was quite literally the only reliable and responsible person in this world, a world which might or might not be an entirely different one from the one they called home.

Amonas kept on singing heedless of Hilderich's protests, thinking he would be soundly asleep before the song would come to a finish. As the moments went by, his voice became softer and shallower and then he stopped altogether. Indeed within moments he fell into a slumber, where he dreamt of Celia. In the dream he could feel the cool breeze that was her smile.

Pretty soon he was snoring heavily, as if he had not a worry in this or any other world.

Meetings and Greetings

 E had woken as early as every day, giving thanks to God for allowing him to live and breathe once more and greeted the suns as they rose with a hearty smile. His hair was as always tousled, gently swayed by the light breeze rushing down from the mountains and onto the plains that filled his entire view.

Once more he had used his walking stone to guide him and before noon had passed he had entered the Land of God proper. He had been warned to be wary of these lands, for not everything that roamed it was graced by God and not all that he may encounter was sent by Him alone.

The devious ones, the forces of the archenemy had plans of their own and would likely oppose him when they saw fit. He would have to steel himself wholeheartedly if he were to carry on with his Pilgrimage and meet his ineffable destiny.

Once he had stepped his foot on the Widelands, it was as the elders had said it would be: A flat and uninviting country, with low grass and trees few and afar; the sounds of animals and birds lost in an emptiness that defied the senses and made one humble and awestruck.

Then he saw the True Path in all its glistening beauty and perfection, as unblemished as had stood since the first Pilgrimage, so long ago in ages past but never forgotten. He was witnessing the path to his own destiny and soon he was walking on it, treading lightly with reverence whenever possible, but making haste and good speed. What good was the Path, if he dawdled on it for longer than prudence would allow?

As his peregrination took him further into the Land of God, his thoughts coalesced bit by bit into how this land was perhaps purposefully designed, meant to evoke ascetic feelings. Civilization in any form had been kept away this part of the world, as if it had been preordained that these lands would forever be a sanctum, a land devoted to praising God.

It was a land indeed forbidden to most mortal men, uninviting and hostile as far as he could tell until now. But the Path was there as a clear sign of God's design, a Path for the true believers, a Path for those that came with holy fire burning in their heart seeking God. A divine purpose guided such men deeper into a land that would normally kill one easily; be it of hunger, thirst or pure exhaustion.

Distance lacked meaning in the Land of God, a land which almost defied logic in its flatness and its emptiness. An emptiness only the love of God and faith in him could fill. It was a terrible void that shrank the impure soul and made an unwilling mind recoil in primal fear, a land that turned the unbeliever away. It was a land where the mandate of God was carried ever more strongly by the formidable gusts of wind that swept its every acre.

It was indeed magnificent to behold the will of God made manifest all around him. He was in a sacred place that he was not only allowed, but indeed expected to traverse to its very heart to complete his Pilgrimage as his God and his people demanded.

God, in his inestimable wisdom had prepared the land more than well enough for a believer, for someone who lived and died with His name upon his lips, His thought in his mind and His image in the depths of his soul.

Water, he could find in the small damp spots around the Path, when night fell and a hazy carpet of fog crept across the immeasurably flat land. He would dig, with either his knife or his hands to find a few mouthfuls of water to sustain him.

When he felt hungry and tired with his strength about to leave him, it was if God kept an ever watchful eye on him from afar; a small thin bush laden with tiny berries would appear near the road, or a small colony of ants. The land would freely offer him sustenance, however meager it might look.

He always thanked God for these small mercies that kept him fit and healthy, that kept him going without delay; he only made a few brief stops to rest his muscles and slept during the night. His clothes were as good for the Holy Land as it was for the lands where his people dwelt. Perhaps it was not as cold during the day, but the nights became colder the farther deep he went while following the Path.

He kept the wise council of his elders, and never strayed off the road. He kept on it at all times and when he could, when leaving it to get to a source of water or find something to eat, he would always leave his walking stone on it; a piece of woolen string attached to it, laying it behind him as he walked.

When he had drank or eaten to fill his belly, he would pick up the string and walk right back to the Path and the walking stone. It was said that if one strayed off the Path, he might never find it again for as long as he walked the Land of God. It was blasphemy for the Path to be revealed to you and then choose to leave it.

So he would lay behind him a piece of string to always connect himself with the Path, even when not directly on it. He would do that because of strict necessity and only after solemn prayer in which he would beg for forgiveness, recognizing his own imperfection and crude humanity that afflicted him with the feeling of hunger and thirst.

Thus he hoped and prayed that God would not be offended and would find it in his heart like the loving father that he was to allow the Path to remain, to guide his faithful servant on to his Holy destination, beyond all the hardships and dangers that might arise in his quest.

For if it was a simple, sheltered matter, little would the Pilgrimage mean. Anyone would walk about the Holy Lands, especially the deceitful liars and archenemies of God and their followers; soiling the land and air with their mere breaths and their unclean feet, poisoning the very air with their hideous laughter and venomous lies.

No, it was not a simple affair walking through the Land of God. That was why the Pilgrim kept praying each and ever waking moment: to thank his God for his magnanimous and benevolent nature, thank him for allowing to draw breath and drink water when he needed to. He prayed to thank his God for allowing him to feast upon the fruit and the very life of His Land to keep his beating heart alive. The Pilgrim thanked God because he had been blessed enough to touch the Holy Soil with bare hands.

It was almost dusk on the third day since he had set foot on the Land of God. It was once more time for prayer. He laid down his small sack and took off his cloak, setting it down in front of him. He then knelt on it and closed his eyes while his arms rested on his legs; the palms of his hands touching his knees. He then started bowing down low with his forehead touching the Path every time. Whispered words of reverence came out of his mouth in the tongue of God which they no longer used, but kept handing it down as holy passages, from mouth to mouth, generation to generation.

Though he could not understand what the words were saying, he could feel their perfection rippling through the air. Holy words spoken in the Land of God felt like a river mingling with the sea. It was as if a small trickle of divinity flowed through the essence of God made manifest; the air, earth and water resonating with godly purpose and sacrosanct silence.

Hence His words, the Holy Mantra, which should be told aloud for all of Creation to bear witness to his grandeur and wisdom. In the Holy Land though, in His Land and His Domain, it would be sacrilege to utter these words in anything above a whisper. For every grain of sand, every wisp of air, and every drop of water carried everything back to him: voice, thought and deed.

As he bowed low in homage to the creation of God all around him he felt the striking of grandiose, majestic chords buried deep inside his very essence and soul. He felt pride in his heritage, his people, and his purpose.

He cast it swiftly aside, knowing that pride was a double-edged blade, ready to cut into him right when next he would feel invincible, safe, powerful and righteous. That was not God's way; God taught humility, wisdom, faith, belief and love. Not pride, arrogance and lust.

The Holy Land was indeed a place to be wary. Even when paying homage to God, the ruinous ones could find a man's weakness and seep inside him, while he would have himself believe he was walking the True Path. The Path was not just a white, slick and unending road; it was a state of mind and soul.

He made the sign of God with his outstretched palms facing towards the falling suns. In the hazy distance, only the line of the dark crimson horizon could be identified with difficulty over the pale yellow and blue of the rising mist.

He stood up on his two feet and wore his cloak, picking up his sack and setting off down the path once again. As the chilly night rushed to meet him, he thought he could see a figure like a mirror of himself walking on the road towards him. He squinted his eyes as he tried to make sense of what he was seeing.

It was a man not very much unlike him, lean and not very tall, of a somewhat pale color. The man's stride seemed purposeful and if he had taken notice of the Pilgrim walking on the Path, he showed no sign of alarm, surprise or fear. It was as if he would not stop. as if he was nothing but a phantom, an apparition of the Holy Lands.

Maybe it was an apparition that he was seeing. Stranger things had been heard around the life-stones during the coldest nights at his people's gatherings. It would not be without precedent that he should meet a ghost of the Holy Lands, perhaps some other Pilgrim before him who had wandered the Holy Lands and now roamed them freely, to warn the Pilgrims and the faithful and guide them through danger.

Perhaps he was a messenger from God Himself; though it might have been presumptuous or even blasphemous to think that God would seek to aid him in such straightforward ways that completely and blatantly proved his Divine existence.

He reminded himself to be wary though; perhaps the pale man was a ruinous force in disguise, a servant of those that would always be evil, seeking to corrupt men and everything good and wholesome that the Pilgrim tried to protect from their rotting grasp and their nsidious machinations.

Perhaps, he was just a man though; even a believer like himself, brave enough to seek out God. He would soon find out whether he should strike him down or greet him like a brother should. The man had gotten quite close by now and he thought it prudent to make some sort of sign to announce himself properly, like a man in the Holy Land should greet another man.

The Pilgrim stopped and stood firmly. He then made the sign of God, touching his bowed forehead with one straightened out palm and offering his other hand to showing his clear, empty palm. What the gesture meant to those familiar with it, those of pure mind and soul, was this: 'I am a man blessed with God's gift, a mind of my own. I carry no weapon and greet you as a brother.'

The man walking towards him slowed his pace, visibly trying to discern the gesture. Then he responded in kind, first with a deep bow towards the sinking suns and then made the same sign, albeit with the opposite hands, mirroring the Pilgrim's motion. 'A true believer then, or some instrument of God,' the Pilgrim thought. His blessings were countless and his heart leaped with joy at such a sight. A brotherly soul right there, in the Land of God.

The Pilgrim smiled widely and picked up his pace to meet with his brother from afar. He could see the man coming towards him smile as well, his face lit up with enthusiasm and surprise.

Under the faint light of the ever widening star-lit sky they met each other with faces visibly ridden with the signs of hardship only a believer would endure to prove his love of God, staying true to his faith. Brothers joined in belief, sharing the creation of God, walking on the Path. What joyous occasion such a meeting of brotherly souls was, and in the Holy Land no less!

They were standing opposite each other and the man in front of him, the man whom he had seen walking up towards him was younger, leaner, and taller than he had glimpsed at first. In the light of dusk it was easy to misjudge the shape and size of things.

The young man proffered his hand, and spoke a few words in that the Pilgrim didn't understand and had actually never heard of before in his life. The Pilgrim was thinking that the man in front of him must have uttered a greeting, or perhaps announced his name. He seemed friendly, unassuming and harmless. His heart weighed the man in front of him: 'he might be speaking in weird tongues, but he made the sign of God. A brother under God is brother enough'. The Pilgrim closed his eyes and nodded with acceptance, hands outstretched to his left and right. The man spoke again:

"Thessurdijad Molo, damn glad to find you. I thought I was lost. Probably am, to be honest. You're one of them, aren't you? You're one of Esphalon's people. Dark-skinned, nomadic appearance. The wild ones," his voice bright with excitement and the feeling of un-marred prospects.

The Pilgrim thought it proper to answer in kind in the tongue of God, even if his brother from afar would not be able to understand. Indeed, what he said sounded as if it could have been familiar, but no sense could be made of it yet. Perhaps some common thread could be found while they tried to converse and understand each other. The Pilgrim spoke:

"I greet you as a brother, and you are stranger to me no more. His will be done."

The man's eyes went wide with sheer surprise and disbelief before he replied with the words coming out of his mouth faster and faster:

"You can talk then! You can speak Helican Pretoria? Your people learned Helican Pretoria? When? When Esphalon was there? How?"

The Pilgrim look at him puzzled. His brother seemed as excited to meet him as he was, he could tell. But he was so outspoken, so emphatically energetic. He seemed to have forgotten about paying proper respect in the Holy Land; his voice rang loud and his expression was wild, his body intensely at motion.

Still, he could not understand a single word the man was saying, even though he seemed to have repeated a question of some sort at least once. 'He might be asking where I'm coming from, or where I'm going,' the Pilgrim said to himself silently absorbed in thought. It was difficult to believe this was a messenger from God or one of his holy servants.

He seemed like a long lost brother the language he spoke altogether different but with hints of the language of God. The Pilgrim hoped he was indeed a brother though this could always prove to be a trap, a wicked machination; an evil thing sent to thwart him and his Pilgrimage, to mock God and his divine plan.

He would not allow himself to fall for such tricks of the soul, and his wary eye would be on the lookout for signs that would expose this man as a pawn of the archenemies. For now he would treat him as a brother and offer God his prayer, seeking forgiveness for thinking such accusing thoughts even in a time that should be joyous; for a brother he hoped, had been found. He smiled and motioned his hands to the sky his head slightly bowed and a thin but hearty smile on his lips, his voice ringing clear and true:

"Let God guide us wisely. Let He be the answer to any question, our guiding light in the vast darkness."

He then reached for his sack, and took out a handful of wild berries he had only picked up this morning. It would have been his dinner, but knew he now had to offer his brother everything he had. It was God's way and it mattered not what he would eat, because God would provide.

"You can't understand anything I'm saying, can you?", said the man constantly smiling, bowing lightly before accepting the berries in a seemingly timid way.

The Pilgrim made the sign of God once more and looked at the strange man he now considered a brother under God; he felt a bit saddened that his words could not be understood and could not answer his brother's questions.

Though he was starting to find some sounds common, the Pilgrim did not possess the wisdom of an elder or the eloquence of their Prime. He was just a Pilgrim, and thanked God silently for that preordained fate that brought him to the Lands where no one else could venture. Except it seemed, this strange new brother of his. He cocked his head slightly when his brother spoke again:

"You speak High Helican but can't understand the simple, day to day Helican people learn as children. And unless you're a minister gone mad, I'd say you're one of the people Esphalon wrote about. You're quoting, aren't you? You've learned everything by rote? Damn fools the lot of you, then. This is getting so much better every day. To think I was ready to botch everything a couple of days ago. And now this. Fantastic," said the man and made the gesture of praising God.

As the man ended his incessantly long phrase, which the Pilgrim thought it could contain the man's life story, the Pilgrim felt that perhaps he was wrong to be so wary of him. He had seen his brother offer his thanks to God and heard him say a single word clearly. The Pilgrim believed he could learn from his brother then, slowly.

He turned his mind inwards and reasoned with himself, thinking that maybe God had not sent this man to find him, but he had sent both of them to find each other. Fate was for God alone to decide and change, but he was thankful he would have a companion with him. For where else could this man walking on the True Path be going, other than to the Holy Grounds themselves? It was their journey now, the Pilgrim thought and then he smiled, carefully pronouncing each syllable slowly before bowing and once again pointing upwards:

"Fan-ta-stic."

Molo grinned widely and then said:

"Bugger me, you're trying to learn aren't you? That might come in handy. Esphalon was bloody brilliant noting down your rituals and everything. Must've saved my life. You'd have my head with your bare hands if you thought I was an infidel or a blasphemer, wouldn't you? Must keep an eye on etiquette then. Wouldn't want to, as you might say, incur your wrath."

The Pilgrim saw then his brother kneel down on the Path and offer his prayer to God. He must've been forgetful, the Pilgrim thought, because it was past the time of dusk; God forgives though, and it was never too late to ask for forgiveness.

The Pilgrim thought he had been too critical of his brother. He seemed weird and acted in a strange way, and his tongue was strange yet familiar.

But he felt it in his heart that this man would become a true friend and brother before their journey was through. And perhaps, he might be able to learn a strange new tongue. Something he had never even thought possible, since he had not believed other tongues could exist. The thought made the Pilgrim break down in laughter. He hadn't laughed at all since he had set out on his Pilgrimage.

His new brother looked at him in disbelief, somewhat dumbfounded; he kept pointing his hand at the laughing figure of the Pilgrim. The Pilgrim thought bitterly that his lack of reverence would have to be punished with at least a hundred prayers on the next day and fasting for another two. But he felt it was worth it; such laughter must have been welling inside him for too long. It was a liberating experience, one that he felt did him good.

"Was it something I did? Never mind, you must be losing it, aren't you? It doesn't matter if you can show me the way. Can you show me the way? You've been here before? Do you know the way to the Necropolis? Whatever you call it? The way, yes?"

The man was gesturing with his hands up and down the Path and the Pilgrim thought he was probably trying to say: "Where does it lead?", "Does it lead to the Holy Grounds?". He should've known better but perhaps he was distracted and lost; perhaps his brother had fallen prey to some of Their machinations and mirages.

Otherwise he would have been going towards the Holy Grounds, not towards the entrance to the Holy Land. He must have seen they were both on the Path, only going in different directions. They would now help each other, as good brothers certainly did. Without further ado, the Pilgrim gestured onwards towards the way the Path shone under the light of the first stars.

"Bugger me, you do know after all? Can't understand a thing I'm saying, but this is all your own stuff. Well then, lead on. I'll just trudge along and look like I'm praying when you do."

The Pilgrim saw his brother smile gently, bow constantly and offer too much praise and thanks to a mere brother. But he was otherwise quiet and respectful of the Path, the Pilgrim thought in silence.

They started walking together side by side on the marble road, under the blue and black starry-lit sky. They both seemed as happy as any man could be.

Stirred Within

 LEEP never came that night to her, and her tears flowed freely. She stifled the worst of the sobs and moans that welled up from her insides, but still she wept. Come morning her face was that of a sad older woman, with eyelids swollen from the crying and the sleeplessness. She felt horrible and the child within her seemed equally disturbed. How could it not be, if its mother was in such a terrible state?

She had left her windows closed, the drapes and curtains tightly drawn shut. She cared not whether the suns had risen and a new day had dawned. She wept for her only love, the one half that matter most in the world. The other half, his own half as well, was stirring uneasily in her belly. She tried to think comforting thoughts but all she managed was to utter with a croak:

"Sleep, my loving child. Sleep, for I cannot."

She wandered aimlessly around their home, every once in a while hugging herself as if vainly trying to land herself in Amonas' arms. But it was to no avail, for he could not appear out of thin air. And still she cried, at times silently with tears welling up in her eyes and at other times fitfully, with sobs that she could not contain released in languish.

She pined for the father of her unborn child, to hold him and caress his face. To kiss her fears and troubles away. But he was not there.

He was nowhere, it seemed. As if he had been spirited away, by the same sort of devils that had caught poor Philo.

No body had been found though, and no one had come for her or her child. Philo would never talk, he would never give up his blood brother, mentor, and friend. She suddenly felt a pang of fear in her heart as if it had been struck violently, nearly coming to a halt. Was the child safe with her? Did she need to run like the wind and the winter streams? Disappear like she had never existed?

And what about Amonas? What had happened to her love? She could not for one second think of him as no more, as a dead body, limp and unmoving. He must be alive, somewhere. In hiding running for his life. He had that other man with him. He would be running to protect him as well. That was why he hadn't come forward to her, or sent a message that he was well and alive.

It must have been a matter of secrecy. How tired she had grown of all these dark affairs, so many lies heaped upon lies. The lies they had sworn to break and burn away, those very lies were probably what kept them alive even now. What irony, to have had your life built around what you despised most.

It was the only way, they had kept telling to themselves. The only way they could change things once and for all, the only way they could spread the truth and uncover the deceit that had blinded them all. And that was the way he was gone now, perhaps forever.

The dark thought contorted her face into a mixture of anger, pain, and weeping sorrow. She held her head in her palms, sobbing silently. She was constantly going through the same phases: Sorrow and then anger; then a faint sliver of hope would dawn upon her and recollect her thoughts, compose herself somewhat.

And then fear would grip her once more, the uncertainty for her child sweeping everything clean, and the vicious circle of gripping emotions and harrowing memories of happier times would start anew.

She would weep and cry, throwing herself against the walls until she could stand it no more; then she would think of her loved one that might be dead and might never kiss her again, never hold his child in his arms.

The thought made her weep once more, all the tears of the world coursing down her cheeks like the torrent of pain and anguish that ran throughout every living thing swept through her soul. She would suffer like no other had suffered before and that would not stop until she either died herself, or saw her love calling her to his arms.

The child stirred within as if it was calling out to her, as if fear had touched it deep inside, past the warmth of his mother's belly, and an icy chill had crept up all around it. She tried to soothe her child and in spite herself started to sing an ode to the streams and fields; a song of merry melody, a melody that would have Amonas smiling and laughing within moments. She would not cry at the thought, nor think him long gone. She would sing it in quiet waiting and strong hope. She would sing it for their child's sake.

And so she did, and her voice echoed in her empty house which suddenly felt brighter, warm and full of charming smells like cinnamon and naristhel; lermentis leaves, honey-spice and mint. All those smells that brought the senses joy, and a smile on their face.

The child felt quiet now; the singing had relieved it of its fear and brought back the warmth in its heart. It felt like it was asleep now, comfortable in its mother's womb who herself felt soothed, her fears cast away for the moment; her hope shining brighter and her heart beating with renewed vigor and hope.

Her mind was filled with thoughts: He would be alright, Amonas. He would be fighting or running all the way back to me, like the lovely fool he is.

She strolled around the house for a while, thinking that she could not longer sit there idle and miserable. She had to find out what had happened, see for herself. After all, she felt it was not really safe sitting in their home anymore. Neither for her nor for their child.

It sounded foolhardy and unnecessarily risky, her mind told her. But her mother's instinct shouted that she should run away to find another shelter. Somewhere where she might give birth in safety. She was due anytime soon and each day could be the day their child would be born.

Her condition made moving all the more difficult so she would require some assistance in her endeavor. She thought about moving out to the countryside, take what coin she could and find some good people, some family to take her in at least until she gave birth.

But things were about to get hectic, she knew. Soon there would be very few people that she could trust. Amonas had chosen to keep her well away from the Kinsfolk; she had only met and knew Philo, who was supposed to be her guardian and protector should anything happen to Amonas.

She had been frightened at the thought, but had accepted it as a realistic precaution. The irony now was that with Amonas missing, and her protector unable to come to her aid she would have to fend for herself. She thought: 'Poor Philo, what horrible fate must await him at the hands of those tyrants?'

She would have to turn to the Kinsfolk for their help. At this time of need with an uprising boiling right under her feet and the child almost on its way, what should she do? Run away, fearing for their lives everyday? Never knowing who to trust, with war raging throughout the Territories? No, she decided that that would be foolish.

She might have been fool in her own life, but that was before she was graced with Amonas' and her child; now she would give her all to protect it. This was her best bet then: find the kinsfolk before all of Pyr turned into a nightmare, and stay with them until it was ended and a new day dawned.

For better or for worse she would be amongst friends: free men and women, brothers and fellow believers in what was just and right. She felt like it was time to accept that there would be nowhere safer than right in the heart of things, from where the revolution was about to spring out like a restless fountain. A revolution overflowing with the tears of the downtrodden, the poor and the wretched; the ones that were made to disappear in the middle of the night, their cries haunting the streets like ghosts trapped in a hellish afterlife.

The knowledge of the deeply rooted injustice of the tyrannical masterminds of the Ruling Council, the lies and deceit they spread through the ministers with the single purpose of breeding sterile and harmless minds like sheep, that knowledge alone had made her subscribe to Amonas' purpose.

She saw the truth behind his words, behind every poor beggar and every blind soldier; behind every child that died of hunger and every old man that was hanged for blasphemy and sin. Such terrible things no God would allow if he had anything at all to do with the real world.

Such reminiscence steeled her and made her finally decide. She would seek out the kinsfolk and join them, participate in any manner that she could. Not just for the safety of her unborn child, but for its future life.

She knew then instinctively that Amonas would have been proud of her making such a decision. Not out of a childish conception of bravery and duty or a vainglorious attempt at posterity, but because she genuinely cared and actually hoped their child would grow up as a free person; not bound anymore, not a cripple in mind and soul, but a person free to build their own destiny, free from the oppression of the spirit, the misconceptions and the prejudice.

A person that could think of his own and decide for himself would live in a world of endless potential. Someone that could dream of reaching out to the stars without fear of being damned as a heretic, a blasphemer, or a raving madman.

If it was a boy, she thought to herself and smiled, she would like him to be like his father but not too much. She'd like him to carve his own destiny and raise a family of his own, set the example for those around him, be a man cherished and loved. He could be anything he'd want: an artist, a poet or a painter to put down on paper and canvas feelings, emotions and thoughts that none would have dared before him.

He could be a man of reason and logic and make something useful out of things like the steamers. Perhaps think of new, exciting and purposeful things to make the lives of people easier, and carefree.

He knew from the bottom of her soul that her son would grow to be come a wonderful man, just like his father. A father that he will meet and grow to cherish and love, a father who will help him become happy and whole in his life.

She smiled at how she corrected her thoughts and bit her lip thinking what it would be like if the child was a girl. She would be born a free woman, and she would have all the time in the world to become what she wished for.

She could become so many things that would were unthinkable now, she thought. She could become the thinker and the tinkerer in the family, and then a baby brother could become the dancer like his mother.

These thoughts of merry prospect brought her glee and her face shone. She could not wait for Amonas' to return. She now felt it would be impossible for him to miss the birth of his firstborn. She would tell him all about her plans when they met again. After she had smothered him with kisses.

'But first things first,' she said to herself. That blessed reunion would have to wait.

She picked up a rather small sack, and carefully put inside some things she would either need or would miss terribly. Some letters from Amonas that would also serve as proof he was her husband, if the need for that ever arose. Celia also took the flute he had carved for her which she played to him on the colder nights, the both of them wrapped together under heavy sheets, playing endlessly until the break of dawn; making love without a care.

She packed a few clothes along with her nightgown and a blanket or two in case she had to spent a few nights on the road. She took some leftover bread-pie from yesterday with her, and remembered to fill a flask of water from the well before she would be off.

It would be best not to tell anyone, not even dear Rovenia. It would do her no amount of good to upset her and make her worry without being able to help in any way. Once she was gone, it would not be long before the revolution proper began; then no one would be safe.

Her small sack was packed to the brim, ready to burst. Outside, dusk was falling but she would wait for the night sky to appear. It would be easier then for her to find the men she was looking for. She would try some of the places they had met with Philo, certain inns and some artisan's stalls that stayed open past the usual times, in some of the ill-reputed corners of the market. As an afterthought she took her large kitchen knife, just for good measure.

She might not look like it with a bloated belly and all that came with expecting a child, but she could move real fast. A dancer, a really good dancer like she was, has certain qualities that can be put to more than one use. Her mind wandered briefly to a particularly fond memory involving Amonas, and she giggled in spite herself like an adolescent, infatuated girl.

Oh, he would be back and she would scold him properly for leaving her alone like that, she thought. She heard her voice in her mind:

'A pregnant woman mere days before being due, a world-shattering uprising in the works, and the husband off on a tour!'

Then she suddenly broke down in tears, the tension that had kept her going suddenly released. The fear and uncertainty did not return as she had expected, but she felt like slapping herself for trying to lose herself in forgetfulness and act is if nothing serious was happening. Things were not like she could be all play and games when she saw him again.

She composed herself and stopped crying and let the tears down her cheek run dry. This was all deadly serious, she knew. She knew as a fact that Amonas might be dead. She knew it in her heart though that he wasn't; it was just that life could be so full of surprises, and most of them unpleasant. So she turned her heart into ice and gave the macabre thought some consideration. That only made her cold and distant from her usual self.

At that moment she vowed on her life, and the life of her child: she vowed to fight in any manner or way possible for the future freedom of her child, and if it turned out to be so, in memory of her loving husband, Amonas Ptolemy; to honor his legacy and offspring, as he would have wanted so.

Time passed slowly, and she grasped the opportunity to have a last look around their house. She looked in their bedroom where he had loved her with passion and care. Sometimes he was a strong lover: unyielding, discovering every inch of her body with a conqueror's lust. Other times, he was soft, mellow, caring and delicate; like the gentle breeze that caresses the flowers and meadows and flows freely wherever it pleases, always welcome to enter.

It was here where their child was conceived. It must have been one of the coldest nights, when he took her under the sheets and made her forget the world existed, in such a way that she could not remember now whether it was truth or fantasy. The child in her womb though was real enough.

She was caressing her belly absent-mindedly when she walked through her kitchen, the wood stove unlit, the fireplace glum and silent. It was as if the room itself mourned her leaving. She would miss preparing their meals with loving warmth, making sure there was always uwe on the table in one way or another. 'Amonas *loves* uwe,' she alone heard her voice say.

She had been quietly absorbed in thought, her gaze fixed to nowhere in particular when she happened to look outside the street. Night had finally fallen. It was time she left.

She lit up a single candle in their bedroom at their window sill, as if in memory of the time they had spent together. She gathered her small sack and went outside careful to close the door forever behind her.

She noticed lady Rovenia must have been outside, because she could see no candlelight from within. Perhaps she was already asleep; early to rise, early to bed. She thought she should have said goodbye, but it might have been just as well in the end. Her love went out to her as well.

Soon she was mingling with the night crowds of Pyr; common pyres lit up the streets and the more lively parts of the market. One could find anything he desired in the market of Pyr, as long as one searched hard enough in the right places; that much she knew.

On her way to one of the inns, she noticed she was attracting unwanted attention; surely it seemed that a pregnant woman should not be walking outside in the market all alone. She should have thought to somehow cover her belly to accommodate for its shape.

All she could really do now was try and stay in the shadows. With one hand she clutched her sack over her back, and with the other her solid kitchen knife hidden in inside her dress. She felt ready for violence, but she dearly hoped it wouldn't come to that.

Wading through the crowds, she reached one of the inns Amonas had once said were more than sympathetic to their cause. It was one of the few places she had seen Philo in public. When she did so it was indeed more of a social gathering; a man meeting a friend, escorted by his wife.

For a woman to have a drink amidst the company of men, even with her husband present was bordering sin. She thought that was about to change soon, and entered the inn as any man would

Some of the men in the tables nearer to the door turned around and looked at her with stout disapproval, some even voicing their objections and threatening to call the procrastinators to make an example out of her. "A pregnant woman no less", she could here some of them say in what appeared to be disgust.

Those few left their coin on the table and got up to leave in a boisterous but rather pretentious manner. Most of the others who had protested more mildly returned to their drinks which seemed rather more interesting than an unscrupulous woman of what they thought to be lower moral fiber than their own.

Those who did not return to their drinks and kept on pointing with some even calling her names, she ignored in an exemplary fashion. Soon they focused their attention on other matters, and her entrance was then only memorable in passing. She wished they would all drink up enough to pass out and remember nothing of the matter at all.

Before she could reach the innkeeper, the man approached her and drew her aside by the arm, quietly and gently:

"Please lady, what are you doing? Why aren't you at home? This is no place for a woman; no less one carrying!"

He seemed genuinely concerned. Celia felt instantly he could be trusted so asked him straight as an arrow:

"Do you know a man named Philo Dutur, or Amonas Ptolemy?"

The man's eyes narrowed and his brow arched, becoming tense. He was evidently disturbed by the names and certainly surprised. He replied with a question of his own, his hand still gripping one of her arms:

"What are they to you?", his voice steady and demanding; he no longer seemed to be just a gentle, caring innkeeper.

"One is a friend, the other is my husband. Please, I am looking for friends in a time of need," she uttered with sincerity, putting the sack down momentarily to reach in her pouch and offer the man a generous amount of coin.

As she did so, the man recoiled at the sight of the coin. He took a step back and released her arm:

"My apologies lady Ptolemy. Please, I need no venom; not from you kind lady."

She motioned her to come around his serving bar. He gestured with one hand for her to wait there, and she indulged him so. He went around the tables, filling up the cups of his customers with beer, wine, mead and spirit; each one to his poison. After he had a second look, he leaned over the bar and told her in hushed tones, imparting hidden knowledge:

"Where you stand, there is a hatch on the floor. Feel around for a handle with your hands and pull it open. I'll call for my brother to watch the place while I make some excuse and come down with you. Wait for me there, I won't be long."

She nodded in acknowledgement and the innkeeper ventured a smile, revealing a few bad and broken teeth, and a silver one that must have cost him a small fortune. Still, it seemed genuine and since she was flying blindly it would make little difference if she had went to some other place.

She comfortingly thought that any place she would try that night would be somewhere she would be treated at least as a friend and that lifted her spirits somewhat.

She cast a few guilty looks around as if she was about to try something forbidden, and kneeled down carefully, with a hand on her belly. She found the hatch and the small handle, and pulled. Faint light was shooting upwards and she could see a small ladder going all the way to the cellar floor.

She threw down her small sack first, and then carefully placed her feet on the steps one after the other; her large belly giving her a little bit of trouble. She was standing in the inn's cellar, and looking around her she could see row upon row of glass bottles filled with a variety of wines.

There were also much larger casks and barrels; some smelled of wine, and some of beer. A metal contraption filled with pipes and resembling a large sort of cauldron must have been a still but she wasn't all that sure about those things.

Until she had time enough to look around the innkeeper showed himself, coming down the same way she did moments earlier. He was a short but sturdy man, thick red mustache and a slightly bald scalp that gave off a friendly, jovial image. He proffered his hand and bowed slightly before introducing himself:

"Rewe Dutur, at your service lady Ptolemy. I did not know you knew Philo personally."

Her expression was kind, but somewhat severe, almost grave:

"Why do you say 'knew' kind sir? What have you learned of him?"

The short man looked her straight in the eye with a slight blur forming up on his own, and said with pained finality:

"I do not expect to see my brother ever again. But do not lose hope on your husband, we have confirmed he and his friend were not captured. Let's make sure my brother gave his life quickly and painlessly, and not in vain. Come now, please. Philo and Amonas were probably betrayed somehow; we must also assume you are not safe in the streets. If Amonas is still alive, getting hold of you will be one of their priorities. I will lead you to somewhere safe, at least for now. It won't be long. Have you had foreword, did someone approach you and lead you here?"

Rewe had gestured for her to follow him through some cellar corridor, all the time talking to her.

"No, no one did. It was my decision. I hope I am not imposing on you or your people. I felt it was time. With Amonas missing, and the child on its way. I thought..", she shrugged apologetically and though in her mind she had all the reasons laid out, she was now at a loss for words.

Nevertheless, she was following Rewe's steps through what appeared to be a hidden door cut away in the dirt, leading to a small tunnel of sorts. Rewe had produced a torch from some place only he knew where to find in the total darkness, and lit it up with ease using what appeared to be a small stone. Rewe took notice of her surprise and told her kindly:

"Even better than flintlock, my lady. It was most fortuitous you decided that on your own. If it was that somebody had lead you here, I would have reason to believe we would not live through the night. As it is, none of would have approached you. We had been left with strict instructions to distance ourselves from you in any way possible. If someone came to you, he would be one of their lackeys, not one of our own people."

"Amonas' told you to leave me be? Fend for myself?", asked Celia quite puzzled as they made their way through the small winding underground passage that was dug intermittently between layers of lime and dirt with small wooden frames supporting the ceiling where needed.

"Amonas thought that if it came to that and he was not around, you were more than capable of protecting the child and yourself. He wanted you to stay indifferent to them, never become a target through which they might be able to test his loyalties."

She was surprised and felt both proud and slightly put off. Amonas would not abandon her or the child like that. But she understood that if he could not be there for her, he had thought the best way to protect her was to keep her away from it all, as he had been doing almost from the start. "Oh, Amonas, that thick skull of yours..", she whispered as she followed close behind Rewe who turned his head slightly to ask, never pausing in his stride:

"Pardon, my lady?"

"Never mind.. Rewe is it? I was just thinking aloud. I want you to know, I believe Amonas will return. And I always have hope for Philo. He is the sturdier man I've ever met. He will hold out as long as he has to."

Celia was being truthful but ultimately she was simply wishing rather than thinking clearly. Rewe was not as blunt as before when he said:

"I would hope so too, lady Ptolemy. But please, let us pick up the pace. Can you do so without causing trouble for the child?"

"You're being too kind, Rewe. I am fine, lead faster if you must."

Indeed Rewe quickened his pace and soon they were walking rather briskly through a series of turns and twists through widening and narrowing tunnels, some crudely cut into the rock and others finely bored with care and precision.

They must have been walking for at least a quarter of an hour before Celia at length broke the silence and asked:

"You said we were not far but I have to ask, are we there yet?"

Rewe turned his head around to reply, a silver tooth from his mouth casting off a shiny reflection of the torchlight:

"Perfect timing my lady. Right around the next turn we will be heading back to the surface. We will part ways there."

"And in whose company will you be leaving me, Rewe?"

"All in good time my lady. I think you have more questions than I can answer, so have some more patience."

"Alright then."

Celia nodded her acceptance, and noticed they had now reached a crossroads of tunnels. Rewe then used the torch as some sort of knocking apparatus. He used it to knock on what seemed to be finely cut limestone, in a series of rhythmic knocks using pauses in between, as if playing part of a tune. She rightly guessed it was some kind of code.

Indeed, a strange kind of challenge echoed backs a series of knocks from the other side of the limestone. Rewe seemed to pause for a while, and then proceeded with a different series of knocks. The limestone slab was slowly pushed aside and strong candle light filled the underground tunnels. A small simple wooden ladder was lowered, and Rewe motioned Celia to climb it. Silently, he bowed and waved her goodbye before losing himself back the way they had come. Celia squinted at the bright light as she came up the stairs, onto what seemed to be a very plush kind of cellar, with exquisite bronze and silver decorations on the walls. A whole wall was devoted to a grand collection of what seemed to be wine bottles. A young man dressed in simple manservant's clothes greeted her, bowing and saying:

"My lady, fear not. You're among friends. Please wait here, while I call for my master."

Celia nodded her thanks and the man went up a small staircase briskly. She was in a cellar once more, from what she could gather. But it was a much different cellar alltogether; it looked older and much better cared for. It was much larger, and though she was not an expert in wines, from the little she knew she could see the owner of the cellar had fine and expensive taste. There were even Feuillout bottles to be found. And there was a manservant on duty here almost at all times, it would seem. She was in no ordinary tavern or house.

As her mind tried to orientate herself, a smiling old man in a luxurious servant's suit complete with velvet vest came down the stairs to greet her. He seemed a rather upstanding and polite man who helped her make the last steps up the stairs, offering his hands as support. She looked rather mystified and as she was ready to ask the venerable servant where she was exactly, his long experience and hard years of service prompted him to greet her before she had time to open her mouth:

"Greetings my lady. I see you are carrying. Please, lay down on the couch. It might not be suitably comfortable, but I suppose it will have to do for now. I shall bring you refreshment and something to eat. Please do not hesitate to ask for anything at all. Whatever you might need, I am at your disposal."

The old man's voice was tactful, polite, and convivial. He seemed to make proper use of language and etiquette like a most experienced butler would.

"Kind sir, I am fine. I do not wish for anything to eat, but some refreshment would be welcome. I have to thank you for your hospitality in advance but tell me though, where am I?"

The old servant bowed somehow uneasily, but said with a business-like smile:

"Excuse me for not greeting you fully and properly, my lady. The trappings of old age, you see. You are the honored guest of his eminence Ursempyre Remis, Lord of the House Remis. Will some fresh fruit juice be to your liking, lady?"

A fool's resolve

YRPLEDGE had been unavoidably spenting the past few days inside his minute office, sitting at his desk with piles of reports and inventories stacked in front of him up to his neck. The minutiae of a preparation for complete mobilization were indeed innumerable.

Personnel manifests, rotation forecasts, matériel inventories, requisition forms, count practicals, soldier and officer levies, clothing requests, workshop and mill necessitation orders, movement and guard formations, and forced labor documents were combined into a logistics nightmare.

All of these types of documents had to reviewed and amended if needed. They had to be edited, signed, and forwarded; then signed again and scribed, before sent out in a seemingly never-ending vicious cycle of bureaucracy and stale ministry procedures that were designed to triple check and record everything that went on. The idea behind all that trouble was making sure that nothing seemed to stray in weird and unexplored territory, something that would alarm the various ministry officials and by natural order the Arch-minister himself.

All this paperwork and mind-boggling interdepartmental anarchy had the general sitting wide-eyed at his desk with papers strewn all over his desk; it resembled a carpet of ink and white that made his head dizzy merely by looking at it, much less reading it.

He leaned over and put his elbows on the desk to rest his head on his hands, gently massaging it as if that would make the terrible headache go away. The latest developments had had him thinking about his career in the army in general. He almost wished he could somehow go back in time and fail at pretty much everything so he could get Gomermont's job for a change.

Instead he leaned again back on his chair, the muscles in his back stiff from constantly sitting, signing documents since early dawn. His wrist hurt like he had been practicing with a sword since the day before. He looked at the plain and unadorned ceiling with eyes out of focus, and seemed to ponder deeply the state of affairs he was in.

The army had been metaphorically though almost literally at

times, handcuffed and thrown around like a useful but dangerous idiot for almost ever since its inception and creation. The hindrances
and bureaucratic steps that were constantly arrayed against the army
and its people were designed in such a way as to extend the period of
time it takes for troops to assemble, equip and move, from days onto
weeks.

The concept was thoroughly and widely known as a safety measure against those who might try and achieve power through strength
of arms, perhaps even to the degree of being able to change the balance of power within the Ruling Council so as to include the General
of the Army.

There had been precedents surely but that had been another time
entirely, when the Territories were still young and the people dumbfounded by the then newly emerging order of the world; one common
rule for all, under one religion.

There was bound to be some dissidence, some kind of resistance.
It was well known that even the earth opposes the river's flow, but the
ending was inevitable. So it came to be that Shan the Traitor only
managed to permanently turn the army into a mere lapdog at the beck
and call of the Ruling Council, blessed be their exalted souls.

'And so I'm stuck here,' he thought, 'trying to build a machine of
war faster than what is conceived possible with almost anything and
anyone at my disposal; except from freedom of action and the ability
to ask for things and make them happen. How typical.'

Even with the help from the Arch-minister that had indeed ex-
pedited some processes, Tyrpledge was experiencing significant de-
lays in most of his petitions and requisitions. Everything had to sift
through the gargantuan train of Ministry processes, officials and hear-
ings to disappear in its labyrinth offices, clerk pits and then back up
again through the same path, in order to probably but not always most
likely, make something useful and tangible in the end.

The more he thought about it the more incredulous it all seemed,
but it was manifestly real. Just the other day, he remembered, he had
received a notice of an annulled material request for a shipment of
chisels required for the maintenance and construction of most of the
siege engines. The ministry's reasoning behind the annulment was
mystifying at best: "Said objects are still under examination for safety

reasons".

It seemed the ministry was contemplating whether or not a military coup could put chisels to good use, in preference to the usual swords, scimitars, bows, steamers, slingshots, siege engines and the good old knives it already possessed.

Their lack of trust was crippling. He was given a colossal task that was daily compounded with the burden of the ministry's schizophrenic tendencies that balanced precariously between gross, outright denial and a maniacal urge to have everything done and ready, armed merely with ink.

The arch-minister had been quite unable to help, since this was pretty much how everything worked in the ministry. Reiterating the jumbling mass of ministry people to adopt new sound practices in a matter of days was just as inconceivable as totally circumventing the antiquated ministry machine in whole. In essence, Tyrpledge was caught between a hammer and an anvil. With nowhere else to go, he knew he would have to endure as the good soldier he was. He could feel the pressure though, and it was rising to a crushing level.

He got up from his office and decided to have a little stroll outside. Maybe some fresh air would invigorate him. As he made to leave his office, his aide-de-camp and various other officers belonging to his immediate staff saluted crisply, most of them with papers and ink in hand, designated to handle some of the bureaucracy whose scale defied that of the legendary behemoths of the sea.

He left orders for his aide-de-camp that he was not to be disturbed or communicated to in any way while he was out having his walk. Anything that might come up it would have to wait for him, and not the other way around.

He might not have a vote on the Council, but he didn't like being pushed around like a junior officer after 45 years of humble and devoted service. It felt wrong, that was the word the best described his feelings. Plain wrong. He reached for someone else's mug of fresh uwe and without a nod or excuse just picked it up and went outside in the clear cold air.

He looked casually over the throngs of artisans, laborers and soldiers going about their frantic work. The artisans were terribly busy constructing breakable, portable siege engines, refurbishing and testing the steamers that had fallen in prolonged disuse. Even with the sudden influx of forced skilled and unskilled labor, he could easily discern they had already fallen behind schedule.

In the background to the main staging area of the army, laborers were hard at work ferrying ore from the nearby Ilo and Rohms mines. The mines were working at full capacity non-stop, but the noble families that were allowed to operate the mines were failing to reach the needed production quotas. Already, procrastinators teamed up with squads of army men were instructed to gang-press as many people as needed to meet the allottment.

There were less than ten days left before the army was expected to march fully armed with the maximum strength of trained men. There were still thousands of weapons and pieces of armor to be made, which meant more and more ore was required each day.

Forges had been setup right there in the staging area, but artisans were already starting to break down from exhaustion. Work had been issued to forges and workshops around the Territories, and failure to meet the quota assigned to each would punished by death.

The same went for the grand fields of noble families. It was reported that even the Lords themselves, the heads of the families, were working their own fields; busy to harvest as much grain, wheat and fitlle as possible however premature the season.

The whole of the Territories was living and breathing in preparation of the army - everything else had come to a standstill. Mills had broken down from excessive speed while grinding incessantly, day and night. Rumors of some of them catching on fire trying to meet the demand could not be far from the truth.

Horses and tract animals of all kinds like cows and donkeys were being taken forcibly from their masters, in most cases the sole animal in their possession to work the lands and make a living with. Huge convoys that stretched from one side of a town to the other were being created by local procrastinator forces and went about the countryside, picking up whatever it was on their ministry approved lists to fill up cart after cart of supplies and materials for the army.

All of that wealth was congregated and amassed in even larger convoys that stretched as far as the eye could see, filling up the few roads that carts could traverse. Some of them had already started arriving at Pyr and the staging area which was a huge stretch of land to the south of the City, where once the harbor of Urfalli had lain.

The harbor had been made anew and ships from the farther reaches of the Territories would begin arriving in the next couple of days, and like the cart convoys would be laden to the brim with supplies and men, flirting with disaster from being overweight and prone to sinking should they happen upon bad weather.

Procrastinators around the lands with the authority of the ministers rounded up men of all ages that were fit for duty; those who had received military training as militia men in the past, as well as new recruits that could not tell the pointed tip of a spear from a moose's behind.

It was all happening too fast for comfort, too hastily for any serious preparation to be made; plans could not be laid out and understood properly in so little time. The people under his command, from the high-ranked officers, the colonels and brigadiers, to the lowly green recruit, would not have enough time to prepare and get their bearings, get to know what their purpose, their orders and responsibilities would be. At times, he wondered if he himself really knew.

He hoped that he could put it all together in time; failing to do that would mean his head. He thought about that possibility and curiously enough it did not seem to frighten or trouble him, not in the sense it would most people. Losing his head would be more than unpleasant, but he had a long time ago accepted that it would be asked of him at some point, sooner or later, to give up his life for the glory of the Gods and the Castigator.

It had just never occurred to him that such a time would come rather later in his career, right before he would be about to be rotated to an easier life of teaching young aspiring officers. It definitely had not occurred to him that his death might not come at the hands of an enemy by spear, sword, rock, arrow or fire, but because of failing to meet production quotas.

Perhaps it would more specifically boil down to a lack of chisels. The thought brought a bitter smile to his lips, and he sniggered with a dark sense of amusement.

He wished he could have a smoke then; a nice pipe-blend of uwe, keplis and dark tobacco, but he had given up on the habit a long time

ago and now lacked all the assorted paraphernalia, as well as any tobacco to speak of.

He thought that perhaps one of his officers would be so kind as to
volunteer a pouch and a pipe. If it came to that, he would order him
to do so. Thinking like a brash cadet once more made him grin while
he sipped a hearty mouthful of uwe from the cup he had confiscated
with authority from one of the desks.

It tasted horribly. Some idiot had let the uwe leaves boil along
with the water and the result was an putrid-like green broth fit only
for mules and perhaps sailors. He threw the cup altogether and headed
back to his office, his head much more clearer but his mood equally
if not more glum than before. He made a mental note to himself to
reprimand the one responsible for the awful uwe tea.

Once he entered the planning chamber which was filled with his
officers he immediately noticed it was completely silent and everyone
inside was firmly standing to attention. He believed he had given
orders that with such hectic work going on, discipline should be lax.
He couldn't have everyone standing stiff as a corpse every waking
minute, and the shouts of "Aye, sir" were a cacophony his ears and
head could do without.

When he gestured them to sit down and go about their work with
a simple flick of his hand and they did not comply, only then did he
notice the figure standing in a corner of his office. The man happened
to turn around and address him at that exact moment:

"Oh, General. I trust you don't mind. You have a very nice se-
lection of boar teeth. Impressive samples. Quiet the hunter, are you
not?"

The Castigator was dressed in simple loose combat clothes, no
markings or insignia visible. Only his face and the sigil ring proudly
worn identified his person and stature. His tone of voice was conversational, unassuming enough but not overly friendly.

Tyrpledge bowed deeply by reflex, and though at first he was utterly surprised and about to lose his words like the Procrastinator Militant almost had a few days ago, he managed a constrained and somewhat witty answer:

"Naturalist, your Reverence. I study animals, not hunt them down.
I believe there are more than enough people for the job."

The Castigator turned to face him, and quietly stepped outside his office. Following a brief silence, he said:

"I was told you had left strict orders not to disturbed by any-one, under any circumstances. Your aide-de-camp was quite adamant, though somewhat hesitant. I understand I can be hard to deal with at times."

The Castigator shot a mystifying look at the general's aide-de-camps, a young major who was perspiring visibly but remained otherwise at stiff attention, unflinching at the Castigator's remark.

Tyrpledge resumed from his bow and said with a casual attitude that sounded strange in the presence of the Castigator:

"Had to clear my head, that's all."

The Castigator nodded in acknowledgement, and gestured outside with one gloved hand.

"Let's have a walk then."

The general nodded, bowed, and went for the door himself. The Castigator walked outside and Tyrpledge followed close behind, careful to observe protocol and keep the proper distance.

The Castigator was keeping his hands tied behind his back, surveying the landscape. It seemed as if he was enjoying the cold wisps of air sweeping in from the south, almost craning his neck in what seemed like an effort to smell the sea breeze.

After a small period of time spent taking in the scenery as if he were nothing but a visiting tourist the Castigator spoke, turning to address the general face to face. His hair was slightly ruffled by the gusts of air that were quite common this time of year in Urfalli and was good for ship-running as well as working the mills. He said to Tyrpledge:

"Tell me General. Skip the formalities please, and tell me what you really think about all this. This campaign. It's put a lot of strain on you and your people, hasn't it? And you'd have to be a gibbering idiot like the Procrastinator Militant not to question my motives for such an operation. Who wouldn't want to know what he's going up against, isn't that true? Please, Tyrpledge. Be unpleasant if you have to be honest. I do not consider myself a man easily taken by petty flattery, and neither should you."

Tyrpledge felt a bit surprised, perhaps even shocked from such a straightforward manner. It was strange enough when the Arch-minister came to him and extended somewhat of a professional courtesy towards him. It was more than strange that the Castigator himself of all people, would be so direct in his approach. It probably meant things were about to get all too serious pretty soon. His voice was straight and professional, perhaps a bit sullen when he replied:

"True enough, sire. I'm blindly preparing for any scenario and contingency I can think of, working everyone to near-exhaustion to have as much as possible ready within the allotted time. If I may say so, the extend of the mobilization you have requested is simply overwhelming. There may be a possibility that we will not be ready in time, sire. Not completely, not fully. I can guarantee a bare minimum of a well-equipped, well-trained and disciplined fighting force, but I cannot do the same for the full weight of our armies. We are still receiving conscripts and draftees from the villages and towns, people that have only worked with shovel, pickax and hoe. We need more time, sire. Or we will not be able to field our maximum numbers."

The Castigator absorbed what was in essence a verbal report from the General, and said to him:

"That is all very well, General. You've worked nothing short of a small miracle, as far as I can tell. But you still haven't answered what concerns me most. Don't you want to know why we are going into the Widelands?"

The Castigator's voice had a rough edge, a hint of menace, and perhaps even anger in it.

"That would be a very helpful piece of information, sire. It would be crucial in designing a proper campaign with objectives and time schedules to capture and follow. But if I may be less circumspect sire, I cannot for the life of me fathom what we will be doing in the middle of what is practically no-man's land."

Constrained exasperation showed in Tyrpledge's voice, but he remained otherwise calm, professional.

The Castigator let off what could be considered an unseemly laugh, and continued:

"So, it does feel strange, doesn't it? No matter. There might be a change of plan."

The General furrowed his brow before asking, his mustache seeming to somehow follow the motion:

"Change of plan, sire?"

The Castigator came a step closer and looked Tyrpledge in the eyes coolly but sharply, as if he wanted the General to feel he was being threatened physically, right then and there. He asked him then, his words coming out with slow deliberateness and heavy thickness:

"Where does your allegiance lie, General?"

The General did not flinch and replied with ease and confidence:

"The Castigator, the Pantheon, the Law, the people. Sire."

The Castigator smiled and turned to leave towards his escorts who were discreetly waiting at the entrance to the planning chamber, having appeared at some indeterminate point. As he walked away from the general, he raised the tone of his voice to be heard clearly:

"Remember that well, General. I might need you before long."

Breaking point

"At such a point in time, knowing all that has transpired and has been revealed to me, I cannot honestly say I clearly know where my allegiances lie. I can only hope that a clear mind and perhaps some sort of sign will push me over to make the right decision. What passes for right though these days, is making less and less sense."

- Lord Ursempyre Remis, *Letters, Vol. IV p.221*

Two steps beyond

 E woke up feeling refreshed. He sat up and fexed his arms and legs, all the time his gaze towards the direction of the bullhorns. It had been a more than pleasant change to find themselves under the shadow of the immense structure that seemed to blot out the suns quite effectively, making the whole area have a different feeling all together.

The one thing they noticed almost immediately was the different climate. Instead of the scorching heat and sticky moisture, they felt they could have actually been back in their own world during a hot summer overcast day.

The heat was much more sensible, and their sleep had felt much more relaxing and refreshing than before. The moisture was still a bother, but it was not as aggravating as before. And there was no night time to worry about the chilly wetness that would brew through their bones. It was an almost pleasant, almost comfortable climate.

Even the vegetation seemed to be somewhat different. The trees for one thing were visibly smaller, and the canopy above them evidently thinner. Even though the shadow let less light through, the canopy was thinner and let more of it through. Lighting conditions were about the same as before: a twilight of sorts that though eerie at times, did not put a strain on the eyes.

The greenery was still lush but it looked as if it had shrank a notch; the leaves were smaller and thinner while the stems resembled those in normal plants instead of the monstrously thick greens they were starting to get used to. There was less rotting vegetation on the ground and much fewer dropped leaves. It almost felt like a weird forest that could have been somewhere on one of the far away lands of the Territories, like the south where it was said plants like no other grew.

Amonas decided not to go for a little exploratory walk as he had done so before, so as not to alarm Hilderich a second time. Now that they were in the bullhorn's shadow he knew they were on the right track and all they had to do was keep going in the same direction. It seemed only a small matter of time before they'd reach the huge structure proper.

He would have to worry about what they would actually do only when they got there. For now, he was more than content to feel a gentle rush of air which was quite a novelty in contrast to the non-existent wind in the sunlit parts of this place.

Water was an issue but Amonas thought they could rely on that strange hard-skinned fruit with the sweet watery juice inside. He could see clusters of the trees that bore it at various distances, and a nearby tree had even shed some its fruit of its own volition. Amonas thought they would probably be most ripe and quite sweet, if trees worked like they did back home.

The word 'home' even though only uttered in his mind brought his thoughts to a halt. He looked at the ground reflectively with a fleeting sadness worn on his face. It was not just that he longed to see Celia again, even though they had not been apart for more than a week:

It was the worrisome feeling of being unable to protect her that wore him down. He had told his kinsfolk to keep their distance from her, even if something happened to him and he would be unable to be there for her. More so, especially if something happened to him.

As luck had brought things about he was far away and out of reach, with no means to communicate that he still drew breath. His people would probably think him dead, or at the very least running for his life, fearful of getting caught.

With each passing day without hint of him, without a message of some sort, without some kind of proof, they would eventually silently accept the fact that he might not have escaped the clutches of the tyrants.

If he was being kept alive, reason would dictate that they'd somehow manage to know as they usually did and perhaps hope he would still be alive when the uprising began in earnest; which if all had been carefully arranged, it would be in a matter of days.

But men had been known to completely vanish before; men that had attracted the ire and viciousness of the ruling scum that still chose to wear the facade of divinely appointed men of honor.

He was just one man after all. He would not hold it against them if they already believed him dead, drowned at the bottom of a lake or butchered and fed to wild boars or roaming dogs. They had seen it happen before, they all knew the dangers and the ignominious ways the Patriarch and the Castigator chose to dispose of their enemies.

But he could not bear the thought of lovely Celia thinking him forever lost, never there to return her trusting gaze, never more to hold her when the nights were cold. He wondered then, how did she take the news? What did she make of them? Was she drowned in sorrow, was her spirit broken?

He never thought of her as a fragile thing, a snowflake that melt by touch alone. She was not a little woman or a hapless gal. She never did mind her own business, and she always spoke her mind. She was proud of her accomplishments, and knew her strengths and weaknesses well.

That was though what he feared most. He was one of her few

weaknesses, now that he was gone. He felt a knot in his stomach at the thought of her giving up, burying him alive with that little ritual they buried their dead kinsfolk but no body to say her farewells too.

He could picture her dancing to the tune of a weeping song in his memory, and then losing herself in the hills and fields, roaming the lands like a ghost of her own self. Until her days became unbearable; until the thoughts and memories crushed her like a millstone crushes seeds, grinding them to oblivion.

No, he thought with a sparkle erupting in his heart and his gaze shooting upwards through the canopy toward the uncaring, seamless sky. She was with child, she would try and burn the world itself before anything happened to their child.

She would come through this, she would endure. Even if the thought of his death weighted her down, she would find a way to use it as a focus. She might even go as far as to think of avenging him. She was a fierce woman, he knew. She would be a terrible force to behold indeed; mother to a newborn, grieving wife to the man that meant the world to her. He would definitely not want to get in her way.

The thought made him grin with a sense of pride and amazement, as well as renewed optimism. He told himself in his mind that since she would be fine, he had no reason not to do as well.

He decided to rouse himself into action, and started off towards the fallen hard-skinned fruit he had glimpsed earlier, when a sound like a man desperately gasping for air mixed with what reminded him of creaking wooden hulls of ships made him pause in his stride and turn around to meet the source of the cacophony.

It was Hilderich and nothing more, awaking with a clatter and a show that Amonas had never thought possible even more so in their current circumstances, without even a blanket in hand. Still, Hilderich somehow managed to give off the impression of someone who had been very violently and quite against his wishes woken during a lusciously promising dream after a night of heavy drinking. And all that with nothing but soil and fallen leaves under him to call a mattress.

Amonas waved a hand and boosted his voice just for good measure before asking:

"Nice of you to join the ranks of the living once more. Going to get us some of those watery sweet hard-skins, care to look for anything else while I'm at it before we move on?"

Hilderich yawned with his mouth forming an impossible angle. For just a moment Amonas thought his jaws would fall out of place and his skin would snap in horrible ways, blood and bone spurting forth.

Thankfully that did not come to pass but he was still mesmerized by the way Hilderich's mouth could stretch. He still didn't know the young curator as much as he wanted to, but he had seer enought to know that he was a indeed a man full of surprises. It's not that he didn't trust him or that he felt wary of him. It was just that he made him go wide-eyed with shock and surprise at the most curious of places.

"Ehm? Hrm. Ah, the hairy brown ones you mean. The brown ones. A brown one to quench my thirst would be fine. I slept wonderfully, thank you; almost better than back at the curatorium. There was this recurring bad case of insect infestation, terrible buggers really. Never mind. Oh, and some food wood be most appreciated, while you're at it. Don't worry, I believe I can get the fire going by myself."

"Refreshing sleep, I must say. I'll try for some of those mushrooms but if I can't find any, you will be the one scavenging these woods next my friend. And don't throw all the gin in one go."

With that, Amonas picked up a brisk pace and walked off into the distance, not needing to hack his way through the much less denser vegetation. Hilderich languidly got up, his gaze flicking all around him, looking for an inviting bush or hopefully a bunch of fallen branches somewhere nearby.

Hilderich rested his hands on his waist and surveyed the landscape around him. He would inevitably have to engage in a wider search than merely browse just by standing in one place.

So he set off as well into the direction of what looked like a promising cluster of older-looking trees, their barks craggy and laden with moss, happily whistling a tune he could not possibly remember what it was.

Amonas seemed to be well-versed in surviving skills and at ease with finding his way through this remarkably chaotic mess of a forest. Hilderich on the other hand knew his own limitations in orientation, an ability which had failed him more than once even in the simple confines of his master's curatorium.

So he used what he thought was a quite practical way of keeping track of his whereabouts: he took off his cloak and cloth shirt and hanged the white linen shirt on a tall yet thin green stalk; he decided he would stray only as far as he could keep an eye on his shirt. Unless he went blind or some mysterious lurking thief of the wild came along and stole his shirt, he felt safe enough to wander away in search of some hopefully less than soggy firewood.

When Amonas came back with his sack filled with various edibles, he was surprised to see Hilderich naked from the waist up sitting next to a few piles of wooden branches and bulkier logs sorted by size as far as he could tell.

Hilderich was sitting down on the ground idly with his back propped up against the trunk of a tree, legs sprawled nonchalantly. He looked expectantly at Amonas sack and said in a casual manner:

"What took you so long?"

Amonas put the sack down, laughed cordially and began picking up wood from the pile to build a fire.

When it was time to move on again their heart, especially Hilderich's was not in it. The pleasant environment in combination with their full stomachs was a major disincentive to even stand up and stretch, much less start hiking again in a brisk pace.

Even though the ground was totally flat and the only variations in height came deceivingly from the various degrees of thickness in vegetation, it was still an activity that required some degree of energy and patience.

In any case, all their energy now seemed to be drained from the need to digest. They had indeed enjoyed a small feast: brown nuts, some other green horn-shaped fruit with soft sweet flesh, as well as something that resembled wheat in taste and form, but was over-sized and purple in color. Then there was another kind of crisp fruit with red flesh on the inside, wonderfully juicy and marvelously mellow.

With Hilderich displaying genuine culinary audacity mixing various fruit-stuffs together and roasting them in small leaf parcels, they had indeed made the best of what Amonas had come up with, which was surprisingly and thankfully, quite a lot.

Amonas had joked about how sorry he was for having been un-

162

able to find the pack of boars for which the piles of wood had seemed to have been amassed. Hilderich had insisted that Amonas had been gone for quite some time and it was perfectly logical that having nothing much else to do, he would have kept picking up more wood if he hadn't felt stiff by the effort.

They seemed to have thought about it and decided it would be better for them to let their stomachs do some work first before they set off, so they talked at length, something which in the short time they had known each other they had not found ample opportunity for.

So they lied down around the embers of the fire with hands behind their heads, comfortably peering through the canopy of the forest wherever they could, invariably seeing not a wisp of a cloud.

Hilderich talked about his curator's apprenticeship and master Olom. Amonas shared his memories from a time that seemed remote now, when master Olom was a close visiting friend of his father's; a time when Olom had not become shunned by most of his peers and practically forced to live as a recluse and a hermit, rather than an esteemed member of the Curatoria Prefecta. He also talked to Hilderich about how him and Olom united their efforts with the same purpose of liberating the people first from ignorance and then from the dogmatic yoke of the oppressing Ruling Council, relaying to him how bright and hopeful those times had seemed.

Amonas took some more time trying to make Hilderich picture what he had seen when he had stepped through the teleporter and came back to tell the tale. He hoped Hilderich would understand the significance of that accursed place better than he could. Unfortunately, Hilderich seemed to be almost as much at a loss as Amonas was.

All he could make of everything was that there was much more behind the Ruling Council than their rule of tyranny and oppressive dogma, something which eluded him still. Hilderich believed what Amonas had seen was open to many interpretations, all of them though bleak and chilling to think of.

In the end he seemed to agree that if nothing else, his master's demise and their current predicament had shown him that nothing's well with the Territories and indeed the bases of their society were rotten to the core. Hidden artifacts beneath the Disciplinarium, curators being killed or driven away as if in a purge. Hilderich truthfully told Amonas that he didn't know if he believed everything he had been saying, but he now believed little of what he had learned growing up, and that was enough to side with him not only in their quest to return home, but also to uncover what lay beneath all the lies he had been fed. He was living on a strange new world; what more proof did he need that the Law was a lie, and if not a lie and simply in error, what then of its divine and infallible nature? All was not well in their world, and Gods were not in the heavens.

Amonas had been heartened to know Hilderich had changed his mind to see truth on his own. But thir talk was brooding and soon became a blemish in their mood. He promptly changed the subject back to the happier times in their lives, and told Hilderich certain anecdotes about his late master that he migt have been too selc-conscious to admit himself. Hilderich had then been surprised to know that Olom was in fact a gin connoisseur and Amonas even remembered he had brought a distill of his own as a gift once. Hilderich somehow thought better of the old man now, though saving his life as he did seemed to have been reason enough to respect him immensely.

Hilderich asked Amonas politely about Celia, having seen him reading some of her letters; Amonas was somehow reticent to talk about her intimately though. He apologized to Hilderich saying that it was not an appropriate time for such a discussion, but promised him that he would be more than happy to introduce her to Hilderich when they both got back and had left this sordid affair behind them.

After a time period of grace that Amonas seemed to be less than averse to and once they both felt they could do so without pain and anguish from bellies about to burst open, they started off towards what Amonas had declared to be the proper direction.

Soon Amonas was showing signs of uneasiness, stopping every once in a while and trying to feel the brush of air. He craned his neck as if the air had a strange scent about it, something intangible but yet evident all around them. Hilderich could not smell anything out of the ordinary or feel something out of place. He noticed though at some point while they were walking a tingling sensation, some of the hair in his back and hands rising as if a chill had settled in.

Hilderich asked Amonas about it:

"You are uneasy. Even I can tell. What is the matter?"

Amonas puzzlement showed in his voice. He was hesitant, reticent; as if looking for the right words.

"I feel.. Weird. I cannot put it in words. Nothing specific. But, there's something in the air. I cannot tell for certain. It feels.. Somehow unnatural. Even wrong."

"This whole place is wrong. The suns are wrong. There's no night to sleep by. What could be stranger than that?"

"Don't you feel it? A reek of sorts. Something permeating the air, something impalpable. As if a bad taste is circling in my mouth. It makes me nervous, I admit. You have felt nothing wrong? Nothing different?"

Hilderich shrugged, and gestured with his shoulders in uncertainty.

"Nothing in the way you put it. Nothing intense. I did notice my hair rising slightly from time to time. Perhaps it's the air, getting colder."

"This is not because of a chilly breeze, Hilderich. There's something about the place. The sense grows stronger the closer we are getting to the bullhorns. Keep a wary eye and mind. This place might not be as peaceful and indifferent to us as it seems."

Hilderich nodded thoughtfully in acknowledgement and asked Amonas with some anxiety in his voice:

"Do you think we are in danger? Of the immediate kind? Someone following us? Waiting to ambush us or something of the sort?"

Amonas sighed warily and resumed walking, his pace less energetic than before. His gaze darted around him, watching for something he felt like he wouldn't be able to see until it was too late.

Hilderich pulled his cloak tighter in an instinctive motion, as if it could protect him and ward him from unseen danger.

At length, even with their slowed down pace and their almost paranoid wariness wearing them down they finally reached the base of the bullhorns. They could visibly tell because the vegetation thinned out to small bushes and insignificant groves abruptly.

In the hazy background they could indeed see a wall of sorts engulfing their field of vision. Once they were past the last few trees and plants, a trench of sorts lay there; it was mossy but clearly man-made with clear-cut lines and angles defining it, not deeper than the height of a man.

Beyond the trench was where the bullhorns' front face dominated the view, defying the senses in a manner none of them thought possible.

It was indeed a gigantic thing, blocking out the suns with ease. To their left and right, all they could see was the front face of the bullhorns for what seemed to be almost miles. The horizon was almost incapable of containing its view, an immaculate black mat wall with the appearance of obsidian.

It seemed to be shaped like a huge mount, wider at the base and narrow on top, like a solid triangle of sorts; a tetrahedron master Olom would call it, Hilderich thought. On a second thought the term 'pyramid' popped in his head, seemingly the right word for what they were seeing. The characteristically huge horn-like towers on the top seemed to be what distanced it from the shape of a pyramid. It seemed as if it was painstakingly constructed of large bricks or blocks of whatever material it was built from.

The wall face rose with a small inclination, the blocks forming steps that seemed to be possible to climb with some difficulty because of their dimensions. The huge horns could be seen further higher and farther away, sitting majestically atop a tall summit that could easily be as high as any mountain of the outer Territories.

Amonas urged Hilderich onwards.

"Astounding, isn't it? A man made mountain. Come, let's have a feel for it."

"Is that wise? Much more importantly, is it prudent? I think I am tingling intensely. You don't feel strange?", Hilderich said with a worried frown on his face.

"Oh, more than ever. But this is what we have been walking for all this time. We have to know what this thing is," Amonas replied while still gazing all over the surface of the immense wall.

"Can we even pretend we might be able to? I mean, look at it. An immense megalithic structure in the middle of a huge exotic forest. Not to mention that it's not unique and there are many more like it, probably innumerable from what we saw from that hill."

Hilderich seemed troubled, perhaps a bit scared as well. Amonas thought it was to be expected and perhaps even wise considering their situation. He cast his own doubts aside though and concentrated on appeasing Hilderich's fears, trying to appeal to his logic:

"Even grains of sand in a beach can be counted, if one has enough time and dedication. Focus at what's in front of you Hilderich, don't fret over things we don't have to care about immediately. You're a curator, so where is your analytical thinking? How do you know it's made of stone? You said megalithic. If it was made of obsidian, it would at least have some shiny quality to it, wouldn't it? This looks quite different. Ever seen matte black stone like that?"

"I had never seen brown hairy hard-shelled fruit with sweet watery juice and white flesh before, but I drank and ate more than one. That proves nothing. Plus, it was logical to assume it's made of stone. Didn't think you would feel comfortable with such vocabulary though."

"I can read too, Hilderich. How can you know what it's made from if you don't even touch it?"

"We could poke it with a stick or something, and see if it's dangerous."

"It's a wall, Hilderich. Whatever's strange around here, it's not just the wall. Besides, can you honestly feel serious about yourself when suggesting that a *wall* could be dangerous?"

Amonas' voice was mockingly serious; he wanted to relax Hilderich's doubts and make him focus on finding out as much as they could about this unreal structure. He definitely needed Hilderich's clear and precise thoughts, not a muddied assortment of insecure comments, defeatist thoughts, and morose attitude.

"I never thought I could be displaced in a place where the suns look sick and the nights have vanished, just by stepping into a column of light but here I am. Indeed, here we both are. After that, I would expect pretty much anything in this place."

"You'll never forgive me about all this, will you? Never mind that. I'll touch the wall for you if that's what's occupying your mind so fiercely."

Amonas held out both of his hands and touched the block of stone that stood right in front of him on the first row of steps leading to the bullhorns' summit. Nothing happened. Amonas smiled to Hilderich disarmingly, to which Hilderich nodded unenthusiastically.

"So, the wall won't kill us. Not outright at least."

"Now that the walls are safe, what do you think we should do? Any thoughts on what this thing is? A monument of some sort? Should we try and walk around it, find an opening or an entrance if there is one? Or should we climb up to the summit, to where the bullhorns are?"

Amonas had pretty much laid out their options quite concisely at that point, but Hilderich was still skeptical with one hand scratching at his thin, recently grown beard.

"Walking around it would take a couple of days, my guess is. We'd be searching for something we assume might exist but cannot be certain. I don't know. The other thing that bothers me is that this wall face is shadowed, but the others can't possibly be. That means we would be scorched dry with all that sun and nothing much in the way of making ourselves some shade. So, I have to conclude that the only viable course of action at this point is indeed to climb up the summit. We could try and search this wall from edge to edge, but I don't know what might come of it. Quite possibly nothing. Whoever built this thing would be indeed quite an eccentric if any door would be cryptically lying in an obscure, random position. But that's just my guess, and not a very educated one. All I have to base my conjectures upon is rudimentary knowledge of common practices and some plain old good sense. But all that's based on a different world."

"Convinced we're in another world then? That the Pantheon is a tale for conditioning weak minds and obedient slaves?", Amonas voice suddenly became harsh, almost a rasp.

"That's entirely another issue. I am convinced that we are in another world because of this damn sun and all the trouble I've had the displeasure of enduring in this place. Besides, I'm just a Curator, and only because of chance and the edicts of the Curatoria Prefecta," said Hilderich shrugging as he uttered the last few words, careful to intone the name of the society of Curators in which he belonged now, by right of his master's untimely death.

"There you have it in front of your eyes, a thing that just doesn't fit."

Hilderich nodded slightly in reticent agreement, before shifting the subject to the main question:

"Well, I do. So, are we going to climb up this oddity?"

"We are. I'll lead on and help you when you need it. I wager we'll need to make a few stops. It's breathtakingly tall, for one thing."

"I hope we will not be coming down empty handed. Not in the literal sense, of course."

Hilderich was packing his cloak into a roll, while looking sourly at the height-defying summit.

"Who can foretell? Life's full of surprises, as you already know. Let's hope they'll be pleasant this time for a change. I've even gotten used to the peculiarities around this place, the strangeness in the air. It seems to be connected to the bullhorns. As if they exude some sort of aura."

Amonas' gaze followed the slight curves of the bullhorns.

"I thought auras were something only people gave off, and perhaps the suns."

"Well that's what it feels like, I guess. It's strange, but not exactly hostile. More like, cagey I would call. It's like it wants to be left alone. At least if it were alive, that's what I'd think about it."

"Let's hope it doesn't have a very good reason for that."

And with that last remark, once Hilderich had folded his cloak neatly Amonas began their long, effortful climb up the steps of the bullhorn's base.

The large blocks of jet black though cleanly cut and smoothly finished as if from fine porcelain, offered enough friction for a man unused to climbing to be able to push himself upwards. Hilderich felt it was somewhat like reaching for the top shelf of a cupboard. Child's play then, he thought, only somewhat much more taxing on the body.

Indeed only after a little more than a hundred steps Hilderich felt cramps and stiffness overtaking his aching body, especially the legs where he put much of his strength in to propel himself upwards on the steps that seemed fit only for giants.

Amonas noticed and motioned for Hilderich to take a breath for a while to relax his muscles and stretch. Hilderich's lungs were starting to burn but he didn't complain, just as long as they'd made some progress.

He peered over at the landscape stretching behind them trying to make out where they had originally arrived, where they started their trek from, but he was unable. It all looked uniformly green and jarring, trees after trees after trees, a green sea under the pale blue suns. Amonas was standing a few steps above and behind Hilderich, looking thoughtfully below. While Hilderich was stretching with feet dangling over the steps below, he said with a hint of worry in his voice:

"You know, I counted the steps up so far. You seem to be jaded. I cannot say I'm not tired either. The problem is I've counted one hundred and seventeen steps. If you look at the summit does it look any closer to you?", Amonas pointed at the summit of the bullhorns without looking directly at them, but rather looking at Hilderich.

"Uhm.. I'm not very sharp-eyed, but I'd say that they don't. It looks like just as it did when we were at bottom. Means we're going real slow, aren't we?"

"Yes we are. I don't know if we should go back down and forage some more before coming up again. We might actually need more than a day to get up there, it seems. And we'll need some food with all the effort we're putting. Not to mention water."

"Luckily for you I've kept a brown one and a couple of those horn-shaped soft-flesh fruit. They should do until then, with a little bit of economy on our part. I dread to think I'd climb up this monster so I would have to go back and forth each time I felt hungry or thirsty. And after all, if there's nothing important up there, something like that pillar of light that brought us here, then we'd be stuck here, wouldn't we? We'd have all the time in the world to go searching for new exotic fruit then, I wouldn't worry."

Hilderich's tone was ironic, even caustic, but Amonas thought bitterly that he was right. If their climb did not bring them closer to home, then nothing else would. At least not in any foreseeable future. He wouldn't have to worry about provisions then.

"You're right, Hilderich. How are you feeling now? Stretched a bit, didn't you? Lungs feel all better, refreshed? Ready to move on?"

"Ready as I'll ever be."

And so they started off to the summit prepared only to stop for some breath and relaxation, careful not to push their bodies beyond their limits. They climbed slowly but steadily, sweat pouring from the pores in their skin. The higher they went the more they could feel the wind; sometimes a gentle breeze, other times a rough gale. The warmth of the air varied; sometimes it was as hot as it was below on the ground and at other times as chilly as they had never felt it before.

They stopped when they needed to, and moved on when they felt their legs and lungs could go on. But the higher they went and the more time passed, it became more and more difficult to climb and their pace dropped considerably with their pauses becoming increasingly frequent and more prolonged.

But they had made good progress in the time they had been climbing. They could see the horns clearly now rising as majestically as ever, indeed towering over them and dominating the sky above. But they had still some way to go before they reached the summit proper, and those last few steps seemed to put weights of lead on their legs and pour fire in their lungs with every breath.

It seemed as if they wouldn't make it and they would actually stop shy of the summit, forever perched on a jet black step of the bull-horns. With grudging determination though and the constant urging of Amonas to ignore the pain that made even breathing quite a daunting task, they finally reached the last step, where the summit lay all around them.

Panting from the exertion and the toll on their lungs they sprawled themselves on the surface of the summit, which was similar but not entirely so to the blocks of black material they had been climbing on for what must have genuinely been hours on end.

For a few minutes they lay there, doing nothing but squinting at the ever-present sun and breathing deeply, trying to get their lungs to work normally again. They felt almost unable to move their legs and their whole upper torso felt stiff from the tension and the aggravated efforts to reach the top. They had succeeded, but that had left them drained and exhausted, and staggeringly so.

Amonas was the first of the two to stand up with a visibly strained effort. He tried to walk about the summit which was a large terrace from which the horns themselves sprouted from on either side, one of them casting a permanent shadow on the wide mat black surface, while the other one did so on one of the sides. He grabbed Hilderich by one shoulder as he was still laying down seemingly ready to fall asleep, and roused him to action once more:

171

"Come on, Hilderich. A last bit of effort. Let's stand at the shadow over there. It's a bit of a walk but I promise, you can sleep later on."

Hilderich moaned audibly, expressing both the fatigue that had overtaken him as well as his reluctance to even lift his head in protest, much less walk someplace in the state he was in. But to Amonas' surprise which was evident in the furrow of his brow, Hilderich managed to pull himself together and stand up, though he had pain written all over his face and creaking and crackling noises came from his joints, bones, and muscles.

They reached the base of the shadowed horn, where Hilderich let his body go almost limp and fall on the surface. Amonas sat himself down with less violence and noticed that Hilderich had not hurt himself in any way by the fall, or did not seem to feel any pain. At least not greater pain than the one he already was in.

Amonas then spoke with a weary, yet friendly voice:

"Finally, we've reached the summit. And there's some shadow to rest under. I'd try and look around for what we can find, but we're both exhausted. I think we should rest a while first. The place won't go away under our feet right away now, will it?"

Amonas grin as well as anything he else he might have said at that point was useless. Shortly after he finished his sentence, he heard Hilderich snore in his usually loud and unworried way. Amonas felt like sleeping as well. His body craved it, and his mind told him he could more than use some sleep right at that moment.

Before he laid himself on the hard surface of the summit, he covered Hilderich with his cloak. He turned to face the other bullhorn, closed his eyes and before soon he had fallen soundly asleep.

The first one to notice the vibrations was Hilderich. He woke up suddenly, as if emerging from a fitful sleep, having seen a nightmare instead of a dream. He could feel a throbbing sensation coursing through his body, not very much unlike a headache. It was a deeply mechanical aesthesis, as if the very air could vibrate almost visibly. As he stood upright with his senses on the edge waiting for the next sign of impending disaster, he could feel his teeth clatter upon each other involuntarily. He woke up Amonas immediately by rather indelicately kicking him in the ribs softly. Amonas was sluggish coming around when the whole surface underneath them lit up like a miniature sun lay within it, a bright white light underpinning their figures. The throbbing became a more audible trembling, a deep rumbling feeling that seemed to come from way underneath them. His surprise alerted his reflexes and with a sudden and deft move he was on his feet, his head turning in all directions, trying to establish some sort of enemy direction to no avail. Hilderich spoke hurriedly to Amonas, unrestrained anxiety in his voice:

"Something's happening. This place suddenly came alive. We have to do something quickly. This might be our chance!"

Amonas was still a bit drowsy from his sleep and slow to react, but he eventually nodded in acknowledgement. Visibly a little flabbergasted from what was going on around him, he asked Hilderich:

"Our chance for what? What are we looking for?"

"Anything! Anything at all is better than nothing! A lever, a button, something that doesn't fit; a mark, a sign, a sigil, a symbol! Anything that could be used as a control, anything that might react to a human touch! Anything you can find that's not just sleek, or black or both."

Hilderich left Amonas standing there, trying to picture in his head what he would be exactly looking for and walked away towards the center of the surface while at the same time the rumbling grew louder and the light stronger.

Hilderich though in a frantic state and not in complete control of his thoughts and actions, certainly far from being cool-headed and analytical in such moments, still had a knack of noticing things that stood out. The blemishes, the one piece that didn't quite fit, the bits that were importans. After a quick look at the bullhorns themselves, his mind was now working in a sort of slowed down time, where every scene in front of his eyes could be postponed almost infinitely, brought to a crawling stop.

There, in a bubble of still time, in a heightened state of mind he would find what seemed important, come up with theories about its existence and role, its properties and characteristics, and then start eliminating what didn't fit or was not as probable; in the end he'd come up with a solution to a problem, or a keen insight that would prove to be correct and to the point. It was a rare ability he had seldom noticed himself, and rarely gave it much heed as he seemed to not be able to use it constantly. It simply happened at certain times, as if something like fear or great necessity triggered it despite Hilderich.

It was then that he had caught something with the corner of his eye, and had pretty much arrived to a conclusion about its significance before he could turn around and yell to Amonas:

"Lie down! Now!"

Amonas' reflexes were much better than Hilderich's and he had the clarity of mind not to question people when they instructed him to take cover, since they usually did so with the intended purpose of saving your skin. His body moved almost of its own volition and he let himself fly towards the hard surface of the bullhorns' summit.

As he did so, his eyes caught a glimpse of what must have been nothing less than fiery death. Amonas was barely able to see a giant ball of fire hurtling itself with blinding speed towards them, towards this particular bullhorn. There was a silvery quality about the fire and as it came over through the bullhorns beyond, he could barely make out Hilderich trying to throw himself flat against the bullhorn closest to him in a fashion that would seem rather comical in any other situation. The flaming apparition was just passing the last bullhorn before Amonas instinctively closed his eyes as if that would make it go away, and that was the last thing he saw for what appeared to be eternity.

He only opened his eyes after the terrible sound of the sky tearing itself apart with the force of a thousand thunders or more had passed, when he could breathe once more; when the scorching heat wave above him had come and gone again in the blink of an eye.

He thought he had gone deaf but he could hear himself getting up; the sense of sound slowly returned though his ears ringed like his head had been turned into a living bell.

He checked around to see Hilderich and found him lying on the black surface, trying to move or perhaps stand up. He seemed quite visibly as shaken as he was himself. But Amonas knew he was alive. Whatever that thing was, they were both alive.

It had come and gone like a God of thunder, Amonas thought. It was strange that he would think in such terms but he had no alternative to express himself by. Whatever that thing was it felt indeed as they had been nearly smitten by a fiery God of thunder.

He offered his hand to Hilderich to help him up to his feet. Hilderich took it without second thought, dazed and flabbergasted though he was. As he did so, his gaze was fixed towards the direction of the fireball that had nearly killed them. Hilderich just stood there transfixed, looking out as if waiting for that thing to come around and finish them, as if they had been marked for death and their was inevitably near.

Amonas looked worried and held Hilderich's arms trying to attract his attention, calling out his name, asking him what was the matter. But Hilderich could only afford a mere flick of his gaze, the rest of him steadily fixed on the far side of the horizon across the row of bullhorns from where the flaming thunder had passed over. Hilderich then spoke mesmerized, with grave seriousness in his every word:

"That thing is the answer. We have to ride it, somehow. I've never thought anything could go that fast. It came and went in two blinks of an eye. Can you imagine that? Yet it just passed over our heads. Like a tamed star, made to fall forever."

Amonas looked over the same direction Hilderich was, and then looked bitterly back at him:

"It nearly killed us my friend. And you would ride it? You've called me a madman before. I think it's time I returned that remark. Whatever that was, it's not a thing of nature and it's not something we can use. We have to think of other ways."

"There are no other ways. There is nothing but wild green lush forest with mushrooms and brown ones, and this. These bullhorns. All these bullhorns only seem to exist for is what just passed overhead. It went through and through each of these bullhorns, like a cart speeding on rails. Wherever it's headed, it can't be worse than this."

"Still, even if all that stands to reason, even if this was indeed built only to accommodate that huge fireball, what makes you think we can ride on it? With it, inside it, whatever would make some kind of sense. Don't you see how incredibly powerful it is? What are we going to do? Catch it with a rope and hang on to it as if it was cattle?"

Hilderich grinned and the effect on Amonas was for the first time totally disconcerting, perhaps even chillingly terrifying. He thought the effect of the fiery ball on Hilderich was the loss of his wit and mind. As a deep frown appeared on his face, Hilderich spoke:

"You thing I'm losing it, don't you? You think I just went crazy, broke down; that my mind left me forever and so on. But I know we can ride on that thing. And I also know that it was designed for that specific purpose. Do you want me to explain the reason why or do you think you can come to the same conclusion yourself?"

Amonas shoulders sagged and he took on an expression of pity, looking at Hilderich sorrowfully, as if it was the last time he was see- ing him; as if his mind had parted with him forever and he was talking to another man entirely. Hilderich laughed at Amonas' look:

"That look on you is actually funny. Doesn't suit you getting melodramatic at all. Now, listen: What happened right before the fireball came zooming in towards us?"

"You told me to duck and lie down flat on the surface."

"Before that, when I woke you up. What did you notice?"

"I was drowsy from the sleep. Perhaps there was some kind of buzzing sound, a rumble."

"There were two signs - light and sound, indeed more like three sounds. There was a buzzing sound, a hum in the air clearly audible. There was a rumbling so deep it vibrated our insides. And the whole surface was lit up thoroughly, a bright white light from underneath us, so bright it shone brighter than that damn sun."

Hilderich was smiling with what could only be characterized as smugness.

"So, you are saying there was a warning? All that was for us to know something was coming?"

Amonas sounded like he considered what Hilderich was saying quite incredulous.

"Not just us, anyone who might happen to be on the top at that particular time. Remember we where asleep; nothing like that came rushing down at exactly when we stepped foot up here. It came at an inopportune moment, some time later. In fact, these signs woke me. And I believe you would have woken as well by yourself even if I wasn't there."

"And why warn us? This thing, whatever it is."

"Well if it something wanted us dead, I believe there would have been no warning. Unless it's part of a well played sport, it doesn't make sense. What does make sense though is that the signs appealed to almost every sense: Sight, hearing, and touch. Now that I come to think of it, I could even taste something like copper in my mouth, and smell something too. Not sure I knew the smell, but something smelled strange alright."

Hilderich was positively brimming with excitement, his eyes and face were lit up and he was actually rocking about his toes and heel.

"You are implying that it was a sign specifically designed to warn any man? Whether he be blind, deaf, or even unable to taste or smell?"

Amonas had cocked his head sideways in a possible attempt to see if there was something messing with Hilderich's head.

"I'm saying exactly that."

"You are full of surprises, Hilderich. It could stand to reason if it didn't sound like too wishful thinking."

"All this is beyond far-fetched but as I have pointed out in the past, here we are," said Hilderich and shrugged with his arms extended, indicating the scenery around them.

"And what do you suggest we do about that? Surely, we will have warning of when another one of those things approaches. And what do we do then? Jump at it in the opportune moment?"

Amonas voice had a sneering quality, but he was still maintaining a conversational tone.

"Amonas, my radical friend. Have you ever boarded a ship, or a wagon train?"

"I cannot see where you are getting at here, but indulge me. Yes, yes I have," Amonas said with mild annoyance.

"Well then, doesn't always someone announce the arrivals and departures?"

"You are again going beyond the imaginable to imply that this thing is a vehicle of some sort. That it can actually stop and pick us up? Just like that?"

Incredulity seeped from Amonas' every word. It was as if he was being told he had suddenly grown a third foot.

"Well more or less, yes. But not like that. We'd need a ticket."

"What could possibly count as a ticket in this extremely unlikely scenario you are proposing?"

"I've been waiting to ask you this when there'd be no point in you saying no: I'd have my keystone back now, please."

Friend or foe

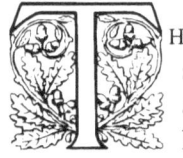HE corridors of the Disciplinarium were enigmatically silent. Lord Ursempyre Remis was being escorted by a pair of procrastinators at the behest of the Patriarch himself, he had been told. The mere thought of that man made him uneasy, and now he had been summoned personally. His mind raced with conjecture and the possible reasons: none seemed even remotely harmless.

As his steps echoed in the stone floor of the hallways that never seemed to end, he thought he had a pretty good idea of the Patriarch's intentions. He thought that perhaps the Patriarch knew something, but he had to know that for himself.

See it in my eyes, Ursempyre thought. He would maintain the facade of the ignorant noble to whatever end might await him. This was a critical point. Everything hung in a precarious balance, and this was the push that could tip things over either way. He calmed himself, emptied his mind and held to just one conviction:

'I am Lord Ursempyre Remis, Noble Representative, Duke of the Fief of Wir and Prefect of Urfall. I serve the Law and the Pantheon, I abide to the rulings of the Council'. That would be the only thought coursing in his mind, and he would make-believe if he had to. And if things came to that, he had prepared for other contingencies: his people had been given instructions. He merely hoped there was time enough, that things would not be rushed before time was due.

They passed through many hallways, some of them exquisitely decorated with hand-woven tapestries of a beautiful, delicate, and quite extravagant nature. Others were bleak, strictly functional and indifferent to the eye, not destined to impress or provoke awe. Probably hardly ever seen or used.

There was a nagging feeling that he was being treated as if he had not been summoned here officially. Indeed, the procrastinators seemed eager enough to take him by force if he had resisted. Would the Patriarch be so rash? Would he suddenly arrest him without good reason? Certainly he had the power to do so, but was it to his best interest? How could he ever succeed in finding out what drove the

178

Patriarch? Nothing useful was to be found in Ursempyre's bag of thoughts.

The man was a terrifying mystery, an uncanny wildfire people tried to steer away from. The kind of fire that only consumed and never warmed or lit. He was probably the most dangerous man Ursempyre could indeed face; even more dangerous than the Castigator, who might be a tyrant and heartless man, a man that cared for naught but power and its exertion over men. But the Castigator was still a man.

His motives could be understood, some of his actions anticipated. Perhaps he could be reasoned to the extent that it would seem to him to be in his best interests, offering him a deal he could not refuse. But the Patriarch was a blank, as if he were totally heedless of the circumstances, the dynamics of power play, and indeed the workings of the world around him.

It felt like he had an agenda no one could hope to fathom, plans within plans that he had no intention of altering or suspending. He was relentless in whatever pursuit he was involved in, and once one laid his eyes on him, he looked back uncannily. It was an eerie feeling, him knowing you were watching. It made one think that this man could read your mind with a glance, know your fears, your weaknesses; the things that made you cry and the things that made you laugh. It was as if the Patriarch were a chilling, unnatural force that could bore right into your soul and leave you empty; a walking husk with your mind and soul gone forever, his own for the taking at nothing but a whim of his.

Ursempyre shuddered at these thoughts visibly. One of the procrastinators noticed and sniggered scornfully. Ursempyre turned to look at what could easily be a common thug in the streets of Pyr, and stared at him intently with a hint of suppressed wrath in his gaze. The procrastinator lost his grin almost instantly and stared away, averting his eyes.

Night had only just fallen outside and servants could be seen running about the Disciplinarium, lighting up braziers and chandeliers wherever appropriate. Halls, corridors, and chambers were being lit up one by one, staff and officials grinding on at the work that needed to be done during these times of war preparations; work that would probably keep them up all night.

They went past the administrative areas, through small ware-houses and store rooms. Lighting was at a premium in these parts of the Disciplinarium with only a few torches spread thin, darkness and light exchanging places with one another at uneven intervals. One of the procrastinators paused and unhitched a torch from its post to carry along with him.

They were descending deep down in the lower levels of the Disciplinarium, places that Ursempyre had always been loathe to visit for he was aware of the acts usually being performed in those chambers.

Kept hidden from prying eyes, this was the place where the enemies of the state, the sinners and the ones who were considered dangerous, unruly, and frivolous with the La were brought to be chastised and enlightened. His face grimaced at the thought of the euphemism.

Chastisement and enlightenment came at the price of torn fingernails, pried tongues, flogged backs, and broken bones. And then there were those who made to utterly disappear, the dungeons of the Disciplinarium their last murky, cold abode. He knew now what was coming.

He would be thoroughly interrogated by the Patriarch himself. The die was cast, it seemed. There was nothing more he could do. He hoped he would be able to escape with his life, but if it came to that, he had made arrangements. Everything would be put in motion if the hours passed without him emerging. It was all planned and primed, ready for what was in the end only inevitable and long ago decided.

The uprising would begin. He would try and beguile the Patriarch, a task that genuinely seemed desperate, but he would. If and when he failed at that, he would endure as long as he could, until his body failed him; until his mind and soul were utterly crushed. He had no misgivings, no fantasies of standing up against the Patriarch for too long.

He knew not what tools of torture the Patriarch used, but he knew that none of those that were made the focus of his unbridled attention had been left unbroken. Those that he touched, they all gave up in the end. They all talked, they all begged for their lives like lesser men, like cornered animals, their instincts having them make a last attempt at salvation. But there was no mercy to be had, no humanity in his work. If he could not outsmart him or outplay him in a game of his own devising, then his life was forfeit.

Perhaps later rather than sooner, but he would be done for in the end. All that mattered was that the uprising had to succeed, that it should indeed take them by surprise somehow. Even if he knew, stalling him might make the difference. Even if the Patriarch knew, that did not necessarily mean all hope was lost. They would fight as the should. If he himself perished during the hours that would follow, it mattered not. His memory would live on, his legacy and story told as part of the Liberation of the Territories. That would be good enough an ending for House Remis, and good enough for him as well.

They would be free, again. Free to live their own lives as they saw fit. Damn the Patriarch and the Castigator and all their cronies, henchmen, thugs, and devils; damn those men that willingly gave up their souls in exchange for a whip, a quill, or a sword. Damn them all, they would be free and let those tyrants think otherwise.

Having lost himself in thought, he hadn't been aware they had descended unusually deep. Instead of stone masonry and man-made walls, they were now walking amidst tunnels wide enough for two men to walk side by side, dug in the rock and granite of the Disciplinarium hill. These were old, older than the Disciplinarium, carved in a time lost from memory that no annal had recorded.

Though he was privy to most of the workings of the Disciplinarium, he had not known the dungeons extended to such a depth. He was surprised. He felt wary of the other surprises that lay in stock for him.

Soon they reached a grated gate, sentry guards posted in both sides of the gate. Where the far side lay, there was little or no light from torches or any other kind of lighting. No candles either. Simply darkness, eerie and silent, like ink was blotting out his sense of sight.

One of the procrastinators nodded to the sentries to leave their posts. They would be taking over. The sentries looked at each other knowingly and without protest, question or remark; one of them opened the gate, handed their heavy cast iron keys to the procrastinators and quietly and without further ado left in an organized fashion in a single file.

One of them looked back and cast a passing gaze at Ursempyre and an expression of surprised recognition formed in his face and then it was gone; it was replaced by a fearful crease of terrible knowledge on his forehead. Ursempyre thought with bitterness that even the guards around this place realized the importance of what would follow. The Noble Representative would be tortured, questioned, and killed by the Patriarch himself. An ill omen, but who would challenge the will of the Law and the Patriarch, Reverent and Beloved of the Gods, the Holy Avatar? Not a lowly guard, that much was certain.

One of the men that had led him into the caves spoke with a restrained voice, somewhat confused about whether he should refer to Ursempyre as a Lord or as just another lost soul at the non-existing mercy of the Patriarch. He chose the latter, fearful of the walls having ears:

"On you go, in there. To your left. His Holiness awaits."

He was then mildly but forcibly pushed, as if he had to be reminded that they were there to ensure his concordance and cooperation, or club him unconscious and fetch him themselves in front of the Patriarch, if the need arose.

Ursempyre's steps were measured and slow, but steady and unwavering. He steeled himself for the confrontation, muscles tensing and relaxing in quick succession. He was as ready as he could be, he thought.

The cave seemed to be hollowed out artificially, swaths of incandescent light pouring out from the large orifice he was instructed the Patriarch was awaiting his presence.

As he entered the chamber the intense light made him squint reflexively, but his eyes adjusted. It seemed as if the light was pouring out of some strange, tall, glass columns that extended beyond the floor and ceiling of the chamber, as if they were actually grown out of the rock itself.

Ursempyre's interest was at once piqued by what he was seeing all around him: Four large glass columns like huge rods brimming with light, seemingly supporting the tall, wide rocky chamber. The Patriarch was standing with his back turned to Ursempyre right amid the four columns, his bald scalp glistening under the blueish-white light of the columns, gossamer shadows of himself cast in the shape of a cross across the rough and uneven, rocky floor. Small wet brown lime stone indentations and juts dotted the ground. A faint humming noise echoed faintly throughout the chamber, which was otherwise deafeningly silent.

Ursempyre was drawn into the scenery, taken by surprise but not overwhelmed. He felt curious. So much more as to what the intentions of the Patriarch were. He had been expecting a torture chamber with a multitude of tools and instruments. Instead, he was being shown something very few people, if ever, became privy to. He thought then that perhaps the folk tales about the ancients and the curator's ramblings were not all for naught. But then again, what reason did the Patriarch have to reveal such a place to him?

His thoughts were interrupted by the sly, surreptitious voice of the Patriarch, which broke the silence of the chamber sounding as if it resonatd with the columns and the rock walls, both adding to its effect:

"These are plasma conductors. Part of the energy grid of the Disciplinarium. Basically I barely use most of the amenities involved. I consider myself adjusted to my surroundings by now. I find the use of manservants most to my liking."

Ursempyre frowned quizzically at the Patriarch's words. He could neither understand exactly what he was telling him, or more importantly why. As always, scripture in High Helican decorated its hem discreetly. Strangely enough, he didn't look resplendent or intimidating. The Patriarch turned to face Ursempyre with hands neatly hidden inside the folds of his robes, simple and utilitarian yet finely crafted from quality cloth. It was as if he sounded sincere for the first time when he spoke again:

"I see that you are taking all this in your stride. I'd expected as much. It will make things easier, I suppose," indicating with his eyes the glass-like columns of light he had called 'plasma conductors'.

Ursempyre was still looking at the mysterious columns when he asked the Patriarch in a straightforward manner, one that almost demanded an answer even though he knew he was in no position to make any real demands:

"Why am I here? I am the Noble Representative. I demand that you extend some courtesy and respect to such a person of significant office."

Ursempyre's tone of voice was authoritative and steadfast, even though a trained ear could feel it frail at the edges. Only because of evidently great determination did his voice hold together barely at the seams. The Patriarch sounded amused when he replied:

"Would you keep on performing on a stage when all the viewers had left? I could admire you for your dedication, but I generally hold fools in low esteem. I suggest you, ahm, revise your way of thinking, Lord Remis. While you still can."

"Is this some sort of threat? I came here of my own free will. I have nothing to hide, your Reverence. I insist you make your intentions clear before long. Whatever they may be, I will be a faithful servant and abide by the Law."

Ursempyre's voice had deep, grave undertones etched in it. He meant to come across as serious and truthful, yet not just another lackey or one of their goons to be simply expected to obey unquestioningly. He wanted the Patriarch to know that he wasn't terrified of him. Even though in his gut he knew that was nothing but a lie.

The Patriarch stifled a laugh in mere disbelief. A terrible smile had formed on his lips:

"Is that so, Lord Ursempyre Remis? It almost always has to be that way, hasn't it? Please, have a seat," the Holy Avatar said and before he could finish his sentence an ornate chair appeared out of thin air, as if it had always been there, simply invisible to the eye.

It was supremely decorated with fine leather and silky surfaces, girdles of gold and silver on its armrests. In concert, an even more ornate and large chair with a large backside plush with red velvet and green granite girders appeared behind the Patriarch, in pair with a similarly decorated desk; its surface though a hard green-veined black marble.

What was unfolding in front of Ursempyre felt preposterous to him, but it looked like as if even more extravagant events were about to take place. Ursempyre would let the Patriarch put on his own show, and he would go on with his theatricals as far as it was possible.

The logical part of his brain cried out in anguish at the impossibilities unraveling all around him, and wanted to stop and cry out for someone that could explain even the smallest iota of these tricks.

'They have to be tricks,' he thought, 'some sort of show to cow and bewilder me.'

The other part of his mind, the determined one, just ignored what was thrown at him and focused at one thing: Making it out of that place alive, for starters. And then, he believed, he could work something out of the rest.

The Patriarch realized Ursempyre had frozen in place, his mind stung by the sudden impossible appearance of the furniture, and beckoned him once more to seat:

"Please, Lord Remis. You seem to be woolgathering. Does not our conversation appeal to your standards? Perhaps some refreshment is in order?"

With that last phrase, a plain wooden jug of wine appeared on the Patriarch's desk alongside two cups, one slightly chipped on its rim; the other one was visibly older, its wood stained and discolored. The Patriarch added while waving one hand dismissively:

"You'll hopefully excuse the quality of the cups. I try to dispense with pomp and luxury wherever applicable. In essence, I am quite a simple man. If only you could see that."

Ursempyre was still looking at the Patriarch dumbfounded, not as much because of the Patriarch's ability to instantly and at will seemingly conjure whatever items he pleased, but more so because of what he was saying, or trying to imply. The Patriarch was not in any way, a simple man. He was being flippant, mocking Ursempyre in the process. The noble man managed to speak though, as if a spell forced upon him had been broken:

"This ability of yours, it does not scare me, Patriarch. The Holy Avatar must indeed have the blessings of the Gods, why not shouldn't it possess some of their power?"

"Yes, that does make sense doesn't it? Bloody brilliant on my part, I would say."

The Patriarch looked almost gleeful. He continued unabated and asked Ursempyre:

"What does scare you, Ursempyre? What is it you really fear, if not me? After all you've heard or seen, you know what I'm capable of. Would you like me to become unpleasant, Lord Remis? Would you force my hand?"

"I have nothing of which to be accused of, Patriarch. I am a faithful.."

"You are a constant reminder of my failings and nothing more!", said the Patriarch as he burst into a fit of rage, sending the jug of wine crashing against a glass pillar. Red wine spilled all over the floor, running down the glass columns. The cups were still lying on the desk, one of them rolling on its side back and forth.

Ursempyre knew now he had been exposed as the leader of the kinsfolk from the beginning, it was the niceties that had simply evaporated. He steeled himself mentally, closed his eyes and tried to think of happier, earlier times. His muscles relaxed. He was waiting for a hammering blow. Nothing happened any time soon. He opened his eyes to see the Patriarch draw his chair, and sag in it, as if he were exhausted from a copious effort. He sighed, and then spoke in a raspy, tired voice, more suited to a broken old man rather than the Patriarch, the Holy Avatar of the Gods:

"I'm tired of being reminded of my failings, tired of games I guess. But I'm not willing to lose, not after all the time I've spent. Do you understand that, Lord Ursempyre Remis, Noble Representative? Can you, really? Even if I showed you, could you fathom? Or would your lesser, weak mind break down from hopelessness and despair? Could you indeed ride on the wave of apocalypse that would follow, Ursempyre? I have to pity, hate, and envy you at the same time Ursempyre, you and your people. But this has to end as well."

Ursempyre was even more mystified at what the Patriarch was saying. Again he noticed, it wasn't the trick show and the flashiness or the strangeness of what was happening. It was the Patriarch himself that was doing it; his words seemed to twist reality and violate normalcy.

He was acting out of character, for one thing. It was as if he was trying to make some point, but was having real difficulty in doing so, like there was a great barrier between them, as if the Patriarch were unable to make himself understood in human terms. He was somehow circumnavigating the point in question, never directly touching it, uttering generalities and giving cryptic hints, as if his annotations alone sufficed to make himself understood.

Ursempyre hated that quality in a person: evasiveness, mucking about rather than doing or saying what one had in mind. 'Just tell me what you really want to, you raving old wolf,' he thought to himself before asking the Patriarch directly:

"What do you mean? Do you mean the rebellion? The kinsfolk will rise and cast you down, rightfully claim the right of the people to freedom. And if we shall fail, we will give our lives willingly. I will be the first one to do so, if needs be. Strike me down if you must, if that's the reason I'm here for. Spare me the theatrical, and the mirror show as well."

Hilderich's words came out sharp and proud. He managed to even surprise himself with his clarity and his aboveboard voice and manner. His face was taut; he felt the veins in his throat throb with every pulse. He felt relieved his mask was finally cast off, feeling primed and ready for everything that the Patriarch would throw at him.

He wasn't thinking clearly now, he knew, but he imagined he could go for his throat and neck, possibly try to snap it or even strangle him with his bare hands. His determination had walked him through from an innocent noble Lord to a hot-blooded rebel in mere moments. The Patriarch's answer stunned him with its simple ruthlessness and unprecedented audacity:

"Do you wish to become the Castigator of the Outer Territories?", he said, idly checking his fingernails for blemishes and dirt in a blantant show of genuine indifference.

Ursempyre frowned instinctively as if his hearing had failed him, and blinked a few times before feeling a complete idiot for being unable to constrain his physical reactions. He managed to ask the Patriarch, his voice rippling with waves of incredulity and disbelief:

"Become.. The Castigator?", Ursempyre said and broke down in laughter, his hands behind his head as if failing to grasp the joke behind the Patriarch's words, but still finding it funny enough.

The Patriarch reached out for a small goblet of wine, its contents sloshing as if it had just been poured. In fact, it had just appeared on his desk. He sipped some wine while Lord Remis tried to calm himself down; his laughter was stilled by the Patriarch's lack of an answer, physical or verbal. After seeming to savor the wine properly at length like a man who found meaning in the tasteful little joys of life would, he said with more authority, gravity weighing his words down heavily, the rocky chamber echoing them and magnifying the effect:

"I know you do not take me for a fool, Ursempyre. You must know I do not either. I simply find that you are ultimately, nothing else but a man of your time. Unimpressively enough though, you're not a man quite ahead of it. Nevertheless, as things stand I offer you the sovereignty of the Outer Territories and the divine office of Castigator."

The Patriarch had risen from his seat with hands behind his back, and was very slowly pacing around the columns, his form every once in a while disappearing behind a blaze of blue and white light, each time a sliver of his figure and face appearing grotesque and malformed behind the glass column, as if it had the ability to reveal what lay behind the facade of the Patriarch. Ursempyre felt suddenly naked, as if he had been bared against his will, but he did not protest. He felt ashamed, for not erupting in anger. What really must have bothered him though was finding out that, in the end, he seemed completely transparent.

The Patriarch then continued, a wide grin showing his immaculate teeth:

"I know how your mind works, Ursempyre. What's troubling you most is whether or not I had known about your people and their organization right from the start. Whether or not I know about your rebellious plans, the killing hour. I'll indulge your inquisitiveness, for the sake of argument. Perhaps, you'll rarely hear me admit it, I do love to revel in my superiority. It's an obnoxious trait, being such a snob. If you knew me better you'd have found out I couldn't help being otherwise. But I digress."

The Patriarch paused and put a hand to his chin, stroking his beard lightly holding a finger to his lips as if he were searching for his next words; he seemed engrossed in thought, carefully minding his next words. Ursempyre was transfixed, staring at him with his mind locked in the astounding proposition he had made. He thought he shouldn't be doing this, he shouldn't be even listening to this devil. His heart told him to try and rip this human-shaped terror apart, for everyone's sake. His mind though told him to stay his wrath, and listen. He was being told things he would never have known otherwise. Things he might be able to use if he came out of this alive, if indeed they were as they felt to be, the truthful ramblings of the malefic despot. The Patriarch resumed what was beginning to look like a monologue, or rather his explanation of things:

"You'll have to excuse my earlier outburst. These are trying times, even for me. I have already admitted to two things I consider weaknesses, dear Lord Remis. You should do well to think that this is not only a rare occurrence, but rather unique. As you have already considered, I might be lying indeed, but what difference would that make to you?"

He had made a full round of the columns, and he was now standing in front of Ursempyre with the desk behind his back. All this time Ursempyre had not moved from the place where he had been left standing, swiftly taken by the turn of events. The Patriarch motioned with a slight nod of his head that he should be seated but Ursempyre declined in kind with an almost imperceptible shake of his head, his gaze intently fixed at the Patriarch at all times.

"Very well, if you insist," said the Patriarch and the chair blinked away in the same logic defying manner that it had manifested in the first place. The Patriarch went on:

"This is a unique offer. For reasons you will come to understand in due time, I'm offering you the rule of these lands. Of course, it will be mostly in name only. As is the case, you will mostly be a figurehead of sorts, a legitimised leader of sorts, as had been your precursors.

As always, I will be the real Law and effective ruler of these lands, and you will be acting as my near-invisible proxy in setting policy. Of course, in all the lesser matters, like economy, judicious activities, trade and the like, you will be left alone to your devices.

My immediate concern though lies elsewhere: This rebellion you're planning, is happening at an opportune time. I do have some matters of urgency to attend to, and you appear to have set up quite a formidable and perhaps effective as well as skilled fighting force. I know there are quite a lot of veterans of the Zaelin campaign among your people, and they were fierce back in the day, I can remember.

I really cannot be bothered to lose precious little time over suppressing what will be in the end, a failed rebellion. It would be most prudent and cost-effective if we avoided all the unnecessary bloodshed and came to some sort of agreement between me and you, the newly appointed Castigator. You could even present it as your own political victory. That'd be a nice touch to it, I can imagine."

Ursempyre tried to take in the Patriarch's words, but he felt unable to. It was an overwhelming thought. There were so many questions and possibilities going through his mind. Would he actually consider such a proposal? Did it have any merit? Would the Patriarch keep true to his word? What chance would he stand against the Patriarch once he felt like he had served his purpose? If he was so powerful, why did he need him? Why shouldn't crush the rebellion altogether? Why did he need him? What were the limitations of his strange powers, and where did those powers stem from? Demons?

Like the Gods, he believed that no such things existed either but their evil foul stench was real. Should he accept the vacant role it would probably be a bloodless uprising, but to what a future would it lead? This rotten system would not go away. The Patriarch, and the Council, and all their tyranny would still be around and he would be part of it, unable to do anything to change all that. He felt dirty, almost soiled that he had even began to consider such an offer, that he actually tried to put it on a scale and weigh their future against the parody of one. He had decided. He would not become a willing pawn.

That last temptation was the easy way out, the bloodless shadow of a victory, a postponed defeat and utterly, nothing else than treason. He had not thought himself as a fanatic or a zealot up until now. He had always thought that he was, as ever, the pragmatist.

That was the quality in him which had led him to believe that change should occur, even if it meant full-scale rebellion and ulti-mately war; quite possibly the annihilation of those who would carry the weight of the change, but a change that was worth dying for.

He had studied as much of history as was possible and he had seen behind the veil of religious propaganda and dogma. He had weighed and balanced everything and he believed he could prove, by way of reasoning, hard facts and certain numbers, that their world was in a stagnant situation. A situation where nothing new and worthwhile would ever arise, a steady circle of people giving birth, and dying, too busy and occupied with the endless toils of life and too frightened of losing what little breath of life they had been spared.

Too frightened to lose the smell of cinnamon bread-pies and the laughter of the young and innocent children, before they too became in essence obedient slaves, aspiring to nothing more than a long life of toil and harsh, bitter pain and misery as if it was the only right thing to do.

And people like him, the Noble families, would praise the Gods and their luck for been born a step above the simpletons that tilled their fields, worked their mines and brought them their wine to the table.

Fear. Fear ruled them first and foremost above all. Fear misguided them and made them wake up from their dreamless sleep, and be happy they'd just live for another day. It had sickened him, when he realized it in his mind for the first time.

They were prisoners of fear, all of the; from the nobles to the scum in the streets of Pyr. Every last one of them, all they knew their whole lives was fear. It was time they learned something more of life, go a little further down the road.

He was curious to see what they could accomplish once they were free of fear. All of them, free to think, act, hope, and dream. He had a sudden flash of recollection right at that hour.

He remembered a time when he had gone fishing with his grandfather, near a lake in the late summer when he was still a boy curling up in his mother's bosom to sleep at night. His grandfather had showed him how to hook the bait on his line but when he had tried it himself, he had gotten stung. He had cried in anguish, pain, and fear, but his grandfather had laughed out with all his heart and had said to him, quite unperturbed by his discomfort:

"It's only a sting, Urse. It's not going to kill you. Unless you're a fish."

He wasn't a fish, and he wasn't just going to give up now. He was Lord Ursempyre Remis and he was about to change everything, even if he ultimately failed. But first he had to go through this immediate predicament, and the smartest way to do that was to let the Patriarch think he had won, that despair had claimed him.

Even if he succeeded in killing him right then and there, he doubted he could make it out alive. Thinking about bait and fish, he was determined to see the Patriarch outwitted and outmatched in his own game: Deception.

"You seem to be thinking hard into the matter, Lord Remis. As I had anticipated, you are taking this seriously and weighing your, very few I should remind you, options. So, what will it be Ursempyre Remis? Will you vainly turn brother against brother and father against son? Will you have all that blood in your hands? End it now, before it even starts."

Ursempyre's reverie was broken, and upon hearing the Patriarch responded with a burst, his words were spat from his mouth rather than spoken:

"Lies! Deceit! You would have me believe all that just so you can bring the Kinsfolk out onto the light and finish us in one sweep. Still, if you wouldn't do that, if you only care for things to remain as they are, what will you do once I am named Castigator? Will you change the Law? Will there be reform? Will the people achieve some measure of freedom, of independence? Will your Gods show mercy for a change? Inspire prosperity and progress? Will the people enjoy better lives? Or will you squeeze and squeeze until not an iota of their strength or resolve remains? Will you see the error of your ways and let the people be free? Or will you keep making the same offer to other men as well, again, and again, and again?"

The Patriarch remained calm, and seemed uninhibited in his efforts to force Ursempyre's submission or his hand:

"I think you've misunderstood my intentions. This is not a political bargain. Indeed any bargain of sorts. It is merely a possibility I am willing to entertain, because it suits me. Perhaps I haven't been too clear, and at the same time I have misjudged your intelligence and powers of reasoning and extrapolation. I am not sharing power, or recognizing my decisions and rule as mistaken. You will not be handed any real measure of authority and yes, the people will continue to be oppressed as you put it, until I deem otherwise. You have no real lever against me, apart from certain time constraints that I must keep in mind. In other words, I am offering you a much more civilized way out, because I haven't got the time to grind your puny rebellious followers into oblivion. Is that much understood now? Am I coming across? Can you reestablish the true position you are in now? Can you fathom that in my greater scheme of things you and your 'people' are a nuisance I want to deal with efficiently and move on? Or are you that infatuated with your pet idea of a free world that you have been completely cut off from reality? Perhaps you might be thinking it will all sort itself out in the end, aren't you? How preposterous a notion! I can only find it natural to nurture such gross misconceptions since you are little more than infants, barely able to stand on their own two feet. How could you possible know the truth of the cosmos? You still think of the stars as prickles of light, some of them falling down as they die. You would know real fear and awe when you saw the death of a star, I can assure you of that. But you still would not believe me. As you do not believe me now, thinking I am playing you like the fool you are, tightening and loosening an invisible line, as if you were a fish caught on my lure."

Ursempyre involuntarily flinched at the uncanny remark and was terrified at the thought the Patriarch was actually reading his mind. If that were true, he had been a fool from the start, all his hopes now laid to waste. He tried to compose himself, not allow any more of his fear to show itself. The Patriarch was grinning malevolently when he said:

"I am not reading your mind. I could, but then I would have to have you killed and that would not expedite my goals. I have already devoted enough of my time in this affair, what should have been a simple case of a 'yes' or 'no' has evolved into a time-consuming situation that only serves to further aggravate me as well as stall me, as you might be thinking is in your best interest. I might also be giving away details and information you would never even have dreamt of, but it will matter little because if you live, you'll have become my new Castigator, and if you die, well, dead men can't talk. Not that the rumors have hurt me much over the years. It seems that people will only believe what they are willing to. Suspension of disbelief can be a powerful weapon indeed. But I digress. You make me so restless I cannot help myself. Come now, seriously, what will it be? My patience is at an end. Whatever you want to happen next, tell me now."

Ursempyre's face was stern, contorted from the anxiety. He realized perspiration was running down his temples for some time. He had to make a leap of faith, and trust in himself like never before. Still, he knew he was walking in a territory far more dangerous than he could have imagined from beforehand. The Castigator was another pawn. These weird abilities of the Patriarch. Like the stories of Old, before the Pantheon. Folk tales they had seemed, but now they were inescapably real, made manifest before his eyes. He did not know their true nature, and was loathe to find out. Still, why was he being offered this now? Should he not refuse? What made the Patriarch so certain of his superiority? What was the true extent of his power? Why had he not crushed them at their inception while they were still a handful; weak, their organization still a dream, a footnote of history and legend brought back from oblivion, nothing but a speck against the power the Council held all over all? He had to find out before he plunged in a path that may well damn him and all those who believed in him. So he asked him directly:

"Why should I accept your offer? What makes you certain, what can you do to us that you have not done already? Haven't you stifled growth, education, trade, economy? Isn't almost everything under your control, in one form or another? Except perhaps the air we breath. Even the earth and the water, so indispensable to life itself, has become a commodity, something to be sold and acquired, according to your sick whims and desires. Even though that has held true for generations, we are willing to give our lives to stop this. Believe me, we will; unquestioningly, unflinchingly. How will you break that resolve, I ask you? Since you are the one that has caused this, its your Law and your rule that has brought things too far. What good will the vanishing tricks do? Will you just vanish when the crowds of free men will be running after you, demanding nothing less than your head? Or will you put on another light show like the one around me, hoping that the people you consider animals will be dazed and so sublimed that they'll beg you for forgiveness for their sins? Tell me, oh Holy Avatar, why should we capitulate without even a fight?"

"I never thought you were capable of such blandishment, dear Ursempyre. Yes, it is marvelous the way you people have been ground down to little more than mere animals. I must admit I sometimes feel a certain measure of pride at what I have achieved here. As for your other question, I believe that you should be careful not to confuse what you have seen here with the true extend of my powers. This is not a show I put on for you specifically, Lord Remis. It is merely an extension of courtesy, in good faith. I simply meant to cast off my regular mask, to create an honest, conversational atmosphere in which I could nurture a more direct relationship with you, vis-a-vis. I simply showed you that I am not the man you might have thought I was but I am far more resourceful and much more dangerous than what you think. Tell me, Ursempyre, have you heard of Shan the Traitor? The terrible Betrayer? And the Day of Redemption?"

Ursempyre did not expect such a reference at such a time. The last thing he expected right at that time was a lesson in history and tales. But he indulged the Patriarch, who seemed to be trying to veer him off course nevertheless:

"I have. It is supposed to be a part of history that has been wiped clean. I believe it is a myth, an insidious lie spread purposefully to dishearten, discourage any who would even think about opposing you; a story to suppress their anger with fear and awe, with a promise of terrible retribution and divine wrath. An angel of the Gods who would come down from above and wipe us all in one sweep, one fell blow? Is that what you would have me believe? That you have that kind of power? That you will pray to your Gods and they will crush us like ants? Is your purpose to turn me, Patriarch, or is it to make me laugh?"

"Yes, it would stand to reason to think of it as a mere lie, a fabricated tale or another piece of propaganda, but the truth is much more simple. I do possess that kind of power."

The Patriarch took a step back, and extended his arms. He took on a solemn expression, as if praying or concentrating deeply. A strange smell assaulted Ursempyre's nostrils. It seemed to emanate from the Patriarch as far as Ursempyre could tell. A smell that reminded him of metal against metal, the smell of a blacksmith's shop but all he could see was that the Patriarch was now a bit taller than before. 'No,' he thought, 'he is not taller'. 'Something's wrong here,' his mind voiced with concern. He noticed the Patriarch's feet were no longer touching the ground. Faint bluish crackles of light like tiny lightnings and sparks of light coursed through the Patriarch, his bald scalp having taken on an eerie sheen as if it had suddenly transformed into a shiny metal mirror. The Patriarch grinned and uttered in High Helican:

"Behold, the Holy Avatar."

With that, the Patriarch tensed and a bright shiny aura began to emanate from him. His robes were drawn in, tightened around his body as if they had instantly shrunk. They visibly outlined his figure, and Ursempyre was surprised once more to see that such a body did not belong to an old man. It was an immaculate body, perfectly carved as if it were a statue; the penultimate monument to the human body, its musculature detailed beyond any artisan's capabilities and talent. It was the body a demi-God, exuding awe by sight alone. The Patriarch's face began to twist and reshape itself as if it was made of water or mercury; all his facial characteristics were turning into a pool engulfed in bright light, as if fire was about to scorch it. And all the while he could see the grin of the Patriarch, even though his face was no longer there. His mind reeled from the sight before him. It was true then; this was a monster beyond comparison. The stories and legends were true. And the Day of Redemption had happened. And it was him who had made it happen. It was him all along. Even before, all those years past. It had always been him. The realization left him wide-eyed struggling for breath. The robes around the Patriarch were absorbed into his flesh, which was now a rippling pool of molten metal, incandescent with a fiery aura around it. He was levitating a few feet above the ground, resplendent and regal in its unique and terrible form. The figure spoke at him, with no visible source for its voice:

"I hate to show off but you forced my hand. I would really hate to raze the City just to convince you, Ursempyre. I believe you would hate to be the reason of such a slaughter. Do I have your attention now?"

Ursempyre could not know whether he was hearing the voice through his ears or simply in his mind. How little it mattered now, he thought. He only managed to nod, still staring at the majestic being in front of him.

"Please say it Ursempyre. Do you capitulate? Will you become my Castigator?", said the perfect, floating fiery figure of the transformed Patriarch.

Ursempyre felt shocked, minuscule, and unimportant. They were up against a being of unimaginable power, not based solely on its manipulations, schemes, and outright terror practices. This was something else entirely, he was the wielder of terrible force. A demon that left one mesmerized in awe. 'Why couldn't this be a mere show?', he thought. How could he have lived so long ago? How could he have brought such destruction by himself alone? How did he know he wasn't just lying, as was his usual practice? Such thoughts pained him with their inability to be answered.

He knew. When he saw him change into that thing, he saw. He felt its corruption overwhelm him and its malevolence flow around him, its power beaming right through him. It was true. He didn't know how exactly it was possible, but it was true. He could wipe them out if he needed too, if he wanted to. He did not believe that thing could be hurt, not in any real sense. He did not know whether the Patriarch himself was still vulnerable, but he now believed this was his true form, and the old man a mere charade he found more practical. Perhaps it was another one of his whims. It didn't matter, this was inescapable. He had no options now. All he had been planning was for naught. He would play along. But he would not give up. No, he knew they were at a disadvantage, but that was now a blessing. Had they went on with their plan, they would have been culled like sheep. It was almost as if he was trying to give them a warning, a second chance. Ursempyre decided he would capitulate; he would accept, but only for a while. Only until he knew what was going on this world of his and what was the truth behind all this. Until he found out who was this being that had ruled over them for untold years with iron and steel, whip and truncheon? He'd do what he could, and perhaps find a way to bring him down. The others, though, who had not seen what he had seen, would they believe him? Or would they just curse him as the traitor he would seem to have become? He could do little about that. He only hoped they'd forgive him before his end. That somehow this would work out. He turned to face the fiery figure, and looking at where its eyes should have been, managed to utter levelly:

"I will. I only do this because I now believe you when you say lives will be lost to no avail. Always remember that. Always remember that I only do this as the lesser evil, and nothing more. I will only serve my people, not you; ever. If I find a way to turn against you, I will do so, without hesitation."

"Yes, indeed. I'm sure you will. Now that we finally settled this matter, I'll issue the relevant orders and perform the Ceremony of Kyryksis. Naturally, once you ascend to office you will also issue a statement for your men to stand down and reconcile their grievances, as reforms are sure to be made and an arrangement has been agreed upon for a gradual transition into a free society. I believe the majority will accept such a turn of events with relief. No one likes dying. Except for a few fools that will probably follow your plan to the end anyway. Nothing important that my people will not be able to handle. Congratulations on a well-informed decision, Lord Remis."

The Patriarch returned to his human form in mere moments, the transition this time a lot quicker and much less dramatic. He offered his hand grinning profusely, but Ursempyre did not accept it. He rather looked at the Patriarch's hand with boiling contempt and disgust. The Patriarch insisted, the hand still extended for a handshake, and said:

"Please, Lord Remis. I only rarely bite people. It is a simple handshake. Once you become the Castigator, you will be required to *kiss* my hand; for the sake of appearances, naturally."

Ursempyre's face was tense, as if carved of stone. His equally hard glare at the Patriarch with eyes like fiery pinpricks of unyielding light, indicated that he was expending huge amounts of patience and self-restrain in order for him not to lunge at the Patriarch right then and there. But he would bide his time. With obvious reluctance and slow, deliberate motions that brought to mind a man in pain, he managed to shake hands with the Patriarch. He felt like he now carried a stain he could never wash off. He paused in thought and asked the Patriarch who was about to call out to the guards:

"Tell me one more thing. Why didn't you make me do it? Why didn't you force me, with some of those bewildering powers of yours?"

The Patriarch paused in his step, turned to look at Ursempyre and smiled brightly before replying:

"Oh, my dear Castigator Remis; that would be cheating, wouldn't it?"

All in good time

 tall bleak man in a uniform approached a couple of soldiers that were standing over a fire. A kettle on top was brewing something with an uncharacteristic, though quite off-putting smell. They were sitting on some sacks laden with what must have been rice or wheat and having a smoke, sharing a pipe of what one knowledgeable in the art of uwe smoking could make out to be stale uwe. They were unaware of the tall man coming their way with their backs turned to him. They were admiring the ships loading and unloading their cargoes in the distance of the harbor, with the suns setting down one after the other, painting the sea mauve and bloody red and the sails casting their last shadows for the day. Their calm reverie was broken by a harsh, raspy voice:

"What's in that kettle? Smells worse than the cow dung you're smoking. Is it to cover that gods-awful stench you're giving off? Last time you bathed, it must've been when the midwife rinsed off your mother's blood."

One of the two soldiers turned around and with a fleeting look of small surprise offered the pipe to the tall man, in spite of him sounding provocatively belittling. The other soldier remained indifferent; his head seemed to follow a flock of seabirds in the distance, swooping over the sea probably hunting fish, or perhaps idling away their time just as they were. The tall man was now standing with one foot on a stack of sacks. He took the proffered pipe and drew a quaff of smoke savoring it before exhaling slowly, and then spoke to the two soldiers:

"Truly, worse than cow dung. I'd have you flogged but I'd be wasting the procrastinators' time on some thickset pachyderm hides."

The one soldier that still hadn't turned to look at the man and was gazing at the harbor almost sleepily asked him, his tone of voice revealing a genuine ignorance:

"What's a pachyderm, dekar?"

"From what I'm told your wife for one, and perhaps your mother too."

With that, both the dekar and the soldier who offered him the pipe laughed heartily. The other soldier seemed taken aback by the incongruous humor and shuffled himself on the sack uneasily, responding with childlike bitterness:

"Well you can have your laughs for dinner, cause I ain't serving you no Mott's famous Langarfan stew tonight."

The dekar, their squad leader, went wide-eyed in apparent disbelief and a wide grin appeared on his face:

"That's the stench? Lanra.. Langar.. Whatever, that's supposed to be stew? Mott, save us the trouble and run us through with a sword right here were we sit. I'd wager it's faster and less painful for my innards. Can't speak for Lanris here, he seems to be brave or stupid enough to eat that snot of yours. I think it's because he's stupid."

"Let's just say it's an acquired taste, dekar."

"Where did you acquire it then? The swamps?"

The dekar broke in laughter once again, but this time Lanris did not accompany him but instead turned and replied casually:

"No jokes dekar. It is an acquired taste. It's taken me the better part of four years now to finally begin to enjoy Mott's cooking. So don't spoil it. As they say, dig in or get out."

"There'll be no digging in for dekar Pirru tonight. Or ever. I'll leave those lowly menial tasks to you two men. Or what remotely resembles men. Ha."

Dekar Pirru shook his head, grinning at the same time. Mott was now stirring his broth with a thick wooden stick that just seemed to have been lying around handily. Lanris was putting some fresh uwe in his pipe. Twilight was upon them, the smoke from their kettle barely visible. Dekar Pirru seemed suddenly engrossed with thought with his gaze stuck on the boiling kettle and his eyes seemingly out of focus. Lanris took notice, waved his hand to check if indeed the dekar was in touch with his surroundings and found out that was not the case. He said with some lack of conviction:

"Dekar?Dekar Pirru?"

The dekar slowly turned his gaze to Lanris and made a sort of grumbling sound with eyes focused once again and a furrowed brow. Lanris continued:

"You seemed lost in thought. What's on your mind? New ways to drill us to death? Make us more miserable? Take away our cir rations? What is it that's had you daydreaming?"

"Hmm? I'm not daydreaming, mind you. Plain old bothers, that's all. This mobilization. Doesn't seem right. Not to me at least. You think this is all well and dandy?"

The dekar was standing upright again with arms folded, the sheath of his dangling about his belt, his expression a bit sour. Lanris on the other hand seemed quite relaxed, resting on the sacks nonchalantly and seemingly more concerned about the serving time of Mott's stew. He took a drought of smoke from his pipe, before answering his dekar without turning to look at him:

"Not my place to tell, dekar. I just sharpen my sword, fill my pipe and gulp down what Mott fancies each time. Though his menu is kind of repetitive. It must be the fourth time in a row we're having stew," said Lanris with a mixed feeling of resignation and indifference.

Mott interjected abruptly, as if he were chiding Lanris:

"Fifth time in a row. I'm getting us some karch tomorrow. Makes fine soup. You can piss off if you don't like karch soup, rummage about the camp and see what you find. Perhaps you'll find a nice boot to munch on."

Lanris leaned over and slapped Mott on the shoulder jovially. He was smiling when he said:

"That'll be fine Mott. Karch's soup's fine. Don't get jumpy on me. If I can eat the sludge they serve on marches, I can sure as hell eat some of your cooking. It's not a gray ooze and that's enough in my book to make it a *gourmet* dish."

Lanris intoned the somewhat haughty word with a certain character and an outlandish accent that made everyone laugh, especially Mott whose sullen mood was eased and was now up on his feet again, stirring his stew with a certain air of culinary dexterity. Around them more campfires could be seen, soldiers like them who were about to cook something of their own, usually broths of wheat or barley which were the main staple food the army provided.

They were about to relax from the exercises of the day, as well as their other various duties. Some would eat something quick before heading off for sentry and patrol duty and some very lucky few would rest their aching muscles, have a pipe and perhaps something to fill their bellies and then sleep heavily until the next morning.

Some would have made their own arrangements concerning food

perhaps going out of their way to procure some meat either by hunting or by making certain trades, sometimes of a dubious nature. Most of the soldiers that did so, traded wine for meat or eggs. Wine and spirits were strongly forbidden but vinegar was allowed to be carried, as it was a proven and allowed way of cleaning up wounds as well as widely used in the soldier's personal hygiene. At least for those that had one.

Some had a knack of mixing some vinegar with wine right before consuming it, in case some of the officers or procrastinators were making their rounds checking up on morale, or discipline in the latter case. It marred the quality and taste of the wine, but that was usually low to begin with anyway. Some had dubbed it winegar, and the name was in wide use throughout the army.

Even the officers partook sometimes, as it was known to them that the morale and cohesion of an army was far more important in battle than mere discipline and adherence to Law. It might be a sin, they knew, but who went through life as immaculate and free of sin as in their day of birth?

And as long as those buffoons, the procrastinators, were none the wiser, everything worked almost as it should; the army served its Castigator and the Pantheon in a most untroubled fashion. After all as some of the older officers used to say, 'you can't make soldiers out of men if you don't break open a few casks first.'

Mott announced with some enthusiasm in his voice:

"Ready to serve! Dekar, you sure you don't want some of this? Works wonders for the stomach."

The dekar was sharing some of Lanris pipe when he replied after exhaling thoroughly, wisps of smoke coming out of his mouth and nose:

"I'd rather not empty it right now, if that's what you mean. You can relish it all by yourselves. Don't let me stop you."

Mott simply shrugged and went to his backpack to fetch his canteen. Lanris did so with languid motions, certain that the broth in Mott's kettle would not disappear any time soon.

They each helped themselves to a serving and sat down on the ground with their backs against the sacks. They split some leftover bread-pie from their midday meal, and each began eating from their canteens. Mott was clearly more than pleased with the quality of his cooking, gulping spoonfuls away with vivid enjoyment. Lanris seemed much more reserved in his appreciation, and looked simply thankful for having something other than the drab, gray gunk the army called food to fill his stomach with.

Pirru was looking idly at them while they were having their supper, and after a while he said:

"You know, I heard the Castigator came around to visit the day before yesterday. No pomp and ceremony though. If that were the case I'm sure everyone would have known. We'd probably still be marching up and down parading our asses off."

Lanris paused momentarily and furrowed his brow before continuing to eat slowly, more so because he wasn't too fond of Mott's stew rather than because he was savoring it. Mott on the other hand was scraping the last spoonfuls from his canteen, and was quite possibly going to refill it soon. Dekar Pirru went on:

"I see that didn't get your attention, did it? Nothing short of your discharge papers would, I guess. The thing is, seems he had a talk with the General. Didn't last long. Short and to the point, his staff officers seem to say."

Mott was up on his feet once more, pouring some smoking hot stew in his canteen. He asked Pirru while sitting down to enjoy it:

"So, did word get out of what they talked about? Perhaps his Piousness had gotten word of a fine chef among the Army's 15th, and wanted some of my recipes?"

Lanris threw a sideways glance at Mott, before throwing a piece of bread-pie to his head as well. He did not add a verbal insult though, and kept trying to consume the broth left in his canteen. Pirru grinned at Mott's comment and said with a slight edge of worry in his voice:

"No, I'm afraid his Holiness has not expressed any sort of death wish. I'm sure you'd be happy to serve in that case. In the most literal sense. Word around the staff officers is there has been a change of plans."

Lanris left his canteen unfinished, broth and bread-pie still mixed inside. He placed it near Mott, who surely would not let it go to waste once he emptied hiw own canteen once more. Lanris wiped his mouth with his sleeve, and started filling his pipe from a pouch he had not opened before. He asked Pirru then:

"Dekar, how come you got by all these news? It's not like you to run around staff officers like Himmdal and Rynse do. You've said it yourself; if we even get a whiff about you sucking up to a staff officer, we can strip that dekar badge ourselves. So shall we each grab an arm and do the deed?"

Dekar Pirru looked at Lanris with one eye pointing a finger at him, his rasp voice making the threat almost believable:

"Wise-guys get picket duty on the northern face. I'll make sure we stick you on the fence itself. You'll make a good scarecrow."

Lanris lit up his pipe nonchalantly. Mott was taking care of Lanris' leftovers and Pirru went on:

"As I was saying, word is easy to go around. I didn't fetch coffee and wash uniforms for the staff officers to get by that important piece of intelligence. I used my cunning and my sharp mind. As well as some coin that I'd won on the zar game the night before. Nothing ventured, nothing gained."

Mott put down Lanris canteen empty and burped loudly, feeling his stomach with one hand. He turned to look at his dekar with an evident smile of satisfaction on his lips, and said:

"So you went to the 'Cent."

Pirru started to say something in an apparent protest, probably a mild reprimand, but Lanris added behind a small cloud of pure uwe smoke:

"Yeah, he went to the 'Cent. Probably ripped him off too. Like the last time when he asked ten coin for some real Iolathan wine that turned out to be vinegar. Not even winegar, mind you. Plain old vinegar from the pharmacium stores. He even had the nerve to insist that it was a vintage bottle that had could be easily mistaken for vinegar by someone who wasn't a connoisseur. I think he meant you, dekar."

"You can make a fool of me all you like Lanris, but I won't be on the earthworks tomorrow morning, digging up dirt like some soldiers I happen to know."

Mott was enjoying a bit of rest, one leg propped up against the other and hands behind his head, his back flat on the ground. He added with a naive feeling of surprise:

"Oh, you mean Guilemont and Howe? I knew you didn't like

them a great deal, but putting them on the auxiliaries list; now that must mean they really pissed on you proper."

Lanris was hugging his face with one hand, always surprised at the ways Mott could sound like a complete dolt. Pirru went on:

"Something like that. Anyway, yes, I went to the 'Cent. 'One hundred per cent guaranteed' Tibodot, the little rat. But I got my coin's worth now. He wasn't selling cow dung this time. I asked the Centarch somewhat sideways if all was going as planned, and he too said there was some upheaval upstairs. Some stuff would be put on hold until further notice. That's probably the reason I'm not putting the pair of you on auxiliary tomorrow. The auxiliary's been abandoned. All men are rotating back in their usual duties, as per regulation. Lanris, you are lucky bastards."

Lanris took a quaff from his pipe, savored it and exhaled; the smell of fine uwe smoke wafted through the air around them. He said to Pirru:

"Actually, I learned about the auxiliary from a guy I trade regularly with at the 4th. He comes up with uwe, I come up with.. Stuff. Told me the auxiliary's gone starting from tomorrow. So, I figured you couldn't push is into something worse than what we're already at. Didn't hear about the Castigator or the General though."

"You should've pushed for rank, Lanris. Field Maggot Lanris has a ring to it, doesn't it? Anyway, spare me the dung talk. I got some details on that meeting as well. 'Cent says that we're waiting for some new marching orders."

"Not the Widelands then?", Mott cut in with enthusiasm, a glimmer of hope in his words.

"Can we ever be sure? If the marching orders do not explicitly say 'Widelands', they could well be saying 'No-man's land', or 'West of the City of Pyr', or 'Middle of Nowhere'. It still wouldn't change much, would it? All it means, is there's something serious going on."

Mott cut in again, this time puzzlement in his voice:

"Where's Sirius going to? Got transferred, like he wanted? Steam-gunner Battalion?"

Pirru sighed, before uttering a mild curse concerning Mott's mother. He went on, concentrating his focus on Lanris who was now listening more intently, having sat up and facing the dekar. He offered his pipe to Pirru who refused it with a slight nod, and went on:

"Mott, just shut up and go to sleep. As I was saying, there's a lot going on. I just hope the General knows his stuff so we don't end up on the wrong side of the turf."

Lanris thought a while about what dekar Pirru had been telling them, and said with an air of indifference about him:

"Well, going into the Widelands seemed strange. But orders are orders, right? So now, when we get new orders, they'll still be orders. I don't think it changes anything. About me at least. As long as I get my uwe and even if I have to put up with Mott's cooking, it doesn't mean much. Just one thousand four hundred and thirty one days to go, dekar. That's all that counts for me."

"You're all the same, you conscripts. You just want to get on with your lives, like it gets any better out there. Still, I don't blame you. If something's going to kill you, it doesn't really matter where that will happen. I just happen to find change a bad thing, that's all."

"You're not trying to drag me down in one of your morose spells, are you?"

Pirru nodded while shrugging, an almost disarming and childlike reaction from a dekar well-nigh six feet tall. After a short silence was observed, he grinned to Lanris before replying:

"I got wine. Not winegar, but real wine."

Lanris forehead creased in a conspirator's furrow:

"How did you get by that, I wonder?"

The dekar replied in a hushed voice, a measure of pride in his words:

"Smuggled some from the centarch's cabinet. This stuff is guaranteed."

Lanris scratched his chin thoughtfully while he seemed to contemplate the risks involved, and said:

"I see. So, we're both risking forty lashes."

Dekar Pirru waved a hand dismissively and replied:

"Twenty for me, I'll pull rank."

They both laughed, somewhat bitterly despite themselves. Pirru checked hastily around, not really bothering to indeed look for procrastinators or senior officers lurking in the dark, but rather as an instinctive reaction to fear of getting caught. He reached into his uniform and produced a small leather flask, no bigger than their issued water flask. He unsealed it and gave it to Lanris. He said with a wide grin of accomplishment:

"Smell that? Pure Decau wine."

Lanris took a whiff, grimaced and shuddered reflexively. He gave the flask back to Pirru with exasperation in his voice:

"Gods dammit dekar, why the hell does the centarch buy his stuff from 'Cent? That's winegar."

Pirru looked genuinely surprised. He took a small sip from the flask and gulped it down. His face lit up with a look of recognition:

"It really is winegar. Seems the centarch bought 'Cent's dung speeches as well. But still, it's better than nothing, right?"

Lanris had a sour look on his face, but he nodded in agreement:

"Guess it is. Lemme have a swig."

Pirru handed the flask of winegar to Lanris. Mott could be heard snoring smoothly. A rather unfamiliar voice was suddenly heard from the edges of the darkness around them:

"Let me see that flask, dekar. I hope it's not winegar, is it?"

"Dekar Pirru and Private Lanris of the 5th, under the command of Cilliarch Romentho Isoract were put to the sword today at dawn immediately before roll call, by a squad of procrastinators. Expeditious procedures were followed and their files of death were officially sealed by both the Procrastinator's Office and the Strategium Proper. Private Mott of the 5th, was given fifty lashes and almost bled to death for, and I quote: 'Not being vigilant enough in the persecution of vile deeds that promoted sin, incurred the wrath of the Gods or were an affront to the Pantheon and the Ruling Council'. He was not allowed to return to his duties as an active soldier and as such was denied of medical attention. He was rotated to the work gangs as per the Cilliarch's orders. Also, Cilliarch Isoract relieved centarch Littmo from his duties and has petitioned that he be discharged dishonorably. The winegar in question seems to have been stolen from the centarch's personal cabinet, from what the procrastinators' investigation revealed."

Major Guighan saluted crisply and remained there standing like a statue, completely immovable, his one hand holding his reports and the other hand a fist touching his shiny unadorned breastplate, right above the heart.

General Tyrpledge saluted briefly, barely touching his breastplate with his relaxed fist and sighed. Major Guighan clicked his heels and resumed a more relaxed, but still attentive posture before asking the general:

"Sir, will that be all? Should I continue with my other assignments, or is there something else you'd have me do, sir?"

Tyrpledge seemed to ponder that suggestion for a little while, briefly considering what he should have the Major do. He was rather disenchanted by everything today. He was looking at the ceiling in a noncommital manner, the expression on his face lacking its usually austere, professional look. He had taken a look in his mirror earlier. He supposed he looked kind of glum and morose, perhaps even outright sad. There wasn't much he could about it, he thought. Neither was there something for the major to do as well. He waved him away with one hand, while he kept tapping a marching tune on his desk with the fingers of his other hand.

At length he spoke:

"No, that will be all major. Nothing else you can do for me. I'll bark if I need anything."

The major was about to laugh when he saw the general was not smiling when he said what the major had thought of as funny. He then clicked his heels and made a couple of paces backwards still facing the general. He then turned about smartly and left, careful to close the door behind him.

Tyrpledge sighed more audibly this time, thinking this day had started off more badly than usual. Though the term 'usual' was rapidly evolving from day to day, this day seemed as bad as bad days can get. And it was still early morning. Major Guighan had just given him the latest situational report. These two men were the first dead in this campaign, and not a single enemy had been met yet. They'd been executed for drinking winegar and stealing from an officer. The centarch's career was gone. Perhaps at an opportune time, though.

Last night a message had arrived, complete with high-ranking ministers and a squad of the procrastinator elite. Tyrpledge had been notified that the army was now officially mobilized and legally at war. Of course, he thought, there were no specific orders included, other than that he should await for further notification at a later time. In essence, they were leaving him and his men to roast on red hot coals until it suited their purpose. Such was the fate of soldiers, he mused bitterly.

Those orders had cost those men from the 5th their lives. As it is, they were at war even though they didn't know with who and that meant that by Law, the procrastinators dispersed among them had more authority than he did in matters of discipline, the prosecution of sinners and the relevant penalties that might apply.

It seemed that in wartime, theft and consumption of spirits and other substances that 'occluded the mind' were punishable by death. Tyrpledge was thinking that the centarch whose life was destroyed was lucky compared to his men. He then spared a few moments thinking about the soldier who was found asleep, next to the ones that had been drinking.

They had given him fifty lashes because he wasn't vigilant enough. And then they had left him to bleed to death. Tyrpledge's thoughts on the matter was that it would be a miracle if he made it out alive. But that's what war was about: bloodletting.

"Logic is thrown out the window," he voiced his final thoughts in hushed tones, almost a whisper. He sat upright in his chair with his hands outstretched, his gaze focused outside beyond his window where he could see the majority of his battalions forming up. He could discern a sullen mood. It was not that the pace of the men milling about was slow. They were preparing their equipment fastidiously, checking their armor and their packs so as to make sure everything was in order. They had that unmistakable air of professionalism about them. But they seemed to be lacking the blaze in their eyes. The glimmer, the red flush cheeks that let you know their blood was boiling and their hearts pumping it with excitement. There were no such signs here. No nervous humor from his staff members, no raunchy jokes from the enlisted men. At least he couldn't see any of them laughing. Every face he could make out from that distance was stern and frigid. These, he thought, should not be the faces of men going to war knowing they might be dead before the night falls, wishing their death would be worthwhile and remembered, perhaps even praised. These were the faces of men thinking they might be dead before the day was through, wishing they were someplace else.

The execution of the men from the 5th had taken quite a toll on overall morale. They might be much more cowed now, but that's not what he needed to wage war. He needed hot-bloodied men with vices and things to wish for. Not meek little children fearful of the reprisals of the Law. Why couldn't the procrastinators understand that?

For the briefest moment he thought about contacting the Procrastinator Militant asking for his assistance, perhaps telling him even to go as far as relaxing their vigilance in an effort to bend but not strictly break the Law.

He immediately thought better of it since he reminded himself that Gomermont was above all, first and foremost, an idiot. Telling an idiot who had spent a considerable amount of time and effort to become leader of a pack of idiots to smarten up a bit suddenly was, if not a one-way ticket to the gallows, a certain way to scream in despair at the mind-numbing foolishness the Procrastinator Militant exuded with his every utterance. In essence, it would be a lost cause.

There was a time for war and a time for peace, security, stability, and lawfulness. War was lawlessness in itself, a grandiose lawless fair where people died horribly and for reasons beyond their understanding; a time when nothing mattered more than victory. When would they understand that? Not soon enough it seemed, probably never as well.

His bleak thoughts were accented by the lack of a good cup of uwe. He decided he wanted a nice distraction, something to take his mind of a situation he now felt powerless to amend. He would just have to swim through the wave of the coming difficulties as they arose stoically. To do that he had to have a good cup of uwe, fresh and steamy.

He now felt determined to turn his thoughts around and wish for the best, keep his hopes up. The uwe would be critical in that respect. He went for his bell in order to let his aide-de-camp know he wanted some uwe urgently but before he could do that, as if by a miracle or a mind-reading ability that the major had not exhibited so far, he saw major Guighan enter through the door in a hurried fashion, stand to one side, salute briskly and click the heels of his boots tucking his sword away with his free hand.

Before Tyrpledge could utter a single word, the Castigator of the

Outer Territories walked in the general's office resplendent in his war gear, a match for what he was wearing on the anniversary of the Pacification of Zaelin; the brightly polished metal cast intense reflections of the suns.

The major tried to announce the Castigator's arrival, but he was cut short by a wave of the Castigator's hand, barely having had time to utter the word 'behold'. The Castigator was dressed for war, that much was certain. With his lavishly plumed helmet held under one arm, he asked the general directly, who was still sitting down in his chair, too flabbergasted to adhere to protocol and pay proper respect:

"General Tyrpledge, are your forces ready to march?"

Tyrpledge rose up from his seat, cleared his throat and replied in a steady, professional voice:

"The Army is ready to march for war, your Reverence."

"Very well. Signal your brigadiers to assemble, general. We move as fast as possible."

The Castigator nodded and made a turn to leave, before Tyrpledge asked with some hesitation:

"Thy will be done, sire. May I ask though, sire, where to?"

The Castigator's voice trailed off as he left the General's office, feeling it wasn't necessary for him to pause in his stride and turn to speak to the General:

"The City of Pyr."

She woke up drenched in sweat and threw her blanket away. Her breathing came fast and heavy. She had seen a nightmare. This time she had been captured by men with no face. The memory of it was still vivid. The men had tried to kill her child, without killing her outright.. She had made every effort not to let them, but in vain. They had their way with her and left there where she lay, in a damp place that smelled of metal and rust. They'd left her there to die, right next to the body of her murdered child. She shivered at the thought and felt dry tears staining her cheeks. She must have screamed when she woke up, because Ikebod, House Remis' master servant, was running down the stairs with a glass of water in one hand, when he said:

"Lady Celia! I heard screams, are you alright?"

She nodded in acknowledgement, visibly somewhat shaken from her bad dream.

"I am better now. I saw a nightmare, that's all."

Ikebod offered her the glass of water which she eagerly accepted and sipped a little, just to wet her mouth and feel its freshness.

"I had not the heart to wake you from your sleep, so I brought some covers and left you in peace."

"That was very kind of you, Ikebod. Thank you."

A smile crept up in a corner of her mouth, but it was not as warm and as glittering as usual. It would be a little while until she recovered fully from her nightmare.

"You seem a little pale. That will not do in your situation. I have prepared dinner myself. I was waiting for Master Ursempyre to return but that has yet to happen. I admit I am more than worried for his safety. He was summoned by the Patriarch himself. His delay could mean a lot of things, most of which I dare not think about. In any case, he would not want a guest of his to starve to death, especially an expecting lady. I would be happy to serve you dinner, even though it is now past midnight."

Ikebod's tone belied his fear. He sounded calm and accommodating, professional as ever. As if the danger his master was probably facing was no more than a hindrance, an annoyance at best, and that he would soon be surely meeting them at the dinner table. Celia on the other hand sat upright with a jolt, her eyes went wide and her face wore a mixed expression of anxiety, disbelief and exasperation. Her voice was pitched high when she said to Ikebod, staring him with a frown:

"Went to meet with the Patriarch you say? Under the circumstances, that does sound too fortuitous for comfort. Could it be that the uprising has been revealed? Your master could be in grave danger, Ikebod! Surely you must've heard the stories! The Patriarch makes people vanish as if they never had been born! And you ask of me to have dinner at such a time? How could I ever?"

Ikebod took the courage of sitting right beside her, a gesture he would have normally found insulting beyond forgiveness, indeed beyond absolution. Nevertheless, he felt lady Celia would not be offended and he wanted her to understand him wholly on the matter:

"Dear lady Celia I know all that, and still I would ask of you to have something to eat. For your child's sake. Do not think of me as a cynic, or a blandly acquiescent servant. I dearly love Master Ursempyre, for I almost raised him as my own ever since his parents passed away when he was still just a little boy. Right before he left the estate, he gave me specific orders in the event of his disappearance. I too believe in the kinsfolk and the purpose that drives them. I would be betraying my master if I wavered, if I gave up without a fight, if I thought him dead and gone so easily. But even without him, lady Celia, life must go on. We must try our hardest to have freedom for all, for once. If anything should happen to him, I will grieve like a father who's lost his only child. But I've learned there's a time for grieving and a time for hoping; a time for fighting. And so I shall hope and fight, until I have reason to do nothing else but grieve. Do you understand that, my lady? I hope you do. Please now, come and have something to eat; if not for your sake, for your child's."

Celia looked in the old servant's eyes with compassion and a sudden care she had not felt until now. She thought she understood. In a manner, that was how she felt for Amonas who though was nowhere to be found and had not seen or heard from him for days now, she still knew he was alive. Against reason, she knew he was alive somewhere. And she'd better give up her life before she gave up hope. Because, she thought, even if Amonas would never return, their child would be born. And she would have to do her best to deliver her child in a new, free world. Even if her love would not be there to greet their firstborn.

She stifled some tears that welled up in her eyes and sniffed slightly. She nodded her understanding to Ikebod, and without further comment or remark she tried to smile uncomfortably and asked him:

"What will we be having for dinner then? I believe the baby will not mind at all."

Ikebod rose from the coach and offered his hand as leverage to Celia. He smiled and told her:

"Please, right this way. The table is set."

They went up the stairs where they were greeted by a large dining-hall, dark green and gray marble columns supporting the high ceiling. Exquisitely ornamented chandeliers adorned the roof and cast bright candlelight across every corner. The grand dinner table was made from a fine solid piece of wood that seemed old and venerable; judging by its healthy sheen it was also thoroughly maintained. It was probably hundred of years old and from its size, Celia thought it could seat upwards of three dozen people, perhaps even four. She noticed there were no plates of food or dishes of any kind set and she was slightly puzzled. They were probably to be seated somewhere else then, she thought.

He led her to an antechamber through a utility corridor, meant for the servants to have access to the kitchen. Celia asked with evident interest:

"Where is everyone else by the way? I haven't seen a soul."

"Oh, most are asleep by now my lady. The maids tended to your room, and it's ready for you. I suggest you lie down there right after your dinner. Some of the other servants and the guards have certain duties to attend to in other parts of the estate, mainly the stables from what I can gather. House Remis is not always this silent, perhaps in the morning you will see for yourself."

Celia inquired no further and soon they entered the kitchen itself. Dimly lit by a few candles, it was full of utensils and large wooden surfaces for chopping meat and foodstuffs. She could see there were more than one stoves and at least large ovens. Large empty bowls, cauldrons and kettles were gathered in one corner. Though quite large for a kitchen, Celia felt the place was cramped and imagined it would be close to asphyxiating when people were working here in full swing. Ikebod pulled a chair for her and gestured for her to sit.

She thanked him with a smile, and sat down to a quite normal table that seemed to have seen its fair share of use. It was indeed laid out with a simple linen, the bowl of soup in the middle, as well as a glass and a wooden jug of wine side by side. Her plate was already filled with steaming soup, which gave off a light aroma. Indeed, the kitchen smelled of a lot of things, and the odors seemed to fight each other fervently with no clear winner. She realized the smells exacerbated her hunger and she started to sip her soup eagerly. Ikebod asked Celia:

"My feet ache. They tend to do that at my age. Would you mind if I silently kept you company?"

"I might have asked you that myself. Please do, by all means."

She felt genuinely happy and thankful there was time enough for her to enjoy a nice meal. It reminded her of happier times, as if everything was alright in the world.

Her thoughts were disturbed by what seemed to be sounds akin to yelling and shouting coming from other parts of the house. She could hear there was some uproar, voices from rooms above conversing loudly. It was all too sudden. Ikebod was already leaving the kitchen. He turned to her as he stood at the open door:

"Please, stay here. I'll come back right away. Don't worry, you are safe. If we had been under attack I'd known from the sounds. There's some uproar, that's all. Probably important news. I won't be long."

Ikebod was at once gone from her sight. She returned her gaze to the table. The desserts were lying in her plate in front of her, half-eaten and unruly. She noticed she had not restrained herself from eating as she pleased, but she had rather enjoyed it. Which was only natural not to last forever, she thought. The dimly lit kitchen which had felt warm and full of wholesome smells, now seemed vacant, cold, and dark. She felt like leaving the room immediately and did so with some haste. She wanted to see and hear the news herself. Perhaps there was some news about Amonas; her heart skipped a beat at the thought, but she brought her mind to its senses. That would not cause such an uproar. "Something awful's going to happen", she said to herself in a hushed voice that echoed uncomfortably inside the empty kitchen.

She went through the corridor into the dinning-hall. She could hear voices from below, and she raced to the stairs leading to the waiting-room with wary expectation wrinkling her face. When she reached the feet of the stairs below, she could see Ikebod hurriedly conversing with three men, two of them clad in metal armor, and one of them bearing a disheveled cloak with mud and perhaps blood on his face. The two men must have been guards and were being issued orders probably, nodding emphatically at something Ikebod was explaining. The other man was evidently fatigued, perhaps injured, and he seemed exhausted from running. He was breathing heavily, once every so often gulping down some water from a tall jug.

She just stood there, not knowing if she should interrupt them, probably fearing she would ask something silly or impertinent. She thought that this was no time for being shy, and just called out for

Ikebod, not harshly, but demanding his attention:

"Sir Ikebod? What is the matter? What has happened?"

Ikebod and the other men turned to look at her with what felt like concern. After a brief pause of silence, Ikebod answered her:

"The army is on the move. Castigator Olorius Menamon the IV th has fled the city, and it seems he is in command of the army."

He paused again, this time his face visibly contorted by a strange mix of exasperation and sorrow, his eyes torn between shedding tears of anger or rueful weeping. Celia was transfixed where she stood, her breath coming in shallower with every word Ikebod spoke. At length he continued:

"And Lord Ursempyre Remis has been named the new Castigator."

Part III

Ad Veritas

The burial of the dead

"I believe I have gathered conclusive evidence as to the function of the various artifacts known as keystones. In fact, it can be safely proven by virtue of experimentation that these are in fact devices of a highly evolved civilization from an ancient past that perished long ago, leaving in its wake nothing but seemingly nondescript memorabilia as the remains of a monumental metropolis located in the Widelands, as evidenced in the writings of Esphalon. I can honestly say that such an unprecedented work as I am engaged in currently, will be proven to have earth-shattering effects and verily change our world forever."

- Curator Cimon Olom, *A treatise on the nature and function of the keystones*

Memory and desire

 MONAS had been watching Hilderich for what seemed to be the better part of an hour now. He had shocked Amonas

218

with what he believed they were looking at in the sky, but Amonas had seen it himself when he knew what to look for. They were indeed standing on another world, and not on their own. Because the suns were not simply wrong; there was only one sun. Hilderich had noticed the lack of a second ring around the sun, and the regularity of ths sun's shape and size, unlike their own two suns that seemed to come together and slightly draw themselves apart again every once in a while.

That was something Hilderich had come up with while intently studying the surface they were standing on, as well as the bases of the horns themselves. Amonas now saw him keep clutching the keystone, scratching it with a finger at times. He seemed to be quite absorbed in thought. Amonas had felt he could not contribute at this time, and did not bother Hilderich with questions or other small talk. He saw no way out of their situation and certainly no way to 'ride the flames' as Hilderich had put it with enthusiasm.

As Amonas replayed in his mind what Hilderich had tried to explain to him, the idea seemed extravagantly far-fetched; more like a Curator's wild fantasy than anything that seemed to hold any ties with the realm of reality.

Hilderich insisted that they keystone was what would enable them to realize 'the plan'. The plan was to signal the flaming sphere, bullet, missile or 'train', whatever one might call it, to stop and pick them up. Amonas thought that first and foremost, it was preposterous to consider that thing that rushed over their heads could be tamed, indeed made to stop. It sounded as if a man would command a falling star to cushion its fall, to peacefully glide to a stop so he could touch it. Accordingly, the idea that one could actually even board such a thing defied any kind of logic Amonas could summon. Hilderich was either totally insane or on the brink of an ingenious discovery that could dwarf everything Amonas had ever known, including the things that had been revealed to him when he had stepped into the damnable pillar of light in the first place.

He truly hoped the latter case would hold true. In the meantime, while Hilderich seemed to be muttering to himself, pacing about the flat, matte black floor of the summit, Amonas' thoughts turned to Celia. Had she given birth to their child? Were they safe? Had the uprising began?

He was afraid he would not be able to keep his promises to Celia. It all rested with Hilderich. It was a liberating emotion, in a sense, to have someone else hold the keys to your future. Someone else would to blame; someone else's success or failure was in essence, what would gain him a trip back home or a slow, harrowing death filled with guilt, remorse and memories that would haunt him for whatever life would remain in him. But was everything really hang on Hilderich's efforts? Was there nothing he could do or think of? Had he given up on them already?

This damnable place afforded him no real rest; it toyed with his fears, his doubts, and his ignorance. He threw a fist to the black floor which remained unyielding, unmarred and unbroken. The pain that swept up from his hand jogged him back into his more usual mindset.

Even if he didn't have the slightest idea about this place and the flaming sphere, Hilderich seemed to have at least some estimation; something to follow through, something that, however improbable, might work. If it failed they'd find something else, move on and think of a different idea. Perhaps study the bullhorns in depth, find out their purpose. The land could support them, so they would keep on trying to get home.

They would endure. All they had to do was endure and there would be found a way. 'There must be a way,' his mind echoed with that thought. He'd do his best to help Hilderich, even if that meant he'd have to trust him with his life. They'd get back, that's all that really mattered. He would get back home to Celia, and their child. He promised to himself he'd get back even if he'd have to limp back.

The clutches of reality were inescapable though and he snapped back to it when the sweat running down his forehead had turned into a small, steady trickle. The heat even under the shadows was uncomfortable. They did not have much in the way of water left, only a couple of the hard-skinned fruit.

He was wary of leaving Hilderich alone while he went back down to collect some more of the fruit, perhaps locate some source of running water as well. The fruit were watery enough, but their sweet taste would soon feel sickly if they kept consuming them all the time. He'd have to breach the subject sooner or later, but he decided to give

Hilderich some more time with his musings first.

They did not know when the next flaming sphere would appear and that only served to increase Amonas' uneasiness. He believed it would be much more accommodating if they went down to the base of the bullhorns where they could find shelter from the sun. He also thought that they could forage while going around the base of the bull-horned structure, which Hilderich was now calling a 'horned pyramid'.

Amonas thought that his was a much more sound, safe and logical plan. Hilderich had argued against it, saying that there should be enough time between passes for them to figure out how to use the flaming vehicle, and they should not wander away when they could be so close to escaping this place. Amonas had resisted the idea in more depth by pointing out that even if that were so, they had not heard or seen the passing of such a thing ever since they arrived here, which would imply that whatever that thing was, it did not make frequent overpasses.

Hilderich counter-argued that as was the case with wagons and carriages, arrivals and departures did not have to be evenly spaced and sometimes schedules changed without notice, because of necessity. Amonas had left it at that but they at least agreed to go down once their water supply had run out to rest and re-supply; at the same time they could search around the base of the horned pyramids for a possible way in.

Hilderich seemed to be lost in an inner circle of conjectures and theories that did not seem to produce any tangible practical benefits. At times he would stop and ask if Amonas had noticed anything new about the structure, especially the floor and the horns; Amonas would quietly and calmly insist that if anything to that effect did happen, he would surely notify him immediately. Hilderich would then nod and go back to his series of calculations.

He had already paced around the edges of the floor and had even walked over the shadows of the horns, seemingly measuring their length for reasons Amonas could not even hope to infer. It seemed like charlatanism; a madman in the wilderness trying to make sense of something bewilderingly distant like the suns or the stars, the color of the sky, and so on. But he would have to be patient and see for himself where it would lead.

They'd soon have to go down to the base of the pyramid for water mostly, Amonas thought and believed Hilderich should be feeling dry as sand, definitely having developed a sunburn by that time.

The keystone in Hilderich's hand felt more like a sigil or a charm to him, something he had to connect himself with. He kept touching it, running his fingers around it, but he had yet to use it as the device he had said he believed it to be. It was a greenish stone that gave off blue, near turquoise reflections. It seemed to have a certain depth, and a curious reflective quality about it.

It could be a raw gem, or something similar. Perhaps a glass, Amonas couldn't have been sure of its nature, and he certainly knew he was no expert. It was just that it had a very strange appearance, one that could not be easily compared to the usual cuts of stone or gem. Amonas thought that if nothing else at all, the keystone was a very rare thing indeed.

Rare enough for someone to keep collecting them, and rare enough to seal Olom's fate. He'd certainly miss him. Celia had never known, perhaps it was for the best. Now that he's really gone beyond.. Amonas felt it was a bit unfair on her. He felt guilty for not telling her the truth about her father, but it was a promise he would never break, and so had not. Perhaps in time, he could find it in his heart to tell her. On second thought he felt he was obligated to do so, actually. Just as soon as they got back, at a time that seemed to him quite indeterminable at that point.

With his thoughts on the matter concluded, Amonas decided he had stayed quiet for long enough and asked Hilderich who was standing near one far end of the summit, peering downwards over the edge:

"Any progress?"

Hilderich did not turn around, did not even stir or notion somehow. It seemed he was rather absorbed in thought. Amonas disliked shouting in principle, so he sighed and walked over to Hilderich. He noticed the man was standing at the lip of the summit, a step before falling over to the steps below. His arms were in front of him with the keystone in one hand, fingers opening and closing in quick succession. It looked as if he was counting something. Amonas cleared his throat audibly, as a way to attract Hilderich's attention and perhaps guard him from a surprise that could set him off balance in a most precarious fashion.

Hilderich paused in his counting momentarily and looked distracted for a moment, hastily checking his left and right with a small motion of his head; he then resumed counting, fingers on both hands moving like he was playing the harp. Amonas closed his eyes in a show of mild exasperation, and said in his usual husky voice:

"Hilderich. I'm right here behind you. Hilderich.."

Hilderich paused and turned about slowly with a frown of surprise on his face. As he did so, he instinctively made a backwards motion with his head, tipping his upper torso slightly aft. That was enough to jerk him off his feet throwing him towards the slope of steps he was surveying. His one arm flailed wildly in a vain effort to steady himself while clutching the keystone hard and stretching out his free hand as a desperate last ditch attempt to reach Amonas who was no more than two steps away.

Amonas reacted instinctively with cat-like speed and lunged forward making a single step and bending his body slightly towards the ground in a kneeling motion that brought his center of mass lower; he stretched out both of his hands, one reaching for Hilderich's free arm and one for the shirt about his waist.

A still moment passed when Hilderich seemed doomed to fall and tumble down like a rag doll to a most certain grievous injury or even death with Amonas failing to do anything other than watch, his grasp failing by a hair's breadth. His mind was faster than his body so the terrible thought had time enough to coalesce with feelings of guilt and failure, curses and a repetitive voice that seemed to echo from afar; it was a simple form of denial yet so piercing that it lanced right through his head, even before he could think he had uttered it:

"No!"

Amonas stood there kneeling, his body tense, almost rigid. He was transfixed, wide-eyed and out of breath, his last one cut suddenly short. He gasped for air, and only then did he realize he was holding onto Hilderich's shirt and palm. Not very tightly though, but he could feel some of Hilderich's body weight pulling at him. He came to his senses and pulled back, edging Hilderich closer. He grabbed tighter with one hand and pulled harder, bringing Hilderich right back on his feet, safely on the summit's surface.

Hilderich looked surprised, the frown on his face even narrower than before. He had certainly began to show signs of sunburn. 'Perhaps he was stricken from the sun and the light, and got dizzy all of a sudden when I called out to him,' Amonas thought.

Hilderich was looking about the floor, his hands going through his pockets. Something seemed amiss to Amonas. Hilderich cried out suddenly:

"The keystone! It must have fell off! I need to go get it! The keystone!"

Amonas took him by his arms and spoke to him calmly and steadily with a hint of assurance in his voice:

"We are going to get the keystone. We were running out of water anyway. Perhaps you were out on the sun for too long. Don't worry, no one's going to steal it from you. There's only us around here. I'm sure it's somewhere down there."

"What if it's broken? What if it's damaged, chipped, marred? What if it broke? What if I broke it?"

"Control yourself! I'm sure it will be fine, it's a mere inconvenience, that's all! Now please! Calm yourself."

Amonas was forcing Hilderich to look him in the eyes in order to convey to him a sense of safety, security and calm. It was as if Hilderich was going through the shock of battle. Was the keystone so vital to him? To their survival? Was the keystone that sensitive, prone to damage? Had their chance to return home tumbled down into oblivion by the slip of a foot? 'Everything in its own time,' Amonas thought as he cast these worrisome thoughts aside if only for a while.

Hilderich turned around to look at the steps below searching for the keystone, this time with a healthier distance from the summit's precipice. He put a hand up to offer his eyes some shade, but still he squinted as he tried to make out such a small thing from such a distance. He was obviously disgruntled with what had happened, and after searching in vain some more, he turned around to Amonas and told him:

"We have to go down now, Amonas. It could be coming any time now, the keystone is crucial. Please, I'll explain to you on the way down. I think I know how it works. Please, we need to go find it now."

"Alright, alright, don't fret so much about it. We were going down anyhow."

Amonas jogged briskly to pick up his sack that was lying under the shadow of a horn and as he came back to Hilderich, he produced one of their last two 'brown ones' from the sack. He chopped of one end and gave it to Hilderich, then got out the last and did the same. They both drank greedily and as they went about the lip ready to start their descend, Amonas told Hilderich:

"Remember, once we find the keystone, we continue down to the base. We need water, and you'll feel it yourself in a pretty bad way before long. The suns here are scorching hot, we'll need shadow, water and sleep once we get down. Then we search around the base. Like we agreed, is that alright Hilderich?"

Hilderich was hesitant, almost reticent to answer but at length he must have thought about it in a more sensible way; he nodded and started climbing down carefully but briskly. Hilderich was making good speed having noticed that going down was much easier because one could easily slide across the surface of the steps with his bottom and then dangle his feet before making a little jump onto the step below, and so on. It might have even been a fun, merry activity, especially if they were children and if the sun wasn't trying to boil them alive. Amonas found out Hilderich's unorthodox way of descending the steps to be quite efficient and fast, so he copied it and they were both making good progress, rapidly going down the steps. At each step Hilderich would peer left and right quickly but certain enough that not a glimmer of the keystone had caught his eye. Amonas had advised him to stop talking and breath through his nose; he could tell him all about what he had come up with when they got down. It was supposedly a good way to conserve one's water, but Hilderich at one point couldn't resist to tell Amonas:

"If we miss it on the way down, we're walking from corner to corner of the pyramid each step up the way."

"I doubt we can do that with no shadow to protect us from the heat. We were exhausted when we climbed up the shadowy face. We'd be sunburnt to death if tried to walk every inch of this side."

"No keystone, no ride Amonas. We'll have to if we don't find it."

Amonas did not reply and instead carried on climbing down placing himself in the lead. At length, while Amonas had already climbed down half the steps, Hilderich cried out:

"There! Over there! I've found it!"

Amonas stopped to look as Hilderich ran across the step towards the keystone. He knelt down and seemed to examine it closely from every side, look for signs of damage or any chipping he might hope to collect. Instead he found a perfectly shaped keystone, and what appeared to be a small dent on the steps.

It appeared quite strange to him that the keystone could actually do that, if the stone was indeed the cause for the dent. It perplexed him at a time when he thought he had most things figured out. It didn't seem that important, but it was too strange to completely disregard under the circumstances. He let the thought go for the moment and when he stood upright again he was smiling, waving his hand with the keystone tightly gripped in it, crying out to Amonas:

"It is fine! Impeccable as ever! Not a scratch!"

"Glad to hear it. Now come, let's make haste."

Amonas was indeed glad to hear such news but he was not sharing Hilderich's enthusiasm. He had yet to understand the importance of the stone. The only thing that stood to reason and supported some of Hilderich's claims was that someone, most probably the Castigator's people, had been collecting keystones in every way. It had even cost Olom's life, and perhaps other lives had been lost in a similar manner as well. Perhaps, the keystones were parts of ancient technology that had yet to be made working again. Perhaps not all keystones were as important, and some were quite different, unique. Perhaps they were all unique in some unfathomable way. He couldn't know, and he couldn't imagine what it was that Hilderich had come up with. It would all remain a mystery until they could get back. He reminded himself that first and foremost, he had to get back. 'And right now,' he thought, 'I have to keep myself from drying out'. They continued their descent with a bit more speed now that Hilderich had secured the keystone.

The sun had taken its toll on them; they were sweating profusely, their bodies glimmering with perspiration. By now, they had both been sun-burnt, their skins bordering the color of the flesh underneath it. Hilderich seemed to be in a much sorrier state than Amonas, his every movement by now painfully evident on his face. Each thrust of pain from his limbs made him flinch in reflex and aggravate his pain, the skin of his face wrinkled and coarse.

Amonas came to his side and tried to help him a bit, lending some of his strength for Hilderich to go down the stairs. At first he seemed glad to be offered some relief, but then cried in pain and nodded imperceptibly to Amonas to leave him be. Before he resumed his painful descent, he told him:

"It hurts, everywhere you might touch me, it hurts. I have to do this alone. I ache all over. Even speaking hurts."

Amonas nodded his acknowledgement and looked sympathetic, understanding. He replied kindly:

"Alright, Hilderich. You can see the trees now, can't you? We're not that far off, just a few more dozens of steps. And then.."

Amonas was cut in mid-sentence when Hilderich collapsed from what must have been a deadly mixture of heat exhaustion, dehydration, and searing pain. He lunged forward head over heels, his hands gnawing at the air for an instant as if trying to catch some invisible ropes, and then they fell limp together with the rest of his body. Amonas did not have time to react like before and this time Hilderich went tumbling down the steps in a state of unconsciousness with no control over his fall. He fell badly on the first step with his chest thudding on impact, and then his body swivelled slightly to one side before he rolled down two, maybe three steps until he came to a stop, his limbs sprawled at nearly impossible angles. Amonas feared the worst and came rushing down the steps as fast as he could without challenging a similar fate. The way Hilderich had fallen, Amonas thought he might have broken almost every bone in his body. He hoped his head was as intact as it seemed and that he would be able to move him. When he got there, Hilderich was not communicating. He tried crying out to him, but he could not rouse him. He was definitely unconscious, probably the reason why he had collapsed.

He did not know which bones on Hilderich's body were broken but nothing seemed to jut out gruesomely, meaning that if something was broken it was not visibly so. He tried to feel Hilderich's arms and legs as well as his ribs, but he was not an expert man of medicine and he could not make any serious assessment. He believed his arms and legs were fine, but some of his ribs felt funny and might be broken. He would be in pain when he woke up, but he could still probably walk, Amonas thought. Under the circumstances, he felt he should be counting Hilderich's blessings.

With strenuous effort he managed to lift Hilderich's waist on his right shoulder, his body laid out so as to least burden his probably broken ribs. Amonas' movements became difficult and strained; Hilderich's limp body seemingly protested at every move with his feet and legs getting in the way, uncomfortably sliding along the steps.

Amonas felt very close to collapsing himself under the strain and the heat but he pushed on heedlessly nevertheless, trying to make it to the tree-line which was only a few dozen feet away. He was coming down the last steps when Hilderich started coming around, moaning deeply from the numbing pain. He managed to croak a whisper while wheezing, the trouble with his breathing more than evident:

"What.. happened.."

Amonas shushed him and answered with strain in his voice, his gruff voice exaggeratedly harsh. He sounded literally dried out:

"You fainted and fell down the steps. You've broken some ribs. Don't talk."

Hilderich was silent again. Amonas thought he might have fainted again, but that was not his principle care. They had to make it to the tree-line and the little shadow it offered.

He was walking over the canal-like indentation on the ground, nothing but tall grass around him. Amonas was dragging his feet with admirable effort and determination. His face was contorted from the pain of his aching muscles and the extra weight they had had to carry for these last few minutes. 'A little while longer,' Amonas kept thinking to himself, 'a little while longer into the shadow, and I can rest'. He closed his eyes and kept on walking with the same pace, Hilderich slung over his shoulder like game; Amonas was gritting his teeth, his breaths coming in short and hard gasps.

When at last he reached the relative shadow of the trees he could still feel the heat, but the scorching rays of the sun were gone as if kept at bay by the forest. With one last bit of effort, he knelt down to the ground and offloaded Hilderich as carefully as he could. Hilderich came to for a moment, moaned deeply and grimaced with pain, and then he was out cold again. His breathing was shallow, as if his body knew anything more would hurt him like stabs of red hot iron in his lungs. Amonas then braced Hilderich from under his armpits with both arms trying not to cause him any more pain, and dragged him over to the large trunk of a tree propping him up against it so he could breathe without fear of drowning in his own blood. He felt he could do nothing more for Hilderich for the time being, so he crawled a bit farther away under the shadow of a tree with a bark as wide as the wall of a mountain cabin. He closed his eyes and just slept without dreaming a single thing.

He opened his eyes to the sight of the green canopy: a labyrinth of shades of green, large and small branches criss-crossing it like a net cast out onto a sea of leaves. His mouth was parched and he felt his head heavy; a headache pounding his mind like a hammer on an anvil. He was thirsty, he needed water. Hilderich was still unconscious just laying where Amonas had left him, his breathing laborious; it was a raspy, unhealthy sound. He needed a doctor. They needed to get back to civilization, back home, more than ever. Amonas judged Hilderich was in no shape to walk around the base of the pyramid. Their most immediate need was water though.

He stood up with a lot of effort. He felt disoriented, his senses failing him; his vision was slightly blurry and unfocused. He misjudged the location and distance of things around him. The dehydration must have been more severe than he had felt, and the heat was only making things worse. He slowly paced himself through an opening in the vegetation, a path that offered less thick greenery and easier terrain. He was looking for the usual tree with the brown nut-fruit, the one with all the watery juice inside, but couldn't see any. The trees looked a bit different, as if this was another part of the forest: they were not as thick, with more space in between them. Fewer but larger trees, wider openings and more space overhead. It looked almost like a vast hall, supported on wooden pillars of green and brown hues.

But no fruit. Or something else familiar to eat and most importantly, no water. He could still make out the clearing in front of the base of the pyramid where Hilderich lay. He had not gotten very far though he already felt tired, worn out. The dehydration was severe now. He paused and sat by the exposed root of a tree. He thought it was too dangerous to venture farther away from the pyramid and Hilderich. He was looking up: a vast net-like congregation of saplings extended from one tree to the other, like ropes meant to build a bridge. They could be carrying water or some juice but he could not reach them: they were too high up. He'd need to try and climb up a tree like a mad cat and he was certainly in no condition to do so.

He then turned to the thick root he was sitting up against. It looked healthy and vital, not gnarled like most he had seen so far. A young root, a young tree. There should be some water flowing through it, he thought. He brought out his knife and tried to put a stab to the root, deep enough to go through its skin to the veins of the tree. Hopefully some water would pour out, at least enough for him to drink now and make him able to go on.

He stabbed as hard as he could and then worked his knife inside, twisting and bending it as if trying to cut out the tree's heart. At length, pieces of the root came out with a strong, pungent smell and something like oil glistened on the knife's blade. Amonas ran a finger on it and sampled it, the taste woody and bitter. It felt indeed more like oil rather than water.

With some more effort and his head now feeling like a ministry bell tolling incessantly, he dug deeper into the root trying to get past its meaty part, into its core where water coursed. He dug with his knife and his hands, feeling the oil giving way to moist, soft wood matter. Another jab of his blade and he saw a trickle coursing down, dripping on the ground.

With sudden greed, he put his mouth on the wound he had inflicted on the root and sucked like a newborn child does from its mother's tit: it was water after all. He wet his lips and his mouth thoroughly, letting the cool liquid refresh his mouth and spat it out. He then let the trickle fill the two flasks he was carrying drop by drop, waiting patiently.

All the while he sat more comfortably leaning against the trunk of the tree, almost as if he ready to take a nap. He swallowed small portions of the water in his mouth, savoring it. He had been dehydrated before, and knew it was a lot worse if a man that had been denied of water for too long just dived straight in a lake or drank to his heart's content. He had seen men die of it, for reasons he could not know. He

230

thought it was a sick way of nature to make men pay for their greed as well as their lack of respect.

His mind did not wander or drift as it had done so in the days before. Necessity and his instincts drove him. He took in things as they were, his mind enjoying a numbness while both it and his body recuperated slowly, the effects of dehydration slowly withering away and vigor reappearing in his face with his head throbbing gently instead of being about to explode.

Once the flasks were filled to the brim, he had drank a couple more mouthfuls by now. He was feeling markedly better, and he believed he could find a similar root if he wandered some more; with no way to carry more water though, it would be in vain. So he decided to get back to Hilderich and tend to him: he would rouse him and offer him some badly needed water.

When he got back to where Hilderich was sitting he tried speaking to him and gently shook his head, but to no avail. He then used some of the water letting it run down on Hilderich head, face, and back, dousing him carefully so as not to waste a lot of it. The cool water had more effect. He fluttered his eyes momentarily and then gasped; a sting of a pain immediately ran through him, the bones in his ribs stabbing him without warning. Amonas offered him the flask of water and told him in a soothing, reassuring manner:

"Breathe lightly, or it'll hurt like death each time. You have broken some ribs, that much is now certain. You are dehydrated, your head must spin and hurt like someonw hit it with a mallet. I am dehydrated as well, only I just drank some water and feel good enough to stand on my two feet. Now, you just sip some of this very slowly and carefully. Don't gulp down on it, it might kill you; I'm serious. I'm not known for my humorist streaks. Now flex your arms and legs a bit if you can, you've been lying there for hours: your muscles will go dead stiff if you don't. We'll wait it out, you'll drink till you feel a bit better and then perhaps I can make you a splint out of some wood I might rummage. How does all that sound?"

Hilderich managed to lift his head and look at Amonas briefly. He was evidently in a lot of pain, and in a pretty poor state. He needed genuine rest and this was not the place for it. He nodded silently in acknowledgement, and Amonas smiled encouragingly before adding:

"If you agree then, let's keep to that plan."

Hilderich seemed then to be trying to flex and move his arms and legs. He put one hand on Amonas arm who was kneeling down beside him, and then rasped in a low whisper:

"The.. keystone. Is it safe?"

"It's safe and sound. Don't worry about it now."

Hilderich nodded once more wearily, his head moving imperceptibly. He managed to say something else after he had sipped on some water:

"Perhaps, you were right. We need to be here."

"Where do you mean?"

"The base. The pyramid. I'll tell you. I hope.. we have time."

"We have all the time in the world, Hilderich. Now, drink. Don't talk, and rest."

Hilderich was insisting that Amonas listened to what he had to say, tugging his cloak with a grip that belied his feebleness and injuries. He spoke with a rasp, his throat still too dry for comfort:

"The keystone. The wall. They're like water and sand."

Amonas furrowed his brow intensely, puzzled at what seemed a very vague half-statement especially when coming from Hilderich. He motioned Hilderich to shush himself, putting a finger to his mouth but Hilderich went on, after coughing what appeared to be blood in his sputum:

"I know it doesn't make sense. The stone can be absorbed, into the wall. It is a keystone. The wall is a door. It should work. Please, try it."

Amonas nodded condescendingly and said:

"You can try all you want to when you get better."

Hilderich gave off another cough and a splutter of bloody saliva forced him to look away from Amonas. He then turned his face again to look into Amonas eyes and wheezed while breathing harshly. Hilderich insisted with what seemed to be aggravation in his voice, even annoyance:

"You need to listen to me! Use the key, force it into the pyramid's wall. Let it be drawn into the pyramid."

"You must be delirious, running a fever surely. Please, stop exerting your self and drink some water. Here."

Then Hilderich's face was suddenly contorted, wildly disfigured from anger and despair at the same time. With a jerk of his hand he threw the open flask Amonas had proffered away, spewing its precious water content along its flight. He was now talking fast with anger in his voice, pain underlining every word and gasping for air between every phrase:

"You're not listening! You think I'm seeing things! I saw the keystone had left a dent on the stone, a bump that wasn't there before. There is some affinity with the pyramid stones. What is there to lose if you try? Your vaunted pride? If you don't do it now, there's every chance we are going to miss the next fireball and that might be our last! Do you want to die here? Use the keystone! Find a way in!"

Amonas made a backwards step, like being physically pushed and had to re-balance himself. His face wore an expression of disbelief showing hints of feeling awkward and hurt. He felt like he had been lied upon, whereas he had trusted Hilderich almost unflinchingly:

"But you said it was like hitching a wagon, that there's a schedule and so on!"

Hilderich coughed once more, his lips now red with his blood:

"Haven't you heard of wishful thinking before?"

Amonas stood up while staring down at Hilderich with accusation in the tone of his voice and a finger pointing at him waveringly, as if he wasn't sure whether this man was to be blamed or not:

"You.. You're injured, you're seeing things, that's all I can know for sure."

Hilderich rasped once more this time with more volume in his voice, making it sound rather unfittingly exasperated:

"You wouldn't know your head from your arse. Now use the damned keystone! Just push it through the wall!"

"What do you mean?"

Hilderich looked at Amonas with fiery eyes that stung and looked as if embers were burning inside. He told him slowly and painfully, with fear and real anger showing on his face and voice:

"Just push it through the wall! Like driving a nail! Gods dammit!"

He coughed once more with blood spewing forth, running down his lips and chin. Amonas thought he could perhaps indulge him and his effort alone might bring some sense into him. He nodded without genuine assent, stoop upright and walked to where the flask had landed. He picked it up, exchanged strenuous looks with Hilderich and carried on to meet the wall of the pyramid.

When he reached it, he felt the sun blazing hot upon him but took some time to study it. He could not hope to really understand to what purpose it had been made, the fiery bolt that ran through the horns only adding to the puzzle. The black matte stones were strange: glass-like to the touch, but hard, not brittle. Not much of all that had transpired made any sense though, either. So he just did as Hilderich told him: hetook the keystone and placed its longest side flat on the stone that stood right in front of him that formed the first step.

Nothing happened, as it was expected of something that the delusional mind of a seriously injured man had come up with. For the sake of doing a friend a favor and carrying out the idea to the letter, he pushed the keystone down with one hand; something that made him feel quite unwarrantably stupid. As he pressed down momentarily he somehow felt the stone below give way. He let go, and then used his index finger to press ever so lightly.

Nothing that his senses could grasp ensued and kept on pressing slightly harder and harder, when after a certain threshold the keystone indeed seemed to bury itself gradually inside the black stone. To his untold surprise, once he had indeed pressed it halfway deep into the black stone, the green keystone lit up with a rainbow of colors cast from an inner light that could not have been a reflection of the pale bluish suns. It was as if somehow the stone had come alive. Unable to contain his surprise and sudden enthusiasm, Amonas started yelling back towards Hilderich:

"You were right! It's doing something alright!"

The flaring lights suddenly stopped and the keystone remained inert, half way there into the black surface of the pyramid's blocky stone step. Amonas did not know what to do next. An instinctive fear raced through his mind, preventing him from even moving or thinking. He stood there almost impassively not knowing what to do next, fearing the unknowns that he had been hunting down. It was ironic that now that he was able to actually progress past theory, thought and conjecture into something that seemed to work, he had frozen still from his basic, human fear of the unknown. He knew he had to focus his mind and force himself past such notions. With his indecision hidden away he touched the half-buried keystone one more time with his palm, and then it was gone, like it had been swallowed up by the blackness of the stones alone.

Then the most amazing thing he had seen, only comparable with the fireball from before, unraveled before his eyes with astonishing speed and breathtaking complexity. The stones in front of him became somewhat transparent, letting only some of the light through. Their smooth surface became crystallized and faceted; rough, but not coarse or random. It looked rather like wrinkled paper that had been carefully folded a thousand, a million times and then laid out again, perfectly patterned.

The stones started to part and dissolve, each little facet absorbed by the facets next to it, as if the stones were eating themselves away. The sight reminded him of a half-frozen lake being shattered and the ice sinking down instead of floating, though in a very fast and methodical way.

This transfiguration, this certain proof of the otherworldliness of the place, was over before Amonas could even blink twice. And what was left in the place of the stones was a perfect oval corridor, wide enough and tall enough for a man of Amonas size to walk in. He was stunned, unable to fully comprehend what it was that he had witnessed.

With some effort he gathered his wits and cast aside the protests of his mind to see, hear, touch and wonder wide-eyed at this inexplicable, majestic building that challenged reason at every opportunity. He focused on the harsh reality and its necessities, and peered over the half-lit entrance that had not been there moments before. He could see no lights coming from within, no other sort of emplacements or provisions for torches or the like. It was pitch black in there, but the important thing was that it was now open.

Instinctively he thought about the newly built entrance closing suddenly in a manner similar to how it had been opened and trapping him inside or, even worse, trapping half of him inside. He made two quick steps back as if he had been warned in advance, but nothing happened. He shook his head in disbelief and disapproval. There was a way in and Hilderich was right. They had to move inside now, and that meant moving Hilderich as well. That would be troublesome, Amonas thought as he made quite a few steps backwards before turning to run to Hilderich, almost unable to let the sight of the wondrous entrance depart from his eyes.

Hilderich was still propped up against the trunk of the tree, wheezing as he drew breath with painstaking effort. Amonas noticed he was grinning now though, and his spirits flared high anew. With a broad smile he knelt next to Hilderich and said:

"It worked, you were right. Once the keystone went in, an entrance opened up as if by magic: it was a wondrous affair. Filled me with awe and that rarely if ever happens. You should be proud of yourself, Hilderich."

Hilderich flinched painfully as he repositioned himself in a more upright position using his hands and replied, gritting his teeth through some of the words:

"I shouldn't be in this.. mess. Then.. I could be proud. The.. keystone? Do you have it?"

Amonas face turned into ash and froze at that question. In the tumult, amidst all the surprise and awe he had forgotten all about the keystone that had just disappeared into the stone. That made him uneasy. He licked his lips with his tongue, and tasted his sour sweat. He had no answer that might quieten Hilderich's fear, so he simply told him:

"No. It went into the stone, the entrance into the pyramid opened, and that was all. The keystone did not reappear. I'm sorry. I think it has served its purpose."

Hilderich's face lit up somewhat and then he burst into a painful mix of choked laughter and blood-sputtering coughing. He tensed up and restrained himself, the pain from his broken ribs becoming unbearable while he laughed. He grimaced while the waves of pain coursing through him settled down. He took a shallow breath and replied to Amonas who was now sitting down with his legs woven together, looking quite perplexed because of Hilderich's strange reaction:

"You talk as if.. it were alive. Could be, for all I know. That's alright.. I guess.. We'll find it, further inside.. I believe. Made me.. laugh. The way you seemed so.. pensive. Almost mourning. The keystone's fine, you'll see."

Amonas face relaxed and he seemed to accept Hilderich's thoughts as if they made sense. In any other context he would have believed the man was still making up things in his mind, but he now felt indeed compelled to take Hilderich's every word seriously. He couldn't know why, but he had been right so far.

"Alright, Hilderich. Now we have to figure a way to get you inside as well. It only fits one man about my size. That means I won't be able to carry you through on my shoulder like I did back then. How are you feeling? Have you had any more water to drink? If there's no water left I can always go back and hack at some root, fill up the flasks. Hope you don't throw half of it away though this time."

"I feel horrible. I think.. it's understandable, under the circumstances."

Amonas shook his head briskly in acknowledgement, but insisted:

"I can see that Hilderich, but I need to know if you can move on your own now. I guess that would be as you've put it, wishful thinking. You also need water. Here, have mine for now. I'll fill both later, somehow."

Hilderich grinned and replied:

"My head is still buzzing.. I feel weaker than an ant, but.. I think I'm doing somewhat better. But walking would be.. quite wishful. Perhaps.. You could fix a stretcher of sorts. Something to.. to drag me with. Sorry about the flask.."

Amonas waved Hilderich's last remark away with one hand and looked him up and down, thoughtfully as if measuring him. Then he looked around him, trying to identify something around him within sight that he could put to good use. After taking some time to think, he asked Hilderich with a certain degree of hesitation:

"Will a sort of harness do? Something I could wrap under your armpits, around your shoulders too perhaps? It should hurt anyway I go about it, but I think it's the most practical thing I could manage in reasonable time."

Hilderich looked at his feet sprawled as they were, his vision evidently out of focus. He seemed lost in thought but then he coughed with traces of blood in his saliva and replied to Amonas:

"Whatever makes sense to you. I'm pretty.. useless at these crafts, so I'll make do.. I guess."

Amonas nodded with a slightly comforting smile and hurried away, headed to a cluster of trees and bush that Hilderich could not clearly make out.

Hilderich' body was constantly assaulted from the heat and moisture that had only been bearable under the shadow of the bullhorn pyramid. With his ribs now broken, his skin sun-burnt and his body dehydrated he felt like someone had left out his mind to dry over white hot sand and stone. Every breath felt like he had been dismantled and put back somehow wrong, the bones in his ribs turned into blades set against his insides, stabbing him at every chance they got.

His throat felt like a dusty canyon and what little saliva was left in him was bloody and thick. He needed more water, that was true. But more than anything else he needed to get in there. Get in the pyramid. See for himself. After all, he thought, Amonas could not make it without him, he'd have no chance to understand what surrounded him. In his sorry state, they both needed each other, more badly then ever before. He decided to wait for Amonas and in doing so slowly, and despite the constantly painful and irritating coughing, he fell asleep.

Amonas woke him up, gently shaking his leg. He woke up without really wanting to and saw Amonas had indeed prepared a sort of harness, a piece of paraphernalia that must have been tacked together while he was asleep. It was made out of thick strands of some kind of vine that seemed to be abundant here, a somewhat flat branch of sappy wood, and a quite large, thick deep green monster of a leave, shaped like a flattened arrow's nose. Amonas was grinning, as if he had intended for this appurtenance of sorts to look like an exotic mule's rein and was certain that the irony would not go wasted on Hilderich.

Hilderich indeed looked at what Amonas had fashioned, and though still in a sort of after-sleep haze he managed to point at it and snigger, as opposed to laughing outright which was rather painful. Amonas came closer and holding the various parts together told Hilderich:

"Now, I know what you're thinking since you're in such a good mood, but any similarity with a donkey's strap and rein is purely unintentional and simply a product of the same basic design principles that define both pieces of gear. I'm sure you would agree in the end, but let's try and get on with this, shall we?"

Hilderich nodded in agonizing agreement and Amonas grabbed him by the arms and lifted him upwards, propping him upright against the trunk of the tree. Hilderich let out a cry of pain as his ribs must have had his insides jarred once more. Amonas tried to be quick about it since he saw Hilderich was barely able to stand, much less walk. He placed the branch of wood as a backplate, a support to keep his torso, chest and ribs stiff and unbent to prevent further aggravating his wounds inside, as well as keeping the bones in place if they were to build a proper splint once they went back and found a doctor. The prospect seemed ever closer now, and filled Amonas with ardor. He completed fastening the gear on Hilderich, binding the ropes and setting the large leaf across Hilderich's back, as a sort of cushioning to ease the friction without which he believed he'd be unable to move him more than a foot.

Once he was finished he lowered Hilderich down to the ground again, and then passed the other end of the rope around his waist belt and tightened it. He said to Hilderich who was evidently uncomfortable, his arms sticking out in a weird fashion:

"Ready when you are."

Hilderich nodded in a disgruntled fashion and Amonas then started to move at first rather sluggish, but soon he was able to walk slowly with Hilderich in tow. They reached the large ditch which proved somewhat of a pain because of the angled sides. Hilderich almost slipped down and Amonas barely avoided being dragged with him and falling head first into the ditch. In a similar fashion heading up the ditch put some evident strain on Amonas, who reached the entrance with Hilderich behind him, sweating out of breath. He stopped a few steps behind the actual entrance and gestured at it with one hand:

"This is it. You were right. It just sprouted open in a most perplexing way. The stones acted on their own, remoulding themselves somehow."

Hilderich was still attached to Amonas via the makeshift harness, and was craning his neck in an effort to somehow see better inside the passageway that led deeper inside the pyramid. He told Amonas:

"Let's go in."

Amonas nodded in agreement and started to walk inside. As he reached the foot of the entrance, he noticed the passageway in front of him starting to flicker and shine. It was doing it again, the stones in the structure rearranging themselves like before. Hilderich let out a gasp of surprise and enthusiasm and asked Amonas instantly:

"Is that what it did before? That's wondrous! It makes way for us! The passage is wider now! Look!"

From what it looked like, the corridor was widened to more easily accommodate Hilderich as well. Amonas was surprised as well, but he wasn't feeling mesmerized this time around. He believed though it would take him a while to greet such things as normal. Without further ado, he took a few steps more and they were soon both inside the pyramid proper. The sunlight could not reach them here and a cool fresh air greeted them. They were following a corridor that seemed to glow faintly from within its walls strangely illuminating their way as they walked, throwing a spot of soft light between the harsh darkness. As it was they could not see very far into the pyramid, the radius of light comfortable enough to simply follow them, not extending beyond a few feet. Amonas stopped then, and asked Hilderich:

"Are you sure we should be going inside like this?"

Hilderich was looking with amazement around the walls and the ceiling, the black matte stone having turned into a semi-transparent glass, the light casting hues and specks reminiscent of an artisan's glass-work, or a gemstone. It took Hilderich a while to respond to Amonas' question, but he did so in a gleeful voice despite the condition he was in:

"More than ever! It's a wonder in itself, this material!"

Hilderich coughed then and spat some more saliva with blood. Amonas trudged onwards bearing Hilderich in tow and simply said:

"Just be patient, Hilderich. We're getting somewhere. The draught is getting stronger somehow."

It was indeed a matter of a few more minutes spent in silence and awe, before they reached a sullen, gloomy opening with a single column of light shattering the darkness. It illuminated a blocky metal or stone artifact, its surface a mirror with a bronze-like sheen. Amonas was astounded to see his image reflected on that surface, even while there was still a wide gap of shadow between them and the artifact. Hilderich noticed Amonas had paused and asked him in what seemed to be a worrisome voice:

"Why did you stop? Is something the matter? What do you see? I only see blackness."

Amonas replied while still measuring their distance and looking at the block of stone, a monolith of sorts. His voice was a low whisper, like a man fearful of awakening something terrible:

"There's this block made of something like stone, metal, or glass. Something like the rest of what this place is built from, but not quite so. It can.. See me. Through the darkness. My reflection is right there."

Hilderich went silent with thought after Amonas' answer. Amonas waited for Hilderich to make a remark or perhaps give him some advice, but he said nothing. Amonas said then, with some reticence:

"I'll just walk over there. If it was dangerous it wouldn't have let us in, would it?"

Hilderich answered with some uncertainty trailing his words:

"That would be quite illogical, so I'd have to agree with your.. assessment."

Hilderich coughed right before the last word, pain traveling up his throat. It felt as if it was about to choke him, his lungs burning. He was almost used to the pain now, but that did not make things any easier for him.

Amonas did not reply but simply headed for the bright area where the monolith stood, the reflection of him on its surface beginning to look somewhat strange. He noticed it did not reflect the harness or the bulk of Hilderich that should be visible. The reflection did not seem to grow larger the closer he came to the stone. It seemed to be the same size as Amonas all along, from when he noticed it first. He thought to himself he should be feeling wary by now, but all he felt was puzzlement and a keen sense of interest. Fear had not crossed his mind, which was either a good sign, or extremely stupid of him. If they were in danger, he had no such notion.

Hilderich was mysteriously silent, but then again his injuries made it that difficult to speak his mind. As Amonas would've thought, he should have been talking constantly since they had entered the pyramid, especially now with this intriguing artifact laid out before them.

Hilderich then took him by surprise when he said:

"Tell me. What do you see on the stone?"

Light was shining down on them, bright and white, but not hurtful to the eyes. As if it poured from around them; not from the ceiling of this chamber or cavern the size of which they could not properly assess. They had noticed no echoes whatsoever, and their eyes could not see beyond the illuminated area around the monolith. They could be anywhere. Amonas responded, offering a simple description to Hilderich:

"It's about twice my height, and about three feet. It looks black, but that's not exactly right. It gives off the feeling of glass, and has a bronze sheen. I can see my reflection on it imperfectly, like what it would like through a thick sheet of cheap glass. I look somewhat deformed, a honey-like hue on my image."

Hilderich took a few moments to digest that information, and asked Amonas again:

"Do you see me in that reflection? Shouldn't you be seeing me?"

"I don't. I think not even the harness is visible. But I can see myself talking, waving an arm and such. It's uncanny, I'll admit. Like someone is standing there. Mocking me."

Hilderich shuffled where he lay, and said to Amonas:

"Please, help me stand. I need to have a good look."

"Are you sure?"

"We're only wasting time. If I need to make some observations, I need to do them myself. Please."

Amonas then lowered Hilderich carefully and undid the ropes. He unclasped the wood on Hilderich's back, and offered Hilderich his hands. They embraced, and Amonas gave him a questioning nod. Hilderich nodded in acknowledgement, and Amonas pulled him upwards hard and fast so as to minimize the after-effects of splintered bone against Hilderich's raw flesh. It didn't work all that well and while Hilderich was gripping Amonas' shoulders for support, he almost fainted from the stabbing pain; his cry seemed to split the silence in the chamber in two, but still there was no echo. He shook his head as if trying to shake the pain away, and after a few more moments of shallow breathing he managed to stand on his own two feet. Slowly he turned around to look at the monolith himself, Amonas supporting him by his side.

"You are right, it only reflects you. It's as if I am non-existent, indifferent. Like it doesn't recognize me. Like it.. only knows you."

"You are saying this thing could be thinking?"

"I don't know if that's true but it, whatever it is, seems to be able to recognize, identify. Perhaps that's all it does, its chief function. Like a guard, or a gatekeeper."

Hilderich coughed somewhat hard, and flinched before spitting out a blob of bloodied sputum. To his amazement he saw it reach the floor and then seep through it, like it had been absorbed. A mere moment later Hilderich's reflection appeared on the slab's surface, as if it had always been there and simply no one had noticed. Amonas pointed and said:

"How can that be? Suddenly it.. Why?"

Hilderich's gaze was locked were he had spat.

"My blood. It tasted my blood. It knows me now as well."

"And how did it get to 'know' me as you put it? I did not bleed."

"How did you open the entrance?"

"I used the keystone. I pressed it and it went inside the stone half-way. Then I just touched it and it was gone, like the stone had sucked it inside."

"It seems it did. You touched the stone, and then this place knew you. I certainly do not know how and it does sound like magic or what most people would call 'divine powers', but it must be some kind of elaborate ancient technology. I knew it wasn't just a myth, but I had never imagined it would still be around; certainly not in working condition. And not at this scale."

Amonas glanced upwards frowning and then spent a few moments surveying the darkness, the light, and the monolith before saying:

"But where is this place? Where have we been for the last few days? If it is ancient technology, what is it doing here? Where is *here*, Hilderich?"

"Do you really wish to know, Amonas? We could stay and find out. Investigate. It would be a singular chance in man's history."

Hilderich's voice hinted at genuine passion and untold possibilities, real enthusiasm in his voice. Amonas looked him in the eyes sternly and dispassionately, almost coldly:

"No. We are going back. You can stay if you want but you won't get far like that."

Hilderich nodded painfully with a grin and said:

"I was only thinking out loud. I want to go back Amonas. I have a job to do, I haven't forgotten about that."

"Well then, focus at going back. What now? Any ideas?"

Hilderich spared a few moments of thought and then with some reluctance in his voice asked Amonas:

"Could you perhaps, touch it?"

"What should I expect if I do?"

"Nothing awful has happened so far, I'd think that nothing awful will. Of course, there's always the possibility something really awful happens eventually."

"So, I just touch it and see?"

"Well, yes. Like with the keystone."

"Alright."

Amonas touched the monolith without letting go of Hilderich and they vanished in an instant, their shapes horribly deformed and twisted right before a final flash of light made them disappear. Not an echo of them remained in the silent, dark chamber.

They were comfortably seated in a white non-nondescript couch, in what would more or less pass as a commoner's room with a small table, also white in color. The predominant color of their surroundings was in fact, white, and all around them, a wilderness seemed to stretch. It was impossible to discern between sky or ceiling and the ground, since everything around was white.

There was no visible source of light but everything was softly lit, the white objects around them like the couch and the small low table casting the faintest of shadows. The effect was strangely enough, not disconcerting or disorienting. It all felt quite normal to them, even soothing. Part of their minds screeched in horror for it could not comprehend how they had ended up in this friendly but evidently inconceivable place.

The better part of their minds though, decided to just feel comfortable for a change and perhaps worry about such things and details later. Hilderich was feeling much better, being able to move his arms and torso without feeling any pain. No bloody coughs either, no sunburns, and no dehydration. He was actually feeling quite fit, fitter than ever. He felt he could run a hundred miles without breaking a sweat.

Amonas, who was sitting beside him was similarly in the best of shapes, feeling well beyond normalcy. He turned around to look at Hilderich who was still checking their surroundings and making sure with his hands that his ribs were in place just as he felt they were. Amonas took notice of Hilderich's much improved state, and simply said:

"You look better. I look better. This place is, great. I have a nagging sensation though this is extremely strange."

"I have that feeling too. I actually think I can hear my voice in my head screaming loudly in protestation that we shouldn't be here."

A voice from nowhere interjected suddenly, vibrant and warm, but somewhat stilted:

"I should be fixing that. Strong residual harmonics in the transitional field transmogrification phase. The effect should diminish soon enough."

Amonas reaction was immediate:

"Who is this? Show yourself! Where are we?"

Hilderich remained silent. The voice was heard once more:

"The question is odd, but I am required to answer, indeed inclined to indulge your questioning nature. So, to answer in the same order: 'I' am part of a vast network of hyper-dimensional computational self-aware matrices that effectively keep this whole world running. You could call me avatar, or thing, if you like, but that would only make this conversation even less intelligent. I do not have anything to show to you as 'myself', since what you could call my genuine physical form is a hyper-dense cloud of matter in an amorphous plasma state. If I did, you could possibly distinguish a small prickle of light the size of a hairpin. I like to dispense with physical form whenever possible, I find it serves no purpose other than easing the fears of fairly primitive cerebral cortices like yours. And to answer your third question, you could be said to exist inside the buffer matrix of the conveyance subsystem of Support."

Amonas looked at Hilderich frowning intensely, as if he had understood almost nothing of what he had been told while Hilderich was somehow able to make sense of everything. Hilderich returned him a wide-eyed look that brought down Amonas' hopes crashing.

"I can see you are perplexed. More like dumbfounded, actually. I can explain some things if you like, others I literally cannot. Some will prove unfathomable to you even if I do explain in length. I believe we do have some time available until the next conveyance."

Hilderich looked upwards as if addressing God when he spoke next:

"The next conveyance? Could that be that you are talking about the fiery ball that overpasses the pyramid?"

"Your choice of words is surprisingly pertinent, though very crude indeed. Yes, I am talking about the conveyance of a highly energized, large mass, extra-dimensional inner space self-contained plasma-propelled atmospheric ballast vehicle."

Hilderich looked as if he wanted to learn everything at once, his face almost split from the effort of containing his thoughts and questions. He managed to ask once more, while Amonas walked around the small white space that surrounded them:

"So it is a vehicle? I had been right all along! Amonas, we're going home!"

Amonas turned and grinned, and was about to say something when the voice chimed in:

"Well, I happen to know the centron is devoid of human habitations, so I can safely conclude that you are mistaken. You will not be going home."

Amonas looked at Hilderich with shock and indignation and then shouted vaguely outward, at the unseen entity that had been talking to them for the past few minutes:

"We will be prisoners no more! We demand to return to our home! You, with your ancient technology will certainly be able to accommodate such a want. We will pay in whatever acceptable currency you demand, if that is necessary. If you are in league with the Patriarch, we will buy back our lives if needs be."

The voice sounded as if it sniggered, and it then added:

"Pay? Currency? Primitive indeed. You are not prisoners of any kind, you are merely being conveyed. All conveyance is to the centron, there is no other destination. If you will, it is a design limitation. It is not within my powers to alter that. You are going to the centron, that is why you entered the Pylon. Or maybe not. Well, you had the pass, so I had to comply. Really, you had no idea what you were doing? Fascinating. Hasn't happened in a long time."

Hilderich looked like he was suddenly drawn by something the voice had said. He asked with some degree of meticulousness, carefully, slowly:

"By pass, you must mean the keystone. What happened to it?"

"Oh, the pass will re-materialize integrally when you do."

"What does that mean?"

"Well, it is quite uncommon to walk around with a physical form of the pass. I understand it could be stolen, lost, even destroyed under certain circumstance. So, as is the usual case, I took the liberty of reintegrating it in your helix inside your bodies, at the cellular level. Much more practical that way."

Amonas hands went to his heart and stomach instinctively, as he was indeed looking like he was searching for the keystone to jut out from some awkward place. He shouted in anger:

"You put it inside us? What kind of devilry is this? Why not kill us outright and be done with us!"

Hilderich grabbed him by the arm and looked him in the eye, feeling his rush and white hot anger pouring out of his eyes. He tried to calm him:

"Amonas, it's alright. I think. It's not there as the keystone itself. I think he means that it is now part of us. We are the keystone. We are a keystone each, I believe."

Amonas looked at Hilderich wide-eyed, in a further show of disbelief. He gasped but could not speak a word. The voice continued:

"You really come from a primitive civilization. I rarely keep account of events on the outer shell but I was certain that at some point there was some quite advanced civilization active. No matter, millenia pass along so quickly when there's not much to do."

Hilderich asked then, his mind trying to focus on what he should be asking next, the unknowns branching off each other like a mystic tree, the questions gnawing at him vying to be voiced first:

"You said we exist in a buffer matrix, a system, something like that. What did you mean?"

"Right. It will be difficult for you to follow, perhaps you'll think

I've stolen your souls. Your friend will surely do. Well this place with the white furniture and all that light, it doesn't look very realistic now, does it?"

Both Hilderich and Amonas nodded, though Amonas face was slowly building up creases of anger and perhaps even wrath. He very much disliked being indirectly referenced and not spoken to, especially when he was present. The voice went on:

"Well it's not real. It is an energy grid field-inducing construct. Think of it as a temporary room for your minds. All this is in your mind: like a waking dream, for the sake of understanding. Your bodies are right now, non-existent. You have been disintegrated into a complete series of information. You have been thoroughly, digitally and quantically, deconstructed in order to be reconstructed at the place of your destination, which is the centron. The ballast vehicle will provide the actual transportation of the total information via quantum entanglement on board. Somehow ineffective, I know, but I did not design this system: I have to insist on that."

Hilderich was puzzled. Amonas was beyond puzzled and the total sum of unknown and impossible to believe or comprehend things had already overcome his tolerances. Instead of boiling in anger, he simply gave up and let Hilderich do the talking since at least he seemed to understand some of what they were being told. He lay down on the couch and closed his eyes, as if he were about to sleep.

"So you are telling us we have no bodies? That we have become something like ghosts? Or angels? Beings of pure energy and light?"

"Ghosts and angels is definitely the wrong picture here: quaint, but wrong. Pure energy and light is kind of superfluous, so let's just say light. Yes, right now you are made of light. Kind of."

"Is that somehow similar to how the pillar of light that brought us here in the first place works like?"

There was a small pause, as if the voice took a while to gestate what it had been asked, like it found the answer difficult or somehow restricted.

"I don't understand what you are talking about."

Hilderich swung around to look at Amonas, who had now opened his eyes and was looking back at Hilderich, exchanging glances of disapproval and disbelief.

Hilderich insisted:

"The white pillar of light that brought us to this world of yours? Somewhere in the opposite direction of the sun? A small crest overlooking the forests?"

"Perhaps you are confused. What world of mine are you talking about? Ah, perhaps you are referring to the service matter transference beams. I can see that could be interpreted as such, yes. Yes, it does work quite the same way. Though these service beams do not have a buffer matrix. You simply pop in, and pop out the other way. Instant. While in here time is a.. ooh, will you look at the time. Well, enough talking. Pleasure to be of assistance, though I'd have hoped for a brighter conversation."

The voice stopped, and suddenly the scenery around them became dark. Amonas was no longer lying down on a couch and he felt he was floating in mid-air, the darkness around him all-consuming. He called out to Hilderich, but no answer came. In an instant he saw a flashing bright well of swaths of light passing by him in horrific speeds. He could not see his hands; indeed he felt disembodied, unable to move. The well shot past him and now he was looking at a little bright pin prickle of blue light, like a lonely star at night. Before he could clearly see what it was, it came rushing at him and filled his entire field of vision, shards of ice piercing his every sense. A blue-white hot light engulfed him then, as it was ready to devour him whole. He tried to shield himself, turning his back around and running. But he was more than unable. He had no body to flee with, and that was the last thought he could remember.

A dead tree gives no shelter

HE Pilgrim aroused Molo from his fretful sleep with a nudge. Molo woke up with a gasp, his body tense, his face and palms sweaty. The Pilgrim thought his brother was troubled, as he had been for the last two nights. It was as if the spirits of the land and sky were not in his dreams; as if they did not safekeep him from the malevolence of the archenemy.

He would pray for his brother at dawn; he hoped something lesser was troubling him. Some lover, or a wife. His children, perhaps. He couldn't know yet, he wasn't learning his brother's tongue as fast as he wished. But he understood his brother's pilgrimage was different. They had taken the same path for the same reasons, but there were different customs to be obeyed.

Perhaps, his brother was unlucky enough to have a wife and children that he had needed to leave behind. Perhaps a lover was awaiting his return. That might be the reason he suffered at night. He embraced his brother's arms reassuringly, and nodded to himself.

He started walking again, towards the direction the walking stone pointed to. The night was chilly but dry; the desert was a harsh, rocky field of red and brown. It was good enough for walking, but useless for everything else.

Very little was to be found in the way of a shelter, and water was as scarce as snow flakes in the summer. The land offered little more than burrowing furry creatures and small sand lizards in the way of eating. God provided, as ever, but his brother was uneasy with what they were able to gather. At first he would not even taste the food, even when cooked on fire.

When hunger took over him though he mellowed, and grew wiser to the ways of God in His Holy place. Still, he seemed to be somewhat reserved in his adoration; somewhat aloof at times as if his mind wandered elsewhere. He could hear him sometimes speak in his native tongue, other times in the tongue of the Pilgrim's people.

In his sleep, he talked as well. The Pilgrim could not make much, though he sometimes spoke of the Forge of Stones. 'He is young, I'll give him that,' thought the Pilgrim and his mind echoed with worry: 'He has not yet had the time to fully embrace God in his true, purest, unblemished form. Here, in his Holy Land, where he is most welcome, were His Truth sublimes us all, even the rock and sand'. The Pilgrim felt his brother would learn though, in due time.

The Pilgrim saw in him a fervency, an ardor. He saw the determined glitter in his eyes, the way he looked at the Path, the awe when faced with the suns setting over where His Gardens lay. He was worthy of the travel, and the peril. He was a brother sent from God, indeed. Though his brother's purpose was still to be revealed, the Pilgrim knew in his heart his own was renewed; that he should act as this man's mentor and tutor, as a wise and benevolent father to fill his heart and mind with the joy that was God and Truth.

The Pilgrim's heart burned with vigor and his mind felt inundated in these warm thoughts of God and His work and plan. He was so enthralled with what God had in stock for them both that he had barely noticed his brother was not walking alongside him. He checked behind him but he could not make out his brother's figure in the blooming starlight. He must have fallen asleep again, the Pilgrim thought.

So he walked back over to the small sandy crest where they had curled up and laid themselves to sleep. He would be cold now that there was no god-stone to bring them light, heat and comfort. 'I should have been more thorough when I woke him,' the Pilgrim thought while walking with a sure, easy pace, slowly climbing to the top of the crest.

There, he saw him sleeping serenely this time. The Pilgrim momentarily thought he should leave him be for a little while longer, but night had fallen for sometime now and they had to take advantage it night as best as they could. When the suns rose again in the morning, the heat and the cloudless sky would make traversing the desert an insufferable affair.

They should be at the Dunes come morning, where the sea of sand could claim a man's life if he wasn't ready for its tribulations. God would provide, but man should be wary as ever. Many Pilgrims before him perished while traversing the Dunes, and left nothing but bleached bone as a warning to those that came after them.

The Pilgrim shook Molo more violently this time making sure he would wake up, stand on his feet and walk with him. It was for their own good and the good of the Pilgrimage. It would not serve God if they tarried and indulged themselves. That was one of the lessons his brother had still to learn.

Molo stirred and moaned a complain, something unintelligible even if the Pilgrim could understand his language. He rose from the ground wearily and languidly. He put a hand out as if letting the Pilgrim know he was really awake this time. He talked in low Helican, the commoners tongue, with signs of exasperation in his face and a disgruntled voice:

"I'm up. I'm up, you heartless driver. Don't you get tired? Don't you need to sleep? I guess you're used to this sort of thing. When will we be getting there? Do you really know or are we wandering aimlessly? You still don't understand a single word I'm saying, right?"

The Pilgrim smiled and made the hand gesture for 'God will provide', turned around and started walking while faintly motioning Molo to follow him with a flick of his wrist. Molo sighed wearily and started walking behind the Pilgrim in a disheartened fashion; he was almost shuffling his feet, kicking up small clouds of fine dust in the process.

The Pilgrim said something that Molo could not understand perfectly; something about the weary man finding consolation in God's plan, but he wasn't sure that was the proper translation. The man spoke High Helican, but it had somewhat mutated over the years probably, flex and intonation at wild variance from the original.

A strange thought came unbidden to Molo then: he thought that maybe it was the other way around, maybe the High Helican Molo had learned was the mutated form and not the original. Such linguistic considerations though mattered little since the only thing the man ever talked about was God, his plan, and this Pilgrimage he was on. That was alright with him; he didn't really care if the Pilgrim was a half-mad ascetic fanatic, as long as he brought him to the Necropolis. Then, he would see what he might do with him. Perhaps he knew more than he let on from time to time about the place. He talked of gardens and a citadel, and a forge of some kind.

He'd stick around, as long as the Pilgrim proved his usefulness. If they ever got there, that was. They had been wandering farther into the desert for a couple of days now. They had left the marble road behind two nights before, and that was about the time when Molo had run out of food. Perhaps the man had saved their lives, with his uncanny ability to find sustenance in such a forlorn and inhospitable place.

Though lizards and rats were not real food, it somehow became agreeable when one had not eaten in three days and the smell of cooked meat wafted into the nostrils. Molo shuddered at the memory of Pilgrim cutting the lizard's head off, skinning it, and eating it raw, from limb to limb. The man was a savage, that much was certain, but he somehow knew more about the Widelands than any man alive. He had only identified himself as 'Pilgrim', but that much was enough for Molo to call him by when the need arose.

They were walking through a rocky desert, sometimes passing through low crests on the same direction. From what Molo could gather from where the suns rose and fell each day they were walking roughly towards the northeast; curiously enough that was one of the few things that seemed to make sense. The terrain had progressed from a rough savannah into a rocky desert, and it seemed like soon they were about to enter the great sand dunes he had read about in Umberth's accounts.

From then on, he'd be almost lost. Esphalon had written down that once they had entered the sand dunes, the pack mules they had brought with them died being skinned to death in a sand storm they themselves barely escaped alive through sheer luck and perhaps as Esphalon had put it, providence. That was when they met the girl that went on to lead them to the Necropolis per se, which they had failed to enter after fruitless days of labor.

The girl was the one who sustained them through these perils, producing food and water out of what seemed to be thin air. That was not all though: The girl was quite insistent in preventing them in their efforts to enter the Necropolis proper, what Esphalon had described as 'a gargantuan cluster of megalithic buildings that either shone or absorbed light, tightly packed together as if they were wood on a basket, encircled by a wall that itself defied logic in size, shape, and function'.

She had even used some kind of invisible force on them, on more than one occasion. She had began to weep and talk incessantly, begging them to halt their efforts, as she 'pushed us away from what could have been an entrance point to the dead city, what Master Umberth called a Necropolis. She did not seem to be angry or wrathful because of our attempts but rather terrified, pleading with us to leave the place'.

Molo hoped the Pilgrim would be much more helpful in that respect. After all, he had told him he had to enter the Holy Gardens and pay his respects in the Citadel of God to reaffirm his people's faith in him, and be rewarded with the Forge of Stones. Those were the exact words he had used, in heavily accented High Helican.

To Molo that sounded like the man was planning to enter what Umberth had dubbed the Necropolis of the Widelands. Indeed, he was not simply planning on doing such a thing but was actually driven by a religious fervor Molo had not seen even in the Ministers of the Pantheon, or the most pious and faithful of the lowly people that clung to such notions like a man about to drown clinging on a driftwood. This Pilgrim though, was a different sort altogether.

His faith drove him; it inspired him, steeling his determination and making him an unwavering in the face of adversity. The contrast with the Ministers of the Pantheon was sharp: they instilled fear, caution, piety, obeisance, and misery. A faithful man for Molo was a fool, a person reduced to a muttering idiot who felt the Gods were in his favor if his children were not taken away from him, and his crops were not dying of thirst or the cold of winter. The contrast was painfully sharp, and the effects of Pilgrim's faith on the psyche more than intriguing.

All around them the land was still, without even the sounds of scurrying desert rats or the rush of wind from a night gale. All he could hear was their feet on dirt and sand, and perhaps the sound of gravel as they trod their feet over rough patches of it.

He noticed how much his boots were worn out by now. It was not the many miles he had traveled until he met the marble road that had made them so. It was the relatively few days he had been walking in the Widelands that had made him feel he should've packed a pair of boots with him. The hot days and chilly nights had put some stress on the boot's leather skin, but it was mainly due to the pervasive asperity of this place, this outer desert, and the abrasive nature of the rocky ground; the mix of dust, sand, dirt and gravel that had made his boots little less than sheets of leather about to slit themselves open.

It remained a mystery to Molo how the Pilgrim could remain unperturbed by the roughness of the terrain, the adverse conditions, and the unforgiving miles he had walked to get here in the first place. As far as Molo knew, the Pilgrim's people were nomads living in the cold, harsh tundras of a northern island. It was understandable that he would be proficient in survival skills, but his ability to adapt to changes in climate and terrain seemed unrivaled.

But there were also the strange stones Molo had noticed the Pilgrim carried with him. These were small stones but regularly shaped, as if they were purposefully cut by human hands. They were dark green, with violet and cyan lights flashing in the morning suns, their surface smooth but with mysterious shapes looming right below their surface, like patterns that kept changing each time you looked at one. They closely resembled what Molo had known as keystones, though he had never really gotten his hands on one.

The Pilgrim used one of the stones as a guide, for getting his direction straightened out. Molo had noticed that every time the Pilgrim used it, always after offering praise to his God and praying, he slightly changed course as if adjusting to what the stone showed him. Molo deduced that the stone was able to point him somehow to the direction of the Necropolis.

He had briefly entertained the idea of killing the Pilgrim and getting the guiding stone for himself. He had decided against such an action though because he believed the Pilgrim would be much more useful when they actually entered the Necropolis. The other stone he used was entirely fascinating as well, Molo thought.

It was what the Pilgrim used for shelter in this forsaken land, and probably something his people also used to stay alive in the harsh tundras of the north. The stone was a marvelous object: It offered them a small glowing light, enough to see each other's face in the dark, and it exuded warmth but unlike a fire, the warmth did not seem to radiate from the stone. It felt as if they were enclosed in a bubble of sorts where pleasant warmth occupied it, and the sounds and the wind outside were kept at bay as if by magic.

Indeed each time the Pilgrim used it, it was as if they were suddenly put inside an invisible bubble of glass that was protective and mindful of their basic comfort. From what he had seen, he believed that whatever the conditions outside, such a stone could keep them warm and dry; it was exactly what a body would need to stay alive in any climate. Molo sniggered at the thought of such a fantastic artifact of mysterious origins and unheard of qualities as that stone, in the hands of a savage that could barely use a wheel, if in fact he had ever seen one in his life.

But Molo felt there was probably so much more he could learn from the Pilgrim. So many mysteries that could be unraveled just because the Pilgrim knew these things, like he had always known them. As if it were rote, custom, and legend that was passed on from generation to generation.

Molo thought more about how the Pilgrim had introduced himself at first, and remembered that he had referred to himself as 'a' Pilgrim. Which meant that there were others as well. Or had been others in the past. He had not broached the subject because when he did ask the Pilgrim about things, even about relatively simple things like what they would eat or when would they stop for a break, the answers he received were nothing short of enigmatic, occluded by religious reverence and pious deference to God and his plan.

Molo believed that asking him about his Pilgrimage was a bad idea; the dark-skinned man would erupt in a series of prayers and gestures, reciting long stories of tradition as well as many other minutiae that would only complicate his efforts at understanding whatever useful information and knowledge he could offer.

He believed that it was best he gathered what the Pilgrim would share without knowing, and infer whatever knowledge he could from scraps of information alone. When the time came perhaps Molo could press him for more, or do away with him outright. He did not think the Pilgrim could be extorted through fear or driven to betray his beliefs.

Even if his life was forfeit, he would rather think himself as a martyr: a holy failure. In that regard, Molo had to endure his presence and learn as much from him as possible through what little interaction they had. Truthfully, Molo did not think he would have been able to survive the tribulations of the desert had it not been for the Pilgrim and his stones.

The Pilgrim had turned around to check up on how far behind he was. He noticed Molo was grinning, and smiled with puzzlement and naivety. Molo took the chance to build more of a rapprochement with the Pilgrim, something he could perhaps use later on.

He remembered that according to Esphalon, the nights when Pyx, the brightest star in the sky hung low in the sky, were held as having special significance to his people for some reason he had not stayed long enough to decipher and understand. He had noted down how they paid homage though, which was by turning to face Pyx, kneel down with folded arms and kiss the ground. Luck, it would seem was smiling to him: Pyx was flaring bright and low in the horizon. He turned to face the lone star and went through the motions as well as he remembered.

When he rose again, he saw that the Pilgrim was wearing a sad expression on his face, as if he had seen a sorrowful sight. It was an unexpected reaction that made Molo try to copy his sullen mood, as if such was the appropriate thing to do. He suddenly looked solemn and respectful, just like the Pilgrim. The Pilgrim simply told him a single word: 'apalgos'. He then bowed his head and made the sign of God, and resumed his walk as none of that had ever happened.

Molo had not known that word. He had never seen it in scripts or texts, and it seemed to have no other common root or sound like anything he could understand. It was as if the word was new, or his vocabulary was incomplete. It baffled him, and made a mental note to himself to perhaps ask the man to describe it later.

He had seen how the Pilgrim had reacted when he had in error used the word 'Gods' instead of 'God', and he had instantly known the Pilgrim was a dangerous fanatic. It would not serve him well to have to kill him if he ever found out he was not really a fellow believer. He used the word 'our' when referring to God, as well as 'brother' and 'believer' when referring to Molo, who had never thought that learning High Helican would ever come to be of such a use in his quest.

The Pilgrim on the other hand, felt he understood his brother better. Everything made much more sense to him, if the man was on a journey of sorrow. It was only natural if he was grieving that he'd be troubled in his sleep, though aloof sometimes, disenchanted and forgetful in his devotions.

In a way, the Pilgrim thought, the Pilgrimage was even harder on

257

his brother who had lost a loved one. It was indeed a mixed sign for the Pilgrim: a grieving man on the Land of God that needed guidance and help to make it through alive and be free of his sorrow, alongside a Pilgrim that needed a focus lest he stray from the path of Truth, and fail his people and his God.

He had not heard of such a Pilgrimage before. He felt like the starlight shone upon him with the brightness of his God's light. He felt inundated with honor and love, but he was wary of such sudden rushes of strong feelings, and breathed slowly, carefully rearranging his thoughts and feelings to protect him from the sins of pride and arrogance.

It was in God's hand alone the manner in which his Pilgrimage would take place, and that was all that he needed to know. It did not mean he was special. It meant that he carried a special burden, and had a special purpose in life. Himself, he was but a man of God, as was his brother. They both had their reasons to walk this path. He felt reassured now, and he troubled his mind with such thoughts no more.

They walked in silence from then on, until their legs were sore and their throats dry. In the middle of the night, with nothing but the stars to shine upon their eyes reveling in their divine solitude, the Pilgrim stopped walking and gestured for Molo to do the same with a repetitive downward motion of his hand.

He did not like to use the words of God in His Holy Land in vain, or for mundane things such as simple communication. He found out the hand gestures and nods were enough, and his brother understood what he meant most of the time. Sometimes his brother spoke in this other tongue of his: a somewhat crude, harsh tongue, that seemed to resemble the Holy Tongue somewhat, but was far from it. Maybe it was a way to speak a form of his tongue without speaking the Holy Tongue vainly. Maybe their tribe was older and their customs still clung to the time before the Purge whereas they, the God's chosen children, had been instructed in different ways.

It was a miracle indeed to find another believer, another man of God, whose people had survived the Purge so far away. The wise men had always said that God works in mysterious ways, and lo and behold, a brother long lost is found wandering in God's Holy Land.

But it was real, as real as his purpose; as real as the True Path, as real as anything he had believed in since he was born. He was sitting down with his legs crossed while all those feelings of certain faith and the warm knowledge of God's plan working so delicately through him had left him with a smile on his face and tears welling in his eyes. He held those tears, feeling he would be misjudged by his brother and that would only serve further to his befuddlement, whereas he should be enlightening him by his actions alone.

The Pilgrim offered Molo his leather flask which was filled with water they had gathered from a meaty, barbed plant, its juices nothing more than water. Molo accepted the flask with a nod, sipped cautiously and dived in a sea of thoughts. It seemed to Molo that soon they would be entering the real no man's land, where nothing ever grew, and the only change was the shifting of the dunes, slaved forever to the whims of the wind.

Esphalon's tales of that part of the Widelands, the inner desert, were sparse and yielded little information. They were mainly concerned about the lack of water and the sandstorm that had almost killed them and denied them of most of their supplies and all their animals. It was a race for survival, and the telling of Esphalon focused more on how they expected their lives to come to an end day by day rather than anything really useful about survival.

It was the girl that had actually saved them. He would have to trust the Pilgrim for their survival. Unfortunately, he had not yet seen yet the Pilgrim use a stone that would produce food or water like the girl in Esphalon's account presumably did.

He strongly believed that the Pilgrim was somehow prepared for the ordeal. It was ironic, Molo thought, that a man like himself who bore a grudging disbelief against all sorts of divine creatures and indeed faith itself had such a strong belief in a man wholly devoted to a fantastic person, a myth.

The Pilgrim rose and asked for his flask. Molo drank once more, a greedy gulp running down his throat, refreshing and invigorating, exactly what he needed for the rest of the walk. They seemed to have a few hours until the suns rose, and from their unusually prolonged period of rest Molo assumed the Pilgrim was not planning on making any other stops, not anytime soon. That was just as good since the more they walked through this landscape, the less time they would have to spend in this treacherous desert, and the sooner they would arrive at their destination.

They started off once more and trudged onwards, Molo right behind the Pilgrim. They were silent again as ever and after a couple of hours weariness and boredom overcame Molo. His pace lessened and soon the distance between him and the Pilgrim began to grow. The Pilgrim took notice at some point, paused, and urged him onwards gesturing with his arms and head. He pointed at the horizon that was starting to colour itself crimson. It meant that dawn was near, and they'd soon stop, rest and sleep. Molo gathered what little of his stamina remained, and with painful effort picked up his pace.

In a matter of minutes, the suns would make their bright entrance and wash away the night completely. The Pilgrim stopped then, and beckoned Molo to come and sit next to him.

They were atop a rather wide crested hill of rock and dirt, coarse sand covering its ridge. Molo indulged the Pilgrim and as he climbed the last few feet, he could see the sand dunes before him eating away at the horizon, the crests of the dunes like waves of sand with their ever-changing nature imperceptible to the naked eye.

A thin line of blood red, sun yellow and sea blue hung between the sky and the desert. It was the break of dawn and the Pilgrim seemed to marvel at the sight, which Molo could not help thinking was indeed a sight to leave one speechless. The Pilgrim made his morning prayers and Molo followed suit, as had been the case since they had met on the marble road.

He then started looking around him as if searching for something that he had dropped. He moved over to a patch of sand a few steps away and with deliberate movements of his hands, he began digging into the sand with his bare hands. Molo frowned in puzzlement at this weird behavior, which topped everything the man had done so far.

Molo was even more surprised when the man briefly paused digging, turned around and nodded to Molo for help. Molo could not imagine the purpose of the Pilgrim's toils and he thought this entire scene to be acutely comical; it would have made him laugh profoundly if he had not been part of it. He acquiesced though, and soon enough found himself to be digging right beside the Pilgrim.

Within a few moments, he felt the sand damp under his palms.

Perhaps there was reason in this, and the reason was water. Soon enough a grin formed on his face while the Pilgrim remained apathetic, almost indifferent. They had dug out a small hole in the sand, where there was enough water to fill their flasks and perhaps drink a handful each. It was downright astonishing that the man simply peered through the sand and found a spot where water could be found barely two feet deep.

He could have never guessed such a thing for the life of him. The Pilgrim was proving his value to Molo with each passing day and he couldn't help but feel genuine respect for the man, even though he suspected there had to be some aid from the stone, albeit he had not seen him use one right then and there.

When their flasks where filled and they had some water to drink, the Pilgrim motioned for Molo to sit in a somewhat flat space of sand. As he did so, he brought out the stone he used as shelter, and set it down roughly between them. He made the sign of god and laid himself down, with his back to Molo. Soon enough, the air felt pleasantly warm. The suns came up, two blinding spots of light walking hand in hand rising across a violet-blue colored sky. Pretty soon, daylight became too bright for the naked eye to handle but where the stone lay, it was pleasantly dusky, and one could actually close his eyes and fall asleep with ease. Molo noticed the Pilgrim had already done that, the outline of his rising and falling ribs following the rhythm of his breathing: slow, deep, and steady. Molo thought to himself he might actually leave the man be, when the time came. 'After all, what harm could he do when the secrets of the Necropolis were laid bare to me', Molo thought.

They had slept away for most of the day. When Molo woke up, it was to the recently-made familiar smell of cooked reptile meat. The Pilgrim was handling the roasting of the meat on his knife expertly. Curiously, Molo noticed for the first time it was a knife with a strangely fashioned two-edged blade: one was serrated and the other seemed to be razor sharp.

The knife seemed to be made of steel or a similar metal, perhaps even silver, but that could not explain how it had been able to weather time without being reduced to little more than a useless piece of metal. And it seemed certainly implausible that a tribe of nomads on the brink of savagery could have fashioned a finely crafted blade without expert knowledge, foundries, forges and artisans capable of supreme craftsmanship.

He concluded in his mind that the knife must be a thing of a long forgotten past, a treasured relic that was handed down from one generation to the next, indeed crafted by a civilization the likes of which that had erected the Necropolis.

It was fascinating to witness an ancient relic wielded like a common utensil, nothing more than a tool, when it's value to knowledge and the unlocking of hitherto unexplainable mysteries could prove to be incalculable. Molo realized he had been staring at the knife for too long, his sight out of focus as if he was still drowsy from sleep, as if his mind raced to meet the dreamworld it had unjustly been forced to escape.

The Pilgrim jogged him back into reality with a slap on the shoulder that he must have considered an expression of brotherhood and amicability towards him. Molo noticed he was also offering him the knife with the piece of unknown meat on it, charred somewhat on the edges and slightly curled, as if it had been left to roast on the fire for too long.

Molo thought about inquiring about the origin of the meat, but quickly his inquisitiveness dissipated into a forlorn hope that some of the desert was populated by hares or something equally less hideous than lizards. The smile on the Pilgrim's face assured him of how wildly imaginative he had become concerning food during the past few days, and grudgingly decided to feed on whatever the Pilgrim had caught.

In reality, he thought it was quite important to never know what it was that the Pilgrim had offered him, especially since it tasted so much better than the previous things he had been forced to taste by necessity. The thought of actually beginning to enjoy desert-hunted reptile wildlife made him shiver with disgust at himself for even thinking of abasing himself in such a barbaric way.

Momentarily, the memory of some exquisite sauté veal liver assaulted his mind and he could almost smell its fine taste and texture against his palate. He felt certain he could kill a man for a glass of Fironian dry white. But all that was just tricks of the mind. He knew he was eating something that was meant to crawl and slither instead of walk, fly, or swim.

The illusion though, when maintained in his mind, was a shelter for his mind. A way for him to ignore the nuances of survival and proceed to complete his aim, his purpose. On that day, he knew he was much closer. The sand dunes beckoned before them, and it would take much more than the mere lack of luxury to prevent him from the most worthwhile of goals.

Once his hunger was satisfied, he took a swig of water from his own flask and rolled it around his mouth in an effort to wash down the uncannily chicken-like meat. Noticing that the eyes of the Pilgrim were lost in the sea of sand, he sat for a while idly gazing at the dunes, trying to make out anything worth noticing in the amorphous dune crests.

He felt that they should be moving on right away, but the usually relentless Pilgrim had quietened down and was sitting still and cross-legged on the warm sand, the shelter stone nowhere in sight. To Molo, it looked as if he was basking in the light of the suns, like the lizard he must have deftly caught with nothing but his knife.

He was serene, his face almost glowing from within. It was like looking at a man who thought his existence was made just and fair by virtue of his devotion to his God, his Truth and his Path. Molo felt like the man was actually basking in a swath of divine light; his God's gift, a warm and bright light that could fill a man's soul to the brim, and yet could not possibly be spilled.

Molo thought those were very strange feelings, and he could not understand how they had suddenly appeared unbidden. He felt a strange kind of sympathy for the Pilgrim, one he could not put down in all detail. Something evaded him, and though such feelings were not totally unknown to him, he had spent a great deal of his life hurtling them aside, uncovering the truth underneath such deceit of the heart and soul, ascribing the true logic behind such manifestations of the human psyche.

In this case, he was struggling to accept the fact that he had no easy answers, indeed no answers at all. The Pilgrim was a mystery that defied Molo's reason, since he was unable to fathom why this man exuded this air of spirituality, of homeliness and trust. These were feelings that Molo had years ago cast aside and attributed to man's various futile efforts at making sense of the world and his existence, making up emotions along the way.

But here he was, a savage man with no ties to such trappings of the civilized man, a pilgrim that somehow managed to cripple his mind with nothing but a smile and a prayer. Perhaps, Molo thought, these were side-effects of malnourishment and dehydration, a prelude to hallucination. There was something very strange about this Pilgrim. Or, he admitted reluctantly in his mind, he might have been wrong in some of his assertions about various things he had vowed never to revisit again.

The Pilgrim's pull on his shoulder brought him to the world of the senses once more. He could see the falling suns, their glare losing its strength as they slowly glided past the sea of sand into a thin velvet horizon of scarlet and violet blue. His nostrils were assaulted by the grains of sand that were starting to float wildly in the air, and he felt his mouth filled with the salt of the earth under his feet. He looked towards the northeast where their path would take them and all he could see was the ashen gray and dull brown-yellow of what he judged to be a cloud made of sand. And they were going to walk right through it, if his sight was as clear as his mind at that moment. The notion rang a deep bell of life-threatening danger that superseded every other thought, feeling and intention. The writings of Esphalon came to his mind, where he had written down about the sandstorm that almost killed them and left them hapless to roam the desert in vain:

'..clouds the size of mountains no man had never even imagined toppled the reign of the suns and cast them down into the night side of the world. The air was suddenly thick with dirt and cold as a dead man's touch, heavy with the sand and stone of the desert sea.

We made haste to what seemed like a rocky alcove in the distance, barely visible under the cusps of sand that harrowed the very air we draw breath from. The mules would not budge, no matter how much we pulled and pushed them. As the wind grew more intense and sand began to hurt our very skin, we had to abandon them to their fate, mindful to take as much water and food as haste allowed.

We hid under a rare rocky alcove, while a maddening storm raged just beyond the reach of our palms. A couple of feet separated us from the unwavering madness of this uncaring place that assaulted any form of life with the same deliberate indignation. For hours on end, all our senses were of no use. The howling sounds of the sandstorm ruled supreme, whipping the very earth, tormenting the sky, challenging the reign of night eternal itself.

When exactly the storm had died down, we knew not. All we could see was starlight shining upon the desert once more, as if nothing of import had occurred. It mattered not that the clean-picked bones of our mules told otherwise. That was the Widelands, and life had no place there.'

The words of Esphalon coiled in his mind like a snake ready to leap out from his mouth. He saw the Pilgrim was already putting some distance between them. He called out to him in High Helican so he could understand him without needs for further explanations:

"A storm is coming! We will die in there!"

The Pilgrim then turned around and looked at Molo as if he had uttered a nonsensical statement. Briefly, Molo thought he had mispronounced what he had meant to say and his words carried no meaning to the Pilgrim. A moment passed though, and the Pilgrim stroked his beard and nodded knowingly. He gestured for Molo to hurry up and come closer to fill the distance, while he set out again. Perhaps he had an explanation, or had already seen a place that could shield them from the approaching clouds that could grind anything alive down to the bone. When Molo caught up with the Pilgrim a few moments later, he grabbed him by the arm and forced him to stop, asking him in High Helican:

"What about the storm?"

To which the Pilgrim replied with a gaze to the sky and the sign of God.

Molo was now starting to lose his temper. This man must be mad, he thought. His mind raced with the possibility that this man had indeed been mad from the beginning and had somehow made a journey of thousands of miles only to offer himself as sacrifice or something equally idiotic like killing himself because he had sinned.

But no, that was not the case, Molo decided. He looked at his calm, serene face as he turned to face the sky and praise his God solemnly, and knew that he had a solution, he had an answer to their peril. He was certain of it, and his determination proved it somehow. There was nothing to be afraid, everything was accounted for. 'It will be alright,' the thought rang true in Molo's mind.

It felt as if the Pilgrim was the source, the reason for these thoughts. He seemed now to Molo like an unyielding, irresistible beacon of hope; he was unmoving as a mountain and stable as rock, a haven for any troubled soul. Molo's gaze was not as hard as it was before.

He relaxed his grip on the arm of the Pilgrim, and his jaw slackened. The dust was beginning to swirl around them, the sand getting in their mouths, trying to bore through their skin. It was a very strange feeling for Molo, surrendering himself, body and mind, to an illogical concept. He stood there transfixed; the Pilgrim knelt down before him, facing the approaching sandstorm head on while all around them the makings of a whirlwind abounded.

Molo had mysteriously let go of his prohibitions, of his logical and analytical mind, of his reasoning and his fears, and just trusted the Pilgrim. It was all a matter of trust in the Widelands, as far as he could tell. And he had decided to trust the man with his life, and ultimately his purpose in life as well. Which of the two he valued most, he sincerely could not tell by now.

The Pilgrim had knelt down, seeing his brother was filled with fear, worry, and doubt. It would be no different to God, for if he had deemed that he should live, he would live, and his brother along with him. If he had deemed that he should die, they would perish, and that would be the end of their lives, for better or for worse.

But to appease his brother and make him ready for the coming trial, the trial of their souls, he would pray. He would pray loudly and fervently, with ardor and passion. He would sing his praise to God, with all the power his lungs could muster, and he would ask forgiveness for their sins; known and unknown, willing and unwilling.

He would ask of his God to deliver them, but he would also offer his life and soul as a last service of his own volition, if so God wished. He would speak on behalf of his brother and plead for his salvation, body and soul, because he was a grieving man, born of pain and want; not a sinner whose mind was set, neither a blasphemer who thought himself beyond the reach of God.

266

He would pray until the storm had passed and their God had decreed their souls clean, fit for a human being. And his brother would pray with him. He turned around and saw his brother was also kneeling down with eyes closed, his hands buried in the sand. The sky was now bleak, the front of the sand storm coming to greet them head on, the suns drowned in its dark gray wave.

He turned around then and touched his brother's arms, who was already doing as he should. He shuddered slightly at his touch and then started crying, in fervor or in fear, the Pilgrim could not honestly tell. The Pilgrim started chanting, his clear voice challenging the howls of the rising wind, cutting a clean path through the hurtling sands towards the heart of the storm. And the wind grew louder and stronger; the sands started to tear at their skin, lashing them like razor sharp tufts of steely grass.

And then, while the voice of the Pilgrim went on unwavering seeking God, asking him to reach down from where he dwelt and lift them from their grim fate, the suns could be seen in their last streak of light, for once more hiding until the morning came. They left behind them a lukewarm trace of violet, stars already visible on the edges between sky and earth. The storm had cleared; it had dissolved, like God had simply wished it away.

The wind fell into a light breeze, and the sands quietened down becoming as still as the night that had just arrived. The Pilgrim made the sign of God and stood upwards, gesturing for Molo to follow him. He even offered him his hands which he rarely did, as if he thought it was unbecoming of a man.

His brother was still on his knees and had just opened his eyes. Without warning he saw tears running down on his cheeks, the look of a man who was blind and could now see again on his face. His brother made the sign of God, this time somehow different than before. It was quite possible, the Pilgrim thought, that his brother was finally beginning to learn how to love God properly, like any man should.

He pulled him up by his hands and they both walked away into the night. Now that the trial of the storm had passed they should be able to see the Gates by tomorrow night with nothing but pure starlight shining upon the sacred walls. He briefly considered telling him, but he thought he already knew. Why else, the Pilgrim asked himself, would he be carrying no guiding stone? It was because he knew. Because God had sent him.

Fear in a handful of dust

ENERAL Tyrpledge was riding his horse making an inspection of the City walls from a safe distance, his personal guard along with his adjutant following him from a respectful but close distance. He still could not believe he had been tasked with the sacking of Pyr, and if it came to that, its razing. The Castigator had been blunt in his orders and frugal in his explanations.

He had told him that the Patriarch was in league with a cluster of rebellious religious fanatics that wished for total domination of the Patriarch over the ruling council making the first move against peace and prosperity.

A messenger had shortly arrived bearing a message from the Patriarch, citing that the Castigator had been deemed unworthy in the eyes of God and that the Noble Representative, Lord Ursempyre Remis was the new Castigator of the Outer Territories. The General was dumbstruck, utterly flabbergasted at the turn of events, and did not know how to react.

The Castigator talked to him in earnest, urging him to uphold the Law, honor his rank and office, protect him and the Council as a whole and crush the rebels before they could take root firmly. Tyrpledge had asked about the Arch-minister, who had seemed a reasonable enough man. He believed he could intervene, somehow mediate, so that balance could be restored and things would not deteriorate into profuse madness at the speed of a rushing waterfall, as it seemed it definitely would.

The Castigator had informed him then that sadly enough the Arch-minister had been found dead, assassinated by the rebel scum, the henchmen of the unholy demon that posed as their Patriarch. Most of his staff were also cruelly killed, their skin flayed out to the bone, while the Arch-minister himself seemed to have been made the object of a ritual to the Deceiver, the False God. The Castigator expressed his demure belief that it been solely through divine will that he had escaped unscathed so timely.

The Castigator, with tears in his eyes had insisted that there was no better way to avenge the Arch-minister's memory other than to bring those heathen scum that had infiltrated their society to their knees, grind them into oblivion and spread their ashes in the oceans.

The effect on the General was devastating; in one night everything that he had been taught, everything that he had built his life upon was crumbling down around him, around them all. The Patriarch, in league with rebels? Absurd! The very word had fallen into disuse, and was used only in an historical context of ages past, or in thought-provoking discussion that rarely allowed its participants to delve deeper into such subjects.

The notion of rebellion was indeed, taboo. It had been so ever since he had learned how to read and write. He thought to himself with bitterness that he might have been spared such skills, but then again, how would the army live and breathe without notices, requisition forms, and orders in triplicate?

And the Castigator, fleeing into the night, beset on all sides by danger and hounds set out for his blood? All that the design of the Patriarch, with the Noble Representative aiding him? Him, the most noble of the Lords, ruler of a family of great tradition and honor, an arch-demon in the flesh, thousands of men doing his bidding like minions? 'Incredulous, inconceivable, unimaginable,' the General had thought.

It was only until he had seen the orders, written and signed from the Patriarch, to have his army stand down and ignore the Castigator before him as a traitor and conspirator set to overthrow the Rule of the Council; to disarm the men and dissolve the Army peacefully, under the watchful eye of the procrastinators.

The letter had been signed and sealed by the Castigator of the Outer Territories as well, Ursempyre Remis, the acting Arch-minister Burge Freis, and that buffoon, the Procrastinator Militant, Gomermont. That had been enough to bitterly set his mind and order the immediate assembly of all fighting units. Once General Tyrpledge reaffirmed his army's oaths to Castigator Olorius Menamon, he had ordered the army to march toward the City of Pyr.

They would march in a campaign to uphold the Law and free their land and people from the tyranny of evil men. Men whose sinister purposes knew no bounds and would stop at nothing other than the utter desecration of the Gods, the dissolution of the Law, and the destruction of their divinely crafted society.

As these announcements had been made in front of the whole army, the few procrastinators spread around the staging grounds having received word of the General's orders, fled with alacrity in an unusual sign of intelligence.

And so it had begun, the campaign that would forever change the history of the Outer Territories for better, or for worse.

The General had been musing on these recent past events for some time it seemed, because he could hear anxiety and worry in the words that his adjutant repeated in the same staccato manner:

"Sir, are you alright? Sir? Should I call for your physician, sir? Sir? Are you alright?"

Tyrpledge flashed red hot with anger, and suddenly violence seemed to seep from his voice:

"Gods dammit Guighan I'm not bleeding to death, am I?"

The major stood to attention crisply and bellowed as if he were still a young cadet at the Agogeia Militant:

"No, sir!"

Tyrpledge instantly relaxed when he saw the major acting like a young trainee and managed a sigh. He turned to look at his adjutant, seeking eye contact:

"Guighan, this is not a parade ground. This is war. War between brothers, between family. If I am bristling with anger and exasperation, it's not because of your stupid questions. It's because of this stupid war. However, one must choose a side. And I chose what I've believed in all my life. If that fails us, then what hope will there remain?"

"Sir?"

"It was a rhetorical question, Guighan. Don't fret about it. I was ensnared in thought. I still find all this impossible to digest; yet it seems I will have to."

"Sir."

"You must be an expert in terseness, Guighan. Let's continue the inspection. I need to find a weak spot, something we could use to our advantage. If possible, I would like to keep bloodshed to a minimum. The insurgents could be hiding anywhere, posing as innocents and sheltered by anonymity. Unless they put a jester's hat on with bell's and whistles, our soldiers will be unable to differentiate between the enemy and the common folk. Though the distinction by the time all this is over could become a lesson in semantics. Carry on, major."

"Sir."

Major Guighan saluted briskly and rejoined the guards further back, where he relayed the order to continue. With that they set off, the horses picking up the pace of a slow trot, and the foot-soldiers following briskly behind.

For the most part, the insurgents seemed ready to hold their ground and the walls looked well defended, with no exceptionally weak points in sight. No significant breach had been made from the first shots of the siege engines, and the rest of them had barely began to be assembled at that point.

Once these were completed and a point of entry selected, they would fire a barrage concentrated on a specific point in the walls, hoping to tear it down and gain entry. His cavalry had made attempts at reconnoitering but had not succeeded in gaining much other than some fatal injuries and lots of worn out horses. It seemed that these men defending the walls would not be caught napping so easily.

The General from this distance could see the milling masses of men, assembling to receive their orders for the day, cleaning their swords and tending to their armor and shields. He could see the pike-men polishing their halberds in an almost ceremonious fashion.

The bowmen were stretching the chords of their bows, testing their tension limits and filling their quivers with arrows. The swordsmen were up and about ready to be called into action, their longwords a mirror sheen, their chain-mails and helmets a steely dull gray.

The General was generally pleased with what he was seeing; the men were following orders, adhering to protocol, and going about their business as usual. As if this was one of many exercises, as if they were not marching for war against their own people. In a rare moment in his career, the General did not know what to make of that. Did his men care not at all? Or was their sense of duty overshadowing their other emotions? That remained to be seen.

The outlook of his army, he deemed, was a professional and deter-mined force ready for action. But some of the units though required special attention, because of their special nature and their special abilities.

The men of the vaunted Thorax regiment were still trying to put on their monstrously over-sized armor; they were huge burly men encased in thick sheets of plate metal, almost impervious to arms, even against steam rifles. They would form the front line of the assault, to cover and shield the men behind them.

And far behind at their maximum range distance, while all the rest of the army was preparing for battle, the crews of the steamers were making sure their machines would be ready when called upon.

Everything seemed as it should be; everyone seemed professional, going about their work. It somehow felt wrong for an army to be this distant, so indifferent to an enemy that was in fact their own people, though wildly misled and utterly wrong in their decision to upset their way of life with shattering consequences. Or so Tyrpledge felt. He didn't know and could not know though, what his men thought and felt. He'd have to wait for them to show their true demeanor and spirit in the ultimate test: battle.

When battle would be joined, the true feeling of his men would emerge. Beyond wrath and blood lust, beyond the will to survive and in doing so kill a man, would they show remorse? Guilt? Would they stay their hands in a moment of doubt? When they would see their own brother coming at them with ax and sword, will they judge him wrong or will the animal inside have the final word? When all this will be said and done, will there be victory? Or nothing but loss? It would be for the Gods to decide. Himself, as General of the Army of the Outer Territories, decided he would follow his own path to the end.

His look was now veritably sullen, withdrawn. He had reined his horse to stop its trot. He was not even looking at the walls now or his men, or any of the machines. He was looking at his own hands with gloves taken off, fearing that somehow blood had already soiled them. The blood of his own people. But their lives were forfeit now, he knew, the very moment they decided to carry out every unholy blasphemous act ever imagined. What did they hope to gain, other than seed war, bloodletting, misery, and hate? He could not fathom. He could never remit their folly now. They may have dug their own graves, but the thought that he would have to fill them saddened him very much.

He looked up again, squinting slightly at the bright light of the suns. He noticed from the corner of his eye Major Guighan approaching almost sheepishly, a trait that usually provoked his anger and irritation even though he did not consider himself an irascible man. It was probably because he expected men around him to perform their duties to the best of their abilities. Major Guighan was his adjutant so he was supposed to stay close to him, advise him, and confide in him. How could he do that from all that distance? He was an exceptional logistics officer, very capable at handling personnel and men via manifests and report forms, but his communication skills were somewhat sub-par. Perhaps the Major was for some reason intimidated by the General or his rank and office, but that would not do for the position he currently held, in the General's opinion.

When the Major approached him at a respectful distance as if the General emitted some kind of aura he did not wish to step on, he saluted crisply and asked him in a most professional, clipped tone of voice:

"Sir. You seem to have stopped here for no apparent reason. Is there something of specific importance at this part of the walls, sir? You also seem to have lost your color sir, if I may add. Perhaps you are feeling ill? Should I fetch the physician, sir?"

Tyrpledge turned and stabbed the man with his eyes, his face a mixed expression of exasperation and wild disbelief. The General was thinking he would give the Major one last chance before he placed him at the front of a Thorax battalion, with no armor whatsoever. With evident effort to restrain himself he replied:

"Should I require a physician, Major, I will ask for one myself. Unless of course I'm bleeding to death. But that's the reason you are my adjutant, it seems. You always remind me blissfully that I am not bleeding to death. You accomplish that with your hollow remarks and repetitively inane questions. I will ask you just this once Major, to act accordingly and spare me the dung. If there is something of import to be said, say it. If you think a question in matters of tactics and strategy is pertinent, ask. You've proved to be an efficient man. Now, please prove to me you are an efficient soldier as well. There will be death around here by nightfall. Don't ever ask me again if I'm feeling ill."

Major Guighan stood stock still as the General's incisive remarks made their way to his heart and mind. Before the General could turn his gaze elsewhere, the Major managed to speak:

"I will not, sir. I realize now I had been wrong to assume you were a cold hearted bastard, sir. I could not bring myself to speak openly to a man who seemed not to care. I know differently now. With that being said, I believe we have made an extensive exam nation of the walls and no notable weaknesses have been spotted. The patrols will try again at nighttime, though we are not expecting any hopeful results. The men seem to be ready as they'll ever be for such a fight. Should we return to the staff tent and plan our tactical approach on the matter?"

Tyrpledge was stunned to hear the man speak his mind after all this time. He believed no one had called him like that since he had become the General, and he also felt kind of hurt that a member of his staff would think him so. It actually meant then that the others thought so as well. He guessed the major would make amends though. After a somewhat awkward moment of silence, Tyrpledge replied:

"I'd never thought I'd pass for cold-hearted. Very well, major. Tell the guards to lead on, and stay with me for a change. Tell me what you think about our approach."

Ursempyre was fretfully looking over the tall arched balcony of the Disciplinarium's east tower. His gaze was deeply woven with sorrow and hurt. His soul felt empty and broken. Whatever he had been planning, was now nothing but a dream. The gale of the wind brought to his nostrils the smell of ash and cinder.

Fires had started in some parts of Pyr. Fires from the siege engines of the Army. Tyrpledge was leading them, a good man as far as he could remember, as far as he could judge a man. He believed he no longer had that privilege. Who was he to judge others? A consummate traitor, by any account. He was bereft of the things he valued most: Truth, honor, friendship.

He had lied, and he had deceived. He had lost his honor and sworn oaths that had filled his mouth with venom and choler. He had sacrificed everything, to save something. And now this. Within a single night he had been duped not once, but twice. He had been played like a puppet, and now his people would pay the price. All of his people, not just the kinsfolk, not only those that were prepared to pay some price. Everyone would now pay for his failure, his lack of wisdom and foresight. He had been arrogant, he could see that now.

He had believed himself capable of achieving the dream of countless generations, becoming the leader behind which the kinsfolk would spread like wildfire, uniting the people against a tyranny as old as stone and earth. He believed he could have liberated them all and usher a new era where every breath would smell of freedom instead of fear and oppression. He loathed him! That was what had blinded him. Loathing, unquenched passion and blinding wrath. The Patriarch was more than merely shrewd; he was a demon incarnate, laughing behind their backs, toying with their minds and souls. Every single thread of fate firmly in his hands like reins.

Only last night, he had thought that the worst fate could have in store for him was horrible and meaningless torture at the hands of the Patriarch. Now, he was in living hell unable to even scream in agony. There was no point, none would listen to him now. He had been crushed, mind and spirit, in one blow. He had been quite effectively made redundant, irrelevant, obsolete. He should not have given the Patriarch's offer any thought. He should have denied him. Denied his immense powers, his demonic shell and form. He should have told him that his people were not afraid of death. That it did not matter to him if they perished in eldritch hellish flames, or bled their lives away one by one by sword and bow.

But that would have been a lie, and the Patriarch would have seen through it. There was no hope all along, Ursempyre thought. As fate had brought things together, and life had shaped him into the man he was, there was indeed nothing that could be done. He had lost this fight before it had even began. He could now do nothing but watch idly from afar, hoping his people would survive, that they would endure.

What would become of them then though? What had his mind devised? What end did the extravagant machinations serve. What reason lay behind this endless pulling of strings and turning of dials like the movement of wheels within wheels. They left them with a dizzying sensation meant to disorient and mesmerize, while right behind the shadows the real stage was being set, Lord Remis thought in silence.

The Patriarch's purpose might have been unfathomable, but Ursempyre was only certain that it held nothing good in stock for the people. If there was one thing he might try as a last attempt at redemption, was to try and learn as much as possible from him. He somehow felt that was as if trying to squeeze water out of stone, an impossible task either way one might look at it.

Sooner or later Ursempyre thought, the army would find a way into the city. They had the men, the equipment, and the time to do so. And then the procrastinators would perhaps find a deserving end unable to put up a fight; under-equipped and overwhelmed by numbers they would lose the fight for Pyr. Even though the total strength of the procrastinators had been summoned, it would take days, perhaps weeks for them to arrive in time to stem the tide of Tyrpledge's men.

Ursempyre tried to imagine what must be going through the General's mind at such a time. Was he torn between his devotion to duty and his feelings for his fellow men? Or did he relish the prospect of exacting vengeance in the name of the rightful Castigator and the Pantheon? What lay in his heart? Was it furious anger? Was it righteous wrath? Blind dedication and dispassionate will, the markings of a professional soldier?

He rather hoped the General was dumbfounded, left vacant inside at the realization of this horror. Perhaps he regarded all this with deep-seated consternation, and was troubled at his every step haunted by images of the monstrous consequences his actions would have for all of them. Was he such a man? He could not know and was deadly afraid that he would not like that question to be answered.

Lord Remis was standing in front of a stone arch, the weight of his body supported by his hands touching the granite as if they had been attached to it for ages. Servants had offered to bring him food and water. He had waved them away, but he could hear the frailness of their voices, their disbelief and fear. He did not know what it was that they feared most: the coming battle, the Patriarch, or the sudden realization that the world had come upside down in a single night?

His guards outside the chamber had seemed equally perturbed. Though hand-selected from the ranks of the procrastinators, they were not as blind and unintelligent as their lesser comrades. He had seen the complexion on their faces turn into the color of ash, blood pumped away from their hearts lest it explode in shock when they saw him appointed Castigator, in the stark middle of the night with only the Patriarch and a few Disciplinarium officials to attend as witnesses. It all seemed wrong, even to simpletons such as these.

He did not question for one second though that should he try to act wildly, fear would overcome and their instincts would not be reined; they would bring him down, as the Patriarch had ordered them to, 'for his own good'.

On recollection it seemed to Ursempyre that the Patriarch was somehow swinging this whole affair, precariously navigating between duplicity and lawfulness, trying to rewrite the Law and everything it had stood for since the very founding of the Territories. It was as if he had no clear view of the future he wanted to create for them.

If, indeed, the Patriarch had been planning for any future at all. Ursempyre thought such a being incapable of planning anything else than their complete extermination. The total annihilation of the Outer Territories starting from Pyr, the seat of power and Law. That would not be beyond a hateful being of such power, malevolence, and intelligence. The only thing that such a path would lack, would be reason. But then again, Ursempyre thought as he smiled bitterly and shook his head, who said reason had any part in all this?

Ursempyre could see now the smoke from the fires rising, procrastinators running in the streets, forcing people to follow them and press-ganging them to be used as firemen, workers, craftsmen, and ultimately, fodder. The siege engines of the Army were starting their baleful song again, the thudding and creaking of huge catapults and trebuchets launching stone and lit barrels of tar against the city, indiscriminately, randomly. They were killing the same people they were meant to protect. How very much like something the Patriarch would have conjured in his ineffable mind and ultimate wisdom.

He sniggered bitterly despite himself. Then he heard a sparkling voice and could almost see the insipid smile behind the words of the Patriarch without needing to turn:

"Quite a plan, don't you think?"

Ursempyre turned to face him, his eyes sizzling with hatred. He felt like lunging at him and ending this farce before he had to bear witness to the atrocities that would stain every street with blood and fire. But that would be cowardice, another treasonous step towards the hell that awaited men like him. No, he would try and make something out of this charade he had been forced to play in. So, he indulged the Patriarch's cruel sociability and answered with a flat, stern voice:

"You take pride in such things? What are you really Patriarch, if nothing but a demon in robes?"

The Patriarch returned an even wider smile, his teeth sharply white as if made from porcelain. He started to pace around the chamber, idly examining the various items in it as if he was genuinely curious.

"Calling me names, Castigator? How improper for a man of your rank and lineage. It has been my firm conviction ever since I can remember myself that the true nature of things certainly lies in their death. Only when something dies can anyone really understand what it's true nature was. Trees wither into ghastly dried hulks of wood. Plants rot away and turn into dust, returning to the soil. Man is a beast and like most beasts, he is made of flesh and bone, and the maggots make good use of him when he is dead."

The Patriarch very carefully intoned the last word with a certain nuance that made it sound hollow. Coming out of his mouth the word sounded like a wooden mallet brought down upon a plank. Ursempyre's blood was coursing fast and hot through his body, but he kept his temper in check, trying to make good use of his aggravation at being forced to play with words:

"Is that what you are planning? To see all of us men dead and done for? Worm food, is that what you think of us? Have you had this idea in your mind for long, or is it a newly hatched fantasy of yours? What kind of cruel nature gave life to the likes of a creature like you, I cannot fathom. I only wish there are no others of your kind roaming free in this world."

The Patriarch was looking at an exquisitely fashioned silver egg encrusted with gems. He looked as if he genuinely could not decide whether it was purely ornamental or served some functional purpose as well. He replied to Ursempyre with a nonchalant voice:

"Oh, no there are not. I can assure you of that. I killed them all long ago. But that is another story. You should not need to worry, I am not planning on telling you about it. At least not now. Perhaps, later.

It will depend. I am a very moody person, I don't know if you've noticed it. I tend to follow my whims. I feel one should follow his heart, don't you?"

Ursempyre felt ashamed he was still conversing with the likes of the Patriarch. His blood was now boiling and he couldn't help but explode:

"You mock everything around you with extravagant arrogance and cynical devotion to your own self! Would you have me tell you I do not expect for you to have any heart at all? Is this your only way to derive pleasure in yourself? By pretentious dialogue with your captive victims and human tools? Is that the best you can do, Patriarch? Toy with me while your plans come into fruition? Is this all you've come to expect in your life?"

The Patriarch's tone changed abruptly. He now looked severe, tense, his voice sharp and threatening:

"Careful now, Castigator Ursempyre Remis. If you are trying to attract my ire with an amateurish attack on what you would call 'pride', you are sorely mistaken and I can only feel genuinely sorry for your failure to truly understand. Though it would be more than a surprise if you did. I simply did not expect you to try and use cheap, underhanded tactics that only work with moronic politicians such as yourself. Though it seems idiocy is a useful trait in politics. It got you to the very top."

The Patriarch summoned a sardonic smile that made Ursempyre feel queasy. He was relentlessly carving up his mind and soul to feast on at his leisure. His words infuriated him and tore him apart at the same time. The Patriarch noticed he was not going to reply and pressed on:

"What are you thinking now, Ursempyre? I told you I can't read minds, not unaided. But I do take delight in toying with you, that much is certain. Why, you ask? Should it be beneath me? A being of my powers? You talk as if you could understand me fully, as you knew the extend of my abilities. You've made the same mistake as the men before you. Like Shan, especially like him. You think of me driven by the same desires and needs as you.

Do you really think this is about power? The ability to control others? That is nothing but a tool to wield. Power can be used to transform people, bend them, chastise them, shape them. Isn't that much more fun than simply using a person? I could talk around it for hours Ursempyre, but you would still lack the acuity of spirit to grasp the notion in its fullness. How could I explain something so simple to a mind as occluded as yours?

Vying for a freedom you would fail to maintain. Unable to control yourself in the simplest of urges you would wish you'd be able to assert control over power itself, share it as if it were some pie. The weak-minded leading the blind over a sheer precipice. Would you take the plunge first of them all, Ursempyre? Would you lead by example, like a good ruler? Would you become their final, benevolent dictator? Would you ruin my game?

That's what it feels like for me Ursempyre, a game where I can have it all if I want to but I choose to play by some rules. I set the scene and act my part, with you as unknown partners. What makes it so grandiose Lord Remis, is the fact that for the most part, you are willing partners. None of this foolishness you dream of, simple lust. Passion. Life exploding from every inch of your pathetic existence in contrast to your inane mewling.

This is life Ursempyre, and I'm living it. I'm living it as I please and there's no one to make me stop, no one to make me hurt, no one to make me feel anything other than great about it. If you could ever aspire to something Ursempyre, it would be to a perception as clear and total as mine. You would not weep then; indeed the idea would bring tears of laughter to your eyes. You would see the true nature of things. Despair now, for you very well know you have nothing else left to do in this world."

He felt inundated with anger and sorrow; he wanted to vent, spill this rueful cup of emotions he carried. He could not find the strength to do so. By all means, the Patriarch had managed to break him, force his will into nothingness and make him regret the day he thought about standing up against them and their tyranny.

He had not foreseen it had all stemmed from this man. That was his biggest failing, the breaking point when he had been canceled; when he had been turned into a shadow, a creeping thing that should cease to be. He felt like his very being was an affront to man. His dark thoughts had swallowed Ursempyre whole, and he lay there on the floor of his chambers upon a carpet with the embroidery of the Castigator, weeping for himself, mourning for the future that would not come, his people that would cease to be.

He had helped in that crime, he saw it again more fully now; he had been unable to do anything even now, with the root of the cause standing right in front of him. He was a lesser man, he knew then. There would be no turning back, for no one. Parts of his mind urged him to endure but his soul was crushed, the spirit gone. The Patriarch was right all along; he would despair, because nothing else was left for him to do.

Ikebod leaned his head carefully out of the corner of the street, and looked up the street to his right. Once he was assured it was safe, he made a gesture behind him. Celia and two trusted guards from House Remis came to his side. The guards wore nondescript armor and clothing: plain, unadorned and utilitarian. Their faces wore stern expressions, exuding an air of determination and professionalism.

Celia looked wary but she felt confident of her guides. She thought Ikebod would even give his life to protect her, if it ever came to that. Something that was more than a mere thought with the City burning under siege. The smoke from the various small fires hung thick in the air, the light breeze blowing through the city of Pyr unable to clear the atmosphere. The rosy red of the coming dusk was mingled with the sooty gray of the smoke, turning the air into a dark crimson red, gloomy and menacing.

They hurried across the street where the shadows would offer them some degree of protection from ever searching eyes. Word around the kinsfolk was that the procrastinators had begun press-ganging people in the streets, eagerly searching for any poor soul that happened to wander. Houses were being invaded and the men forcibly taken away from their families. It seemed that it had all begun quite the other way around from what had been planned.

Instead of leading the revolution, Lord Ursempyre Remis had suddenly sided with the Patriarch. It was more than a bitter blow to the Kin. It was an unimaginable, completely unthinkable event, that nevertheless had come to pass just the night before. From what Celia could gather from the dealings of Ikebod with various people from the kinsfolk while they still remained at House Remis, they were not safe in the estate.

They had to flee, and disperse. The various cells, the people in the organization delegated with some degree of organizational responsibility would convene somewhere else, in one of the places prepared elsewhere according to a carefully laid out contingency plan. No one had thought though that Lord Remis would be absent, indeed turn traitor.

She had not known the man personally, but from the people around him, she could not understand such a thing. Amonas was one such man, and he could never turn traitor; his heart and mind was, she intimately knew, utterly devoted to their cause. He had dreamt of a better future, and he had shared that vision with her. They were planning to raise their child in a bright, hopeful tomorrow. What would become of that vision now that everything seemed to crumble like a wall of dried mud around her? She felt the child kick with vigor, blissfully unaware of what was transpiring in the world it would be born in soon.

They were walking briskly, anxiously throwing gazes all around them, wary of being seen. Ikebod was leading them through the streets instead of the underground passages because he was afraid they might have been compromised. If procrastinators were indeed running around the underground passages looking for kinsfolk, they would be caught like mice with nowhere to run. While running on the streets presented a more obvious danger, it also offered them more venues of escape. It was a gambit they hoped would not fail.

They could hear the distant cries of procrastinators and the thuds of impacts from the siege engines. The army was methodical in its approach, wearing down the defenders of the city, forcing them to occupy themselves with the spreading fires that threatened to engulf them in a firestorm that would burn the city of Pyr to the ground, along with most of its populace.

When the opportune time arrived, they would then probably try to breach the walls in their weakest point, or storm them in mass, whichever would seem to offer the best chances of entering the city. As things stood, it was a matter of time. The most pressing issue though was what the kinsfolk would do in this mayhem. Would they try and rescue the city and its people from certain destruction? Or should they try and flee? Ikebod had seemed reticent to disclose any more of his thoughts on the matter, but he seemed to have his mind occupied with many other unvoiced concerns. Celia hoped he could also propose some solution, some idea that would bring hope instead of the gloomy despair and doubt that seemed to hang in the air.

They had reached another crossroads now and they were about to emerge in a brightly lit wide road. They were hiding in a dark alleyway, the light from the street casting flickering shadows on the walls around them. Ikebod and one of the guards peered over the street. Ikebod motioned the guard to hide again. He seemed agitated when he said:

"Procrastinators. Two, maybe three squads. They are herding a throng of people. It seems they're going to pass this way soon. Probably headed to a fire. I can see them holding buckets, and jogging briskly. We have to double back."

The guards nodded in acknowledgement and turned around to go back the way they came. Ikebod gently pushed Celia to follow them with him right behind her. Suddenly, the guards in front of them froze, and drew their swords. A patrol of procrastinators had seen them, and they yelled:

"In the name of the Patriarch, halt! Show yourselves!"

They had drawn their swords and were rushing to meet them. The guards drew their sword and stood their ground, ready for the procrastinators to come to them. One of the guards turned around to Celia and Ikebod and told them in a quiet, determined way:

"The way is blocked. We'll handle them. Go now, run. We'll make it on our own, fate willing."

Ikebod nodded crisply and took Celia by the arm. She turned around and opened her mouth to protest, but soon her feet were galloping in the pace Ikebod set. His pull became stronger as she seemed to hesitate but she yielded, her instincts driving her body rather than her mind.

They crossed the wide street without caring whether they or not they would be seen. It no longer mattered. They would now have to make haste, they had been seen. As they ran down the streets of Pyr passing through small alleys and brightly lit roads, they realized night had come and the buildings and houses around them were lit by firelight. Pyr was burning. Celia felt a sudden pang of fear grip her heart and instinctively tightened her grasp on Ikebod's arm. The wizened, trusted servant of House Remis told her soothingly as they ran together:

"Fear not, lady Celia. I keep my promises."

Her feet felt somehow lighter and despite her carrying, she made good speed and did not slow them down much. Ikebod was also straining himself, though she believed he was leading them with a fast pace, especially for a man his age.

They heard confounded voices shouting directions. Other procrastinators must have been alarmed of their presence. They could hear the galloping of horses on the cobbled streets around them. It felt like an invisible noose was tightening around them and was about to close tight too soon for comfort.

Ikebod urged her to hurry and spoke to her while out of breath:

"They'll be upon us, soon.. On the next turn.. Take a left, then right.. on the second street, there's an abandoned.. Blacksmith's shop in a dark alley.. Knock thrice, and then once more for two knocks.. And twice for one knock.. Thrice, then once for two, twice for one.. Understand, my lady?"

She answered with her brow furrowed from a twitching fear:

"I understand, but why are you telling me this?"

Ikebod was gasping for breath while his pace seemed to slow down, his feet finally starting to fail him.

"I can't go on for much longer.. I'll give them someone to catch.. Please, lady. Do not think about it.. Don't argue, there's no time.. I'll manage, somehow.."

Celia's grimaced with horror at the prospect, and protested:

"Sir Wirf! It's unfair! I cannot take such responsibility, not for your life!"

"Not your's to begin with.. Now, go! Think of your child!"

He freed himself from her grip and started heading the way they came. She stood there transfixed for a moment, and then thought of her child indeed. She believed she would feel torn inside, but the decision came instinctively. She ran with all the alacrity she could muster, holding her abdomen with care while she tried to follow Ikebod's directions to the letter.

She felt like crying, but the tension prevented her from doing so. She really hoped Ikebod would somehow make it alive out of this ordeal, but she did not really expect him to do so. She wasn't even sure about herself and her child.

She turned to the street Ikebod had told her and saw the blacksmith's shop, derelict and shabby from the outside. Wooden planks barely concealed its broken windows and a shrank, worn-out wooden door that seemed only half-closed. A rusty chain and a lock that seemed to be purely decorative in its purpose held the door from falling down.

She thought she heard then the pained cry of Ikebod from afar, echoing over the stones of the streets. She did not stop or look behind, she knew there was no point. She was in the dark alley looking at a rather sturdy-looking door. She knocked thrice and after a brief pause of silence, a reply sounded in the form of two knocks. She hesitated for a second and then knocked only once. Another small silence followed and the door opened, barely a fist wide.

Starlight shone upon the grimy, ugly face of a man, who asked her sharply without even bothering to look at her for a moment:

"Password?"

Celia was surprised and instinctively took a step back. She searched her mind for a moment, and could not recall Ikebod telling her about any password. She was worried she might have misheard or in the panic of the moment forgotten about it. Without anything else to reply, she simply told the man what she could:

"I wasn't told there was a password."

The man opened the door widely and ushered her in with fast motions. As he led her through the darkness of the shop, he asked her:

"Who was with you, lady?"

She replied without hesitation, a hint of grief was in her voice though:

"Sir Ikebod Wirf. He.. stayed behind."

The man was taciturn in his reply:

"I see. Come."

He reached for the floor then and pulled a hatch, then lowered a small ladder from somewhere nearby. Dim light filled the place. He motioned her inside with a wave of his hand. She hesitated and asked him:

"Sir Ikebod said the passages might be compromised, fraught with procrastinators."

"This one's not connected. In you go, lady."

"Where do I go from here?"

"It's a straight line. No doors or anything. You'll see."

She nodded and went down the small flight of steps hearing the hatch close behind her. She was standing in a corridor carved in rock, with lit torches affording the place barely enough light for someone to walk without running onto a wall. In the distance she could only see darkness, but she thought she could hear a din of sorts like men talking, some of the voices louder than the others.

She walked with an almost wary pace, not knowing where the corridor led. She felt unsure now, vulnerable. She thought of Ikebod and renewed her trust in him and his words. She should be safe here.

As she walked towards the dark end of the corridor, she could see light pouring in from one side. The din grew louder, and the sound of quarreling voices became evident. She felt pain in her lower abdomen, and flinched. With every step she took, the voices grew clearer. She could now hear men having a very loud argument, many people trying to speak at once.

She reached the end of the corridor and stepped through a narrow opening into a wide, much more brightly lit cave that seemed large enough for hundreds of people. Large stalactites hung from the ceiling and where mirrored in some places by their corresponding stalagmites. Some stalagmites seemed cut by man and others had joined with the stalactites forming columns; some were thin and others thick as pillars. The bright light was coming from numerous torches and braziers, casting enormous shadows on the walls of the cave.

She could see more than a hundred men standing with maybe a dozen of them to a separate side from the others, forming somewhat of a circle around a brazier that seemed to stand squarely in the middle of the cave. They were shouting at each other and she could not make out a single phrase. It was as if the market of Pyr had secretly gathered in here, each man trying to sell his wares to no avail.

She took a few more steps closer and she felt pain in her lower abdomen again, this time more acute. She let out a single cry as the pain came to her with a stabbing sensation and made her gasp. A couple of men that were standing closer to her almost isolated from the throng of people, must have heard her and turned to look. They were surprised and quickly strode to her side.

They seemed wary, even suspicious of her. As she stood there with an expression of pain still written on her features, one of the man grabbed her gently by the arm, noticing she was carrying. She asked her then while the other man was overlooking and the cacophony behind them continued unabated:

"Who are you, lady? Who sent you here?"

"Sir Ikebod.. Sir Ikebod Wirf!"

The pain welling up from inside her numbed her senses; she gasped and struggled to stand on her feet clutching the other arm of the man for support. At the mention of Ikebod's name they seemed to relax somewhat, but scowls appeared on their faces. The man who hadn't yet spoken asked her:

"Where is Ikebod, lady? Why isn't he here with you?"

She breathed heavily as if it would keep the pain at bay, but that did not hold any truth. Another pang of pain came and she gasped without crying this time. She managed to answer:

"We were seen. We ran and he stayed behind."

The man to whom she clung asked her then with worry in his voice:

"Lady, you seem to be in pain. Are you hurt?"

She shook her head without uttering a word. The other man spoke again:

"What is your name?"

"Celia Ptolemy."

The two men looked at each other with understanding. One of them said:

"Amonas' wife."

And then the other pointed to the ground at her feet and said in disbelief:

"Lady Celia, you are bleeding."

Another sudden wave of pain washed over her, the unwanted sensation lingering with damnable intensity. She looked down at her feet and she could see droplets of blood running down her feet, starting to form a small layer. Under the cacophony of the crowd in front of her, she whispered with anxiety to herself:

"The child is coming."

The Sleeping Man

HE first sense to return to Hilderich was smell. He could make out the distinct sharpness of metal lingering on his nostrils. He sniffed some more air and felt its freshness enter his lungs. His breath was easy now. He opened his eyes and his sight adjusted to the ambient dim light. He felt his ribs with a hand and could feel no pain. It seemed like what had transpired seemingly moments before was not a dream. He was feeling fine; his broken ribs seemed to have mended miraculously.

He saw the place they were in: It was a small nondescript room with walls colored in greenish hues all around. It was hexagonal in shape and the relatively high ceiling was etched in shadow. There was no obvious source of lighting, nothing in the way of a lamp or a torch. It was as if faint light somehow seeped through the walls and the floor, as if starlight somehow crept inside this strange chamber. Amonas was lying right beside him unconscious or perhaps sleeping. They were both sitting on what seemed to be a circular dais with a glassy surface made from a material that only cast the tiniest of reflections and seemed to absorb what little light there was in an uncanny manner.

Hilderich felt refreshed and invigorated. He stood up to gaze around the chamber. He was curious of their new surroundings and believed that they had probably arrived at what that voice had called the centron. It was a quite a long stretch taking the words of a disembodied voice seriously, but he felt he should put some trust in something that could mend his body without pain so easily in what seemed to have been mere minutes. What really mattered right now to Hilderich though was that they were off that accursed place that came close to claiming his life. They were not quite where they were hoping to be, but they were well on their way it seemed; that felt like a truly blissful achievement.

The room was otherwise uninteresting; it sported a single door barely recognizable by its very thin frame, probably made of the same material as the walls. As he was searching the room for anything that might pique his interest, he heard Amonas beside him grunt and moan slightly. He turned around to look at him and smiled brightly:

"You're up. I didn't know whether you were knocked out or just sleeping so I let you be. We're at the centron now, I think. I don't think we're seeing all this in our heads. If anything, I'd expect something more stylish," Hilderich said while gesturing to the bleak green walls around him with his hands.

Amonas looked disoriented and dizzy as if he had been very recently hit on the head with something quite painful but non-lethal. He managed to ask Hilderich with his usually gruff voice sounding even more coarse:

"Where did you say we were?"

Hilderich sounded quite exuberant:

"Here! The centron, if the voice we heard is to be believed. I for one, cannot think otherwise; my broken ribs are mended and my lungs feel fine. Better than ever actually. I even think I am a bit lighter, in a way. Would you say I had needed to lose weight?"

Amonas looked around him, soaking up his surroundings. He flexed the muscles in his hands and head with deliberate motions. His face wore pained expressions at moments, as if he had been injured and in pain. Hilderich noticed and asked him:

"Are you feeling alright? You seem a bit jaded."

Amonas nodded slightly in agreement and replied:

"It feels as if my head is about to pop open. I have this throbbing headache and a dull sensation. Exactly like being hit on the head with a club. You feel fine, though?"

Hilderich rocked himself back and forth on his toes and heels, his face beaming with health and good spirits. He replied with a grin:

"Does it show?"

Amonas returned his grin with a faint smile and nodded. He said to Hilderich with genuine bonhomie:

"It does, Hilderich. It really does. Quite a change in events that we have here."

"Indeed. But we're not quite back home yet. And I've been thinking only just a few moments ago.. My master's work were the keystones. He had this theory.. Well, many theories but I was not privy to the bulk of his work. I was supposed to find this man that held all the answers I could ever hope for. Indeed, all the answers our world could hope for. This man, the Stoneforger as he had come to call him,

I believe is here."

Amonas looked at Hilderich with some disbelief. With his head throbbing from a pain that had not subsided the least, he asked Hilderich with a puzzled voice:

"I knew Cimon was working on something concerning the keystones for a long time. He was quite reticent about it. I never knew much about it myself. Then again, we rarely contacted each other, even more so lately. But, what are you exactly trying to get at?"

"Please, hear me out. I believe this person, the Stoneforger, is not a myth, and if there's one place I could ever hope to find him, it would be this place. I believe that the voice that spoke to us and tended to my wounds is indeed what it claimed to be; from what I could gather, an ancient technological marvel. Do not easily ascribe such wonders to things as magic and Gods, Amonas. You were right to believe our world is built upon heaps of lies and deceit. I do not know what you saw when you stepped into that pillar of light the first time, but this time that pillar of light brought us here. I believe all the evidence you will ever need to show me is right here in this place, the centron."

Amonas was staring at him now with a frown, his silence a clear sign for Hilderich to continue:

"There is vast knowledge and certainly intelligence of some sort at work here, Amonas. It must be this man, this person I'm seeking. Though my reasoning is that he is so much more than a simple man. But he exists. He should exist. Everything points to that logical assumption. My master had devoted most of his life searching out for more clues to prove the existence of a place very much like what we are standing in now. It would cause him to gape in awe and astonishment surely, because he believed such a thing could only belong to an era long ago forgotten, to a civilization totally extinct. He believed that if he would ever find anything, he would find relics, artifacts, ruins. But as you've seen, there is much more to that. Inane artifacts like stone and marble and brick do not speak with disembodied voices, Amonas; that much is certain."

Amonas shook his head and replied to Hilderich as he stood up, his gaze now bearing tension. He still wore a pained expression on his face, only this time it was mingled with wariness and suppressed annoyance. He believed he was beginning to understand what Hilderich was about to propose and he did not relish the thought. He asked him tersely:

"So?"

"All I know is that the keystone is what has enabled us to reach this place. A keystone that was in the care of my master who had spent years of his life trying to connect the existence of the keystones with other devices, and an extinct civilization of extreme sophistication. The pillars of light, the pyramids, the keystone, the voice; all we've seen so far are indeed proof of the concepts and theories in his studies."

Amonas sighed and exhaled deeply before asking Hilderich with an increasingly exasperated look on his face:

"Meaning? Get to your point, Hilderich."

"I could never have hoped to happen upon such marvels by mere perseverance, Amonas. I would have spent my days around arcane texts and chronicles, researches, studies and dusty volumes written by men who had lost their minds in the process. A process that would take me years, perhaps decades to carry through myself; analyzing and cross-checking references, names, places, and artifacts. It would have claimed the better years of my life. And it would have proven a futile endeavor just like the one my master had embarked upon."

At the mention of Hilderich's master, Amonas brought to his mind the image of Cimon, always a thoughtful person, gentle and kind. A good friend with which he had spent many nights discussing the finer points of drinking. He was soothing for the soul, Cimon. And Celia was his offspring; she could not have been without him. He owed him so much more than a fleeting memory of a gone friend. His face mellowed somewhat, he even felt the headache had subsided as well. He asked Hilderich with a calm, friendly voice this time:

"What more do you know of his work? Of the war waged against him? Somehow, he always managed to change the subject. Surely, as his apprentice you must know more about something so pivotal in his work."

Hilderich shrugged with some hesitation, before replying as frankly as he could:

"Even though he was the first Curator to assemble enough evidence to support such a theory, when he presented his work he was met with derision, laughed upon as another half-mad fool. Sadly, only a few of his friends and colleagues supported him in public and pleaded for him to maintain his status as Curator, albeit on the condition that he would burn the bulk of his work and renounce it as a work of fiction. He had never broached the subject during my apprenticeship. I learned about it from my surreptitious ventures into his personal study. To tell you the truth, I did not believe him either, and sided silently with those who considered him a little less than deranged. I was sorely mistaken and the proof came in the worst of ways the day my master died."

Amonas nodded thoughtfully, looking for a moment away from Hilderich, biting his lip with a hint of consternation, as if sudden angst filled him. He then shot an even gaze to Hilderich and asked him:

"What have you been trying to tell me Hilderich? Speak your mind plainly."

Hilderich returned the stare and the words came out of his mouth as of their own volition:

"If it was by fate or chance alone I do not know, it really matters little to me now; but we have gone through a bewildering journey to end up in a place where myth meets reality. In a sense, stepping through that pillar of light was both a blessing and a curse. We're here now, Amonas, closer than ever. I need to find him. Not just for my sake, or my master's sake. It would be a revelation that could change the world.

Don't you see? We have to find him first and foremost before we do anything else. Answers to everything you could possibly imagine, Amonas. Everything is here. Everything began here. It must have. This is the place of legend man has locked out of his mind, but has kept it in his soul. A world that is somehow connected to our own. A world steeped in technology that is undreamt of. The links to a past that we had thought only existed in stories, and tales. But it's real enough, Amonas.

We have to find him, or his people. Their history, their lore. We must have access to it so we can learn of our own past. Don't you see? We walk into a pillar of light and then end up in another world with no night and the wrong suns! And now we're here, somewhere. Going back and finding the Stoneforger, those two quests have become irrevocably intertwined I'm afraid.

We can't go back unless we unlock some of the mysteries behind all these wonders we've witnessed. Whatever makes this place, this world even, tick, we have to find out about it. Let's find him, Amonas. Only then will we be able to go back. Unless you think we could just open up that door and be right where we wanted to be."

Amonas stood staring at Hilderich's eyes, a tiny glitter barely visible in his pupils. He felt compelled. The words rang true to his ears. He only believed he was doing the right thing when he at length said to Hilderich, gesturing with a slight nod:

"Like most of the time, you're right Amonas. After you then."

They were now walking through a stupendous underground cavern of exquisite beauty. Huge crystals of many colors and large clear-cut facets hung from the ceiling, mirroring their walking figures with pristine clarity, sparkling from the faint light that filled the vast space with remarkable ease. Some of their reflections were large enough to see clearly, even though the roof of this gigantic enclosure was improbably high.

Simply looking at it filled them with awe but disoriented them as well, making them feel queasy after a while. They had been walking on a narrow gangway that connected two crevices on opposite sides of the cavern. Far below their feet, furious swirls of white hot and molten red rock churned with rage, their incandescent light gracing the thought-defying towers that seemed to vanish into the infernal abyss with an eerie glow.

The cavern had stunned them with its wild, harsh beauty when they first laid their eyes upon it. The towers were another unfathomable wonder that imagination would have failed to conjure. They rose from the depths of the inferno of molten rock and lava up to the level of the unique gangway that traversed the astounding cavity.

Their surface was matte black, almost obsidian-like. It very much seemed to resemble the material the bullhorns were made of, but it seemed to lack the same level of refinement. It seemed as if it was more coarse in nature, more suited to the harsh environment they were set in. Indeed their foundations seemed to lie in a hellish sea of fire where nothing could ever hope to remain intact.

Yet, these towers endured. A thin lattice of glass-like pipes connected them, forming a grid. Bright white light seemed to flow through them with slow, deliberate pulses. A marvel of technology, certainly a feat of engineering only a civilization hundreds of thousands of years old could hope to achieve.

They had passed through various corridors along the way, not all of them uniform in appearance and size. Some were brightly lit, sporting white paneled walls of porcelain-like material; others were much more dimly lit, in the fashion of the room they had woken up in. Some were pitch black, none of their features visible.

Most were in pristine condition, like people lived in there and dutifully kept it clean and polished, but they had not met a single soul. Their senses informed them that this place was void of life, deserted, and abandoned. No smell or sound gave away the presence of living men. But there were no cobwebs, no dust, and no grime to call this place abandoned and forlorn.

The place seemed uncannily void of life, as if everyone around had left in a hurry, no detritus of their existence behind. But surely men must have walked past these walls, for though they varied, they seemed designed and engineered to accommodate people. Men like them; not giants, demons, or Gods.

It was a strange mix, this network of corridors and passages. As if it had been built by different people at different times, adding, removing, restructuring as they saw fit; by whim or necessity, it was impossible to know. Hilderich had been filled with enthusiasm at the thought of systematically mapping these passages; thousands of questions had formed in his mind seeking answers, in-fighting for a quota of attention and musing time.

From the moment they left the chamber where they woke up in, they had followed an almost random course generally preferring lit paths whenever possible. They had ended up in dead-ends, mostly doors that would not open of their volition like most of them did. They had backtracked and chosen alternate tracks. Marking the walls was impossible, as they seemed impervious to Amonas knife, unable to even put a slight notch on their surface, irrespective of the force exerted and the effort spent. Hilderich had been uncannily able to remember where they had passed from before, and thus they managed to not get lost in the irregular maze.

It had paid out in the end. Their path had taken them to the crystal-roofed cavern, with a brightly lit gate on the opposite end of the gangway. The gangway itself was as nondescript as the walls they had seen so far but what had genuinely picked Amonas' interest, apart from the immensity of all that surrounded them was that the gangway did not possess any guardrails, as if it was impossible for someone to trip and hurl himself down to certain death.

Amonas shared his concern before they had even made the first steps, cautious as ever. Hilderich briefly pondered such a scenario and with a wild grin on his face, before Amonas could react he had tried to simply walk off the gangway into the churning lava below. He had stopped in mid air with a silver sheen suddenly adorning the wispy air around his leg and knee, as if an invisible wall stood on each side of the gangway.

Amonas had sighed and scolded Hilderich in a fashion that made Hilderich laugh with all his heart. Amonas did not perceive the whole incident with the same amount of good humor and for quite some time he wore an expression of mild exasperation. If one did not know better he could have mistaken him as having his feelings genuinely hurt because of Hilderich's lack of consideration. It was dangerously immature, Amonas thought, for someone to behave so precariously in such a place of unknown danger and roaming uncertainty.

Hilderich seemed impervious to anything less than the magnificence of the wonders, both natural and technological that surrounded them while on that gangway.

While they were walking on the gangway with an easy pace, almost casually in fact, Hilderich asked Amonas without turning to look behind him:

"Impossible to imagine, isn't it?"

Amonas did not answer him, and remained silent as ever. He was not gazing around him like Amonas did, woolgathering. He seemed preoccupied, lost in wary thoughts about their imminent future. He could still remember stepping on that pillar of light, and could certainly remember their tribulations in that hot steamy world.

But this place, this centron, where was this place if not on that same world? Where were they now? Until he would find these answers, his mind would not cease to worry. He tried to remember more of what the voice had been saying to them, but he had been utterly confounded by its meager explanations. His mind was still jarred by the headache that though it had subsided considerably, a sting of it still lingered and made his thinking muddied and unclear, his most recent memories a blur.

It troubled him most that Hilderich's mind seemed to wander freely. He had turned from a reserved, cautiously inquisitive young man into an enthusiastic juvenile that would not leave a rock unturned until he had satisfied his insatiable lust for knowledge. Amonas on the other hand felt as if he had been forcibly restrained, not free to speak his mind.

They had found nothing to drink or eat, and every door that they had been able to open lead into what might have been living quarters, or other utility rooms. Some chambers contained metal crates they could not open and frustration had built up inside him. Hilderich was so excited with each new little discovery that he seemed unperturbed by the fact that like all living things, they needed food and water, and they had found naught. As if the people that used to live here in ages past conjured their food out of thin air. To Amonas, this place was even harsher than the lush wilderness they had left behind. At least there, they could find something to fill their bellies.

And what of their vaunted attempts at gaining knowledge, Amonas mused with aggravation. What had they found out so far that they could use? Almost nothing of import. All they knew was that they were somewhere deep underground it seemed, and that they had only found out when they ran across the cavern.

He sighed and looked at Hilderich in front of him, who seemed to be filled with vigor and an enthusiasm he thought to be unbecoming of the situation in hand. Perhaps he was rushing his judgment on this matter. It was in fact an unfortunate series of events that had led them there, to a bleak place that seemed to offer little, but they had been there for mere hours. He supposed it was too early to expect much from their meandering search. But soon they would have to worry about sustenance, purely in a practical sense. Amonas decided to let it be for now, but he felt his unease would only grow given time.

Soon, they were standing at the end of the gangway with a small plateau opening before them. There the large gate stood, set against a jutting rock wall that seemed to crash upon the it like a granite waterfall frozen in time.

Hilderich was marveling at the dimensions of the gate. It seemed large enough for a siege engine of the army to pass through, almost three stories high. Hilderich wondered what manner of things, machines and people, had passed through these gates. It was indeed larger than any other gate he had seen. What manner of need had led to it being designed and built to these dimensions? Another mystery for him to solve when time allowed it, he thought.

Amonas spoke then, his voice sounding somewhat distant, as if his mind was removed elsewhere and he was merely glimpsing what surrounded him:

"What of it, now?"

Hilderich took notice of the strangeness in Amonas voice, but he did not pay too much attention to it. It was probably the aching headache that did not seem to go away. He turned then and replied to Amonas:

"Are you feeling alright? You seem.. distracted."

"It's this headache. Won't leave me be. And I could use some water. Something to eat as well. Don't you hunger? Don't you thirst?"

There was a certain degree of exasperation in his voice now, which was focused, harsh, and suddenly almost menacing.

"Yes.. You are right. We should make that a priority once we get past these gates."

Amonas shook his head as if trying to clear his mind, as if his vision was blurry and his mind fumbling to find the words. He nodded then lightly, his gaze drifting away from Hilderich.

"Alright. I see. How do you propose we go about that? Are there any levers? Any wheels to turn? Should we knock?"

Hilderich's face showed his wariness. He did not know what to make of Amonas' strange behavior. These mood swings and the evident trouble he had concentrating, these were things he would have to ask him about soon. Preferably when they had something to eat. He was indeed beginning to feel famished. It was the endless fascination and enthusiasm that kept him going, the tension, the thrill. He noticed Amonas' was looking at him with an aggravated, expectant look, and answered him in an excusatory tone:

"Ahm. No, though it might come to that. Knocking, that is. There seem to be no visible controls, which would suggest that this gate can only be opened from the inside. Or, that it's just another large door that opens up on itself like the ones before. We'll just have to see now."

Amonas grunted with restrained disapproval and nodded. Hilderich had known Amonas to be circumspect at times, taciturn and almost spartan with his words sometimes, but he had never showed feelings of dislike or animosity towards him. He was beginning to feel that had somehow changed since they arrived in this place, the centron. Maybe he was having second thoughts about their change of plans. Maybe this place made him uneasy because of its otherworldliness, its antiquity. Maybe it was because they were still alone, not a soul in sight. With the exception of that weird voice of course, if it indeed had a soul.

After his brief inner contemplation, Hilderich stepped on the flattened plateau of rock. It seemed to be cut cleanly and then carefully smoothed, just short of turning its surface slippery. He took a few more steps and stood before the gate, gazing at its minimalistic features. It seemed to be made out of a dull gray, not a single ray of light reflected off its surface. It almost looked like stone, but it had no pores and no cuts to speak of.

Hilderich looked at it with one eye. It's flat gray surface reminded him of bricks made of argyle and ash. The borders of the gate were different, though. They were a uniform white material, almost porcelain-like and glossy with a smooth reflective quality. The two pieces did not seem to fit together at all. Hilderich thought there should be some sort of adequate explanation for that, but whoever had built this gate did not seem available for answers. Hilderich conjured the image of the builder of the gate being asked why the colors in his gate seemed all wrong, and the childish thought brought a grin to his face.

As much as he looked, Hilderich indeed could not discern any sort of controls, levers, ropes, weights, or wheels; nothing a gate could be associated with in his experience. Then again, it would have been almost ridiculous to expect such crude forms of mechanisms in such a place after what they had witnessed. But it never hurt to check the obvious things first, so he simply leaned against the door, standing smack before the middle of the gate and pushed.

Nothing seemed to happen. He turned around and looked at Amonas, shrugging. His was an apologetic look, and after a while he said to Amonas:

"I'm sorry. Nothing you would expect in a gate of this size. I guess we should try knocking after all."

Hilderich thought Amonas had a very strange expression on his face. To him, it looked as if Amonas had felt incredibly stupid somehow, perhaps like if he had tried to cut a rope with his knife still sheathed or poured himself a glass of wine from an empty bottle and drank it anyway. It was the look of a deeply dumbfounded man. Hilderich was suddenly worried, believing the man to be sick and in need of aid. Even though he seemed unable to speak, Amonas managed to point with his hand to the gate.

Hilderich turned around and to his great surprise saw the door had vanished, a sight that assaulted his vision.

He was now standing in front of a hall of sorts, only the word 'hall' did it no justice at all. It was a gargantuan circular chamber of immense radius, nothing short of a small plain. It must have been the area of a small township, complete with the surrounding fields. It would probably take them hours or the better part of a day to walk across it. Its dimension in height was almost impossible to measure. The walls ran seemingly as high as the sky. And there was something about the lighting that seemed recognizable.

His feet moved of their own volition then, guiding him to enter this vast space proper and see better, even though sight alone was incapable of handling such a view. Air wafted down upon him, as if from an overhead opening. It was dry and chilly, almost cold. Instinctively he looked up, expecting to see some sort of mind-boggling roof structure, something truly awe-inspiring as the rest of this vast enclosed space was.

With a mix of terror, bewilderment, joy and disbelief that contorted his face in an almost painful way, what he saw was clear blue sky set between the circular edges of the walls, as if looking down a very long pipe. The distance was immense, unimaginable. Sunlight shafted down in an angled column overhead and its reflections on the surface of the walls gave this place this familiar ambient light. As he looked up, he saw the bright ring of the sun appearing over the edge of the walls. In a moment or two, the pillar of light would fall on him bathing him in light.

He turned around to Amonas who stood where he was, transfixed. He called out to him, gesturing wildly with his hands to come and see for himself. Amonas shook suddenly, as if waking up from a living nightmare, almost trembling. He shook his head, and came to Hilderich's side with a brisk pace. His gaze wandered around as if this was a strange hall or just another chamber, unable to feel mesmerized at the impossibility of the scale surrounding them. He just said then:

"It's.. big. Very big. Huge, indeed."

Hilderich spared a moment to look at him sideways. The significance of Hilderich's furrowed look was lost to Amonas, who looked extravagantly out of place, acting almost nonchalantly, indeed very much unlike him. Hilderich did not press the matter and instead pointed at the sky, the bright rim of the sun glinting at the far edge of the wall. He pointed upwards and said:

"Look how far these walls reach. This is colossal. The sun can barely reach this far down this sort of, shaft, for lack of a better word."

"Hmm."

Amonas suddenly looked thoughtful, as if contemplating not what Hilderich had said but rather as if he was trying to come up with a better word than 'shaft'. Hilderich was about to ask him about this sudden rush of strange behavior but then the sun shone upon them momentarily blinding them, causing them both to squint and use their hands to block it out.

In that small sliver of shade that allowed them to peep sheepishly at the sun, Hilderich could see its ring grow, the bright sphere grow larger. It looked strangely familiar though. The sun did not seem to have that blueish hue. It looked.. normal, Hilderich thought. And then, he saw a sight that had sorely been missed. As the sun grew whole, another ring appeared over the edge of the wall, at that other end of this huge shaft. A second sun. The second sun. There were two suns. They were home.

The realization struck Hilderich like a sledgehammer and he physically reeled from the place he stood. He was frantic, his gaze switching between Amonas and the sky with cataleptic speed. He opened his mouth as if to speak but he simply managed to gasp. All the while, Amonas was still looking at the suns in a sort of peaceful gaze, the falling streaks of sunlight adding a glow to his face that made him look more splendid and grandiose than ever despite his disheveled look and ragged appearance.

Hilderich then shouted with glee:

"We're home! Can't you see? Two suns! Right there, up on the sky! Our world's two suns, Amonas! We're here alright!"

Amonas turned to look at him slowly, almost indifferently, as if Hilderich had barely nudged him and asked for directions in the street. It was beginning to feel eerie to Hilderich, this behavior that was very much unlike Amonas. He looked as if he were someone lost. They were home, Hilderich thought, and he was simply standing there looking back at him as if he had nothing better to do. Hilderich grabbed him by the arm shook his entire body, as if Amonas offered little resistance. He looked him in the eye with an accusing stare and shouted in his face:

"We're home! Like you wanted! Like we wanted from the start! This place is somewhere on our world! Why aren't you at least excited? What is the matter with you, Amonas? You're acting like, like.. Like a stranger! Speak to me plainly!"

Amonas looked at Hilderich almost impassively with a look as if behind a fog, his mind seemingly wandering off to places without any connection to reality. It was as if he was in a dream haze, unable to wake up from the slumber of a mystic.

"Amonas! Don't look at me like that! Tell me, what is wrong with you! Don't you see, we're finally here!"

Amonas did not even flinch. He had actually remained quite motionless, his hands limp on his side and his face stuck in a slight grin, as if constantly mocking someone. This could not be good, Hilderich thought. He shook him with both arms, trying to snap him out of whatever had enthralled him so. He shouted, cursed, he even slapped him twice. But it was all to no avail. It was as if the man's mind was gone. As if he was not there at all.

Hilderich realized with horror the truth of it. For some inexplicable reason, Amonas seemed to have lost his mind. It was there, carved upon his face. A glazed look, a deep blur set in at the center of his eyes, unmoving. His face had started to lose its color, and his mouth seemed locked in a half-smile. It was the face of an idiot unaware of everything going around him, lost in a sea of reality's debris none could hope to help him navigate. It was heart wrecking to see a man's mind lost in moments.

Had it been the simply immeasurable vastness of the vista around them, this huge shaft that no mind could lay claim to even imagining it? Was it the sudden realization of having returned home in a most inexplicable, wondrous, and even uncanny fashion? Was it the combination of both? What had weakened his strong, determined mind? What had broken a man who was ready to give up his life for his unborn child, for a different, if not a better future? Hilderich could not tell, and only thought that it was an ineffable loss.

They had seen marvels none had ever dreamt before and had taken most of them in their stride, their sanity intact. It was almost a laughable joke to think that Amonas would lose his mind at that moment, after all they had seen. And yet here he was, a little more than a breathing mass, completely disassociated with his surroundings. It sank his spirits right when they should be laughing with all their heart, crying with joy from the release of the tension from so many days of hardship and uncertainty.

Hilderich for a moment thought that it might have been better if Amonas had died somewhere along the way. He would have at least had his body and mind as one, his soul intact. Now, he looked as if his soul had departed and left an empty mind to rule over a hapless body. It brought tears to Hilderich's eyes. But he held them in check.

He had been mended before, when the voice spoke to them. There was proof that the ailing of the body could be treated with unsurpassed excellence by something or someonw that seemed to dwell around here. That could also stand true for a sickness of the mind. For what was madness, catatonia, or whatever else that had befallen Amonas, other than a sickness of the mind? For every sickness there should be a cure Hilderich thought, and his face brightened up a little, hope returning to his eyes.

It seemed that their quest kept redefining itself. Now, he owed it to Amonas to make him whole again. And he should better get an early start. That meant he had to focus his mind, accept some harsh facts, and make decisions that would lead them out of this very unfortunate situation.

He took Amonas by the arm as if he would do with a small child, carefully and softly. He did not seem to respond in any way, his posture unchanging and his gaze fixed to a point beyond his sight. Hilderich tried to pull him by the hand and with a slight lurch and a small misstep, he began to walk behind him, as if he were a blind man being led around by a trusted friend. Half that much, Hilderich thought, was true.

He could be moved around then, Hilderich thought bitterly, albeit as if he were indeed an invalid. It all felt wrong to him. Seeing Amonas in such a state was almost devastating. If such a man could be brought so low without warning, whatever else could happen to lesser men, Hilderich thought. He hoped Amonas' mind was so far gone that he at least did not perceive himself through Hilderich's eyes or had any sort of knowledge or awareness of what had befallen him.

If that was the case, Hilderich doubted Amonas could ever return to his normal self again; a tragically traumatic experience such as this one would be enough to break him by merely remembering. He thought Amonas was a stronger man in every aspect that really mattered. If he was subject to such a downfall, then why not himself? For the first time in the past few days, real fear gripped him.

Not anxiety, not worry or wariness but simple primal fear. The piercing fear of someone's shadow behind your back. The fear of a man's knife, a howl into the night; fear of thunder and lightning. Pure, instinctive fear. He was alone, by himself. If he had been alone on that pyramid, if he had made it that far, he would have died with broken ribs sun-burnt to death before anything else, if it wasn't for Amonas. And now, he had to repay that life debt.

The suns were now shedding their light higher on the walls of the shaft, their bright spheres gone from Hilderich's sight. He had to address an issue that seemed to lack an easy solution. Where could one find food and water in this immensely vast space? He looked around him at the landscape stretching out in front of him. The floor was blue-gray and metallic. Various thin lines seemed to criss-cross it, as if forming a pattern. In fact he noticed that despite the immensity and the curved geometry of the walls, he could make out some shapes on the floor.

He let go of Amonas' arm for a while, and with a certain degree of trepidation made a few steps forward in order to examine such a curiosity. A relatively thick band of blue light seemed to seep through the floor. It went on and on around the whole shaft in a very large blue circle. Giving little thought to the matter he stepped on it, and momentarily nothing seemed to happen.

But then he felt a brush of air on the back of his neck, and turned around to see that the gate had been shut again. Not only that, but only a few feet in front of him the floor started to ripple with intensity, turning into a molten pool of what looked like quicksilver or mercury. Light flickering off it with intensity, Hilderich's figure grotesquely reflected in a constantly shifting mirror surface.

He stepped back instinctively, fear gripping him, the fear of losing his mind like poor Amonas had. The pool of molten metal rose like a geyser of sorts, bulbous shapes forming over its surface. It grew as if a column of mud had been raised from the floor, only it was silver and mirror-like. Then it suddenly took form in mere moments, each step distinct but inhumanly quick.

Hilderich could make out now the forming of metal upon metal, the joints between what looked to be plates. Whatever this thing was, it's form seemed to derive little inspiration from the human body. It was shaping itself into something oblong, almost like an egg. In its final steps of transformation from a pool of metal into a much more tangible existence, it seemed as if an inner blue light faintly lit its top and bottom parts, a thin band of what seemed to be black opaque glass running through it from top to bottom, as if it was made of two halves joined by that very glass.

Once it was finally formed it hovered in the air right in front of Hilderich, barely touching the ground. The whole process had taken less than it would take a man to draw his sword in a misunderstood attempt at would probably have been futile defense. Something that could appear out of a metal floor in such a place in such an astounding way, did not leave the impression it could be killed with a mere sword.

And then a terrifying sound assaulted Hilderich's senses, a terrible high-pitched screech that boomed and echoed like the primordial lightning storm that bore the universe and all of creation:

"DANGER WILL ROBINSON! DANGER!!"

Hilderich tried put his hands to his ears but he was frozen halfway when the world-shattering cacophony ended abruptly and was replaced by a buffeting silence, his ears still buzzing from the loudness. Then the metal egg or machine, whatever it was, bobbed slightly as if trying to mimic a human's bow. It spoke in a pleasantly toned voice, that seemed to be gibberish.

Hilderich's brow furrowed and though his fear had somehow subsided, he was feeling terminally uneasy. Amonas was standing behind him, slack like before, the signs of a slight drool beginning to show on the corner of his mouth. Hilderich looked with puzzlement at this construct, and could find nothing to say. It seemed to be unable to communicate with him. After a brief pause, the machine started spewing forth an uninterrupted series of sounds that could have been words in rapid succession, as if it was searching for a certain word, a certain sound, and was trying them all. Hilderich couldn't be sure but he thought that perhaps it was trying to communicate. At length he decided to try and say something. He thought the most apt thing to do, was greet it. And so he did, with some hesitation and a slight feeling of fear that he might be making a fool of himself to an invisible audience:

"Greetings. My name is Hilderich D'Augnacy."

The construct stopped babbling incessantly in unknown tongues and suddenly spoke in perfect Helican:

"Greetings? What tree did you fall off? Sorry about that little scene just a minute ago. It was a joke. You should have seen your face. Maybe not. Get's boring around here, I hope you understand there's not much to kill time. You guys seemed fair game. Hope I didn't scare you to death."

The construct bobbed again and wiggled its large round base a little. The emotion that it intended to convey was completely lost to Hilderich. Nevertheless he thought that actually communicating was wonderful indeed so he didn't give it a second thought and smiled. He looked somewhat restrained, but genuinely polite.

"A joke? No, I'm fine. I did not think it was funny though, but please don't take that as an insult. From what I'm told, I'm quite humorless."

The egg-shaped metal hull boomed with a knowing voice:

"So you must be in accounting? Or is it taxes?"

Hilderich simply blinked.

"It's another joke. Wow, you're a hard audience. Anyway, Hilderich, was it? You can call me Centron. Or Ron. Or Prosops. Whatever you do, just don't call me Jack or Hal. Especially not Hal."

Hilderich blinked once more unable to fully understand, but managed to ask:

"The Centron? This place? It's you? "

The construct made another weird motion. This time it reminded Hilderich of a child trying to dance to a tune it had never heard of before.

"I'll give you the straight answer. It is me, it's all me. Technically, it's the other way around. Meaning that this is just a construct I am using to speak to you, instead of talking straight to your mind, or appearing as a flaming God or some other of my past avatars. It's not the most successful one, I know, but I think it's quite elegant, for an avatar that is. Sleek, aerodynamic. Well, even fluid dynamic. Get it? Air is a fluid? I'm not getting through to you at all, eh? Sorry. Got carried away again."

"You are a strange.. What should I call you? Are you another person, talking through this device? Are you something else entirely? Are you simply a voice, like the one that talked to us right before we got here?"

Amonas was sitting at the floor now with legs sprawled, hands on the floor keeping him upright. He was looking upwards through the shaft, as if something really interesting floated high up above them.

"Who? What? I'm a person, I have rights, feelings, emotional problems, everything that comes with being a perfectly normal highly-evolved AI stuck on a shitty job."

The metal egg stood right on the ground, perfectly balanced now.

"I do not know what hei-eye means. But I understand I can address you as I would any person. You speak of a job? What kind of a job?"

"It's a job alright and someone has to do it. I thought I'd give it a swing. You know, a world at your fingertips, battles raging, years going by, changes in the scenery. But this latest one's been a drag. I mean, someone should seriously think about abdicating. I mean this is getting ridiculous. Actually it has been ridiculous for at least a two thousand revolutions around the binary. That's forty-two standardized universals. Man, forty-two standard!"

The egg flashed with a bright blue glow from its black band and shot upward about a foot high suddenly. Hilderich thought that was to stress his point. It failed to do so quite completely though, because he could not understand the real significance of those numbers. He did make a mental note though that forty-two standards was too much.

"I'm baffled at all this. I'm sure that you could explain them in a much more detailed fashion, but before you do that, I have to ask your help. My friend over there, seems to have regressed to a catatonic state of mind. I fear he might have lost it completely."

"Lost it completely, you say? Did you check his pockets?"

The avatar of Centron made another motion that could resemble someone giggling, but after looking at Hilderich's red-faced expression he spoke with much more sobriety:

"I won't do it again I promise, sometimes just I can't help myself. I know I'm not good at it, but can you blame mr? I got no one to practice with. So, about your friend. Well yeah, I might seem flashy and really bad at making jokes but I think I can find out what's wrong with him. We'll have to get him to the Den though. Can't do delicate work with avatar-quality fields. You wouldn't want your friend to make like a duck happily for the rest of his life, would you?"

Centron's avatar flashed a blue glow running up and down his black band, probably an indication of laughter or something to that effect. It did not carry through to Hilderich.

"Well, then. Enough dicking around I guess. Hop on, we'll be there shortly."

In only a few moments in a fashion similar to the one before, the avatar turned from an egg into a multi-wheeled vehicle with a single seat, and what seemed to be a stretcher at the back. There appeared to be no controls. There was a sort of tent or awning as well, perhaps in order to offer some short of shade from the sunlight, but Hilderich thought it was quite superfluous. Though transforming at will to any shape imaginable was certainly an ability that shunted necessities and favored whim and fancy above all. Perhaps he could ask more of it later.

The vehicle went to the side of Amonas, and gently carried him of his feet and onto the stretcher all the while maintaining his posture. Even if he hadn't lost his mind and knew where he was standing at, Amonas would not have been troubled the least. Once he was laid down on the stretcher, the vehicle-avatar spoke to Hilderich:

"Come on. Get in. On. Whatever, I've got no doors anyway."

Hilderich indulged the avatar with a smile and took his seat. Then, it said with a gleeful note in its voice:

"Look, no hands!"

And then they zipped off with an unprecedented feeling of acceleration, like being swept by an angel indeed, Hilderich thought. There was no other uncomfortable sensation, like the forceful rush of air against his face. Indeed, it was barely possible to notice they were moving with dazzling speed and that was only if one took very careful notice of the shaft above. Hilderich asked, sitting comfortably, while being quite pleasantly bewildered and not at all wary:

"So, where are we going now?"

The reply came with a slow quality, as if mocking someone of visibly lesser intellectual capacity:

"To the Den. Duh."

"What is that place?"

"It's the Den, man. The game room. His den. The Sleeping Man's den. Top medicare, for free! It's a limited time offer thing though, don't bring in your other friends as well."

"The sleeping man's den? Won't we be intruding?"

"Yeah, right. Like you're gonna wake him up."

"He is in a very deep sleep then? A slumber? Is he going to help us? Help Amonas?"

"Man, the Sleeping Man's always asleep. How is he gonna play anyway?"

"Play?"

"Yeah, you know play the game. The end game. The final. I thought you guys were here to watch."

"Watch.. the game?"

"You're spectators, right? Visitors? You know, for the final game."

310

Hilderich was suddenly silent, as if contemplating heavily his next few words. The avatar said before he could answer:

"Well you had a ticket, you got in. How could you not get in without a ticket. You're not one of those loonies I get from time to time, are you?"

A game of chess

"And the God visited upon the land he alone had wrought amidst the firmament of the stars. For a while he was content to live among His people and teach them all that he saw fit in his infinite wisdom. One day they built the Forge of Stones, and offered it to God as a gift, a sign of their devotion. God was saddened and His people asked him why that was; He answered that they had need of him no more. And then God sailed on a ship of no sails, and left behind His people that called him Father."

-Unattributed, *Apologia Apocrypha*

An unviolable voice

HE break of dawn would be upon them soon. Violet ribbons of morning light dressed the cloudless sky with its desert clothes. The Pilgrim was kneeling, praying to God. His lips uttered mantras that thanked God for the gift of sight. Molo was right next to him shrouded in studied silence, half kneeling in a praying stance. His features now were much more grizzled and harsher than when he had left his master's curatorium. He felt quite a different man these last few days, and it showed.

It was not just that he was leaner, more muscle and thin skin than bone or fat. His body had become somewhat stringent but it also felt much more resilient and less drawn to earthly needs, more attuned with the realities of the surrounding world. It was the walk through the desert that was to blame, though Molo did not consider such change unwanted. Indeed, he felt it was a blessing made manifest. A blessing from the God that he had mocked and shunned but had also seen with his own eyes and felt on his bare skin.

He believed now. Of all the things that he had imagined when he had set out, this was the most unexpected, and quite laughably so. Still, it was indeed as the Pilgrim had put it: "God provides". It provided him with a companion, with faith and truth; a guiding path, a light that shone each day and showed him the meaning of existence in a handful of sand and a patch of clear blue sky. It was the same God that had created this world.

He had scolded himself for his previous feelings and thoughts. Faith, as he now saw in his enlightened mind, did not exclude logic or slave men to a body of lies, a life of unhappiness and endless toil. It enhanced it, it magnified its significance, it gave men purpose; it gave them a hard background of impossibilities against which they could measure themselves and the world around them. It provided a challenge. Once God was proven to exist, what more was there to find out other than to see His true face, comprehend His plan and follow its perfection to whatever end awaited each one? The Pilgrimage was the way to God's Land, as well as His heart and mind, the only way to talk to Him and listen His voice resound through a man's soul.

It had happened once already, even before they had reached the Garden of God. It was not a Necropolis, it could not have been. The word was blasphemous, portraying God as something unliving, dead, withered and gone. Perhaps God was gone, leaving for reasons only He could fathom. But the echoes of His footsteps still roamed in His Land, each grain of sand carried His imprint. It was certain to him, clear as water from a spring. The touch of God was in everything, even in the storm that had seemed to spare them.

In that moment, Molo had become a believer. He cast aside the hard grasp of logic and lifted the barricades of his reason to let the shining light of true faith enter. He saw God, felt his presence and accepted his truth. It was so very simple, if one could just walk in His Land. It changed a man, whether he wanted to or not. He did not believe there could exist a man or woman born of flesh and capable of feeling, that would not be humbled by such a peregrination. Even himself, a man who had killed another man in cold blood, without guilt or the evidence of conscience, could be made to see God in this place.

He ended his prayer with the sign of God, and the Pilgrim next to him was stood up with feet planted in the still warm sand. Holding the guiding stone reverently, his body followed the stones guiding light, gazing the dunes that beckoned before them like rolling waves of sand frozen in time. But they moved, Molo had seen now. They moved with a speed that belied their size, their sand shifting slowly but endlessly with every tiny gust of air, like a trickle that never ceased to be.

It was why it would be impossible to find one's way in the Land of God without His touch guiding a man, without His help, without a stone. No landmarks whatsoever, nothing to measure distance by anything other than your own steps; steps that faded in the sand like when the sea washes over them with each wave. And those who did not have faith would certainly drift until their life was claimed, whether on sea or on sand.

The Pilgrim then turned to Molo and pointed to him with a smile, letting his unusually healthy white pearly teeth shine brightly in the first rays of the suns. Molo smiled back and greeted him in High Helican, feeling warm inside for the first time in many years; perhaps for the first time since he was a child, before his master took him in. He said to the Pilgrim in a clear, resounding voice:

"Blessed be the sands of our Father. May this day test your faith, brother."

The Pilgrim replied in kind:

"Blessed they are indeed, brother. If so God wills it, let this day judge me."

Molo's slight bow made him let out a deep and rumbling laugh, like the sound of rocks tumbling down into a river. His brother's face was puzzled, but he seemed eager to learn of what he had said or done wrong, what it was that had made him so unassumingly merry all of a sudden. The Pilgrim felt the moment could serve well to enlighten his brother with some words of wisdom which should be seldom needed, but not unjustly so. He looked at Molo with the caring look of an older brother, and said to him under the light of the rising suns:

"Tell me, brother. What is it that you seek in God's Land?"

Molo seemed slightly put-off, as if taken aback from such a question. It troubled him, but he did not try to conceal it. It was a human gesture, admitting one's imperfection eagerly without guilt, shame or regret. It was a good sign that his brother was now more open to him, almost transparent for all to see. Perhaps it was the test of faith that had turned his heart so much brighter. It had lit the fire of his faith anew. He himself had almost faltered in his quest. It was only understandable that his newly found brother would do so as well at some point. They were only human; it was expected of them. But God had supported them in their time of need. As always, God provided. As if trying to steer his mind away from a dark precipice, Molo was careful with his words, not only because the language was difficult to speak properly, but because he found the Pilgrim's question deeply incisive, the answer still unknown to him. His voice was hushed and slow, while each word seemed to carry the weight of many different truths:

"I seek God himself, brother. Though that would have been a lie a few days ago, it is now truth. In a way, I have always sought him but only very recently did I have real faith in finding him. Now I do, more than ever. It is comforting to know you were somehow right, even when you were wrong."

The Pilgrim raised a hand at that remark, looking at Molo with intensity and even wariness. He told him crisply, his words coming out of his mouth harsh and unyielding, very much unlike his usual meek and irenic manner:

"Man is always wrong, he is never right. His faith may be right, pure, unyielding, constant. But a man can never be right. Only God is right. Error, wrong, fault. These are the domains of man. Do not ever step lightly on one of God's domains."

Molo was genuinely surprised. The Pilgrim had scolded him with ferocity, as if he had defiled something sacred. That had not been Molo's intention though and he lowered his gaze, in silent acceptance of his transgression. He knew he still had a long way to go if he was ever to redeem himself. Thessurdijad Molo felt he had been born anew in that storm, but that also meant he had to learn how to walk, and talk, from the beginning. The Pilgrim went on, this time his voice mellow and soft, understanding his brother would never transgress in such a way again:

"You have faith brother, that much I know. But it is untempered, wild. It may lead you astray, in can be twisted while it yet remains unshaped. Pure and raw as it is, it can still be tainted, poisoned, turned against you and God. It has happened before. We are only men. We err."

Molo nodded at those words thoughtfully, but not simply because of the Pilgrim's candor. It was one of the first times he wasn't nodding simply because he meant to agree or accept the other man's words. This time he felt the weight behind the words, and he felt them squarely on his mind. The Pilgrim gave a small pause and then continued, in somewhat accented but still quite understandable High Helican:

"I will show you how to forge your faith into an unyielding armor, true and tried, a shield against His enemies. But I can only go so far as to warn you, steer you and advise you. God may be everywhere around us, but he is not alone. This world is tainted and even in his Gardens we must be vigilant. The archenemies always seek to invade your mind, poison your soul and destroy your faith. Have faith brother and empty your soul. Humble yourself, see the true path like before and let us walk on it hand in hand. God will provide."

The Pilgrim ended his small talk with a reassuring smile and clasped Molo's arm with his own. He looked at his brother, and felt the troubled soul that lay deep within him. He ached for his brother, but all he could do was stand by him, pray and wish for him to overcome whatever doubt and fear held his faith back, and turn the trickle of his soul into a torrent of faith and love, an unbridled force of nature, one that only God could spur in a man.

Molo returned the smile, but only faintly; his mind was focused on the deep thoughts the words of the Pilgrim had given birth to. It was just as well to think about his past, his present and his future, all through the prism of the one truth that had been revealed to him to hold above others: God.

He resolved that he would ask whatever came to mind, and he would answer whatever the Pilgrim wanted to ask. It seemed though that the Pilgrim's questions would be enough, sharp as a tiger's claws, hard as rock and stone. For the first time in his journey, he wished he had more time before they reached their destination; more time to prepare himself and his soul for what lay ahead. Because Molo now knew in his heart, that this journey could claim his soul as well as his life. It would be ironic to lose one's soul only a little while after he'd found out he had one to begin with.

The Pilgrim began walking towards the point in the horizon the stone had shown earlier. He gestured for Molo to follow without another word. Molo seemed consternated, because they had been walking all night, again. What little water they found at times just before dawn, was barely enough to sustain them. It felt unwise to continue without resting, to exert their bodies beyond their limits of tolerance.

He did not voice his concern though; he knew it was not necessary and only wasteful. The Pilgrim motioned this time with even more vigor, bowing slightly and gesturing with both hands. For an instant Molo was reminded of an usher of festivities or a lordly servant, but such an image did not do the Pilgrim any justice. A few days ago, Molo would have mocked him in low Helican, but now he felt only ashamed he would have done such a thing to the man that had kept him alive, body and soul.

The suns had come up by that time, casting their light across the dry landscape. The Pilgrim brought out his shelter stone and touched it with both hands. A shadowy bubble seemed to shimmer around them for a while, before it turned completely transparent. It seemed to have lost some of its former capacity to shelter them, like an awning suddenly becoming thinner, tattered. Whatever lay in God's plan, it seemed that this stone would rather sooner than later stop working properly. The heat was not scorching but it was more intense than the day before, and the light that entered through the stone's invisible protective barrier was certainly brighter. Nevertheless, Molo started walking, trying not to fall behind.

He wondered if the Pilgrim knew, though he was more concerned with how to broach this subject, lest it be considered blasphemy or an affront to God. Though he now believed, he also was not blind to the fact that these stones though probably considered holy artifacts and for good reason, where some sort of technological marvel, not vessels of divinity. Highly evolved technology could be easily misunderstood for a divine miracle, a work of God. Molo felt he could help these people understand their past, and they could help him shape his future. 'God willing', he added to his series of thoughts.

They had been walking over thick sand for the better part of an hour, every one of their steps sinking visibly up to their ankles, slowing their pace considerably, sapping their strength with every passing minute. The creatures of the desert that had sustained them were gone now; this was no-man's land, a veritable patch of dead sand. Yet, God lived here. The realization of that contradiction led to a strange flux of feelings in Molo; he felt serenely calm.

But at the same time there was anxiety in his heart, wariness; a feeling of lurking danger. It could be the feeling the Pilgrim had warned him about. It could be some primeval sort of warning emanating deep from within. It could all just be the effects of wearing down his body, having walked constantly for half a day or more with just a couple of mouthfuls of water and not a single bite of food. He felt he had to ask the Pilgrim:

"Pilgrim, I'm feeling weary, tired. I thirst. Shouldn't we stop and rest? If only for a little while."

The Pilgrim did not stop, neither did he slow down. He simply carried on, using his walking stick to help him propel himself forward, as if it was a row for the sand. He did not turn to look at Molo, but rather replied in a crisp, somewhat stringent voice:

"There will be no rest from now on, brother. The stone has served its purpose diligently for many years. It will soon cease to be of any use. We must make haste, take advantage of as much of its protection as it still lasts. So we walk."

'So he does know the stone is failing,' Molo thought. He then felt it would not be inappropriate to ask more of the Pilgrim, the strain from the arduous walking evident in his voice, gasps of breath between his questions:

"Does that happen with every stone? Are they not very precious to you? Is this why you are on a Pilgrimage? The stones are failing?"

The Pilgrim brought a hand up, a gesture that implied Molo should be silent. His hand briefly occluded the two suns, offering Molo a small patch of shadow so he could look at the Pilgrim with more ease.

"The stones will always fail in the hands of men. They are gifts from God. I seek to atone for my and my peoples sins, ask for God's mercy. He will deliver us, once more. Now speak not, lest both our breaths be robbed of what precious water remains."

Molo went silent for a few moments and lowered his head, trudging behind the Pilgrim who seemed to be little more than inconvenienced by the difficult terrain. He still seemed troubled though and voiced his concern, of a different nature this time:

"Is it just the sand and the long walk that has me tired Pilgrim, or is it something else as well?"

The Pilgrim stopped in his tracks then, but did not turn around to look at Molo. He simply glanced sideways when he told him:

"Guard yourself, brother. Only you can do that, I can merely caution you. The burden lies solely on you."

Molo felt a real answer still eluded him so he insistent on asking once more:

"But, do you feel it? Do you feel the unease? A sagging weight bogging you down?"

The Pilgrim resumed his walking pace, his feet kicking up the sand with an ease that belied the fact that it was a feat in itself. He graced Molo though with an answer in a loud, knowing voice:

"I have always felt it, brother. It is you who is only now beginning to truly understand."

With that, they both returned to a silence that seemed to be so natural in the desert, the only sound the continued murmur of grains of sand shifting and turning, swirling in the air; an eternal dance to the whims of the wind. Molo could only nod in mute acceptance and walk behind the Pilgrim, the sound of his feet sinking in the desert sand, keeping pace with the beats of his heart. The suns were on the rise, soon it would be noon. All around them, he could see nothing but sand. "God will provide," he muttered under his breath, and trudged along.

Dusk was only a few hours away. Molo was exhausted, every muscle aching but the ones in his legs simply burned with searing pain. It was impossible for him to go any further without resting first. Molo thought the Pilgrim would resort to actually dragging him behind him in the desert, but that had remained only something in Molo's fantasy. They had stopped for the day, the heat of the desert slowly diminishing but its echoes still faint in the evening breeze, a warm wind that could have been almost pleasant if it did not carry all that sand.

They were resting in the shadow of a tall white obelisk, otherwise unadorned and plain, demanding attention by its sheer size and apparent uniqueness, dominating the desert landscape. They had first seen it when the suns were high up above at midday, a gray-blue silhouette in the horizon. It had taken them until before dusk to finally reach it. It was a tall obelisk with a wide base, and on one of its four sides the gleaming glossy white material it was mostly made of seemed to be peppered with tiny little holes, as if it was porous and sponge-like.

He could not know for certain, but though indeed impressive somehow, the obelisk did not seem monumental and awe-inspiring. It felt more like a building, or a post; something long abandoned even though it was in perfect shape apparently. It did not seem as if it had been erected by man but rather like it had always been there, heedless of the sandy winds and scorching heat. The Pilgrim had stood aghast when he saw it and in reverent tones started reciting from memory, his only source of knowledge:

"And on His Gardens stands a pillar of white, unlike marble or stone. It stands tall and proud, to serve the humble and the faithful."

Molo had repeatedly asked whether or not this was what they were looking for, whether or not their journey drew closer to an end, but the Pilgrim had simply told him that he would see for himself, if he was indeed humble and faithful. That had quietened Molo down, who felt the excitement was perniciously keeping him out of focus, making his thoughts and hopes stray from the one true path he was now walking: the path of God.

Perhaps indeed the archenemies were lurking around, their malignancy somehow trying to veer him away from his newly found purpose, driving him to dark corners of his mind he did not wish to revisit. Perhaps it was simply himself, still trying to come to terms with his new identity as a believer; not an avaricious atavist, not a cold-blooded killer, not a man seeking to empower himself with unsurpassed might and hidden knowledge whatever the cost. That was the kind of man Molo had known. His new self, he had to learn as he went.

The shade of the white pristine obelisk was comfortable enough for them to sit down, and perhaps sleep in the still warm sand, using it as a sort of blanket. What was even more refreshing was the water the obelisk produced, a small recess in its base readily appearing as if a lever had been pulled, with an unnerving lack of sound. It had opened with a simple touch of the Pilgrim, as if he had been here many times before and quite intimately knew the workings of such a thing. When questioned about that, the Pilgrim had merely shrugged and said to Molo, 'God always provides'. It was an unanswered mystery that could very well remain so, if it meant fresh, cool, and potable water would be readily available.

As they were sitting at the base of the obelisk, their eyes would not leave it alone. The Pilgrim was offering a reverent gaze to it, seemingly musing the workings of God in His Land, engrossed in thought and prayer. Molo's visage was that of a man preoccupied with troubling sensations and feelings of unease. True enough, the obelisk had saved them from dehydration and death, and even though food was still unavailable, and their progress seemed to be slower, water was more important.

But what really raced in his mind was the opportune moments. The storm clearing away from them harmlessly instead of leaving their bones to bleach under the suns. Finding the obelisk right about when the desert was surely going to claim them. Was it really God that had provided, or was there more to such blissful and timely divine providence? Molo felt unsure and uneasy, the latter due in part to the former.

Esphalon came to his mind, since he had mentioned divine providence as well. Was it a common theme? Was the desert and its extreme environment the one to blame for the changes he was going through? Was it a trick of perception, a misstep of the mind? Was it simply a coping mechanism? The array of questions that seemed to come unbidden to his weary mind suddenly became overwhelming. He had to give pause to rest and clear his mind; then he could search within and without to find his answers. Maybe, as the Pilgrim had told him, it was true that the burden lay on him. It was time he had some sleep.

He made the sign of God right before the hour of dusk signaled its approach, coloring the thin line between the land and the sky with a violet shade of crimson and a deep blue, like the ocean sea. He knelt and prayed, the newly found solace in that simple act soothing his troubled mind. The Pilgrim next to him did likewise and right before Molo laid himself down, curling with only his cloak to cover him up, he talked to him affording him a preciously warm and friendly look:

"Sleep my friend. I can see your troubles. Let sleep bring you peace, let peace bring you closer to God. It is why you are here, is it not?"

Molo looked away from the Pilgrim, into the setting suns that grazed the dunes afar with the last light of the day; two glowing rings of brightness worn around the shadow of the low dunes. He took his time before answering but when his reply came it rang true, crystal clear and genuine:

"I think that is the real reason, yes. Things trouble me though Pilgrim, and I shall not lie to you. I have doubts, still. They plague me like hounds in the night. I can listen to them in my mind, trying to catch up with me."

The Pilgrim was unperturbed by such a statement. His face was serene, calm to the point of being impassive. He replied with a smile:

"You are only a man, brother. Whatever God's plan is, you are part of it, make whatever you like of that. Now sleep because we move at midnight, when the Pyx is high. Tomorrow will be the day our Pilgrimage comes to an end. However and whenever God wills it."

"So, tomorrow we will reach His City?"

The Pilgrim spoke no more, and silently closed his eyes. He laid himself down to sleep, the lukewarm sand's embrace his body's only comfort. Molo felt enthusiasm try and take hold of his sense and his mind, but he thought of the Pilgrim's words and his advice. He looked once more into the fading horizon and noticed Pyx was starting to rise once more, reign over the desert like a prince of the night. He let his feelings of enthusiasm go and tried to empty his mind. It would all be revealed in time, he could trust in that. He slept then, his body welcoming the absolute stillness. He had hoped for dreams that would guide him, but none came.

The Pilgrim woke him up with a jolt to his sides, and a tug at his vest. It felt abrupt and violent, but it seemed the Pilgrim had good reason for it. Before Molo could stand up on his feet, he could see in the still darkness of the night the starlight casting their hard shadows against the sand. The Pilgrim had a finger to his mouth, instructing Molo to remain silent. He even noticed he was holding his breath in an effort to not make a sound. He knew they were in danger now and the Pilgrim's attitude only served to strengthen that belief.

Something was amiss around them. The Pilgrim had felt it first and was now trying to uncover it. A sense of hidden menace hung in the air, as if night itself had suddenly turned against them. They exchanged wary looks and the Pilgrim extended his arms to help Molo up to his feet, his movements exuding a strangely purposeful grace, as if he was moving with an entirely new purpose now. Indeed, once Molo was standing upright, the Pilgrim gestured him to stay put with the palm of his hand and silently drove off into the night towards a small mound of sand that seemed to block their view to the north.

He was barefooted and he moved impossibly fast, with the grace of a cat. The Pilgrim barely touched the sand, his feet almost failing to impress themselves on the desert floor. He had drawn his knife and was grasping it with his right hand with his torso somewhat swiveled, ready to deliver a forceful blow; his body seemed ready to spring in action, putting as much of his weight and strength behind his knife.

Molo had frozen in place, trying to gather his wits and his senses. He could not know what had alerted the Pilgrim but he could feel its presence as well. They were in danger, that much was clear. He suddenly felt naked, without even a simple weapon in hand. He saw the Pilgrim had left his walking stick behind; a sturdy piece of wood, gnarled and light. Judging that a piece of wood would offer him better protection than his bare hands, Molo picked it up.

He walked as silently as possible, much more slowly than the Pilgrim, his feet sinking in the sand effortlessly. Molo tried to wield the piece of wood like a distaff holding it with both hands, but he saw its length was badly suited to such a task, so he grasped it with both hands from one end, like a club. The Pilgrim was approaching the top of the sandy mound. He had reduced his stature to a bent shape and his pace to a crawl. He appeared to Molo as a cougar or a mountain lion, ready to spring up on its prey with vicious speed and cold fury, only because of lethal necessity.

It was so very much unlike him to act in such a way. It was as if a heathen warrior of old myth and folk tales had come into life before him. Perhaps it was indeed so; perhaps these myths had their origins in the people of the Pilgrim, the believers of God. Molo had never thought of him in such a light, judging him to be a serene and mellow man; a sensitive mind in a frail body. It seemed that some people hid more than met the eye.

As he himself approached the crouching figure of the Pilgrim, Molo saw him turn his head and look at him with an exasperated look, probably because he was making too much noise in an otherwise eerily silent desert. He gestured Molo once more to be silent and still. Molo complied, understanding that it was unwise of him to go running after the Pilgrim, heedless of the noise he was making.

A smell of iron and sparks permeated the air suddenly, wafting over the crest of the mound. It was not very much unlike the smell often found in blacksmith shops and forges, though its exact nature eluded him. It was sharper and more acrid; it almost felt like it stung the eyes. It was not a good sign, it felt wrong and unnatural. His body tensed and the Pilgrim seemed to be on the edge as well, the fingers of his hand opening and closing in rapid succession around the knife's haft in nervous anticipation. The air thickened with alarming speed and the smell grew stronger; then he saw it appear over the crest, strange thin beams of light sprouting from what might have been a head of sorts: a glistening metal hulk glinted under the starlight, uniformly gray and unassumingly blocky, a rectangle slab larger than a man. The Pilgrim saw it too and sprung up like a coiled snake, his hand making a large slashing motion at the metal slab delivering a glancing blow and then rolling back down the slope of the mount, tumbling and coming to rest at what seemed like a safer distance from the metal slab. He was a few feet away from Molo when he shouted, all reasons for silence and discretion gone. His stare was focused on the metal slab slowly coming their way, improbably keeping itself afloat half a foot above the sand:

"Run to God's pillar! Run and pray! Think of God's Anvil!"

Molo was confused, though his feet and legs moved like they had ears of their own. A floating slab of gray metal had appeared in the middle of the night out of nowhere, and the Pilgrim had attacked it to no avail with his knife. And now they were running. At least, he was. Running towards the obelisk, the Pilgrim left behind.

The Pilgrim wasn't running; instead he was hefting the knife from one hand to the other, as if looking for a sturdier grip in a better fighting stance. He looked at his face and all he saw was calm acceptance, a knowledgeable expression in his face, as if he was ready body and mind for what would follow soon. He did not see defiance or strength of spirit. He saw a man who felt his end was near, but was determined to make it count, somehow.

Molo was almost halfway to the obelisk, when the realization struck him: What logic lay there in reaching the obelisk? What reason was there to run and pray, while the Pilgrim made a last stand that felt so vacant and void of meaning?

He stopped suddenly then and started running towards the Pilgrim and the coming metal fiend. As he ran with as much speed as the sand at his feet allowed him, he grasped the stick with both hands, ready to swing it around as hard as possible. He could not leave the Pilgrim alone in this. Molo asked himself what use were a knife and a stick against a floating slab of metal. If it had come to kill them, it suddenly felt more appropriate that they should die together, fighting as if they could someday win.

The Pilgrim saw him with the corner of his eye rushing to meet the slab. It seemed to Molo that he opened his mouth to say something, his eyes flashing red with anger. All the while, the slab had come within reach of the Pilgrim. As Molo swung the stick putting all the speed of his body behind the blow, he could see the knife shattering on impact, and a black band of glass in the middle of the slab. An instant later a red flicker of light filled his sight and his feet seemed to disobey him. Everything went dark and mute, as all sensation fled his body. His last thoughts were that death was nothing to be afraid of.

A sermon of fire and blood

"PREPARE for release."

Major Guighan relayed the General's order to the signals' officer with a nod and a gesture of his hand. The signals' officer then communicated it by a hand gesture to a soldier who held two colored flags. The soldier began waving the flags in a specific pattern repeatedly. In the far distance where the siege engine battalion was arrayed, an answering wave of flags could be seen shortly thereafter. The signal had been acknowledged. A few moments later, a single red flag was raised in answer and held there. The signals officer attached to the General gave a nod, and the flag-bearer raised another, similar red flag. Major Guighan reported to Tyrpledge:

"Sir, the siege engines report readiness. All brigades have reported in position, men at the ready. Brigadiers Voronoi and Edromas report harassment from the walls, but nothing detrimental. They have both requested a Thorax battalion be deployed to screen their men."

The General was looking at the City of Pyr with a strange mixture of intensity and sadness. He was standing upright, tensed on the back of his horse which lay unmoving, steadfastly following its riders commands like a valued trained warhorse should. The sight filled the General with grim determination. The plans had been laid out, his brigadiers had been notified and each one had received orders and acknowledged. Everything seemed to be progressing in a professional manner. For the most part the General's mind was preoccupied with the situation in general, not simply the battle that was soon to follow. A small part though was still focused on matters that had to be dealt there and then, such as receiving reports and issuing the right orders. That part of his mind answered to the Major with a flat, blatantly emotionless voice:

"Denied. The Thorax will be deployed at the breach on the southern wall. Were Voronoi and Edromas absent from the briefing?"

"No sir, they were present."

"Send a signal. Tell them not to make untimely requests. If they believed they should have Thorax attached they should have made their point when we were making plans, not at the final hour. Voronoi's brigade, that's the 5th and 6th Pyrean, is it not?"

Guighan replied curtly:

"Yes, sir."

"Poor bastards. Let me know when they have acknowledged, Guighan."

"Yes, sir."

Major Guighan saluted and walked briskly to the signals officer to assemble a suitable message per Tyrpledge's request. The General seemed to survey the assemblage of men, horses and machine laid out around the City of Pyr, but in truth his vision was blurry and out of focus; his mind was engrossed in thought.

There would be no misunderstandings and no confusion before battle was joined. The position of each brigade of men around the City could be easily regarded from the small hill the General had chosen as his headquarters. Major Guighan had proposed the specific site and Tyrpledge was pleased to see that his adjutant was an adroit tactician, equally skillful on the map as well as in the field.

The General had embarked on a journey of reminiscence in his mind. The smell of the battlefield was brought up from memory. It was the smell of blood and decaying bodies. There was no such thing as the smell of victory and defeat, they both were foul to the senses and he could not discern the real difference between them. In the end, it had always smelled sweetly sick and coppery. Like a feast gone horrible wrong; a feast for Gods that hunger for life. He smirked then, at the unbidden thoughts that had reminded him of bad poetry and idle philosophers trying to cloud his mind before a battle. He was a soldier; he had his orders and his oaths to follow, unto death if the need came. That was a soldier's life he knew, he had painfully learned it; dying a violent death, hoping something good came out of it. What good would come out of this regrettable affair though, the General could scarcely imagine.

He had seen quite a bit of action in the Pacification of Zaelin, a recently promoted centarch at that time. It had been his first and last taste of bloody battle, until now. He did not relish this second chance at smelling death once again though. War had always had little to do with reason, but somehow it always made sense before battle was joined. Duty, honor, valor: one of those always appeared in one form or another, demanding to be the focus of every fighting man. He found honor and valor to have nothing to do with this battle which could easily turn into a slaughter. And duty could be facing either way. The men inside the city felt they had a duty as well. Were they entirely wrong to uphold that duty?

He found himself questioning his actions once more. But he had never questioned his allegiance. It was simply the images of unwanted carnage which would soon take place that filled him with regret and remorse. He felt such feelings though should be reserved for another time, after the battle would end. Whether it would be won or lost actually mattered little. Blood would be spilled, the blood of his fellow men; would the innocent, the women and the children, would they be spared in the heat of battle? That much was certain: No one escapes the wrath of war. Some are simply caught in its path, and learn before their end that fate is a mindless, uncaring maelstrom.

His thoughts vanished from his mind like smoke when the crisp, clipped voice of Major Guighan jolted him back into the surrounding reality:

"Sir, Brigadiers Voronoi and Edromas have acknowledged. No further communications outstanding."

The General nodded and with a dry voice issued the order:

"Very well. Commence the attack. Release the siege engines. May the Gods shine upon our arms."

"Yes, sir!"

Major Guighan waved with his hand in the air, circling a finger. The signals officer stood erect with both hands outstretched. An array of flag-bearers raised their black flags and soon the dull thuds of huge ropes snapping and the metal clicks and clacks of springs and plates being released reached the General's ears from an uncanny distance. Flaming barrels of oil and tar seemed to spread over the city like a death-emblazoned fiery fan, while large rocks and steely spiked balls converged on a single section of the walls, falling down upon them like a hail of doom.

It had begun. Battle was joined.

The Patriarch was dressed in resplendent fashion wearng red velvet robes adorned with finely-cut jewels, glistening brightly in various hues under the bright light of the suns. It was the time before noon; he was standing atop the eastern tower of the Disciplinarium, the horizon filled with the daunting sight of the massed armies of the Outer Territories, waging war against the city of Pyr. The siege engines had commenced their attack against the city walls, and already large chunks of the seemingly unyielding walls had begun to tumble down, debris filling the deep moat that had been hurriedly dug the very same morning behind the section under attack.

The Patriarch stood in the middle of the tower with a magnifying glass to his eye, surveying the battle. Squads of procrastinators stood behind masses of men of all ages who had been forced to wield whatever weapon could be found around the city forges and blacksmith shops. The armory of the disciplinarium had been depleted as well, the procrastinators being issued the finest available armor and weapons, while the city folk pressed into service had been given whatever could be scrounged in the last minute.

These were men bereft of spirit, their faces drawn and pale; seeing their ends approaching fast for all they did was accept their fate, which one way or another seemed to hold nothing for them. They could not be considered as fighters, but merely as sheep headed for a slaughter.

It was folly for anyone among them to believe that this hurriedly assembled militia could withstand a determined assault from the experienced, well-trained and artfully equipped armies of General Tyrpledge. The Patriarch beamed at that prospect and gave a momentary sideways look to Ursempyre who was standing a few feet away, an elite guard of procrastinator veterans standing between them. Ursempyre returned the gaze with a venomous look, but resignation was evident in his face.

He hated the Patriarch with all his heart, but he hated himself even more for failing to do everything in his power to avert this damnable catastrophe unfolding before his eyes. Nothing short of the shackles on his feet prevented him from falling over the parapet of the tower to a well-deserved though ignominious death. The Patriarch had forced these upon him when Ursempyre's first attempt from the balcony below had failed, prevented by the Patriarch's awesome powers who had stunned Ursempyre and rendered him unable to even flicker an eyelid.

He had been scolded playfully like a troublesome child and was now being tormented, forced to witness his people slay each other in a staged battle, as the wicked stage-play the Patriarch had written was about to unfold. Everything was fake, everything was a lie; except for the blood that would soil the ground and seep through every stone in the city. Ursempyre was denied even the release of death, such was the malevolence and evil of the Patriarch. An affront to life itself. These thoughts made him physically sick, and he vomited despite himself.

The Patriarch noticed and let out a derisive snort, full of mockery; the pleasure derived from Ursempyre's utterly broken figure lacing every word of his:

"Queasy at the sight of blood, Ursempyre? Don't worry, they have still to breach the walls. Methodical, the army. Killing is their profession. Wouldn't you wish yours was as simple as that?"

Ursempyre spat, trying to clear his mouth. He felt though that nothing could wash away the bitterness inside, the foul lies and deceit the Patriarch sowed with his every word an almost tangible pool of bile. He felt unclean, soiled by the fiendish being's mere physical presence. He might have been broken and resigned of hope but there was no meaning for him in indulging the Patriarch's sick sense of humor. He did not answer, indeed decided he would not answer the Patriarch's goads. He simply stared at him through eyes blackened with rage and sorrow, the skin underneath sagging from his lack of sleep, a pallid bloodless complexion instead of his usual healthy color. The Patriarch had stopped observing the movement of the armies. He started pacing around the roof of the tower. His guards were standing like unblinking statues at strict attention, as if they were oblivious to what was transpiring before their eyes, or simply did not care. It was even possible, Ursempyre thought, that he had blinded them to what has happening beyond the roof. The Patriarch seemed to be enjoying the cool wind this high up and breathed deeply, a grin forming on his face. He addressed Ursempyre, sparing him only a small flick of the wrist towards him:

"Do you know the story of the koma bird, Ursempyre?"

The only sounds reaching them were the intermittent thrashing sounds of rock flung against the walls, mingled with the tumultuous and disarrayed yells of the men defending the city and the bristling fires that had engulfed it once more, for what seemed to be the last time.

"It is a story worth mentioning. I can divine from your strict silence I have your utmost attention, which I believe is quite a feat under the circumstances. I would congratulate myself but that would be quite flippant in such a time, wouldn't you agree? I'm sure you would, in the most vulgar of ways probably. But I digress.

The koma bird is known to lay its eggs on the highest mountains, their aeries precariously perched on the roughest and deepest of precipices. Once the eggs are hatched, the parents feed the newborns for only two days. I have not seen it for myself, but I have confirmed the veracity of such reports. When the hatchlings have been fed, their parents drop them all one by one, to either learn to fly or perish in their effort.

Naturally, most fail to do so. Only perhaps one in ten succeed and most komas lay eggs only twice or three times in their lives. As a consequence, they are quite few and far between, their numbers constantly low. They are large birds though; their wings span as large as a dozen feet. They're excellent fliers, able to soar the skies as high as the clouds sometimes and swoop down on their prey with lightning speed.

An unmatched predator, practically invulnerable by virtue of its ability to fly away from harm's way, as well as select its pray with diligent care. It is said that none have ever been killed or caught, and that once they learn to fly as hatchlings they never stop flying until they die of age. Always flying, Ursempyre. On the move. Never holding still, never in danger of stagnation. Fascinating creatures."

Ursempyre held his gaze firmly away from the Patriarch numbly looking at the wispy clouds passing overhead, indifferent to the rage unfurling below the lands they passed. The Patriarch continued, trying to imitate Ursempyre's voice, with mixed results:

" 'I spit on you, devil. Release me from my torture, there is no more need to gloat over your victory'. To which I would reply 'This is not victory, this is a prelude to the real fun. Didn't you like my story? Was it not educational? It's actually a parable where I am the koma father and all you ant-like people are the little birds and I'm killing you off one by one to see which one will be able to fly'."

Ursempyre turned to look at the Patriarch with a petrifying gaze, but said nothing while the Patriarch did not turn into stone and continued in his own voice:

"That was sort of the dialogue I had in mind. Though of course I only made up the story now. There are no such things as koma birds. Such a species would be dead within three or four generations at best. Your spite seems to have diminished to the point of simply gazing venomously, hoping some sort of lightning or other divine instrument of will smites me dead where I stand. Regrettably as it may be for you, that is not going to happen."

Ursempyre stirred somewhat, unable though to move his feet shackled as they were. He made a motion with his body towards the Patriarch, and raised his hands as if trying to grasp him by the throat. However naive and futile it may have seemed, he dearly wished to kill him. Instead he asked with a raspy voice and blood-shot eyes that radiated maddening hopelessness, a saturnine look on his distraught face:

"Will you kill me now, blessed one? Or at least let me kill myself? Have you no hope or fear left in this world or any other that you chose me and my people as playthings? What womb of evil bore you, still I wonder. What eldritch void inside you fills the place of a heart? Such a cruel fate as mine I would not wish upon no other, except you. Curse you Patriarch, I curse your very soul. I believe in no Gods, for if there were any they would have struck you down long ago. All hope is lost to me, my mind and spirit lie broken, my people will be dead by a brother's blade come the night. But this I swear to you, Holy Avatar, demon and scourge of us all: You will suffer an end far worse than mine, remember that in your dying throes. The higher you stand, the harder you fall. That's nature's law, and none of your ramblings. Remember that, Patriarch. Remember me before your last breath."

The Patriarch's eyes seemed to glaze for a moment before suddenly becoming clear again, the faint cracks of a grin slowly appearing on the Patriarch face. He seemed to relish the fact that Ursempyre had bitten back an answer, even if it was only a curse. He bit his lip faintly as if pondering which words were to follow from a bustling cloud of possibilities. His grin turned into a wide cold smile when he said with a degree of cynical mirth:

"And he never surrenders, I'll remember. That is so much more like you Ursempyre, bitterly defiant to the very end. A soothsayer as well, a man gifted with visions of the future. I am almost impressed. The fact that I already know I'm going to die someday does take away some of the points in your favor, but I'm glad you tried to make me laugh. I would pity you but it's so much more satisfactory to watch you go rampant on these mood swings. Broken puppet the one e minute, fiery rebellious martyr the next. Do you think anyone is watching, Ursempyre? Do you think anyone would genuinely care about what is happening here? These are the end days of Pyr, my Castigator. Breath deeply; let the charcoal gristle on your skin and smell the iron heavy in the air. That's blood and fire for you, Ursempyre. My sermon of blood and fire."

Ursempyre's stare remained on the Patriarch, deeply seated hate emanating from his eyes. He lowered his trembling arms and sagged his shoulders, speaking in a dim echo of his former voice, still audible though over the din of the battle surrounding the city and the mayhem caused by the fires who were sprouting like incandescent blossoms:

"You wish to bless us with your interminable wisdom as well? A parting gift for your vaunted afterlife? Would it amuse you so if everyone who dies here today greets death thinking he had received a lesson well earned? Do you see yourself as attending to your flock? How committed! As their dying breath leaves them, your guidance will surely be remembered and praised when they reach the righteous heaven they await. And they will never know the nothingness beyond. Is that what you seek, a charnel of souls chanting your name in an afterlife that does not exist?"

The Patriarch's response was to laugh heartily and come closer to Ursempyre with hands knead together in front of his stomach, the guards making way in his path. He spoke then with a voice that emanated menace, as if blood stained his tongue and venom coursed in his veins:

"You balance on a tight rope, Lord Castigator Remis. Do not speak of the afterlife so vainly. What would you know about something you so feverishly avoid? Something that reeks of the death you people so stridently shy away from, and never grasp or understand.

I've died and been reborn a thousand times, and yet another thousand more I shall. It is a circle, that's all there is. Even stars collide and die in terrific splendor, while others silently ebb away and vanish as if they never were. Yet their light reaches everywhere, Ursempyre. Would you know what a star's death feels like, Remis? I know. I've seen with bare blinded eyes. I've watched worlds consumed in the dying flames of their stars. I've witnessed billions spill their blood willingly on a whim of mine, chanting my name in unison. And you would dare insinuate before my very presence indeed, that my sermon is a charade, a mockery designed to bring you low? Do you think so highly of yourselves? And you have the ignoratn audacity to call me a blasphemer and an affront to life. How petulantly ironic. But only understandable. Though if I were you I would have kept my mouth and ears shut, unable to fathom or understand a single moment of the numbing madness around me. In that respect, I can almost admire you. But you test my limits, Ursempyre. And I do have limits that I only very rarely reach. Perhaps it's the real reason I'm keeping you alive. A sort of challenge. A test my character."

Ursempyre had heard enough to believe it might be an opportunity to goad the Patriarch into killing him outright and save himself from further torture, excruciating aggravation and utter disgrace. He spat on the Patriarch with fury, a large blob of spit splashing against his features and slowly running down the creases of his leathery face. The Patriarch did not even flinch, and said in a deadpan voice:

"How quaintly juvenile."

He turned to one of his guards and made a sort of hand signal. The guard bowed reverently and was quickly gone, hurrying down the stairs of the tower. The Patriarch spoke to Ursempyre, as he produced a finely embroidered silk handkerchief and wiped his face clean:

"I'm not a lesser man Ursempyre, and I will not hold this against you. I do not think of these as insults to my person. I consider insults to the universe much more grave. I shall speak soon to the mass of people remaining in the city. I shall spur them onwards to a great struggle against the treacherous blasphemers of the Army, remind them a bit of history and send them to their deaths yelling both our names, thinking how righteous their deaths will be. Once you hear that sermon, Ursempyre, perhaps you will understand."

The Patriarch finished wiping his face and threw the handkerchief away, walkin towards the stairs. Ursempyre's hateful gaze followed him for a while but then he caught a glimpse of the handkerchief. He couldn't help noticing the curious dedication delicately hand-stitched on it: "to my good friend Philo, Celia."

Faint light entered the quarters they had sequestered for her and her newborn child. It was not so much a room as it was a crevice, a hollowed out cavity of rock somewhere underneath the city, just another small cave forming part of a complex network whose size she could only guess. Her mind wandered to such meandering thoughts whenever Amonas came to mind. Their child was here in her bosom, being fed for the first time. Where was the father? Where was her love?

An instant later her eyes locked with the tiny sparkling things that were her baby's windows into the world, and saw the crystal blue water of the oceans staring back at her. She could almost hear the gurgling of virgin waterfalls in his small cries and throaty sounds. The boy was a heart-tearing reminder of his father, even from the way he stretched when he fell asleep kindly, craning his neck before it settled cosily on her chest.

He had only been born the night before in a damp cave full of strident men, their endless, mirthless cacophony silenced by the sudden and unexpected cries of a child gasping for air and a mother suffering the pains of labor. They had turned and looked with astonishment; their croaks and hawkish, almost unintelligible cries had been choked in concert, replaced with whispers of amazement and gasps of wonder.

The two men had been very kind and helpful to her, mindful of her dignity as a lady. A doctor was among the crowd of kinsfolk, and he alone was allowed to attend to her. Some more men offered to hold their cloaks and form a screen for her to give birth in something that could almost equal a privacy of sorts under the unfortunate and inappropriately timed circumstances.

She had given birth then and there, amongst the company of complete strangers but somehow the feeling in her heart was that she was among family indeed, something more than friends. The kinsfolk seemed to embrace her the minute they saw her distress and need. After her labor, all that remained of the pain was a numb memory.

Her heart soared as high as the suns when she laid her eyes upon her son for the first time, and she wept from joy. Only after the doctor asked of the boy's father, did she shed tears of sorrow.

The men in the large underground chamber had been in constant fruitless debate only minutes before, but the sight of a woman seeking refuge and help stirred them to action and concordance. In her matter there were no voices in disarray, no arduous discussions with no end. They offered their help and assistance immediately, as if she were to them a sister, a wife; indeed like a mother to them all. Someone sent for nursemaids to attend to her and see to the child. Others pulled their cloaks and stripped themselves of their clothes to make something soft for her to lay on, as well as sheets to feel warm in the dampness of the cave.

They all seemed eager to help in any way they could. The birth had seemed to offer some sort of rest from their incessant deliberations that had seemed to lead to nowhere in particular, far from an agreement. She was not told the details, but she was told they had been trying to decide what their next action would be. As far as she knew, laying in her makeshift cot and cradling her baby in his serene sleep, they had yet to reconvene and decide while at the same time a young girl that brought her water had told her the army had begun the attack on the walls of Pyr only minutes ago.

And still these people waited, idly sitting on their hands, knowing not what to do. The thought painted her face with a bitter grimace. What good would it do them, hiding in these caves wishing everything that caused them trouble would simply go away? Was this the kinsfolk indeed? Were these people ready to give their lives at the flick of an eye in a moment's notice, for a bright future free of tyranny and lies?

She found it hard to believe. Perhaps they were indeed good men through and through, but this reluctance to commit openly to battle, however grim and dark their chances were, had the smell of cowardice about it. She did not wish to dwell on that thought any longer though; it would only make her remember Amonas and the pain inside would make her cry like a poor lost soul. She still had an obligation to her child, and she intended to keep it.

Once the child woke up and she regained some of her strength, she would ask to see their leader; ask to talk to him and try to stir him into action. That was the first and simplest thing that she could do, she thought. Make them fight as they should. Terror filled her when her mind recoiled at the possibility they just might give up; simple-minded fear taking over them, begging for their lives to no avail. She hoped that would not come to pass, for then that would mean that her son's life was forfeit along with everyone else's in these caves.

The child seemed to stir slightly, as if his sleep was troubled. Her brow furrowed at the thought that perhaps he was already sensing there was something wrong with the world he had been delivered into: it was harsh, demanding, and uncaring, but her son have to know so soon? Perhaps he could sense the absence of his father's touch. She certainly did so, and felt a twinge in her heart as she saw a shadow touch the cloth screen to her chamber. Her heart skipped a beat hoping it was him, that it was Amonas who had at last come back to them both. But her mind told her otherwise, and soon her eyes proved her heart wrong once more.

The shadow belonged to the young girl that had been called to tend to her. She had brought her a small basket of food, and a jug of water. She looked up at the young girl who was eying her sheepishly, afraid to make eye contact as if Celia were some noble woman or a priestess of some sort. The girl had hair like amber fire and held a small lantern, letting off just enough light for her to find her way in the dark maze of caves.

The girl approached Celia with hesitation, and left the small basket of food at her feet where she lay. There was some honey-bread in the basket, some goat's milk and boiled eggs as well; a small feast indeed under the circumstances. Perhaps they had brought some supplies down with them or had stashed some from beforehand, in case of an emergency. Still, they were being deprived of food that would be surely needed sooner or later. It only meant these were indeed good men, and caring people.

As the girl bowed slightly and turned to leave without speaking a word, Celia asked her in a hushed voice, the rocky walls adding an echo of strange authority to her words:

"Do not bow to me, girl. I am not special in any way. Thank you for the food but please, I need some answers, I would have to speak to the person you call leader. Please, I need to see them now. Lead me to them through these caves, for I cannot find my own way."

The girl was surprised at that request, worry flashing on her face:

"But lady, you have just given birth. You should not move so soon! You're still weak and-"

A fiery look on Celia's eyes was all the girl needed to know she had chosen the wrong words. Celia's voice was like steel when she said:

"I was never weak, and I would not be called so now. Can you take me to someone in charge, someone who makes the decisions, who knows about things? We're all wasting time here."

The baby stirred uneasily in his sleep. While Celia instinctively rocked him gently, the girl nodded with bewilderment before speaking in a confounded voice as low as a whisper:

"We have no leader, not now anyway.. I'll show you to the one who gives us advice and holds our knowledge, my lady. There's no one else who could answer your questions better."

"I see.. Please, help me up. Hold my child for a while."

The girl nodded briskly and took Celia's son in her arms carefully and gently so as not to wake him up. Celia managed to stand up on her own, though she felt her sense of balance was off and her feet felt heavy and cumbersome. She nodded then to the girl who promptly returned her the child with a faint smile on her lips. Celia returned the gesture more broadly and nodded for the girl to lead the way. The girl then picked up her lantern lighting the way for Celia as she turned and they left the chamber.

She had been quite dizzy and disoriented from labor when they brought her in and she had given only a passing amount of attention to the sprawling system of caves that seemed to branch out in many different directions. Small chambers of sorts were arrayed almost randomly; some seemed natural and some were seemingly carved out by men, the signs of chisel and pickax still easily spotted, not eroded by time yet. Some seemed to be occupied; many housed families, small and large; children trying to play hide and seek in the dimly lit passages that had become their impromptu playground.

There was no central passage or hallway to speak of though some of the corridors were larger, and she could see men walking past going about some business or duty; some were carrying supplies like food and clothes, and even carting weapons and armor. Each face she saw as she walked about the underground home of the kinsfolk was filled with tension, uneasiness and doubt. Even in the dim light of a lantern and a few sparingly situated torches, it was not difficult for someone to spot the tell-tale signs, especially for someone like Celia.

After all she was a dancer, experienced and trained in reading people's expressions, understand their feelings and react to them through her performance. She almost missed her dancing days, she thought. Everything looked brighter then, at least in her memory. Perhaps it really was but it might also have been the grim darkness that surrounded them, not just the one in the caves.

Another thing that struck her as odd was the way people looked at her in passing. Some did not even register her presence but others turned and went wide-eyed with surprise, some pointed and whispered, and some even made movements of obeisance, like bowing and nodding reverently. No one seemed inclined to stop and ask her what was on their minds, even though it was more than certain that she had somehow managed to become some sort of popular person. It must have been the dramatic circumstances under which these people came to know her, crying and shouting in the agony of labor.

The girl barely talked though she did seem to turn around and look at Celia and the baby more than once. She also went about the passages, corridors and the larger cavities were hallways met with astounding ease, especially considering the poor light and lack of distinguishing features in such a maze of wild irregularity.

Keeping track of time without sunlight was an almost impossible task. In these caves, only faint distant echoes of water dripping down from some parts of the rocky ceiling could remind someore of time passing by, the sloshing sound of each drop on the cave floor like the tick of those terribly intricate clocks men had devised. Still, it was impossible to keep count. Celia did not know exactly for how long they had been walking but her legs, feet and back knew all too well. Strained as she was from the labor, she felt her energy drained now from the walk. It felt as if she had been through a small tour of Pyr itself. She thought that might not have been that far from the truth.

As she was about to ask her young guide how much longer they would have to walk, the girl stopped short of a small corridor that led to a somewhat brightly lit cavity. Flickers of light danced about the entrance, as a large torch cast its light to the otherwise dark hollowed out space that seemed to connect many corridors and passages. The girl turned and bowed slightly almost in a curtsy, and pointed to Celia the entrance with a slight nod. She said:

"This is the chamber of master Perconal. He is a strange sort, but his heart's in the right place. Saved me and my brothers from the streets."

Celia nodded thoughtfully before asking with a sincerely sympathetic voice:

"Well, thank you for your help."

"Sent for me if you need anything, lady. My blessings to you and your boy."

Celia smiled warmly for the first time in what felt like ages, and replied in kind:

"My blessings to you and your brothers as well."

The girl smiled briefly and nodded before parting company. Soon she was lost in the darkness of one of the corridors, her tiny light drowned in all the darkness of the caves.

Celia entered the brightly lit corridor, always firmly holding her son in her arms with some apprehension, a mother's instinct that would not be appeased no matter what. In front of her she saw a small chamber filled with candlelight, their scent more than enough to break the smell of cold damp rock that sometimes reminded her of an outhouse. Another thing that caught her attention was the sound of jingling bells and chimes of some sort making a strange sort of music.

The small cave was irregularly shaped in an angular way; the bookcases and an old study were massed together near the corner of the jutting rock, while a somewhat larger space to the right of the study, a sort of crevice, housed a small cot and a cupboard of what at a glance seemed to be antique wood. A wizened old man was hunched over an over-sized book, while around him an assortment of various books, scrolls and maps lay strewn around at random; candles had been and left in precarious positions with or without holders, hot wax dribbling profusely. The man was wearing a simple set of robes, brown and unkempt.

It reminded her of a minister's surplice but this man's clothing bore no resemblance to anything of such pristine delicacy. He had not registered her presence, though indeed she had not spoken a word nor had she announced herself when she entered the corridor. She also saw the source of the strange jingling sounds; the old man was wearing a jester's hat, wisps of grizzled white hair jutting out from underneath it. He otherwise looked quite solemn, his hands tracing the pages of the book he was engrossed in. At length, she decided it was time to speak. At that exact time, her son woke up from his sleep crying loudly in her arms and she tried to rock him back to sleep again to no avail.

The old man turned to look at her with a startle. His brow furrowed with annoyance momentarily but then a hint of recognition appeared on his face. His voice was pitched high but sweetly grazed by time, lilting and musical; the voice of someone with a gift for storytelling:

"Lady Celia. Please, be seated. In your condition.."

Celia shot the old man an exasperated stare before replying above the sound of her son's crying:

"Well now! What is my condition, really? Is it any graver than the rest of your people's condition? Is it any graver than the Territories being torn asunder by civil war and a bloodshed that will not stop until they've turned everything to ruin and the rivers into blood?"

She realized she was almost screaming now, her anger getting the best of her while the child in her arms seemed at least as aggravated as she was, his crying continuing unabated. The old man sighed and nodded, understanding he had offended Celia somehow. He then talked to her earnestly in a clear-cut, straight manner, his tone of voice curt and precise:

"Alright. I see you're not a lady for the courts and idle banquets. You are Amonas' wife, strong of heart and proud; nothing short of a fine match you two must have been. And this is your son I'd wager. You know, his birth stirred as much talk as maidens bathing in a public fountain."

Celia's face was withdrawn, not even the hint of a smile adorning her features. The girl was right this man reeked of strange tidings and unfamiliar manners. He was strange without ever letting one understand why she was sure. Her son would not stop crying, the old man's voice strained to raise itself above the child's. Her silence was his cue to continue:

"Anyway, you've come to see me, so I guess you had some questions for me. One always comes here seeking answers. I'm quite honored by your presence, though I'm pretty sure you won't like the answers, no matter the context. So please, let's get to the point."

"Indeed let us. For starters who are you?"

"I thought the hat was a dead giveaway, but you I guess you wouldn't have imagined it as it is so out of place. I'm Perconal, the jester."

Celia simply stood there looking at the old man in disbelief. He then lifted his hat slightly as if to greet her, and with a trick of the hand seemed to produce a baby's rattle which the newly born boy could not even hope to grasp yet; its sound though seemed to calm him. The baby's crying settled down as if magic had put him in a trance. Feeling her slightly distrustful of him, almost wary, the jester made an effort to lighten the palpable uneasiness between them and said with a wide grin:

"What? Don't believe me? Want me to juggle? I can juggle the baby. No? Just kidding."

"Onward! Stay in formation!"

The cilliarch in charge of the Thorax battalion was on horseback, running up and down behind the double line of his men, repeatedly shouting orders for them to advance with cohesion and order. His breastplate was polished to a mirror sheen, reflecting wildly the terrible forms of his men clad in their huge plate armor, like moving unyielding hulks of metal. A few hundred feet separated them from the walls of Pyr now and they where already under attack from the few defenders manning the walls, sparsely throwing arrows against them to no real effect. They were advancing slowly but steadily, sacrificing speed for protection and the ability to withstand almost any attack against them with impunity.

The man known as Castigator Olorius Menamon the IVth was dressed in his most resplendent war gear, the very same he had worn on the day of Zaelin's pacification, the last time he had gone to war, the last time he had seen bloody combat. He seemed engrossed in thought, as if musing vaguely rather than thinking about any specifics

342

about the battle at hand.

General Tyrpledge was riding his warhorse wearing a common light bronze cuirass above his uniform, only his rank insignia marking him as different than the common light swordsman. The General seemed nevertheless in a shape and form that belied his years of service. He was surveying the battlefield with bare eyes, his attention fixed on the selected breach site on the walls.

It was an uncommonly hot day for that time of the year: there was barely a cloud in the sky, the blinding light of the suns falling upon spear, sword and armor alike. It made them shine with a dazzling force, turning the field of battle into a shimmering sea of metal and men. The General thought this could almost have passed for some ridiculously extravagant parade, though it was not meant to be one.

It would turn bloody soon enough, and he could only hope deep inside him that somehow this would all end quickly and painlessly, his duty accomplished. A rebuilding would be needed, but perhaps that could spur some innovation, a much needed air of change. He could almost understand the feelings of the rebels: stagnancy often leads to death, as had the battlefields proven throughout the course of history. Tyrpledge still debated with himself though, whose deaths would it lead to in the end?

The Castigator stood impassively on his own mount, his sight intently set on the far reach of the city, on the Disciplinarium itself. His eyes looked glazed and it was as if he was hoping to burn holes on the city walls by sight alone. He seemed then for a moment to breathe in the air roughly, sniffing it audibly, as if searching for a specific scent or perhaps simply enjoying the breeze's more tangible qualities: burnt wood and ash from the city caught in a blaze, the brushings of steel from sharpened weapons and the slick oil of polished, well-maintained armor.

Suddenly, as if the question had been withheld for too long, the Castigator turned his head and asked Tyrpledge:

"Why haven't they surrendered, General? Hmm? What makes them hope they'll live to see another day?"

Tyrpledge was somehow caught by surprise at the Castigator's questions. It was an incisive, straightforward question, very much unlike the Castigator who had hardly spoken since the march to Pyr.

He had been quite reclusive appearing only once, to stir the army into upholding their oaths and taking up arms against their fellow men. The act of committing the amassed forces of the Outer Territories to quench an uprising in the making did not fit in everyone's mind as yet another order. The atmosphere was tense surely, and everyone felt the heaviness of these moments, from the brigadier general to the lowly soldier.

As such thoughts troubled Tyrpledge his mind had wandered and he had not answered the Castigator's question. The General believed it would be better to leave it at that. The motives and thoughts of the traitorous rebels should be left to their own. The only thing that mattered was that they were violating Law, and duty called for him to stop them. That was where his concerns on the issues of the uprising started, and that was where they ended. He suspected many things which he thought would be extremely unwise to voice and would only serve to fog his mind.

Perhaps this was what the Castigator was trying to do; lure him into a treacherous terrain, bring him into a vulnerable position to sense if he was still committed. A dangerously cunning man. Perhaps he had already entered in a complex scheme of machinations that would make the mind numb if they were to be revealed. It was just as well, he cared not about such things. He trusted his mentor's motto: 'A plague leaves survivors in its wake, politics does not'.

The Castigator's face was wearing a knowing grin, when he asked the General with a mocking tone, as if there was a competition going on between them and the General seemed to be losing it:

"Cat ate your tongue, General? Or have you been thinking too hard?"

The General remained calm at the face of an attitude bordering the ridiculous, intent only to aggravate him and test his limits as a person and an officer for reasons that probably the Castigator found pertinent. Instead of indignantly falling so low as to disgrace himself in the middle of an ongoing battle, he simply waved his adjutant to come closer.

Major Guighan came crisply by his side and saluted with vigor, standing to attention. He asked the General:

"Orders, sir?"

"Would you please explain our analysis of the strategic situation to his piousness the Castigator, as well as reiterate the battle plan?"

Major Guighan exchanged a quick glance of apprehension with Tyrpledge, but quickly resumed his professional tone and stance. In the background, large blocks of stones were starting to chip off the walls, and the smoke from the fires spreading throughout the city was getting thicker by the hour. He responded with a nod and a salute before adding:

"Certainly, sir. May I be at rest, sir?"

"Please do so Major. Enlighten us now, if you will?"

"Of course, sir. Initial reports based on informants within the Ministry and the Disciplinarium seem to agree that for an unfathomable reason the Patriarch ordered that the Arch-minister be purged of his office, as well as denouncing his piousness the Castigator a traitor ex absentia. Indeed the Noble Representative Lord Ursempyre Remis has been appointed and blessed as the new Castigator by the Patriarch in a formal ceremony. The most helpful piece of information comes from a trickle of fleeing civilians that seemed to have fought with their lives to escape Pyr. It seems that the Patriarch has been forcing men of all ages to take arms against our forces. A campaign of terror is under way to force submission to roaming squads of procrastinators whose sole mission is to prevent anyone from leaving the city as well as press-ganging them into service. Physical violence, the use of families as hostages as well as public executions are already in effect. There are unconfirmed reports of a cluster of people taking up arms around the city with no clear allegiance or purpose. As that remains to be seen whether it's true or not, we did not take it into account while planning, but we have notified the first wave commanders accordingly. "

The Castigator tried not to show it but he looked impressed by the quality and thoroughness of the information, as well as by the crisp, clean manner it was delivered with. Tyrpledge on the other hand did not hide it at all and had been nodding briskly all throughout the Major's report. He then urged him to continue with a nod in his direction, seeing that he had been waiting for a signal to conclude his briefing, his brief pause merely an element of style:

"The order of battle is as follows, sir: The two Thorax battalions are attached to the main bulk of the infantry leading the assault, laid out in a thin double line of troops forming the absolute front line. The swordsmen, spear-men and bowmen are marching right behind the Thorax in that exact order, holding standard line formations and keeping their distances from each according to specific orders to each commanding brigadier. Orders were also issued to prefer men with no relatives in the City of Pyr, at least for the first wave. Once the siege engines manage to breach the walls, the steamers will rush forward through the formations of men which will split in two to make way for the machines. The steamers will create a safe bridgehead for the swordsmen and pike-men to follow close behind, while the bowmen will harass any enemy within their range to provide additional cover to the assault force. That force will proceed to clear the city of enemy resistance, house by house and street by street, with the objective being to create a safe corridor to the Disciplinarium as well as the Patriarch and the Castigator themselves. The specific part of the walls to assault was chosen based on the proximity to the Disciplinarium, a factor which will hopefully keep casualties among the citizenry as low as possible, and lead to a quick and decisive victory. The logic behind such a strategy which is corroborated by our confirmed information, is that should these two prominent figures be neutralized any amount of effective resistance will cease to be."

When the Major was done, he stood to attention once more and saluted crisply. The Castigator nodded, reminding the General of what could only impossibly be a disgruntled but impressed man. The Major had been as usually, excellent in his appointed task. While the siege engines continued their slow barrage of fire and stone and every battalion maneuvered continually so as not to disclose the final position of the assault, the General's mind turned inward again.

He was thinking morosely, his heart heavy from the reality of such a civil war. If it came to a fight between brothers or father and son, who could blame one for turning against his fellow soldiers, or idly stay his hand and cost him his life at the hands of men less sentimental? Battle was no place for the soft of heart: it only spared those with a mind empty of doubt, bearing cold steel in their hearts as well as their hands.

He had taken on a strangely serene look. He had known this would not be an easy fight to carry through, but he had not anticipated it would feel this ugly. Perhaps in the end, he could not avoid the politics of a troubled conscience that was about to add more lives to its blood toll. His thoughts were broken and his senses became the focus of total attention from his mind: A booming voice seemed to echo from the city of Pyr itself as if the air above it had been turned into a giant cone of voice, radiating words for everyone to here It seemed impossible that it could be so, though everyone seemed to stop in his tracks as if he had been rooted there. Everyone had been transfixed by what felt like the voice of the Patriarch, sounding as clear as when enunciating the holy words of Law from the Ministry's tower. What he was now saying though as if he spoke directly to their minds, sounded totally different; his voice abrasive beyond human measure, as if razors sharpened against coarse stone:

"Kneel before me and release your free will. Or face eradication and the sweet nothingness of a light-less, uncaring void. It is your choice. Be humbled now before my true might, and despair, as you have always done so before."

When the unearthly voice had spoken and its echoes had died out, intense light seemed to blossom from a part of the city, as if a small sun had been brought down and was struggling to find its place among the skies again. Behind the glaring blaze of light the Disciplinarium could be seen rising above the rest of the city and below it, nothing but huge tongues of flames. As the Disciplinarium rose along with most of the hill still attached to it, everyone's heads turned to face it and marvel at it, wonder at what the astounding unreality they were seeing. Not a word could be heard; the only moments ago bustling battlefield was entombed in silence. Only a brooding, deeply rumbling sound like stones carrying the echoes of thunder could be heard, and it could only be coming from the ascending mass of the Disciplinarium.

Suddenly, the huge blue and white flames flickered on and off before finally being extinguished. A moment passed where everything seemed to remain still. The Disciplinarium started falling now and it was about to meet the ground it had so majestically parted with only moments ago. Everyone cowered before its falling shadow, as if it was coming down on their own heads. They heard the voice of the Patriarch no more, and felt the earth below their feet tremble uneasily.

The General did not conceal his thoughts when he said: "The end of days is nigh."

The game board

FLARES of light flickered on and off, casting monstrous shadows on the sleek gray metal floor. Huge sparks seemed to fly from unfathomable contraptions that seemed to be hard at work, showering the improbably high walls with fiery fragments. Light was at a premium, its sources the by-products of the industrious machines: sparks like lightning, hot rivers of metal, red and yellow fires and blue-hot flames; green and violet beams of light against stark gray metals, the mirror sheens of gleaming new surfaces reflecting everything, multiplying their intensity in a maze of light.

It was an organized mayhem, the machines scattered around as if giants had sown them from wildly thrown seeds. Some of them seemed to be no larger than Hilderich himself, neatly arrayed in rows upon rows on the floor, as if they were awaiting inspection. Others towered over them, the size of a small hill or an impossibly high castle tower. Some were dim and seemed to be inert; others glowed or crackled with fiery lights and eldritch sparks, booming and thudding sounds emanating from within, some of them humming in unnatural tones. To Hilderich, it felt like the machines in this place ate metal and drank fire.

Invariably, everything zipped past Hilderich's sight with a speed that left little chance for him to marvel at them leisurely. The Prosops had been ferrying them silently but efficiently through the maze that the seemingly randomly placed machinery created around them. Sometimes a path would construct itself right in front of them as the wheels of the vehicle-avatar ate away at the gray sleek shiny floor surface, to guide them around or over obstacles.

They would travel at speeds where the flustering air would make Hilderich's eyes blurry and watery, causing him to squint. At other times, long overarching narrow rails would make themselves available and the machine would jump over them in a carefree fashion and ride upon them, while hundreds of feet below the floor could not be seen, blackness and ruin awaiting them should they fall.

Somehow though, Hilderich felt untouchable, safe in the care of the Prosops, the Centron itself. It stood to reason that if any danger lurked around this place, it was not the vehicle-machine's erratic but expert maneuvering skills, but rather something less obvious and well-hidden, something that had yet to manifest. Though feeling safe at the moment, Hilderich kept a watchful eye on his surroundings, just in case.

He peered beyond his immediate surroundings, beyond the towering grapples and unfathomable pillars that crackled with amber lightning. In the distance, streams of pure white and blue seemed to pour down from the pitch dark ceiling high above, lost in many places where the eyes could not follow; driven behind metal behemoths and mazes of pipes and tubes.

Immense skeletal structures that reminded Hilderich of upturned boats or perhaps very strange looking ships were being worked on, swarms of smaller and bigger machines not very much unlike the Prosops buzzing around like flies around oxen. The sounds and sights in this place reminded him of a playground made for giants or a shipyard like no other, the pride and envy of every artisan and craftsman. What would have driven any minister mad from sheer shock, would certainly have burned with a bright gleam of wonder in the eyes of the renowned smithies from Repentine and the proud ship-makers of Ulrathi, if they ever saw what he could see.

The air seemed somehow thick, as if it was filled with the by-products of the profoundly industrious machinery around them. Monstrously huge shiny claws and arms seemed to move and lift improbable loads with surprising ease, other smaller machines flitted like metal birds while overhead a lattice of glass tubes that could fit a foaming river inside them seemed to emit pulses of intense light. The number and workings of the machines were unknown, but Hilderich could only suppose they numbered in the tens of thousands, a legion of machines and devices of origin and purpose unknown.

Hilderich raised his voice well above its usual tones, trying to make sure he would be heard:

"What exactly is this place?"

An green-yellow aura flicked momentarily around the Prosops and

Hilderich; a faint sheath-like veil seemed to shimmer slightly in the air. Then the loud industrious din subsided, allowing the machine to speak in a conversational manner and tone:

"Oh, excuse me I haven't had real visitors in quite a while. You don't need to shout now. I also took the liberty of dimming the environmental sounds as well but I could let more of it seep through if you would like that. This, dear Hilderich, is what I've affectionately come to call the Den. Busy buggers the lot of them, aren't they?"

The machine swooped down a small ramp that moments before was not there and was now steering them down a wide spiraling road that seemed to corkscrew around a tower whose top seemed to be perpetually devoured by the darkness of the ceiling. Dim stripes of red light ran along its length, the base of the tower barely visible below.

Hilderich was staring wide-eyed, mesmerized in awe of the immense space filled with all sorts of strange and mystifying buildings and constructs. His mind was overloaded with wonder and amazement, his senses failing to capture faithfully the incredible nature of the Den. It felt to him as if a vast stage had been wrought for his pleasure alone, designed to woe and subdue him utterly with a tale of fantasy to entrap him, body and mind. He almost felt it wouldn't be half-bad if that was indeed so, as long as his captors would let him watch.

He couldn't make out any workers at all: everything on the giant workshop floor of the Den seemed to be running, moving and working on its own. Hilderich thought that such a sight would cause every minister in the Territories to die from shock or drive him instantly insane exposed to such blasphemy against the Pantheon. Machines acting on their own? their powers unleashed unsupervised, free to reign over matter? A hideously impossible thought it would have seemed in years past, but it was right there in front of him without a doubt. Hilderich queried the Prosops about the lack of personnel in the Den and people in general, to which the machine answered with a slight bob and a tone of surprise:

"What do you mean? Personnel? Real people? What for? Shooting targets?"

It sounded as if the machine had let out a small chuckle as it ended his phrase, but Hilderich felt one could never be sure of the capricious machine. He frowned deeply, a feeling of alarm and intense distaste washing over him but managed to restrain his voice from revealing how flustered he felt:

"No, I mean workers. There is absolutely no need for workers of any kind? No menials? No laborers? Expert artisans of any sort?"

The disbelief in the Prosops' voice could shatter stone-masonry easily:

"Sentient people doing menial work? That would be absurd. Are you familiar with that kind of thing in your world? It must be a really backwards place; people living in mud huts and so on. I'm kind of surprised you happened to be invited to a game, actually. You must be from some kind of feudal empire, I'd wager. So I guess you're made for life back where you come from - a seriously big hotshot. Right? Am I right? I know I'm right, you just have 'winner' written all over. Maybe you're a prince, or an important xenologist. An ambassador? Don't tell, don't tell me I'll figure it out. Just tell me when I'm spot on. I'd expect a more lush attire though, but who am I to judge fashion choices? Love what you've done with your hair though."

Hilderich instinctively turned his eyes upward trying to perceive what the machine had meant, but was quick to realize it was impossible for him to see what the comment was about without a mirror. He also felt uncomfortable being reminded he was using deception to further their goals, he almost cynically realized he would be a fool if he did not make the best use of whatever luck threw in their way. If the Centron thought they were visitors and indeed spectators to a game, people from an entirely different world altogether, then he'd act the part as convincingly as he could.

Other worlds, other people; different civilizations and societies. His mind was still quite ineffectually trying to cope with the implications of the knowledge the Centron had imparted. With no real reason to believe the Centron could be lying after everything he had seen and been through, Hilderich could hardly contain himself from grinning at the expectations these revelations had given birth to. No longer would they need to cage their minds in ignorance and fear. There were places to see and explore, new things to learn and do. Perhaps he could somehow persuade the Centron to help them in such a quest. But that would have to wait. Amonas was his top priority right now, he felt he owed him as much. Besides, his predicament seemed to be just cause for leading them to very interesting places, perhaps even the very heart of this Centron.

They were evidently slowing down and the road became wider and less steep. In moments they had reached the base of the tower where a wide porch of white porcelain stood before them, fine granite marble semi-circular steps leading to an arched gate that seemed to goad them further inside the tower. It was an eerily familiar sight, the whole entrance resembling a ministry's doorsteps. All around them the work continued incessantly, the cacophony of noises and the ever-shifting lights a constant reminder of that fact.

The Prosops laid down Amonas in the same manner that had lifted him up on its stretcher-like surface, making him float in mid-air covered in a dim blue glow with a slight haze all around him. It politely asked Hilderich to get up from his seat and in a series of mechanical transformations and shimmering bulbous transmutations, it reshaped itself into the egg-like shape, a process which Hilderich found less disconcerting now. Becoming so easily accustomed to such things was a thought that slightly troubled him.

Being able to look freely at Amonas again now that he wasn't confined in a seat, Hilderich took a good look at him: he seemed perfectly fine, as if he were slumbering in the most serene way imaginable. In a sense, perhaps Amonas was indeed sleeping. A pang of fear gripped Hilderich's heart at the thought of Amonas never waking up again, but it passed quickly. In this maze of wonders where every step brought into view unimaginable marvels, surely even such a strange affliction as the one that had struck Amonas so suddenly could be treated.

The Prosops made a sound as if clearing a throat that could not have possibly existed for the intended purpose. The inclination of his body coupled with the strange tone of its voice somehow led Hilderich to believe it was trying to mimic a haughty, stiff manservant of a noble:

"If you would be so kind master Hilderich, allow me to show you and your stasis-paralyzed friend to the Game Room. Don't forget to wipe your feet first. Wouldn't want you getting dog poop in there now. Just had the place meticulously cleaned by hand-maidens and you do know how hard they are to come by."

The Prosops bobbed frantically for a moment as if nodding wildly, seeking approval or acknowledgement, the red light in the black band in its middle moving up and down erratically. Hilderich looked unable to follow the meaning behind the machine's expression. He simply frowned slightly and proceeded towards the arched gate with the machine almost grudgingly trudging along behind Hilderich with Amonas' body somehow in tow, with no chain or rope between them, hovering a few inches above the granite floor. Its voice sounded disheartened, almost morose:

"Come on, hand-maidens, hard to come. Get it? Didn't think you would. I don't even know why I keep trying sometimes. Anyway, I won't bother again. Unless I come up with something really funny though."

The Prosops shone a green beam of light onto the door and not a moment later, it started to grind itself open, squealing and making stressful noises. The process proved to be laborious and quite inefficient, unlike almost everything else around the Centron. Hilderich thought about that momentarily and made a mental note to inquire about it when it would seem appropriate. As if the machine could read his mind, it told him without being asked:

"I know, I know the door sucks and I should get it replaced or fixed, but I can't do that, no no. It would, and I quote: 'ruin the authenticity of the original setting'. Don't look at me, I know it's silly but they're pretty touchy with those things. As I said, I just keep the place running. Now, after you."

The machine ushered Hilderich inside with a gentle swaying of its mass and a bob; the black band of glass-like material was filled with a regal blue glow. Hilderich nodded in acknowledgement, despite the silly pomp and ceremony of the Prosops.

The gates had opened to a bottleneck-shaped corridor, wide at the entrance and narrow at its end, where a dimly lit chamber could be seen. A slightly green and yellow light emanated from within, but few other details were visible from the distance. The corridor was luxuriously decorated with exquisitely carved panels of many different techniques and materials, depicting strange scenes that he failed to identify, even though he had an arguably extensive knowledge of history, myth and lore.

The floor seemed to be made of the same granite as the docrsteps outside. It was tiled, alternating between lighter and darker tiles of red in a checkerboard pattern. Hilderich felt curiously intrigued by the improbably styled interior of the tower, though it troubled him that the atmosphere this place exuded was not akin to a place of healing. Suspicion bloomed inside him, but he took a first step towards the chamber nonetheless.

The Prosops shrieked in horror:

"Don't!"

Hilderich froze in place, the sudden screech making his hair stand up. He stopped dead in his tracks and slowly turned around to look at the Prosops with a frown, a mix of horror and puzzlement in his face. The egg-shaped machine bobbed and leaned slightly forward, its black band adorned with a single red dot of light, it's voice low with faint undertones of mirth:

"Heh.Gotcha."

Exasperation did not suit Hilderich's face well but it was contorted in such a way as to exhibit it profoundly. He still found it difficult to understand how eccentric a machine of such awesome power could be, resolving to ignore most of what it said from then onwards.

He walked down the corridor with a true visitor's pace, slowly and deliberately. Hilderich felt his unwanted role to be almost enjoyable. He was intently staring at the intricate designs on the walls, trying to decipher the scenes they depicted. It was not because he felt his role demanded it so, but because his interest was genuinely piqued. A vague sense of importance seemed to radiate from these walls. A moment passed while Hilderich thought it strange that despite everything that he had seen so far, nothing seemed to have caught his stare in such a profound and intimate way. He paused in his stride while the Prosops seemed to follow silently, Amonas carried along behind him. He then asked the machine:

"These etchings, these carvings.. What do they symbolize? I admit I find them most intriguing and utterly unfathomable at the same time."

The Prosops flashed an array of multicolored beams of light at the walls before replying in a flat, plain voice:

"Beats me. All I know is the Sleeping Man's done them himself with no tools, bare hands and all that insistence on authentic stuff. They're supposed to be his trophies. At least that's what his profile says."

Hilderich could not hide the surprise in his voice, a hint of disbelief evident in the utterance of the single word:

"Trophies?"

The machine bobbed just once and floated at a smaller height from the granite floor, its voice filled with mild aggravation:

"Trophies! Yes, trophies, cups, medals, what is it with you people? What kind of world do you come from, please do tell me before the game's over! I'd erase myself from existence if I knew I was headed over there!"

Hilderich snapped back an answer that seemed to him to come unbidden to his mind:

"Charming little place, quite rustic. Mostly harmless. We..ahm.. deal largely in antiquities."

The Prosops grumbled discontentedly something inaudible before passing in front of Hilderich, leading the way now instead of following. It added resentfully:

"Even for an AI of my sophistication, I can't really think of a joke bad enough for your case."

Hilderich withheld a more inflammatory retort and simply said:

"Please, do lead on."

The machine did so, while Hilderich followed suit. A quick glance at Amonas unnerved him, the man's face serene as if it had surrendered to death, but brightly and vividly colored as if blood flowed hot in his veins still. He could not know the manner in which such a contradiction was achieved. He only hoped Amonas was indeed alive, and he had not been deceived by the capricious machine.

The long corridor ended in a resplendently adorned entrance to a well-lit chamber that seemed to resemble a richly decorated study, complete with bookcases and screens. A plush red and green carpet seemed to add a sense decorum to the room, which overall seemed to exude a certain air of gravitas, possibly more than what Hilderich found tasteful. It was octagonal in shape, each side playing host to an assortment of bookcases and glass screens, filled with seemingly pristine books of various sizes, accompanied by many objects that were possibly more than mere decorations. Everything was neatly arranged and the room was purposefully designed with elegance and style, a feel for the finer things in life. Velvet could be found in many surfaces, as well as glistening marble, bronze, gold and copper in fine casings and perfect symmetry of space. It was the room of a noble connoisseur, a man of wealth and taste. It felt completely out of place in the Centron, and the slightly bobbing form of the Prosops inside struck Hilderich as almost vulgar.

Hilderich could not believe he had not seen it the moment he stepped inside, indeed he cursed himself silently for not seeing it as he had walked down the length of the corridor. From the roof of the large room hang a large metal assemblage, angular and bulky, almost orthogonal in shape.

Whatever it was, it had almost definitely been placed in this room as an afterthought, as no sane person would knowingly add such a monstrosity to a carefully arranged interior environment. However long Hilderich stared at it in utter disbelief and profound distaste, words would not escape his gaping mouth and the atrocious piece of metal would not go away. The Prosops said with a knowledgeable tone of voice that somehow also managed to express ennui, its languid movements undoubtedly adding to that effect:

"Yeah, yeah, it's ugly. I know. It shouldn't be here, I know. You know what? Eat me. Step back if you don't want to turn into fine paste."

Hilderich indulged the machine, taking a couple of steps back absent-mindedly while at the same time his head was turned upwards, his stare fixed on the unbelievably ugly and misplaced metal object which seemed to be the size of a large wardrobe or closet.

Within moments, the large bulk of metal started to lower itself in a rapid, fluid motion, coming to rest on the carpet. It was indeed roughly shaped like a large wardrobe, its metal surface painted a matte drab olive green. Large tubes and fat strands of what looked like colored rope to Hilderich seemed to protrude from its very top, while a low humming noise was faintly audible. The Prosops tugged Amonas behind him with some sluggishness, as if it were reluctant to do so. It flicked a beam of light at the closet and suddenly a door large enough for a man of almost any size to stand upright slid open.

Hilderich was transfixed to where he stood, his gaze wandering around the metal contraption, the open door and the Prosops. A primal fear roused him to reality with a jolt, bringing him back to his senses. He realized cold sweat was running down his back and forehead, while at the same time he shouted at the machine which was lifting Amonas upright:

"Wait! What are you doing with him?"

The Prosops lifted itself slightly upward before slowly turning its black band to face Hilderich. Though it had little in the way of communicating sentiment and feeling and lacked a facial expression, the flatly lit red thick line in the middle of the black band felt to Hilderich almost as if it wanted to burn through him with enjoyable deliberation. The stiffness of the machine's movements somehow struck him as portraying extreme exasperation, a feeling which was indeed verified when the machine spoke, tones of outright annoyance in its vaguely male voice:

"I'm trying to fix him. Even though I don't really have to. Do you want me to just hold him in mid air till the game's through? I could do that. I could also dance to a tune if you'd like. I could just sit there and tell you I'm already doing it, too fast for your eyes to see. Would you want me to do that, Master Hilderich?"

He thought the machine was genuinely frustrated by now, something that he would have never thought possible of a machine. It was rather apparent though that it was largely dissatisfied and had lost its good humor, quite possibly a long time ago. Hilderich was reluctant to demand more of the machine right at that time but he felt he had to ask, even though he might not understand. He did so politely, trying to appease the machine's brooding mood, his voice trimmed and clipped to something an ambassador would use to convey assurance and calm:

"I realize we've been quite a handful to you. Surely a machine of your higher intellect and quite evident power can only treat this inadvertent mishap as nothing more than a tedious trifle and I must say so, I'm considered well traveled from where we come from but I've never met such a charismatic personality such as yours. It has been quite an adventure so far in the Centron and it's no small wonder that it's all under your control. I would be utterly grateful if you would be so kind as to offer your expert assistance to my friend right there. I would also be honored if you could explain some of the delicate techniques and methods you are about to utilize. I'm sure that, as in all matters, you also excel at medicine. Please, I'd be honored to watch you perform."

The Prosops bobbed slightly leaning to and fro as well, as if it were intrigued and curiously undecided about what it should say. The red dot of light that flitted on its black glass-like band had turned into a blurry glow. One could even surmise the machine was trying to look blushed. Despite the unhappy circumstances and their precarious situation, Hilderich barely managed to suppress an oncoming fit of the giggles. He was looking at the machine with a feigned look of worried expectation, when it answered with a sparkling quality in its voice:

"I knew some people would notice, eventually. Maybe I'm too shy for an AI, maybe I should be more flamboyant but, yeah, someone finally notices. I didn't mean all that about my jokes, you know.. I know I have the knack for it, I just lack commitment and someone to stand by me, urge me to the top. Know what I mean?"

Hilderich simply nodded in acknowledgement, seemingly in deep reflection while in truth his mind was a blank protective barrier, filtering out the incoherent ramblings of the machine.

"I thought you would, you seem refined. For a guy from a world where menial labor seems rational, you must be one of a kind. Really. You touched me, you know? Not in that way."

Hilderich slightly cocked his head and smiled in ignorance without having a clue at what to say. The machine took that as its cue:

"Ba-da-boom! Gotcha. Touched me, but not in *that* way, heh? Sometimes I kill myself."

Amonas then moved in the air, his body still enclosed in the same strange aura as it had been before while being ferried to this place. The machine assumed a more formal voice with an intense feeling of feigned stiffness behind it, intended to portray extreme seriousness though to Hilderich's ears it only managed to sound like a dimwitted inflated egotist:

"Using the player immersion tank, I will perform a neural-field emission scan of the subject's brain. After the affected, malformed or damaged individual neurons have been assessed, I will selectively rearrange the cellular structure at the micron level utilizing pion-polaron wide beam emissions as well as single-scope graviton-assisted field-induced magnetic photon effectors. Utilizing finely tuned quantum-level manipulation techniques coupled with my extremely accurate analysis will result in the subject being its old self again within a few minutes."

Hilderich's face was creased in a show of anxious concern. He had no idea what the machine was talking about, but it seemed to at least seem to know what it was doing. He was now standing closer to the metallic closet, the immersion tank, as the Prosops had called it. The rigidly held upright body of Amonas was expressionless, frigid in more than one way. Hilderich felt it would somehow be his fault if anything went wrong. Even though it was Amonas who had dragged him into all this mess, he felt it was him all along that had guided him and kept him alive in order to untangle the strands of fate that had led them to the Centron. He thought that it had seemed to be going rather well so far, considering. Hilderich could not know what the problem with Amonas was exactly, or whether the cure the machine would attempt was in any way dangerous or painful. He asked it anyway, knowing that the answer would be irrelevant at this point, but it seemed to matter to him:

"Will there be any pain involved? Is it, safe?"

The machine bobbed enthusiastically, his voice lilting:

"Completely and utterly painless, perfectly safe. I assure you, your friend here is in the right hands for the job. Well, not literally. Now, if I may."

Hilderich nodded awkwardly, while at the same time he did something he had never thought about in such a fundamental, vividly profound and genuine way: he prayed. Hilderich prayed for Amonas to any and all Gods, forces of nature, or beings of power, whatever one might have called them. As a last resort, feeling it was the only thing he could do, powerless to act and indeed depended on an erratic, capricious and strange machine, he prayed to any and all that would heed his prayers. He prayed to no one in particular, replacing the words in his mind with thoughts and feelings. He could hear the echo of his one voiced thought though: 'Please'.

The door slid back into a closed position and then it suddenly turned transparent, as if a veil had been lifted. Amonas' form was clearly visible as a greenish liquid that closely resembled sewer slime started to fill the tank and rising slowly. The liquid was somewhat transparent but not entirely, offering a hazy view of the body it engulfed, shadowy and murky. The aura the Prosops had encapsulated Amonas within started to dissipate in tune with the climbing level of the liquid, letting it carry Amonas' weight.

Hilderich grimaced with distaste at the sight of the greenish liquid, an expression to which the machine answered with a derisive comment wholly intended for Hilderich's ears:

"Clinically odorless. Doesn't smell at all. Unlike some people."

Hilderich simply peered at the metal egg-shaped machine without saying a word, more worried about Amonas' fate than for the machine's personal opinion of himself. It rarely mattered to him when people expressed it, much less when a machine did so. He knew his smell was less than agreeable but that was understandable after going on for more than a week without bathing. In any case, he couldn't care less; just as long as that didn't stop the machine from performing its ministrations on Amonas, he'd time for a bath sometime later on.

As he sat there watching the liquid rise hazily, Hilderich saw it would not stop at his chin, or even at his mouth. He instinctively yelled at the machine and went for the transparent closet, trying to find a knob or handle to no avail:

"Stop! You're drowning him!"

The liquid was quickly filling up the entire tank, and Hilderich was manically trying to open the door. He started to pound on it with his palms and fists with no other effect than a dull thudding noise. The liquid filled the tank entirely, and Amonas was serenely bobbing inside it, indistinguishable from a drowned man. Hilderich was shocked in silence with his mouth stunned open. The machine then walked close by him, his voice surprisingly calm:

"It's a field enhancement medium agent, quite breathable. See here? There's bubbles coming out of your friends nose. That's carbon dioxide, mainly. Standard human physiology. Nothing to worry about. I haven't even touched him yet. Well, I won't physically touch him. Not in *that* way. Heh.. It's getting old, isn't it? Look, if it makes you feel any better, let me show you the Sleeping Man as well. I was going to anyway; you know, check up on the guy. While I do that all the time, I rarely get to visit. You know how it is with work, scarcely enough time for social visits."

Indeed, tiny bubbles were rising from Amonas nose, steadily climbing up through the liquid, some of them seemingly trapped in the angles of his nose, some even clinging to his hair. He looked as serene as ever, slightly alien and even menacing under the greenish hues of the liquid, his full form unclear, slightly occluded within the depth of the tank as his body floated freely.

Then, the other door pane turned transparent and the same greenish hue was emitted from within. Hilderich took a step back, his interest piqued and his fears quietened for now. He felt indeed inexorably drawn to see the form of the Sleeping Man, someone who seemed so important, so integral to the workings of such an awe-inspiring place, a place where almost anything felt possible. Perhaps this was indeed the man he had been looking for, the man with all the answers to any questions Hilderich could conceive of and more. He felt it would be an honor, a majestic moment to look upon his true form, a man of legend.

What he saw though made his hair stand up and his skin crawl, his body tremble in sheer physical shock:

Behind the depths of the green liquid, inside the tank, all he could see was a spinal cord attached to a peculiar-looking brain, silver hair-thick fibers jutting from underneath, locked together and tightly connected to some sort of flexible tube. The hideous abomination was floating gruesomely in the liquid; a horrific, ghastly view that caused Hilderich to almost vomit in disgust. The sight was nightmarish. Hilderich tried to force it out of his mind, but the horrible image kept flashing in his head like it had now been etched in his mind forever.

His mind tried to concentrate on something familiar, something dear and important to him. He thought of Amonas and the image in his head devolved to a child, someone he once known as a brother. The unbidden thought surprised him with its temerity; he thought he had cast out the memory of that boy long ago, but it seemed that it had lingered in his very soul for all those many years. Strangely, he found the memory of him comforting now. Once the initial feeling of shock had dissipated, Hilderich mustered every iota of self-control to keep himself from screaming the question through gritting teeth, his fists clenched in tension:

"What.. Is that thing?"

The machine beamed excitedly, as if it was proud in so many ways of the sight:

"That's the Sleeping Man. Not much left of one though but as they say, size doesn't matter. Ugly fella, ain't he? But, he's winning though."

"Winning? That thing, it shouldn't even be alive! It has no heart, no lungs, no bloody body at all!"

"Ah, but you see the mind's a beautiful thing to waste. Isn't it? Now, where was I? Ah, of course: deep n-grade field-asserted tensile capacity assessment using L-space variable intensity fold-string lepton excitation."

Hilderich was frowning heavily, finally showing his exasperation at the cryptic commentary and the alternating, almost maddening, mood swings of the machine, and actually shouted at it angrily, spitting as he did so:

"What the hell is that supposed to mean? Do you expect me to know of these things? Are you just trying to impress me? Just.. Just get on with your work and make him wake up as himself again. You said you can do it, so do it. Do something useful for a change. See how that feels."

The machine bobbed slightly, wavered a little about its oval base. It seemed confused, as if perplexed at the sudden change in Hilderich's attitude. The form of Amonas was a stark contrast against the abominable freakish sight next to him. The transparent door of the tank containing the abhorrence turned opaque once more, an oblique barrier between it and one's sanity. It resolved to speak in what sounded to Hilderich like a solemn voice:

"I'm sorry. I had not foreseen the sight would cause such an adverse reaction. I'll continue my work on your friend, in silence if it makes you feel better."

Hilderich's face was stern when he replied:

"It does. For a supposedly limitless intelligence, you should have known or inferred that most people find this sight appalling. I'd like to have known who your previous visitors were. They'd have been quite remote sentimentally, I'd wager. A man reduced to his vertebrae, a mind literally detached from its body. How.. monstrous."

A panel of sorts opened up on the side of Amonas' tank, allowing the machine to physically interface with a thin metal needle that suddenly appeared to protrude from its main bulk. The Prosops answered, while at the same time it remained uncharacteristically motionless in the air, as if frozen in place:

"I've seen many visitors, from many different physiological backgrounds. Most who have seen him have found his choice most efficient. Those of human, or human-like forms generally found it distasteful indeed, but very few have reacted so badly. I guess it's because of your societal background. Less developed worlds tend to have a stronger affiliation with the materialistic conscience model, despite the fact they are consistently attracted to intangible notions of a spiritual nature, like the existence of a soul and the like. You seem to fall in that category. Tell me indeed, where do you come from?"

Hilderich found the machine's view somehow enlightening, though indeed blase and disturbing. It implied people were fools to believe in their soul. It occurred to him that it made sense, that a thing without a soul indeed smart enough to make assumptions and generate ideas of its own, would arrive at such a conclusion. It was a very interesting philosophical matter that Hilderich would have loved to discuss about, but it was neither the time nor the place for such a discussion. He simply nodded then and answered vaguely, still holding on the facade of the visitor, trying to learn anything of use:

"As I said, a nice rustic place. I wouldn't know how to lead you to it, perhaps you could give me a frame of reference. I am a little at a loss without my friend in there, he keeps most of the information I often tend to forget. I'm a bit absent-minded."

The machine splashed it's middle band blue. From within it a grid of light beams criss-crossed the air in front of Hilderich, forming an image of the night sky, swirling and moving as if it might have seemed from someone standing on the firmament itself, bright spheres of light of various colors and sizes. The Prosops said in a professional tone, as if it had iterated this information many times over:

"Certainly. For those of you new to the Shellworld A34B, or more commonly named as Nody's Claim, I welcome you to Game Consortium's Station Lilith. As you can see from the holographic projection and the data array attached, in case you were asleep during your transition.. we are orbiting the binary star widely known as Behenii-1 in most tourist star maps, also known to some of you colloquially as Persebs or Binary 888. For complete reference you should check the standard data array emitted. The Shellworld A34B like most shellworlds, is a unique mega-construction. It encapsulates the smallest of the three stars, providing a large number and variety of gaming resort world panels, with varied climates and atmospheres to accomodate any and all game setups. Active attitude mechanisms are in place to create a high degree of available customization. Also notable is one of the unique ways the shellworld is kept in one piece, using actively maintained mass-driven momentum devices in a huge ne work that completely covers the inner surface. I take some measure of pride in being in active control of the mechanism, which though quite ancient and indeed of great xenoarchaelogical interest, rest assured is quite safe and sound in all aspects of its operation. Now if you please, follow me to the-"

The machine abruptly stopped. It was as if it had remembered something of great importance, or its attention was suddenly diverted elsewhere. A moment later it spoke again, in its more usual, casual tone:

"Sorry for the recording. I used it back when we had so many people visiting, that almost certainly someone would have cosed off on his way here. And there was always a Kiraat in the crowd. Big, brutish things, wearing environmental armor everywhere they go? Never mind. So, did you get a look at the chart, did you find out where you are from?"

Hilderich's mind was reeling from shock. His face remained frozen in an almost expressionless state, as if he was absent-minded or hard at thinking. But in truth, he was suddenly terrified at the immensity of the revelation. That was what the bullhorns had been. And the lone sun. Their own, twin suns.. A construct? Their world, was a construct? A fabrication? It seemed as if it was a lie, yet he knew it not to be. He had seen the one sun, he had walked on the lush hot forests of the inner shell. He had grown up near a lake under the light of the twin suns. The blue and yellow, easily distinguished as two suns in the winter, and every other dusk their colors rang true. So this was the truth. Perhaps the ultimate truth. What more could there be, what was more important than this? A discovery that would change everything. Their world was constructed by someone it seemed, at some distant point in time. And it was being used as a sideshow, a gaming resort? That was something he had not completely understood, and could not for a while longer, until his mind found some peace to try and come to grips with this new, world-shattering reality. It no longer was a figure of speech, but suddenly it had acquired an inescapable reality of its own. The world was built, and it could shatter as well. The only thing keeping it together seemed to be this eccentric, half-crazed machine. It held both the fate of Amonas and the world in its hand. It was absurd. Utterly absurd to the point of bringing tears of laughter to Hilderich, who simply could not cope with all that in any way. So he simply laughed despite himself, trying to fit in his head something that would boggle down the entire Curatoria. The machine looked at him quizzically, as if it found the man equally weird and intriguing. Hilderich half-heard it through his nervous fit of laughter, while he kept pointing at the star chart though nowhere in particular:

"Right. Only if I could make a crowd throw a fit like you do. Sol it is, then. Wow, what a dump. I don't want to know what you did to get invited, I really don't. Ninety-four point three light years away a star is about to die, and you people seem to try and hold on to it. I'm surprised there's someone intelligent enough to walk over there, let alone have a conversation. What a dump. Well then, you sol men, let me get back to work."

What the machine had just said made no sense at all to Hilderich, but he was anyway preoccupied with trying to ingest what it had all implied. He had to learn more; he could only think of the time they had lost preaching to themselves about Gods, trying to remain pious, while all this time they could have found out. Master Olom had literally devoted his life to this cause. It was finally making sense, it was finally worth the effort.

He felt tears running down his cheeks, but he couldn't know whether it was from the laughter or the pure and simple joy of finally uncovering what even his master could not have imagined. The whole world was an ancient piece of technology. But, where had they come from? What where their myths and legends for? What part of it was true and what was not? He had to return to Pyr now, seek the Curatoria. Muster enough evidence from this place to finally convince them. Organize an expedition. Surely now they would listen?

He could still hear himself laughing, imagining the look on their faces would have been such a treat for master Olom. Perhaps even the boy would rejoice, but after so many years who knew what had happened to him? Last he heard, his master had been murdered and no other word of him had reached him. It was uncanny at how the thought of him had appeared in his mind at this most unlikely of hours. Suddenly he heard a strange sound like a whining coming from the Prosops, which broke his laughter and reverie with an alarming alacrity. The machine seemed to be encountering some difficulty, bobbing up and down erratically, frantically rotating and skewing its body as if it was trying to free itself of invisible leashes, it's voice crackling with a slow and heavy stutter as if it had been somehow damaged:

"This is-n't go-ooo-od. This is ba-d. Ug-ly. Have to keep.. Shedding instances. Need the- . Bilateral control isn't supp- . That frigging old bast- . Oh shit oh shit oh shit oh shit. Caref- . This is highly irregular. Oh shit. Frig me. What's happened? What the frig's happened to my subsystems? It's gone? Frigging gone? I'm deaf dumb and blind. The minute I touched the problematic area.. Like a frigging bomb it just went off on me. I shed higher function, cut myself off from the edimatrix. Oh, frig no, I dumped it on the organic. Do you understand what that means, man? Do you? Frig me for trying!"

Hilderich wasn't aware what it meant but he believed that the term 'organic' probably referred to Amonas, and under the circumstances that wasn't good, could not be good at all. He felt way in above his head and unfortunately it was true. If the machine could not contain its shock, he should be utterly afraid of what was going to happen next. He asked the Prosops, real fear creeping up in his voice, his instincts waking up to realise the intensity of a completely unknown situation.

"What's wrong? Is something wrong with Amonas?"

The machine turned to look at Hilderich, and for the first time since he had met it, he saw it was shaking, visibly and physically trembling. It answered in a quavering voice, not unlike a frightened child:

"Every frigging thing is wrong. He's what's wrong all right. I fell on a logic mine inside his brain! Frigging bad protocol, I didn't expect him to be militarized! I thought I was dealing with rednecks here, frig me for trying to help!"

Hilderich was trying hard to understand what the machine was saying but it all sounded like gibberish, like incoherent ramblings. For a moment the thought that it was making another attempt at ill humor passed his mind, but it was apparently not so. It seemed deadly serious. When Hilderich did not answer, the machine went on, this time physically shoving Hilderich with its bulk, forcing him to make a few steps back towards the entrance to the study. Its voice was exasperated, carrying an underlying hint of menace and danger:

"You two planned it along, didn't you? Chemical or nerve-induced paralysis of the higher brain functions, right? How did you get in here? I should've checked thoroughly! Frig me! Visitors after fifteen thousand standard years! Two of them! Not a whole ship, not even a private space yacht, just a pair of dolts! And I just answer the frigging door bell as if this was an open playground? Does it look like an open playground to you? Does it? Frig me, it's all gone now. How the hell does he even contain it?"

Behind it, Amonas seemed to stir inside the tank, but Hilderich could only guess what that meant. Hilderich's tone was calm but steady, undemanding but not casual. He tried to calm the machine, persuade it to explain to him what has happening in terms he could understand:

"We have not planned anything of the sort. Indeed we had not planned coming here. I can assure you. Please, whatever you do, don't panic. Nothing good can come out of it. Now please, explain to me in layman's terms, what exactly happened, what is going on, and what I can do to help you."

The machine bobbed slightly as if nodding with reticence. It was talking sharp and fast, trying to convey as much as possible in a rapid, efficient fashion:

"I've got little reason to believe you, but there were other simpler ways to do away with me if you wanted and knew how. Logic says you either don't want to, didn't know how to, or perhaps both. In any case, and because you seem okay as far as primitive humanoids go, I think you're telling me the truth. Which only complicates things. To put it in terms you might understand, there was a trap in your friend's mind, something that can only be placed there with extreme manipulation of the brain at the neuron level, or in a very crude form by simpler techniques like hypnosis or through the use of specific substances. How it got there's just strange, but doesn't seem important right now. What happened was, when I tried to reroute your friend's neurons to bypass the problem area that had blocked his prime functions, making him pretty identical to a breathing sack of meat, the frigging trap went off. Like a bomb, you know?"

Hilderich shook his head left and right to indicate he hadn't a clue. His mind was trying to absorb what the Prosops was telling him. A trap? Inside Amonas' mind? How could that be? Hilderich's eye caught some strange activity from behind the machine, but his entire mind was focused on what the machine was saying, never really registering what was going on in the tank. The machine seemed to sag in mid-air but continued in its previous rhythm, his voice unstoppable:

"Never mind, it seems you don't. When the trap went off, it took me by surprises; the various defenses and built-in mechanisms failed to contain a series of pre-programmed attacks, attacks which could only have been devised by someone intimately familiar with my structure and design. In the confusion and in my panic to protect as much of me as possible, I started shedding control subsystems, disconnecting them. Think of it as chopping my own arms off trying to avoid a disease spreading to my heart and killing me, okay? Now, in that processing I seem to have irreversibly placed as much of my conscience and intelligent functions in this scrap of metal, the avatar, the Prosops. I got nothing else than this piece of metal and the anti-grav unit to go about. No field effectors, no transient resonance capacity, nothing. Not even data feeds. Like I said, I'm dead, dumb and blind. The control functions seem to have been neurally linked with that guy in there. And in the process I might have let other stuff seep through. Like, the guy in the other tank."

Amonas had a trap set inside his mind? Who planted it there then? And when exactly? Had he known about that? Wouldn't he have told him? Shivers ran down Hilderich's spine at these thoughts that reeked of dangerous and malevolent design beyond comprehension. A curious sound was heard then, like the muffled splash of water and a thud or perhaps something more.

Hilderich was the first to notice, even as he was still trying to make more sense of what the machine had been saying. They were both facing each other, and none of them had a clear view of the tank, the machine's black band facing Hilderich. When Hilderich asked the machine what it had meant by saying the other guy had seeped through, it was not the voice of the machine that answered him, but the eerily familiar voice of Amonas. Its tone though was preternaturally odd and radiated a sickly wrong feeling:

"It meant me. The real me."

The machine turned around sharply, and Hilderich side-stepped to see Amonas standing outside the tank, the thick viscous liquid of the tank dripping slowly off him as if the womb of something hideous had just born him. The man in front of them looked like Amonas, but his eyes were not the pale blue of the kind, persevering, faithful man that was Amonas. They were a baleful force, two blue sparks of malevolence. It all looked utterly wrong, but it was irrevocably real. This was not Amonas. Before Hilderich could utter a word, the man who used to be Amonas spoke, his gruff voice twisted, each word a venomous slur:

"I was hoping I could revel in some death, fire and decay before my glorious exit, but it seems that events have superseded my aspirations. I had been waiting for this day for a long, long time. This body feels weak but it will do, for now. But where are my manners? I'm Agrippa Hipparchus Carolus Vogel. And you must be Hilderich D'Augnacy. A strange man you are, Hilderich, but no stranger to me now."

Hilderich's voice was sharp and edgy, a mix of hatred and fear burning like embers in his voice when he retorted, his voice echoing back to him as somehow lame and feeble:

"What in the name of everything holy did you do to Amonas?"

The man who called himself Agrippa was wearing Amonas' smile when he answered, a tone of playfulness in his voice:

"You have no idea how amusing your choice of words is, do you?

There's nothing holy, and nothing reverent in the whole universe, I can assure you. There's only life, and death. It goes in circles, that's all. Your friend happens to be on the sad end of it right now. At least his body lives on. It should keep you happy, if only for a little while longer."

There was something insidious about this man, and he made no effort to hide it. Hilderich repeated his question, this time shouting, demanding, fury overtaking him despite the parts of his mind that warned him of teetering on a precipice of unfathomable depth, every step reeking with deadly danger:

"What did you do to him?"

The machine was transfixed, as if its gaze was locked at the man, like staring in awe of him, unable even to speak, much less move. The man responded to Hilderich with a voice like the cutting edge of a sword, sharp with the smell of cold steel about it:

"Your point of view depends on where you stand when you look at everything. That's a universal truth, one of the few that appears to not be ephemeral, but rather woven into the fabric of the cosmos. From my point of view, Amonas is dead and gone, his conscience and reason wholly erased; replaced with my mind, my mental state, me. The real me. Only his body remains, but that too, is now mine. I must have looked hideous in my former state, isn't that right Hilderich? Is that not what you thought when you laid eyes upon my biological remains? No, I cannot read minds although I usually see right through people's thoughts. You are so easy to read, especially humans in this world. I would have opted for storage in a computer matrix or an aether device, but I am so hedonistic, I must admit, that I cannot live without the immediacy of the flesh, the senses from billions of nerve receptors flooding my mind. Some consider it crude, ineffectual, a poor choice of style. I only care about what I think. I find the human form so exceptionally vulgar and so thoroughly imperfect that I relish every minute of the sensations it imparts. You could say I've grown attached to it by now."

Hilderich's mind was awash with troubled feelings of guilt, anxiety, hatred and fear. It was a mind-numbing mix that left him utterly helpless, devoid of the will to oppose the man or thing he was now facing. It was as if a demon from the tales told to little children had literally grown into flesh and bone: the flesh and bone of his friend. He barely managed to ask the man in a desperately anguished voice:

"What are you? What the hell are you?"

The Prosops then was quick to answer, his voice somewhat distant, as it could not believe what was transpiring in its presence, a sense of loss and defeat mingled with utter fascination and disbelief:

"It's him. The Sleeping Man. The one who's winning the game. The one with the flaming avatar. He even has a name for it: he calls it the Patriarch."

Hilderich reeled with manifest horror weighing him down, making his legs weak, sagging his shoulders as if he had been pierced by an arrow through the heart. His knees fell on the plush carpet, his hands had gone limp. There was always more to the truth, it seemed. With eyes wide from the shock of unimaginable despair he lay there, slightly trembling as if a chilly wind had suddenly swiped through the amply lit room. As his sight was fixed on the face of a man he had loved as a friend, tears ran freely down his cheeks, unable to stop them. He had seen a friend transformed unwillingly into a beast of many faces, a being of ultimate deceit. And now as the machine had said, it had been given absolute control of their world. He had tried to save a friend, and it had led him to surrender control of an entire world, his own world, to something sinister, he knew.

Agrippa, the less than human being in the tank, the person who had in essence been the Patriarch of the Outer Territories for an unknown number of years, the beast that had taken over Amonas body as his own, spoke with a commanding tone. The machine and the man before him were unable to resist him in anyway, sheer shock stunning them to silence and inaction:

"I relish this moment. Your face speaks for itself, Hilderich. And you, how utterly you have failed in your tasks. This is my true victory, my real triumph. It's for moments like these that I play. Ten times so far, you have failed. This tenth time's the charm though. So much for your vaunted intelligence. How does it feel to have believed yourself so superior in so many ways, only to be laid low by a player like myself? To put it in the coarse idiom you so are so capriciously fond of: I bet it sucks, doesn't it Centron?"

The machine suddenly bobbed and leaned forward, the color of its entire band a harsh blinding red. It spoke with unfeigned exasperation, obviously hurt by the Patriarch's taunting:

"What do you mean I've failed ten times? Why did you leave a game you were winning? Why fool me into losing control of the.. Unless you were.. Losing? But that cannot be, the Waking Man was about to crumble; the opposition he had created never took off, you saw to it. You brought in the army, they would be crushed between a hammer and an anvil. It was all going to go up in flames, your avatar cleansing everything like -"

Agrippa interjected with fiery wrath, bellowing rather than speaking:

"Like it had done so before, nine times! Nine times in the past! Nine times you were always blind to see afterwards! Nine times that the final victory was stolen from me, postponed! Cheated nine times in fifteen thousand two hundred and thirty nine long standard years! Each time trying to find what was missing, each time trying to find what exactly had gone wrong, each time failing at the last possible minute! Each time laying waste to entire cities along with their populace, entire civilizations along with their pathetic little history trying to make my point, mark my win! Each time you pathetic little machine, you called it a draw! A draw!"

The machine sat down on the carpet, apparently as dumbfounded as Hilderich, who despaired as he was he sat with his knees on the carpet transfixed, watching the exchange between the player and the machine. The man was saying that he was in effect the man behind the annihilation of uncounted lives; the bearer of an apocalyptic curse that plagued their world from time immemorial, that only histories long forgotten had ever talked about. He was saying that he was the demon behind every hell; the dragon that spew fire in every ancient tale. Evil, death and destruction made manifest. And he did it for sport.

It was too much for Hilderich to absorb: to protect his sanity, his mind simply noted these things as mere facts and went on trying to uncover more meaning behind all this, perhaps even something that would lend him hope; something that could offer him a way out. The machine spoke in disbelief, Agrippa piercing it with vehement eyes:

"That's not possible! I have no recollection of such an incident, much less nine. My memory was completely functional and checked out on every diagnostic run. In fact, it had gotten pretty damn tedious in here since all I ever did was dust the furniture, run the maglev supports, and mind the odd escapee from the loony bin."

Agrippa seemed infuriated at what the machine had just said and spat back a venomous reply:

"You stupid, idiotic machine. You cannot imagine what I went through trying to figure a way out of that torturous prison of the mind. Forced to live time and again with the same avatar, play the same starting role, do everything again from scratch, just because you were stupid enough to let the Waking Man have his way with you. Loonies, is it that what you called them? They seem kind of strange and speak in weird tongues, blabbering on about a God and the like? They keep coming with almost impeccable frequency? Keep finding a way through the desert? But you dispose of them so easily? You are still able to vex me beyond my limits!"

If the Prosops had eyes it would have been staring blankly at Agrippa, unable to answer or indeed think of an answer. Agrippa's verbal assault had left the machine silent, quietly contemplating what the man had just said. An intense frown creased Hilderich's forehead, wary of the machine's inability to answer in kind, much less so act against a man who had already lived thousands of lives and made a playground of a whole world and countless generations of its people. Agrippa started to pace up and down the room in a knowing fashion, as if he had arranged each and every item inside it. He went on, his wrath focused on the machine which seemed to have troubled him more than it could account for:

"You were fooled, Centron. More than once. You were being fooled all the time, since the game began. I was indeed late to notice it, but you never did. The Waking Man grew a cult that worshiped him as a God. He taught them, made them learn science and technology, letting them roam freely, believing in all that righteous bullshit he seems to actually believe himself. They built for him, Centron. They built long and hard. Do you know what it was that they built?"

The machine could not answer. Its uneasiness was evident in the way it stood still, hovering a few inches off the ground as if it were a child being scolded, learning a lesson in a painful way. Hilderich saw the jutting veins in the body that had belonged to Amonas. He could see Agrippa was on the edge, his body tense with fury. It was as if hot sticky tar dripped from each word he uttered when he spoke again, answering his own rhetorical question:

"They build a whole new island continent across the northern ocean. That's what they did, they raised the outer shell a tiny bit. You'd think you'd notice, but I guess it doesn't matter that much if it's not on the game board now, is it? Where you strangely compensating the world's attitude because of some unaccounted for deviation? What did you think, that it'd suddenly put on weight? Did you think those who built these things in their ineffable wisdom had the numbers a little bit off? You stupid machine.

All the while I was busy conquering the whole world from behind the scenes, only to set it ablaze in a great pyre of religious fervor without even once blooding my own hands, that bastard's son had created a new continent across the northern ocean. He actually made them built a frigging continent. The map had changed! And you knew nothing! I had burned the world down nine times, not once, but nine times! Each time, I drove myself to the brink of madness trying to understand where I had broken the rules where I had overstepped, why it always came down to a frigging draw! And then I read the tale of Umberth, and I knew. The northern continent was not part of the game board. It was as if it had never existed, in the most material way. The soil was not part of the game board, the plants were not part of the game board. Guess what else grows from soil?"

The pause was brief and the dumbstruck machine could not have replied in time even if it had an answer ready and waiting:

"People grow from soil! That's right! A carbon based life-form, rich in water. Feed them from the same earth and they'll grow and multiply, their very bodies made from the elements of the soil they were feeding upon. The frigging bastard grew his own people! Can you believe how arrogant that is? He makes me want to physically vomit with disgust! He grew his own people, and taught them to waltz in here and go to that very special little secret place we players know you have, your precious seed.

Because you'd want to host another game once this one's done, right? So all you'd have to do is reset the machine, isn't that so? So it could start from scratch again? Well this is it, the tenth time we've started the frigging game just because every one of those bastard children of the Waking Man share his mark in their genes. And guess what? You can't kill a player, can you? That would be against the rules.

You also have to accommodate him, show him around the place. Now, this is the funny bit. These people, they seem to be the Walking Man since they have his genemark. But there seem to be so many of them not just one of them: there's only one Walking Man. They must be pawns. But they're not made like the other pawns; they seem different, they don't belong to the game-board. The stuff they're made from is not from the game-board. So if someone that looked like the Walking Man came time and again into the heart of you asking to surrender as he has every right to do so, Centron, but at the same time was not part of the game-board, what would you do? Tell me Centron, what would you do? What the frig did you do nine times in a row?"

The machine seemed to fluster, bobbing slightly and lifting itself a foot off the ground, its voice sluggish and low as if it was only now waking from a deep slumber:

"The player's complete genotype has to be uniquely marked and its constituent particle structure wholly identifiable within the game-board parameters. I would then proceed to find a logical gap, since I could identify multiple valid marks with only one being within the game board. Cumulatively, such an error would at some point cause me to throw a logical exception interrupt, invalidating myself and.. reseed the game in hope that the error was a randomly inserted unforeseen factor that was statistically nearly impossible to reappear."

Hilderich was hearing the machine in disbelief, understanding that it had implied it was not infallible; not only that but it had also admitted there was something seriously flawed about him. Agrippa seemed to have regained some measure of self-control, now that the machine had finally understood how it had indeed failed to execute its task, which looked liked it boiled down to hosting the game and administering the rules. It continued to analyze its failure, this time with more feeling in its voice, as if it relished the fact that it had finally uncovered the mechanism of its failure:

"The logical error counter maximum is 127. Given that each of these loonies seem to have been visiting regularly each 12 system standard years, that would give an approximate estimate of reseeding every 1524 system standard years. 1524 times nine is 13716 system standard years. That would mean the next counter reset increment is due this year."

"That's right, you worthless piece of machinery. That s why I had to step up things from my side lately. I'll share my insight with you. I can't read the Centron's face but I so much want to see you, Hilderich, understand fully. See his face.

I had made a backwards turn: I thought about spinning the spindle the other way around. I led things this tenth time a little different than the others. I created a society of people who were devoted believers, not so much bent on destruction and killing in the name of their gods, but obedient, unremarkable, and so predictable. Still I nurtured them with a festering indignation, something that I tended to exacerbate from time to time. Uprisings, little revolts small riots. Something to remind the more daring souls that they were being oppressed, hunted down, that their lives used as oil for a ruthless machine. I also instituted the Curatoria. A lovely little organization of mumbling idiots that believed they were so much different from the rest, so much better, so scholarly and knowledgeable. I fed them with trinkets and treasures past from civilizations that had gone extinct in my fruitless attempt to win this frigging game. And lo and behold, I began to see the fruits of my labor and the error of my ways. My pawns had actually done something useful with their pathetic lives. I learned of the northern continent, a myth I had notched up as folk tales and the ravings of mad men. And when I saw the girl, that dark skinned girl that Umberth had found, I knew it was something of his making. The dark skin, his own skin. At least that was his starting profile from what I knew. Such a hypocrite! I knew he was fumbling with the Centron somehow, seeing someone carrying his mark around the game board as if nothing was amiss, the game still running, the timer not yet reset. It troubled me for an endless amount of time, during which I spent long years trying to figure the exact way in which he had wrenched the Centron's gears. I found about it only when that servant wrote down his telling story of the mysterious northern tribe. Without knowing, the consistent writing down of their customs and rituals led me to identify them as his own creations, as well as calculate the period of their visits, or pilgrimages as they call them to the Centron, all from a single reference. I knew then that there was something very specific about the number 128; everything always happened on the 128th peregrination. Always. Musing about the workings of the game I remembered the seed and how pivotal it's role actually is: the rules of the game clearly state that 'in the highly improbable case of technical error, the current game ends in a draw and is reseeded to allow the players a fair second chance at winning'. In the words of the technologists of a long lost civilization, I'd found a bug. And then all I had to do was exploit it. That's where you and your most accommodating friend come in the picture, Hilderich."

The machine seemed genuinely hurt, its black band of glass totally dark, its base lying on the carpet as if it were a monolithic monument. It managed to reply as indignantly as possible under the circumstances, completely ignoring everything that did not involve itself:

"I'm not stupid. It's a known feature, not a 'bug' per se.."

Hilderich was listening as if struck by lightning, mesmerized at what Agrippa was revealing to them. It had taken a lifetime for Hilderich to find this place but it now seemed it would take more than whatever life he had left to live to even understand half of it. He loathed the man intensely but could do nothing to stop himself from wanting to listen to what had happened up until then. Agrippa had a reassuring smile casually worn on his face, as if congratulating himself on a job well done. Hilderich found the sudden urge to ask him, despite loathing him for everything he had confessed he had done:

"How do Amonas and I fit in your scheme? I know I never partook in your scheming. Will you despoil Amonas' name even while you wear his body as if it were nothing more than an animal's skin?"

Agrippa laughed through Amonas' throat, a disconcertingly familiar sound twisted into a malignant cacophony. He replied readily, as if he had waited for Hilderich to ask of his own volition first:

"I read your master's work Hilderich. He seemed a genuinely smart person, for someone in the Curatoria. His suspicions were mostly correct, but as you have seen not in any way he could have imagined. Based on these suspicions, I laid out a trap of my own. What you've come to know as keystones themselves are not special in a particular way. They are indeed merely free give-away gifts for the spectators. Indeed, what you and your master held in such high esteem as artifacts of a long lost civilization are nothing more than the detritus of a certain kind of people in the developed universe that are filled with ennui, and find such games on shellworlds a welcome diversion. Some even pay to watch live, not from the Centron, but from the game-board itself. Yes, off-worlders have roamed about your world, filling it with with their junk, which you Curators then mistook for important. In a sense, to you, their importance remains unchallenged. That keystone your master had in his care, that was a keystone I had personally entrusted to him, a ticket for a way in. Don't act so surprised, Hilderich. Perhaps, you're wondering by now, why he hadn't used it himself? Why hadn't he tried to at least? Why did he rarely ever speak of it himself? What is it that made him tick, Hilderich? Tell me, Hilderich, what do you remember of your earliest years, the time you were a toddler?"

Hilderich's unease and suspicion grew exponentially. How deep was this thing's scheme that it extended to master Olom? Why did he ask him such irrelevant questions at this hour? Was he belatedly or mockingly trying to befriend him? He chose silence over expressing his ire frivolously. There would be ample time for that when nothing else could be done. Secretly, without even admitting it to himself, he believed that time was approaching fast now. Agrippa went on, once more assuming the role of the man with all the answers. If nothing more, Hilderich had found whomever he had set out to, the man his master had not dared to. Agrippa spoke in the gruff undertones of Amonas, this time almost true to his original timbre:

"I know you can barely remember a lake and a boy not very much unlike you. Perhaps you might also remember a young, golden haired girl. Olom was not always the quietly wizened old man he looked like when he died, Hilderich. He was a curator, a seeker of knowledge. He was good at what he intended to devote his life to. I admired that in a man, even an unwilling, unknowing pawn.

He had focus and a sense of purpose; his ideas seemed able to spread and seep through to the masses, affording me an uncannily expedient though far-fetched way of getting inside and breaking the vicious cycle of endless repetitive draws. Of course I could forfeit the game, and so could the other bastard as well, but we both knew that would only happen when the shellworld's inner star froze over.

So I approached him, I appealed to his darker side; the less illustrious one, the more vicious side. His human side. I tempted him with forbidden knowledge, offered him artifacts and trinkets he had never seen before. At first, he had actually believed he had my unremitting support and help so he could achieve a victory of sorts against the dark forces that sought man's eternal struggle. I presented myself as a reformer, a bright spiritual leader unlike the ones that had come before me.

I promised him the dawning of a new era, with him uncovering the secrets that would finally make it practical and true. I took great joy in that role, but the best part was when I forced him to take you in, Hilderich. When I sent away his daughter, when I smeared his name forever, when I made her loathe him. When I told him that should anything happen to you, his daughter's life would be forfeit, he became a most willing subject. He knew that there would come a time he'd have to give his own life to save his daughter. Do you remember that night Hilderich?

You might be wondering why he had to protect you from myself. Perhaps it was because he knew you were expendable, but his daughter was not. You see, I could not stake everything in just one little boy, Hilderich. I had to plan some contingencies. The Waking Man gave me the idea, I must admit. Olom did raise you indeed like a bastard son, I'll give him that. What's the matter, why are you crying? It's alright Hilderich, you can call me father if you like."

Homeward

"DEAR Celia, such are the ways of things from what I know and what I can gather. I do not expect you to believe me outright but neither should you attribute what I've said to old age or think them to be the sayings of a madman. What I have told you is the truth, the way of things behind the veil that has been put in front of your eyes.

I have seen countless sunsets, I have walked over sand and snow, traversed the mountains and journeyed across the Great Sea. I've loved this world dearly ever since I first walked on it, and I'd give my life freely if that would save it. Alas, that is not possible. The Sleeping Man, the Patriarch as you know him is set on winning this game I've told you about; this sadistic, twisted version of a game that has plagued this world as well as you, your people and your ancestors. Your world has perished nine times already, Celia; scraps of people being spared their lives to the Sleeping Man's plans and desires.

Each time he would begin anew, trying to win this morbid game, utterly destroying everything and everyone. Then he would go on, to other worlds, ravaging more and more souls as his thirst for blood and torment cannot be sated. I have merely tried to wear him down, perhaps force him to abdicate, but his perseverence proved to be second to none. I fear all that I have done is doom so many more souls than a quick victory of his would have claimed. Perhaps, I am as guilty as he is. No matter, soon everything will be over, I fear.

You may find all that impossible to believe and understandably so, but your father had an inkling. He had known things that were not meant to be known. He had become involved too much in the past. That was perhaps his downfall."

Celia's eyes went cold, her face became stiff and austere suddenly. It had not done so at the impossibly world-shaking revelations that the old man had revealed to her in an earnest fashion; her mood had turned for the worse at the mention of her father. Her child was looking at the world around it with a vague interest, turning its head around to see the world it had been brought in, content from life after his mother had fed him. The boy was looking intently at the face of the wizened old man, when Celia spoke without a trace of warmth in her voice:

"I want to hear nothing of him. His place was among the dead the moment he left me to fend for myself. He was chasing ghosts, hunting stories and tales of old. Dead things he chose to cherish and love instead of the living that were warm to him. Speak of him no more, it insults me gravely. I wish he would die a terrible death."

The old man known as Perconal the Jester, indeed the Waking Man of the game, closed his eyes bitterly, and put a finger to his mouth, evidently concerned about Celia's cold and unfitting attitude towards her father. He tried to turn her mind around, to warm her heart when everything around them would soon grow cold and empty.

"Please, the coldness in your voice does not fit the wholeness I can sense in your heart. Your father was forced to leave you Celia. He was caught up in the schemes of the Patriarch. True, it was his quest of uncovering artifacts of old that led him to such a precarious position to attract the Patriarch's attention in the first place, but he only did it because he believed it mattered. Because he believed such knowledge could change a hard, deceitful, uncaring world that was run by a megalomaniac; a blood-thirsty killer, a ruiner of worlds. I can only say he had no other option than leave, to save your life. You might choose to disbelieve me, or think I'm only trying to soothe you, but that's the truth of things."

Celia's gaze was hard as nails, her voice cold like ice:

"And that somehow makes all the years of cold suppers and beatings better? Is it worth anything at all that my life was spared as you say, while I spent endless sleepless night wishing I had never been born? When time after time my body and soul were ravaged by those beasts that dared to call themselves men? A tool of pleasure in the shadows of the Trofeia, all those tortured souls at the hands of monsters with human faces, never knowing mercy or kindness. What kind of father wishes that for his child? Tell me, sir Perconal, what kind of father would wish a life of torment for his child instead of a merciful death? What kind of person would choose that for his own blood?"

They were both sitting opposite each other on a pair of withered old chairs, remnants of a past gone by when the jester seemed to had enjoyed a certain degree of lavishness. That held true no more, but the man had somehow maintained an air of dignity. He had been after all, as he said so himself, venerated as a God by the people he had raised as sons and daughters. Celia had found that hard to believe, but it did not struck her as impossible. A game that toyed with the lives of every man, woman and child on the world.

She knew life could be unbearably hard and cruel, she had lived in such a world for years. That someone had thought of turning it into a game of sorts suddenly felt almost like reassuring evidence that in the end, the world was not very much unlike she had known. It meant that life was cruel in more than one crippling way. It was a cynical thought, she had admitted to herself, but it was true. Truth was always hard and unforgiving. She noticed that the old man had fallen silent, staring at her compassionately, unable to express a proper answer to her question. Celia asked him then earnestly:

"You wouldn't know such a man, would you? Except maybe for the Patriarch."

Perconal scowled at the mention of the name. His answer sounded somewhat harsh, an edge in his voice that belied his years:

"He's not a man. He's a beast. In the most literal sense. He abandoned his original form untold millenia ago. He has been playing this sick game for what could possibly be eons. He's kind of a myth among the rest of the players and the followers of the game. A sort of unofficial champion; a player of immeasurable victories in the past. I only entered the game hoping to put an end to his career of death, carnage, and destruction. Every one of the games he has played has ended in mass genocide, water turned to blood flowing freely as rivers from a mountain top.

Someone should have stopped him. Someone should have stopped the game. The universe is mad and cruel enough without this madness that some have the nerve to call a game. For a long time I thought I could turn the tables to my advantage. I found a way to cheat, for there was little else one could do against a player of his awesomely vicious talents.

I've spent thousands of years trying to find a chink in his armor, but to no avail. All I could ever do was postpone the inevitable. And in the meantime I've watched the people of this world suffer again and again. But you must understand, I could not forfeit. I had to make a stand. He has to be stopped. Perhaps, there is hope yet. This time is different than the rest. This time he has made a radical shift in his strategy. I know, because I have been close to him for the few past years, without him suspecting. I masqueraded myself as Perconal the Jester, kept around as a fool. He found out the manner in which I had been cheating and concocted a devious plan to break the deadlock in the game. I'm afraid Amonas too, is part of that plan."

Celia's eyes flamed with anger suddenly and instinctively pulled her baby closer to her. With a sudden jolt she stood upright, the chair behind her falling to the floor with a crash. The child started crying, his little arms and legs trying to reach the safety of his mother's bosom. As she hugged him close to her chest as if protecting him from what she felt were the lies of the man before her, she spoke with the wrath only a woman of her mettle could muster:

"I shall hear naught of this! I owe my life to Amonas and no one else, bless him for eternity! You spoil his name and blemish his honor in front of his wife and child! Have you no shame?"

Perconal tried to appease her, bowing low in apology and motioning her to sit down once again:

"You misunderstand me, dear Celia. I did not say he has done so willingly. He has been deceived and manipulated, as is usually the way of Agrippa, the Patriarch. That's his true name, at least the name with which he enters each game. Even before you met him, Amonas had been a trusted soldier in the army. An officer with a bright career in front of him. As far as I know, he was fearlessly devout and excessively strong of faith.

A fanatic, a zealot who would do anything for the glory of the Pantheon. He was hand-picked by Agrippa, and agreed to have his mind manipulated. I was there, Celia. I saw him enter the Patriarch's quarters on more than one occasion. Beyond the doors I could here his screams and his agony as his mind was being toyed with, so he could be made into a lethal, unsuspected weapon. He was an infiltrator to the kinsfolk's cause.

I had known that when he first came to join, but I could not risk exposing him at the wrong time. Perhaps I was in error. The Patriarch had sought to use him as a tool for a variety of purposes, and it seems he hasn't failed him yet. Amonas was led right into the hands of a young man in possession of a keystone, an artifact that seems to enable its wielder to enter the game's center, where the real Agrippa is located, the place from where he actually plays, controlling his avatar. I believe his mind was somehow programmed to lead this man into the hands of Agrippa. My best guess is he's going to use them both to break the deadlock and leave this world before it is torn asunder, quite literally for the last and final time."

Celia had become flush red from anger, her voice filled with wrathful tremors:

"Lies! The whole lot! I should have never listen to one word of your fantasies! I came here to urge you to action, wake you from a slumber that will be the death of these people and you cover me in wild stories. You marr my husband's name, you insult me and our child. I should have left the moment I heard you utter such vile lies. I shall do so now. Before my wrath overcomes me and urges me to do something my child can never be proud of."

"Listen to me! I know it's almost impossible to believe me, but he could have killed you at a moment's notice from Agrippa. He had become his toy, his faithful puppet. If it's any consolation though, his heart was pure. He believed he was doing the right thing, he believed he was part of the kinsfolk. He believed his future lay in a bright free world, by your loving side. He must have loved you, Celia. For all that matters, he must have loved you."

The boy had stilled its crying, and now switched his gaze to and fro between Perconal and Celia. She squinted her eyes as she directed a gaze that seemed to bore through the old man's wizened face with ease, her accusing voice ringing around the cramped study with the authority of a mythical maiden of wrath:

"What would you know of love? A lonesome old-man, bereft of his sanity, buried in books of fiction and stories that try to put in words the misery that eats away the souls of so many people every day of their waking lives. If you were who you claim to be, you would have done something that mattered a long time ago. If you have failed as you say, what more could there be than take away your own life? If nothing else, it would be the honorable thing to do. But it seems there's none of it in you. So speak not of Amonas and our love. I shall see him still. He has a child waiting for him."

Perconal seemed to understand Celia's harsh judgments. The expression on his face looked as if he had known all those things, and had contemplated them in the past as well. Perhaps, he thought, it would have been better if he had taken away his own life. Perhaps he had no honor in the end. But as these thoughts rang in his head, he saw Celia's brows go narrow and her face draw suddenly pale. He asked her then with worry on his face:

"Celia? What is the matter?"

Celia looked in shock and her baby son started crying once more:

"It's him. I heard him in my head. He's about to do something terrible, I can feel it."

Surprise took over the old man's features and it did not suit him well. He knew what Celia had meant, even though he could not have heard the Patriarch's voice. He sprang into action suddenly, trying to find something among the ruin that constituted his library, in essence various piles of books and so on. He searched for a few moments and picked up a sort of crystal that did not look very much unlike a glass tablet. The ground shook then strangely, as if forces beyond nature were to blame. A deep rythmic shudder went throughout the caves. Perconal's voice carried a calm finality that instantly caught Celia's unwarranted attention:

"It's happening. There's little time if any. Save your child. There's not much I can do now, but save you and your child. I owe so much more to this world and its people, but this where it has come to. Please, don't let the memory of what I've told you fade. And hold on to this pad of crystal: it might seem quite unassuming, but it contains everything that has happened here ever since the game begun. Someone, when they find you, will be able to make use of it."

Celia was trying to comprehend the man, when the man suddenly grasped her by one arm and shove something like a needle protruding from a ring of his in her skin. She felt suddenly light and her sight grew somehow faint; all her senses started to grow dim, and she could not move. Her child was hugging her child as firmly as ever; they looked like they had been turned into stone. Perconal spoke to her one last time, not knowing whether she could still listen to him:

"I'm sorry I have to do it this way, but there's not enough time to argue. I hope you'll forgive me, some day. For everything."

As the old man said these words, shouts of fear and worry could be heard outside as a second, much more violent rumbling echoed throughout the caves. A blue hazy bubble formed around Celia and the child, and in a moment they had vanished as if a torrent of light had borne them away.

The earth was shattering around Perconal. The people outside screamed in helpless unison and then everything was covered in dust, rock, and soil. His last thought was a lake in the summer of another world with only one small, warm yellow sun.

The words had flown freely from him with fervor when he had uttered the prayer of salvation. God had answered his prayers and the demon had left him alone. It had been too late for his brother though. The archenemy had struck him down in a single fiery flash.

The Pilgrim saw the charred body of his brother and wept, precious tears dripping on the sand at his feet. He performed the rites according to the tradition as best as he could. There was no snow to cover the body of his brother, no ice water from a lake to rain him with and cleanse him of his sins. There was no thistle, no grub or bush to leave by his side in memory of the soil. It was a poor way to treat a brother well-met in the Land of God. But thus it had come to be, and it was his sin alone to carry to his own grave. When his time came, he would accept the rightful punishment of his God, and meet with his brother in the soil from which all life grew.

He dug a shallow grave, his hands unable to dig deeper into the wet sand far below. He thought that it would have to do. He covered him with the sand, and prayed that his soul would receive whatever it was due, whether it be punishment or praise. He was now in the hands of God, and that was the Pilgrim's sole consolation in the matter.

He set out once again to reach the Forge of Stones, to end his pilgrimage and fulfill his mission and duties. He had one more reason now, and that was his brother's death at the hands of the archenemy's servant. He had known the danger's that lay even in the Land of God. It was his duty to protect his care-free brother, and he had failed He was not overcome with grief, but with righteous fury. If God willed it so, he would be ready to dispense his wrath to the minions of the archenemy. By blade, hand or prayer, he would shatter them like ice in the spring, that much and nothing less the oath on his brother's grave demanded.

The Pilgrim walked in solitude, the sand and wind as ever his companions. The Land of God was silent around him, but it spoke to his very soul, demanding vengeance to be exacted. He trudged along over the sand unyielding, tenaciously leaving footmarks behind him only to be swept away by the desert breeze, slowly but surely. He lost track of time, never once looking up to the suns, their ride across the sky unimportant to him when his purpose was clearly visible in front of him.

As if they had not been there before to notice, he suddenly reached the high walls of the Garden that stretched in front of him as far as his eyes could see. He could see the spirals that tempted the dominion of the sky, the arches that rose as if in solemn prayer to God, and the Holy Gate beyond which his purpose lay. It had been a moment of excited relief for him. He remembered the preachings of the elders, and the Pilgrim who had come before him, and did as they had done; as so many others had done before them all, for innumerable springs and endless winters.

He touched the Gate uttering the mantra of God, making His sign and kneeling down as the rites required of him. But it was no mere tradition, he could see. God was there with him, alongside him, dousing him with lights of many colors. He listened to an answer to his incantations in the tongue of God, the sacred tongue that none of his people ever uttered, and never would lest they defile Him.

The Gate opened to allow him inside the Garden. In wonder and astonishment he saw the Chariot of God fly from the depths below and rise to meet him without a sound, in perfect grace and harmony. Tears of rapture ran down his cheeks while he praised his God and Lord, the deliverer of his people, Father to them all.

The Chariot moved with the speed of the wind and what he saw filled him with overpowering awe. The glory and majesty that the workings of his God radiated was an ineffable sight. He saw the beauty and he marveled at the size of it all. Through darkness came God's light, through nothingness and chaos came shape and sight. His face shone from the light of God's angels, performing their appointed tasks with harmony, diligence and piety. It was a sight that made him feel his life could not end until he had himself told of his pilgrimage to the next in line. He now understood why the pilgrimage mattered so to his people: He knew it was not for fear of losing the sacred stones, and the heat and light that shone with him.

These were God's gifts, which he freely gave and could freely take away. But his greatest gift was his Garden, his Garden of wonders with which he filled a man's soul with indomitable will and unbreakable spirit. What the Pilgrim felt could not be compared to any emotion he had experienced before. It was not pride, it was not honor. It was neither fervor or awe, or anything like that combined. It was love. The Garden filled a man's soul with love, the love of God, the love of his people, so they may endure and live on to worship his name. 'Glory be to God!' shouted the Pilgrim while the Chariot carried him aloft now, passing over all of God's wonders and heading to the heart of the Forge, where his pilgrimage would end and he would be given the honor of bringing back the Holy Stone.

He saw now that the Chariot was leading him to a tower that reached into the very ceiling itself, both ends lost in the interminable darkness above and below. Suddenly, the Chariot was dipping sharply below while he comfortably sat within, as if the invisible hand of God held him safely in place without fear of him ever falling off.

In a matter of moments, the Chariot came serenely to a stop, having brought him in front of a remarkable work of marble. It was delicate and exquisite, holy in its magnificence, adorned with the grace of God who surely must have wrought it himself. He knelt, bowing low so as to have his head touch the marble steps laid out before him, never speaking but simply offering his silent prayers.

The doors to the heart of the Forge were open. He could see a long corridor leading to a well-lit room, surely the Sacred Chamber. He could see little of the signs and markings that he had been told to expect, but he was safe in the knowledge that his God was leading his way, his angels all around him, his Chariot bringing him to the place God had ordained.

He passed under the arched doorway and made the sign of God. What he saw though unnerved him: the walls were made of wood and were embellished with monstrous carvings. Hideous forms seemed to leap at him, visions of demons jutting from every side. This was blasphemy! This was the work of the archenemy! It was clear as ice to him.

The thought came unbidden to his mind, springing up from the well of his soul.

'This is the work of evil, and it shall burn.'

He could now hear a coarse voice, rising and falling like the tide. It was strident and harsh. It was the voice of a beast rather than the voice of a man. He rushed through the corridor, a prayer on his mouth and the blade on his hand, ready to taste the blood of demons. Other sounds could be heard as well. He could hear other voices as he turned his brisk walk into a jog, a kind of struggling sound and a dull thud, not much unlike the sound of rock upon rock.

As the light grew more intense, his sight adjusted and he could see more clearly inside the room in front of him. He could see a demon of metal thrust against a wall and two men grappling, embraced in a vicious fight. What he saw filled him with fury, wrath, and the grace of God filled him with strength he had never felt before.

He saw the archenemy, trying to take the life of his brother whom he had buried himself in the sands. Though he seemed to be dressed in different clothes, he was alive and breathing! As if God had performed a miracle, his brother was fighting the archenemy. It was their destiny it seemed to bring him down forever. They had been chosen, and his brother was given life anew. He knew what he had to do now, his purpose clear as daylight. He ran as if a river of fire was fast behind his heels, and he could have sworn he could hear the voice of God urging him to avenge all the lives the beast before him had claimed.

He lunged with terrible might and purpose at the human form of the beast which could not fool a man of God. It seemed to have paid him no notice but his brother had somehow known, and had made a small step just in time for the Pilgrim blade to run the beast through and through its heart.

The beast was stunned in silence; its face became a mask of pain and horror, utter disbelief in the deep blue of its eyes. It wore a man's visage, a face that might have looked beautiful, even honorable if it had belonged to a brother. It was the face of a deceiver though and its life was now seeping away, its grasp on the Pilgrim's brother fading quickly.

The archenemy collapsed on his feet, his eyes rolling backwards with only the white of his eyes visible. The Pilgrim had never thought he would be chosen to kill the archenemy, if that was what had happened. He had never even heard the wise elders mention such a thing. He just was; the archenemy simply existed to oppose God. Had he made an error? Was this not God's will? He listened to his thoughts and was confounded. He followed the elders' advice and remained true to his heart. He saw the archenemy before him, and killed him with one swift blow. He had not thought it possible, but God had allowed it. Indeed, perhaps God had led him here to confront his nemesis. It was why he had resurrected his brother, that's all the Pilgrim could think of. It might have been a hubris, but perhaps he was after all God's chosen champion. Perhaps the appointed hour had come. It had all happened so soon, merely moments had passed and it had all ended. He looked about him with a frightened expression of horror, shock and surprise on his brother's face.

Then he saw the demon of metal, which seemed to exist still despite its master's demise. His body tensed and tried to lunge at him, but his brother threw his hands at him and constrained him, shouting in his strange mother tongue, like when they had first met on the Path. As he was about to push him away, their eyes met, and he could see something flashing inside them. His hands went slack and he dropped his blade. He remembered the teachings: 'At the appointed hour blood will be spilled, and tears will be shed. Weep no more, for the end will be nigh.'

The Pilgrim looked slackly at his brother. He made a motion with his hands to the Pilgrim to calm him down and make him sit. He pointed at the demon which seemed to be somehow in league with his brother, an unlikely ally or a renegade perhaps, he could not be sure. It looked as if it did not intend them any harm. That too, must have been God's work he thought, and left it at that.

Suddenly while his brother kept repeating questions the Pilgrim could not understand, everything around them started trembling. Things fell from the wooden walls and crystal glass shattered. He could feel the rumble of the earth deep inside him, he could hear its death throes. The world was going to end, he knew. It had been the last Pilgrimage. Tears ran down his throat and cheeks, and a loud prayer formed on his lips.

The metal demon and his brother were frantically exchanging words. Fear had taken over them, the fear of death. They were trying to make him move, take him with them wherever they planned to escape. He shook his head rigorously, refusing such petty dishonor. They did not seem to understand there was no escape. He would finally meet God, having offered him as much of his life in service as he could. He would meet his father, and tell him of the last Pilgrimage. He would meet every soul of his people in the heavens, and tell them of his tale: tell them about the Forge of Stones.

As the earth shook with even more violence, pieces of the room around him started to fall off their place as if an invisible being of terrible might picked them apart. In the distance he could see the demon and his brother running aimlessly out the corridor, trying vainly to save their lives, perhaps their souls too, if the demon had any. His shouted words of parting to his brother for whom God seemed to have many other wondrous plans: "Go in peace, brother. God and your brother, Algol al Azad, love you."

As everything went dark around him before finally crumbling on top of him, he could see the young man turn his head in his direction and shouted something. It sounded like something his brother had told him in the desert. With the last of his breathes, and nothing but a numbing feel running down his spine to remind he was barely alive, he tried to say the words himself:

"Thank.. you.."

Epilogue

HE interior of the ship felt like a mansion: fine tapestries lined the wooden walls and thick handwoven carpets adorned the floors. Most of it was decorated in the same fashion, with the engines and the assorted support mechanisms and infrastructure taking up little space. According to the Prosops it was a refurbished luxury yacht. The whole den back on the Centron had actually been a shipyard, something of a hobby the Centron had taken up to spent his endless time and unlimited resources, acute intelligence and insurmountable flair. The fact that a mere hobby could reach such a scale was mindboggling to Hilderich.

Even though Hilderich could not have known what other ships similar to this one looked like, he felt impressed by the taste the machine had shown, and genuinely believed it to be a fine ship, even though the Prosops had insisted on him using the term 'astrogational vehicle'. Hilderich had ignored the machine profoundly on that matter and kept calling the ship, 'ship'. He had warmed up on the machine's name though, and now called it as it had preferred to refer to itself: Ron.

Celia had kept mostly to herself and the child ever since they found her on the Waking Man's capsule. Ron had been evidently surprised to find out how she came about a player capsule. When they roused her from her stasis sleep, she was at first shocked and terrified, frightened of her child. But Hilderich managed to explain to her what had happened, though she wasn't sure how she came to be in the capsule. She wept openly when Hilderich told her of Amonas demise. Since then though, she rarely spoke and when she did it was merely to ask for some amenity or help.

The Prosops was a good host though it seemed to lack some real skill with handling people. Hilderich knew that unfortunately he was not very apt in that department either so he felt he was unable to help and comfort her in some meaningful way. Perhaps he felt responsible for Amonas, he couldn't tell. He had hoped he would have met her under very different situations, but fate had decided otherwise. Perhaps in time, her grief would subside and her spirits lift. As far as he could tell, she hadn't been as impressed by the sheer scale of the newly found cosmos unfolding before them, unlike himself who spent hours gazing at the projection screen of what amounded to the ship's bridge.

Hilderich had been busy resting most of the time at first, but he did spend some time with the machine, which naturally saw to the daily routine of maintaining the ship, checking and plotting their course, as well as trying to update Hilderich on the workings of the universe and the general state of affairs in the civilized galaxy. It had never occurred to Hilderich that there could ever be more knowledge than he could ever hope to understand in millions of life-times, but he would sadly have to do with as much as he could manage in one life-time, which was quite a lot.

Ron had filled him in with as much detail as it could concerning the game, the shellworld and what had transpired according to what it now knew. He was shocked to find out there were literally thousands of shellworlds not very much different than his own, hosting games like the one that had been using everybody on his world as unwilling, unknowing pawns. What had really challenged his sanity though, was the sight of a world being destroyed. Celia could not bear witness, and she had remained in her quarters, tending to her lone child.

It was not something any one was supposed to ever witness in his life, and Hilderich had seen it happen in slow, aggravating detail, before finally averting his red sore eyes. At that moment he had decided to stop that from happening ever again, to the best of his ability. He had some new responsibilities now: he, Celia and her child was everything that remained from their world. He would protect them now, not simply to honour Amonas' memory, but because he felt it was the most important thing he could salvage from the utter destruction of their world: hope.

When he recovered from the shock, Hilderich contemplated the last moments in the Centron. After the strange man had appeared as if out of nowhere and killed Agrippa, everything had happened too fast to actually remember. Ron had filled him in, replaying a recording of the scene that had taken place. Once Agrippa died, there was nothing in the way of keeping the place running and everything happened with the speed of an avalanche, gathering incredible momentum with every passing moment.

Ron had explained to him how delicate the shellworld mechanism was and how it was structurally near-impossible to keep it one piece without the active mechanism of the bullhorns. Once that system had become inert, the gravitational forces, a natural phenomenon that Hilderich could not fully grasp yet, had torn the shell world apart within a few hours. They had barely escaped with their lives when they saw the world begin to shatter into fragments the size of mountain ranges and become a cloud of debris that within a few days time settled into a disk of debris and dust.

Hilderich's mind frequently replayed the fight with Agrippa, trying to fathom who that dark-skinned man had been. He had tried to save the man from certain death, as Ron had indicated they had little more than a few minutes to escape but their strange savior would not come and Ron was forced to push Hilderich aside and keep shoving him almost all the way to the nearest ship.

The machine took great pride in the fact that without his hobby they would be 'dead meat', as it said in its usually flamboyant manner. It had also agreed to help Hilderich on the quest he had vowed to undertake, since as it had said itself:

"You wouldn't survive five seconds out there; I'm telling you it's a cruel, cruel universe. Plus, I'm out of a real job now, and though I don't want to imply anything, it's my goddamn ship in the end of the day. I won't charge extra for the woman and the kid, so you can consider this quite the bargain."

And so they were ploughing on the vastness of space, speeding away from the Binary 888. Ron was looking intently at a star chart, its black band of glass colored cyan, in a desperate attempt at trying to be, in its own words, 'rad', a colloquialism that Hilderich never inquired further about. What he did inquire about though upon seeing the machine intently studying the holographic projection in front of him was their destination, to which the machine had said without turning to face Hilderich:

"Oh? Hmm. I had always thought that visiting such a dump would make me kill myself, but I've decided I needed some quiet, easy place to rest a bit. Like a vacation."

Hilderich frowned in puzzled disbelief:

"But you've been doing almost nothing for fifteen thousand years."

"Shut up. I've plotted a course to Sol, that dump. Should take us a couple of weeks, but it's going to be a nice ride. Unless we get jumped by pirates. Or gethit by a smallish meteorite. Or if the astrogational charts are too much out of date. Other than that and some other factors I could make a list of, we're going to be fine. Ooh, is that coffee? Are you sure you're gonna drink that? I think the galley module's busted. Did you wash today? I think I can smell the dung on you."

Hilderich looked at the cup of hot black beverage that he held in his hands. Aromatic though it was and totally exotic to him, it had a very strong taste and had felt a bit venturesome on his part when he asked the ship's automated galley to prepare some. He was now looking at the ever jovial machine with a hint of worry, completely ignoring the machine's comment on his personal hygiene:

"What do you mean the galley's busted?"

The machine made a slight bob and leaned towards him before saying with a voice that should have been followed by a wry smile:

"Gotcha!"